Not Without You

G·K
Hall
&Co.

Also by Janelle Taylor
in Large Print:

Anything for Love
By Candlelight
Defiant Hearts
Destiny Mine
Love with a Stranger
Savage Ecstasy
Wild Winds

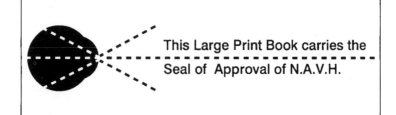

This Large Print Book carries the
Seal of Approval of N.A.V.H.

Not Without You

Janelle Taylor

G.K. Hall & Co. • Waterville, Maine

Published in 2001 by arrangement with Zebra Books, an imprint of Kensington Publishing Corp.

G.K. Hall Large Print Core Series.

The text of this Large Print edition is unabridged.
Other aspects of the book may vary from the original edition.

Set in 16 pt. Plantin by Christina S. Huff.

Printed in the United States on permanent paper.

Library of Congress Cataloging-in-Publication Data

Taylor, Janelle.
    Not without you / Janelle Taylor.
        p.   cm.
    ISBN 0-7838-9531-3 (lg. print : hc : alk. paper)
    1. Survival after airplane accidents, shipwrecks, etc. — Fiction.
    2. Marital conflict — Fiction.   3. Large type books.   I. Title.
PS3570.A934 N68 2001
    813´.54—dc21   2001024845

Dedicated to:
the newest members of our family —
Brandon Michael Thurmond,
born on June 22, 1998,
six days before my birthday; what a marvelous gift!

his parents:
our daughter, Melanie, and son-in-law, Jonathan.

And the other newest member of the family
and my first granddaughter,
Jessie Taylor MacIntyre,
born April 3, 1999,

and her parents:
our daughter, Angela, and son-in-law, Mac.

Prologue

November

Voices. Somewhere in the dark. Watery voices.

. . . lost all memory. Doesn't speak . . .

. . . could be temporary? Couldn't it? Well, couldn't it?

. . . opened his eyes twice and spoke. Didn't know a damn thing. Doctor says it happens sometimes after severe trauma . . .

. . . has to remember . . . has to recover . . . Oh, God, what if he doesn't?

. . . Forget it. We could never be that lucky . . .

The first truly conscious thought that zinged across his brain was: *I'm in agony!* Absolutely everything hurt. Taking the slightest breath crippled his lungs. His ribs, through meant to protect the organs they encased, had become his enemy. Every last one of them hurt.

His eyes opened before he bade them to. The room was unfamiliar, white, sterile. For a moment

7

he lay still in complete bafflement, not even recognizing the woman standing at the window, staring blankly into the dark night beyond.

In disbelief he thought, *I'm in a hospital.*

She suddenly glanced his way and swept in a startled breath. He merely stared at her. She was . . . familiar. She was . . .

My wife.

For the life of him he couldn't remember her name. Nor, he realized with more curiosity than alarm, could he remember his own.

"Jarred?" she said tentatively.

Jarred Bryant. Thirty-eight years old. Head of Bryant Industries. Son of Jonathan and Nola Bryant. Grandson of Hugh Bryant, who was a rogue and a scoundrel, but possessed a genius for buying real estate at dirt-cheap prices and turning that same real estate into some of the most prime pieces of property around the Seattle area. Hugh had also founded several philanthropic projects and one private hospital, Bryant Park, which was undoubtedly where his grandson lay right now.

"Jarred?" she said again, lines of concern narrowing across her fine brow.

He couldn't speak. He could barely respond. The effort was just too great, and he possessed neither the energy nor the inclination to even try. She considered him carefully for several moments, then stepped closer to the bed. Anxiety filled the most amazing amber eyes he'd ever seen. Her skin was soft, clean and imminently touchable.

His wife? Couldn't be.

She reached a hand for something lying out of his line of vision. The call button. He watched her thumb depress the silent beckoning agent.

"Can you hear me?" she tried. When he didn't respond, she moved a half step away, hugging herself protectively.

He realized she was incredibly nervous. The pink tip of her tongue peeked out to moisten her lips. She wore a pale blue blouse and khaki slacks. Her chestnut hair shimmered with good health and curved just beneath her chin. This beautiful woman was — to his mind — perfect.

Moments later a nurse sauntered into the room. She wore the skeptical expression of someone who dealt with others' emotional out-bursts all the time and thought the world, as a whole, was full of overexcitable ninnies. Shooting a glance at the nervous woman, she turned her gaze on him.

"He's awake," she said. "That's good."

"Will you tell Dr. Alastair? Or should I call him? Is he here today?" The woman's voice tightened at the nurse's lackluster response.

"Not at the moment. But I'm sure he'll want to know. Dr. Crissman's on duty today." The nurse leaned her rather formidable bosom his way. "How're you doing there? You've been away from us for a few days. The doctor will be in to see your shortly." She patted his hand, sent the woman a look that could have meant any-thing, then moved away.

His "wife" walked toward the windows again. But was she really his wife? She seemed so reserved and removed. Maybe it was just wishful thinking on his part to believe that this woman could be his.

But he *knew* her. They were involved in some kind of relationship, or she wouldn't be here in the first place. Somewhere outside his vision he heard a hum — a distant sound that filled his head and gradually grew louder and louder. His eyes closed despite his attempts to keep them open, and he thought about rocking gently on soft waves.

The second time he awakened, he breathed deeply, then groaned as fire burst across his rib cage once again. He blinked rapidly several times. The room was half dark. The woman no longer waited at the window.

Kelsey . . .

There it was. So simple. But he'd been unable to think of it while she'd been there.

She is my wife.

He realized his left arm was in a cast and weighted down. His face felt tight and hot, and when he squinched his muscles, a new pain erupted. He didn't think he had the power to move his legs, but a heart-thundering surge of fear abated when he realized he could wiggle his toes. He wasn't paralyzed. At least it didn't seem so.

However, whatever he'd done, he'd done it big time.

He remembered hazily that the doctor had come and examined him, but he'd been lost in a twilight netherworld that felt infinitely safer than this real one. Kelsey had hovered around; he could hear her voice. But her tone was curiously flat, and he had the sense that he was missing vital information.

Now, he felt sharper, and consequently the pain was more acute as well. Carefully — oh, so carefully — he turned his head on the pillow to look out the windows. City lights. Lights. Fitful, smattering rain slapping the panes at irregular intervals.

I'm Jarred Bryant.

He opened his mouth and tried to say the same, but his lips were cracked and the message from brain to tongue and vocal cords seemed to get waylaid somewhere. He shivered. Would he be mute forever?

He tried again, and this time a huffing *ugh* escaped from his throat. Better. Things appeared operational even if they weren't exactly running at capacity.

But the effort cost him dearly. He could feel the sinking exhaustion envelop him again, and this time he did not welcome it. He needed to stay awake. He needed to be alert and ready.

Ready for what? he wondered, realizing that the anxious feeling had come from somewhere in his subconscious. But it flitted briefly through the channels of his brain and was gone, and Jarred sank into deep slumber once again.

The third time he surfaced it felt as if he were literally swimming from the depths of a dark well. He pulled and thrashed and strained until he broke the surface and there she was. His wife. Kelsey Bennett Bryant. Standing at the foot of his bed and gazing at him with mixed emotions, which he sensed had something to do with the events that had brought him here in the first place.

He cleared his throat. She straightened abruptly, lips parting in surprise, amber eyes widening just a bit. This morning she wore a white silk blouse and a black skirt and jacket. She looked as if she were going to a bankers' convention or a funeral. He could not believe this beautiful woman was his wife. For reasons he didn't want to explore too deeply, he felt he didn't deserve her.

"Hello," he managed to say, though his voice sounded rough and scratchy as if from disuse.

Instantly a shadow crossed her face. And Jarred remembered with dampened hopes that she didn't like him much. In fact, he could safely say her feelings verged on loathing and disgust.

"Don't talk too much. I'm glad you can," she assured him quickly, "but don't tax yourself. Dr. Alastair said a lot of things about your condition. Rest was right at the top of his prescription list."

"What happened?" he managed to rasp.

She swept in a sharp, swift breath, disconcerted. Jarred waited for some kind of explanation, but she either couldn't — or wouldn't — enlighten him. Instead she paced to the windows, and he had to turn his head to follow her movements. Outside, the sky and buildings reflected the same color: gray.

"Oh, don't move," she said, catching his wince as she glanced back. "Please. I won't . . . be here long. I'm just trying to figure out what to do. Your parents will be here soon. They're so relieved."

"My parents?" he muttered. His head felt loose and liquidy inside, as if pieces were unattached. Or maybe that was just the effects of the drugs they were obviously running through the intravenous line attached to the back of his right wrist.

"Do you remember anything, anything at all?" she asked tensely, shooting him such a fear-filled look that he could only stare at her return.

Drugs. That caught at the corners of his mind. But it seemed wrong somehow.

"Was it . . . a car wreck?" he asked.

Her shoulders slackened.

She hesitated, then turned to him, eyeing him soberly. "They recommended that I shouldn't tell you what happened. They want you to remember on your own." She paused, then asked in a strained voice, "Do you know who I am?"

. . . has to remember . . . has to recover . . . Oh, God, what if he doesn't?

. . . Forget it. We could never be that lucky . . .

13

Jarred swallowed and considered. Bits of conversation he might have dreamed ran across his brain. Was one of those watery voices hers? A deep, sinking feeling that felt suspiciously like despair filled him, and he closed his eyes. Closed her out. Every instinct he possessed wanted to call out to her and beg her to forgive him and hold him and trust him again.

"Dr. Alastair is coming," she said with relief into the silent void. Footsteps approached and she added, "I'll be back this evening."

She was gone in a heartbeat, a lingering scent following in her wake. He recognized it as one of those natural perfumes concocted in some up-scale bath and body store. He'd called it "Kelsey" because it was what she wore and he associated it with her. She'd been bothered by the endearment even though she'd never voiced her feelings.

"Hello there."

Jarred opened his eyes and gazed up at the gray-haired doctor with the faint smile and intent gaze who stood over him.

"Do you know who I am?"

"The doctor," Jarred answered after a moment.

"Uh-huh. And you're the patient. I'm Dr. Alastair."

"How long have I been here?"

"Four days."

"Four days?" He was mildly shocked that so much time had passed.

"What do you remember about the accident?"

That was a blank. Jarred struggled to recall anything at all, but the effort made his head ache and the doctor placed a hand lightly against his shoulder.

"Don't try too hard. It'll come. Do you know your name?"

A long, intense moment passed while Dr. Alastair regarded him with clinical curiosity. Kelsey had called him by name but the doctor didn't possess that knowledge. For reasons that escaped him he sensed subterfuge was still necessary, and in a split second he decided on what course to travel.

"No," Jarred whispered and the deception began.

Chapter One

Russet leaves spun wildly, a last gasp of movement before they settled to the ground, sticking wetly against the black pavement. Kelsey walked through the growing piles, unconscious of the leaves' slickness as her black heels stepped off the tarmac and headed in the direction of the people grouped at the top of the knoll. The path she traveled was made up of tiny beaten gravel, adding a more natural look to the beauty and serenity of the tall firs and gray headstones that dotted the rolling hillside. Rain slapped at her cheek, and the wind threatened to snatch her black umbrella out of her numbed hands.

November in Seattle — or more accurately, Silverlake, a small suburb tucked outside the ever-growing circle of the city. Seattle itself was surrounded by water: Puget Sound, Lake Washington, Lake Union. A glance to her left and she could see a glimmering reflection off in the distance. Eighteen-mile-long Lake Washington. To her east and south, though she couldn't see it from here, was Lake Sammamish. If her mind were in gear, she would be able to think of its size as well.

But her mind wasn't in gear. There was a great gap between the synapses somewhere inside her brain. Maybe her whole collective nervous system had shut down. Except that she was walking and she managed to tell the cab driver where her destination should be: the graveyard.

The graveyard.

Oh, it had another name. Something more suitable to senses chafed raw by tragedy. But Kelsey had always known it as simply "the graveyard." She and her friends had sneaked over at night when they were in junior high and jumped the graves until something — some sigh of the wind or whisper of the leaves — lifted the hair on their arms and they all ran screaming pell-mell for home and safety.

Today, though, she felt no ghosts, only a gasping sorrow that filled her chest and ached down her limbs and made her want to collapse on the water-soaked ground. Chance was dead, and there was no bringing him back. Gone. Forever.

And it was Jarred's fault.

For an instant, a flash of rage singed across the deadened nerves in her brain. Jarred Bryant. Her husband. The man responsible for Chance's death.

Her grip tightened on the umbrella's curved

handle. Resolve tightened her lips. The same resolve that had kept her going ever since the terrible news of the plane crash. She was going to divorce Jarred and leave this loveless marriage behind her. She should have done it years before. But Chance's death was the impetus that she'd needed so badly to cut the ties that bound her to Jarred.

"Kelsey . . ."

Marlena Rowden reached out a trembling hand. Chance's mother. The woman who had been there for Kelsey all those years of growing up in Silverlake while her childhood friendship with Chance developed into something more. Marlena had always held a special place in her life. She'd taken Kelsey in after the deaths of her own parents: her mother from breast cancer; her father from subsequent loneliness and loss of the will to live.

Chance's parents had picked up the pieces when Kelsey, aged sixteen, was left lost and bewildered. She'd relied on them for love and support just as she'd relied on Chance, and though Chance and she had grown apart after high school, Kelsey had continued to see herself as an "adopted" Rowden. They were her family.

Until Jarred Bryant, that is.

"I'm so sorry," Marlena said now, tears filling her eyes.

"Oh, Marlena . . ." Kelsey hugged her and the grief she'd held back these long, awful days surfaced and filled every space inside her. She wanted to cry out in agony. It was Jarred's fault! He'd been at the controls of the small plane, and if anyone were to blame for the craft's sudden spiral downward into the Columbia River, it was Jarred.

"We — we hadn't seen a lot of Chance lately, you know," Marlena said, pulling away from Kelsey to search in her black faux-leather bag for a Kleenex. "He was having some troubles. You know . . ."

"Yes, I know."

"Robert and I have relied on you more than we should. But Chance couldn't help it." New tears welled and she pressed the Kleenex to her mouth, her face scrunched up in misery.

"I know, I know."

Kelsey couldn't talk about that now. Chance had been a drug user for years. A dabbler, mostly, or so Kelsey liked to think, but the bald truth was that drugs had controlled his life for so long that he was a stranger to everyone, maybe even himself.

"If you hadn't been there for us, I don't know what we would have done."

"You were there for me," Kelsey reminded her gently, hugging her once more. Marlena had been more like a best friend than a woman a generation ahead of her. Even when Kelsey was in high school, Marlena had treated her the way she might have someone her own age, and Kelsey had thrived in the role. Of course, these past years they'd naturally become more distant

19

with each other; Kelsey's marriage had necessitated the change. But it didn't mean they weren't still family, and now, with the Rowdens' only child dead just months shy of his thirtieth birthday, Marlena and Robert only had Kelsey.

And she only had them.

Marlena's face was as white and fragile as old china. Holding her body close, Kelsey sensed the shudder that passed through her thin frame. Over her shoulder Kelsey caught sight of the wheelchair-bound Robert Rowden, a victim of Parkinson's disease, Chance's father. She smiled sadly at the man who seemed to have aged two decades since the accident that had taken his son's life.

"I wish he were still here," Marlena choked out.

"Me, too." Kelsey's voice sounded strangled and raw.

"What are we going to do?"

"I'll be there."

Gently she disentangled herself from Marlena's embrace, hugged Robert, then took a position among the ring of people who'd attended the grave-side service. The group was small. Chance possessed only a few true friends and most of them were scattered to the four winds. Other Silverlake residents who remembered him from high school still called him "the boy with the brightest future." Those attending the grave-side service knew Kelsey as well, and they stopped to talk to her, one by one. But in the back of her head, she considered what they truly must be thinking: She was the wife of the man who'd taken Chance Rowden's life.

A headache started at her temples, but she resolutely refused to succumb. She hadn't lived in the same house as Jarred for the last three years; their marriage had been in trouble even longer. But she was still legally married to the man, and now, with this tremendous burden of grief and blame, which she couldn't quite shake, she wondered why she hadn't taken those steps toward divorce and freedom earlier.

And what had Jarred been doing with Chance in that plane anyway?

A flash of Jarred in the hospital bed burst across the screen of her mind: white bandages, unsteady breathing, bruised cheeks and chin, swollen fingers and lacerations. Unwillingly, a pang of sympathy jarred her. He looked so . . . so *pathetic* that she wanted to comfort him!

Imagine wanting to comfort *Jarred Bryant!*

Inhaling deeply, she mentally shook herself. This service was for Chance. She refused to think about Jarred here.

Marlena's hand fumbled for hers, and Kelsey squeezed it warmly. They stood together like two sentinels and waited. This grave-side service was an add-on for those who knew Chance best. Kelsey listened to the minister's final words through a haze of numb resolve as Chance's body was interred forever. Glancing over the line of black umbrellas rimming the newly dug grave and walnut casket, she couldn't help another thought of Jarred from creeping in. He'd shocked her, opening his eyes like that yesterday, and talking to him again this morning had been surreal and frighteningly *déjà-vu-ish*. He'd been so . . . willing to talk. Just the sound of his voice had raised her heartbeat and lifted the hairs on her arms, and she'd found it difficult to shove him to a distant corner of her mind.

Another flash of memory: herself, meeting Jarred Bryant for the first time, dazzled by his wealth and social status and good looks, standing like a deer caught in headlights as she watched him across a crowded room, dumb-struck when he'd worked his way toward her and they'd been standing face-to-face for the first time.

"I understand you work for Trevor," he'd said by way of introduction.

"Yes."

"Interior design?"

"Yes."

"If you have any influence whatsoever, can you get him to stop designing those milk cartons and littering up the waterfront?"

She'd laughed then, her wonderment over meeting him evaporating as she broke into peals of mirth. Trevor Taggart, one of Seattle's most influential developers and Kelsey's boss, was chock-full of bad taste. He liked ultramodern

22

buildings and had had the Historical Society, the city of Seattle, and most everyone else up in arms at least once every other year. Kelsey sometimes wondered why she aligned herself with Trevor, but he truly thought his ideas were good and often stood around in hurt and confusion at all the slings and arrows thrown his way.

"Those 'milk cartons' aren't so bad," she said, referring to Trevor's latest project, which included a series of look-alike buildings all painted white. "Don't worry. They're going to be taupe."

"Really?" Jarred arched a brow. He was a direct competitor of Trevor's in Bryant Industries' construction division, though his buildings were unfailingly tasteful no matter what the style.

"You should see the interiors. They're fantastic, really."

"Your work?"

She blushed, embarrassed. "The design, I mean."

"I'd like to see them."

She lifted a hand. "Call anytime. Someone will be happy to show you around."

"I'd rather have it be you than Taggart."

Kelsey lifted her shoulders. "That can be arranged . . ."

And so had started her life with Jarred Bryant. It was funny. Shortly after she and Jarred got serious, Chance appeared on her doorstep. He begged her not to marry Jarred, even before Jarred actually popped the question. She'd laughed at his fears, never believing Jarred's intent was that honorable. Then she had been touched when Chance cleaned himself up and suddenly pledged true love. She hadn't listened, of course, because not only was she falling in love with Jarred, but she knew Chance's problems weren't over. They'd just been momentarily put on hold. And she wasn't in love with him anyway. Not in that way. They were friends and "adopted" siblings, and she could never regard him as anything else.

And Kelsey had been entranced with Jarred's extraordinary good looks, intenseness, quick, furtive smile, and business acumen. He'd seemed larger than life, and she'd fallen in love so quickly, so completely, that it was a long time before she faced the fact that she'd made a mistake. She hadn't really known him. She hadn't known then that he possessed the soul of a snake and a miserable, shrunken heart. She'd learned those truths the hard way.

Wincing at her own mental honesty, Kelsey came back to the events currently happening at Chance's grave. The casket was being lowered. People flung roses onto its disappearing satiny lid. Separating from Marlena, she hung back, detached in her own sorrow.

Surprisingly, she'd actually seen Chance last Saturday night, the night before that fateful plane ride. He'd come to her condominium, looking absolutely terrible, a walking skeleton. He'd broken down and cried and said things were just awful. "My life is over," he'd said,

24

words that now lifted the hair on Kelsey's scalp and caused her to shiver.

She'd offered him coffee and food, but he'd seemed to have something on his mind that he couldn't quite force past his lips. Apart from saying, "I'm sorry. I'm sorry. Oh, Kelsey, I'm sorry," he'd been unable to express himself. He kissed her before he left and whispered he loved her near her ear.

And then he was gone.

It hurt. It ached. Chance had never escaped his desire for recreational drugs. He'd battled and lost time and again. He was a drug addict and that was it.

But he didn't deserve to die!

"Are you stopping by the house?" Marlena quavered as everyone began to disperse. She stepped carefully over soggy patches of ground and piles of autumn leaves. Robert waited in his wheelchair, his gaze and thoughts a million miles away.

Kelsey shook her head. She wouldn't be able to stand about while people drank coffee and ate hors d'oeuvres off paper plates and talked in quiet circles about Chance. Her stomach revolted at the image. "I'll come see you another time," she told the woman who had once prayed she would be Kelsey's mother-in-law. But Kelsey had inherited Nola and Jonathan Bryant, instead of Marlena and Robert Rowden, and she knew, regardless of what she felt about Chance, or Jarred, she'd certainly lost out in the in-law department. Jarred's parents were as cold and self-motivated as Chance's were warm and giving.

She shuddered just thinking about how she would have to soon see them.

"How *is* your husband?" a stolid woman in a gray dress asked as she hurried to catch up to Kelsey and Marlena. Florence Wickum. Silverlake's self-appointed know-it-all.

Kelsey couldn't immediately answer. Marlena started to tear up, dabbing at the corners of her eyes with a tissue. It was as if this reminder of how her son had died was the final crack in the dam of her defenses.

Florence blinked. "Oh, I'm so sorry. I didn't want to cause more pain."

Marlena shook her head and tried to wave her away. She was woefully inadequate in fighting off the Florences of the world.

Kelsey surged to her rescue. "Jarred is . . . re-covering," she said tightly.

"I heard he was in a coma." Subtlety was not Florence's forte.

"He was unconscious for several days."

"Oh? So he came out of it?"

"Yes."

Marlena gazed numbly at Kelsey. "Did he say . . . why?"

She knew what Marlena meant. No one understood why Chance and Jarred had been together. They weren't friends. Acquaintances, maybe, but even that was a stretch. "No."

"Is he all right?" Marlena asked.

"Physically he seems to be improving very well. I'm meeting with his doctor tomorrow for a full update."

"What about mentally?" Florence seized on Kelsey's unspoken concern.

"He's . . . alert."

"He spoke to you then?" Florence pressed. "You talked to him?"

"I did." Kelsey took a step backward and her heel sank into water-soaked grass. She struggled to pull her shoe free. Her foot slipped out, one toe dipping into the damp ground. Reaching down, she yanked at the shoe and stepped back inside it, mud and all.

"I'm sure Mr. Bryant had a perfectly good reason for taking Chance with him in that airplane," Florence said soothingly to Marlena. "I have to admit I'd be anxious to hear what it was though!"

"He didn't say anything?" Marlena pressed, needing answers Kelsey was unable to give.

"Jarred hasn't recovered all of his memory yet," Kelsey was forced to explain. "Apparently it's a common enough side effect from trauma to the head."

"Are you saying he has *amnesia?*" Florence demanded.

"No. He's just fuzzy on the details. Please . . ." Kelsey tucked a hand under Marlena's arm and pulled her away from Florence. "I don't know enough yet. Jarred's barely awake. Believe me,

I'll find out what happened."

"I know you will, dear."

"He was heading toward Portland when the plane nose-dived. It crashed into the north bank of the Columbia River, then slid into the water. There were rescuers there immediately. They saw it go down. Otherwise, Chance's body would not have been recovered so quickly."

"And your husband might not have survived."

"Yes, I know."

Kelsey turned her gaze toward the Olympic Mountains. Today they were invisible, their majestic slopes hidden by the arms of gray clouds that so often enfolded the Seattle area in their thick embrace. The crash was still being investigated, but there was no question that Jarred had been at the controls of the small plane. Preliminary reports suggested mechanical malfunction. Detectives involved in the investigation were tight-lipped and unresponsive when the suggestion of foul play was bandied about.

Marlena's drowning eyes gazed up at Kelsey. "You'll tell me, won't you? Please? When you learn the truth?"

Kelsey gazed at her helplessly. "If there's any truth to learn," she agreed.

"Thank you. Thank you . . ." She glanced around distractedly.

Knowing Marlena was searching for her husband, Kelsey's gaze sought out Robert Rowden, who surfaced from his reverie and lifted a hand in their direction. Kelsey made sure Marlena and he connected. Then she gave them hugs and a last sketchy wave good-bye.

She walked back the way she'd come, feeling weary all over. Her feet barely stepped one in front of the other. The cabbie was still there. She'd asked him to wait, and he'd happily complied. "Where to, ma'am?" he asked as she closed the door behind her and simply sat in silence.

"Bryant Park Hospital," she said, leaning her head back against the cushions. She was asleep inside thirty seconds.

Money. That was what made the world go around, not love. One step through the silent sliding doors of the lobby and one was inside Bryant Park Hospital — haven for those with the biggest bank accounts. It sported the Bryant name by no coincidence. Jarred's grandfather had bought up property around Seattle, made a fortune in development and land sale, donated money hand over fist, and left a king's ransom in the upper millions for his son and grandson.

Kelsey turned toward the stairs, which were carpeted on these lower floors in soothing mauve tones. She trudged up six flights, needing the exercise and time before she faced the man she'd married eight years earlier. *Eight years!* For one startling moment, she remembered how good it had been in the beginning; then she shook her head, erasing those treacherous thoughts. It wasn't like that anymore.

The sixth floor sported gleaming linoleum floors and stretches of wide windows along the outside walls. Gray, gray, gray. The weather was as dismal and boring as her life had been since that terrible night when she and Jarred had fought so bitterly and she'd moved out of the house they shared.

Turning the corner toward Jarred's private room, she stutter stepped, then inwardly berated herself for revealing her tumultuous feelings to the people whispering outside the door: Nola and Jonathan Bryant. Jarred's loving parents.

They looked up and frowned in unison. Neither had approved of Jarred's choice of a wife. Not then, and certainly not now. Neither bothered to approach her now with any kind of encouragement whatsoever as she slowly made her way toward them. Politeness did not run in the Bryant household.

"How is he?" Kelsey asked quietly.

"The same." Nola's lips pursed, heightening the lines around her mouth, lines etched by years of smoking. She looked desperate for a cigarette now, her toe tapping, tension emanating from her in palpable waves.

"What was he doing?" Jonathan asked a bit blankly. He leaned heavily on a cane now, a recent addition because his own health was steadily failing. Like Robert Rowden, Jonathan seemed to have aged alarmingly since the accident, and at this rate, it wouldn't be too much longer until Jonathan found himself facing a wheelchair as well. He was an anxious, unhappy man, and Kelsey had never really understood him, though she silently sympathized with anyone who had lived so long with his demanding wife. "What was he doing? Where was he going?" he muttered fretfully, running his free hand over his jaw and shaking his head.

These were the same two questions Jonathan had asked ever since the accident occurred. Kelsey shook her head. She knew Jarred's parents blamed her somehow, but she was at as much of a loss as any of them. Jarred's motives were murky. What *had* he been doing with Chance?

Neither Nola nor Jonathan had expressed any sympathy or even interest in Chance's death. They were as self-absorbed as always, although their fear for their son was real. Kelsey glanced past them to where Jarred lay. She could just see the end of the bed from her position, the small white tent of the covers that indicated his feet. Dim gray afternoon light from the fading day filtered into the room. The weight of depression was so intense she had to take several deep breaths to clear her head.

"Excuse me," she murmured, intending to slip between Jarred's parents.

"I know you want that divorce," Nola said tautly.

"Pardon?" Kelsey turned back in dumb amazement. Nola, for all her faults, was rarely so blunt.

"You've just been waiting. Letting Jarred hang on all these years in the faint hope that you'd come back. Meanwhile everyone's just getting older and nothing happens, and *now this!*"

"I'm sorry," she answered automatically, startled a bit by Nola's vehemence. She reminded herself that the woman was under tremendous strain. "He's going to recover," she added more softly.

"Will he?" Nola demanded through quivering lips. "You'd be happy if he didn't, wouldn't you? So much more convenient for you."

"Oh, Nola," Kelsey protested.

"Don't pretend you care now!" She glanced toward the door of Jarred's room, her hands clenched in agony. "He may not recover, you know. And when I think about how you could have been there for him, all these years, it just breaks my heart. No children. No heirs. Just selfish Kelsey and now my son . . . is . . . lying in there. . . ." One arm gestured futilely toward his room.

"Nola," Jonathan whispered in agony. The cane supported almost all of his weight. Kelsey wondered if she should put her arm around him, but the furious energy emanating from Nola prevented her.

"I don't want to talk. . . ." Turning away quickly, Nola headed blindly down the hallway toward the bank of elevators, her heels clicking angrily against the polished linoleum. A pregnant pause ensued.

Kelsey gazed at Jonathan, who inhaled on a deep, shaking breath. "Where was he going?" he asked again.

Kelsey shook her head. "I don't know."

I'm sorry hung between them, but neither uttered a word. Jonathan turned in the direction of his wife and moved away slowly, his limping steps barely more than a shuffle.

Entering Jarred's room, Kelsey steeled herself for that first look at her husband. He lay asleep, breathing wispily, the bruises on his face starting to turn yellow — the color that meant the blood was dispersing, the patient healing. But even the bruises' sallow ugliness couldn't hide Jarred's innate handsomeness. His nose was straight and aquiline, his brow strong, his lashes dense and unfairly long for a male. She'd teased him about them once, in the first blush of their relationship, and he'd regarded her with that faint smile of indulgence that she had mistaken for affection. One arm lay strapped to his chest, the other limp against the bedcovers. She glanced at his fingers. They were long and sensual, and once upon a time, they had swept across the hill of her cheekbone, his thumb lingering near her lips while his eyes, a strong steely blue, had stared into her own amber ones with a message of pure desire.

"Kelsey?"

She gasped and jumped, whirling at the sound, her heart slamming. Rising from a chair tucked in the corner was Jarred's half brother,

Will Bryant. Will had taken his father's name after his mother sued Jonathan Bryant for parental support and dumped her illegitimate son on Nola and Jonathan.

"Will, you startled me!" she half whispered, half laughed.

"I'm sorry." His answer was a whisper, too. Neither wanted to wake Jarred, nor did they want him to overhear their conversation. "I was just thinking. My father and Nola just left."

"I know. I met them in the hallway." She walked to the back of the room, where Will sat.

He wasn't as tall as Jarred, nor as naturally good-looking, but he possessed qualities Jarred would never have: compassion and interest in others. But today he gazed at Kelsey rather piercingly. She hadn't seen him since the night of the accident, and then they'd all been shocked, raw and dumbly disbelieving.

"How's Danielle?" Kelsey asked automatically.

"Okay." Will shrugged. He was always noncommittal about his wife. The state of their marriage was as bad as Kelsey and Jarred's, although they still resided beneath the same roof.

"You talked to him?" Will asked, inclining his head in Jarred's direction.

"Well . . . we spoke a few words."

"Dr. Alastair said he's come to a couple of times."

"It wasn't exactly enlightening. Jarred doesn't seem to remember much."

"He doesn't remember anything," Will corrected her. "Not even his own name."

Kelsey absorbed that. "It's too early to tell."

"Is it? He didn't say so, but I could tell Dr. Alastair was concerned. Something's not right. Nola and my father suspect it, too. So does Sarah."

Kelsey's nerves jumped. Sarah Ackerman was not someone she cared to think about. It was common knowledge that Sarah, employed by Bryant Industries, was Jarred's right-hand woman at work and, as rumor went, in the bedroom as well. Kelsey had once firmly believed the rumor, though with time she'd grown to wonder exactly where rumor started and truth ended. Nothing was ever as it seemed.

"Sarah came to see him?" she ventured, though the words tasted foul on her tongue.

"We're all worried. For chrissakes, Kelsey, Jarred *is* Bryant Industries. He's the only one who knows what's really going on." He waved away her look. "Sure, I'm with him on most deals, but Jarred's Jarred, you know? It's not like he would relate everything to me. He's not made that way."

"No, he's not," she agreed.

"I've been waiting here for him to wake up. I really need to talk to him. And not just about business," he added swiftly.

"Did I say anything?"

"You didn't have to. I know what that sounded like. But he's my brother."

Silence followed his last words, echoing a

hidden emotion that wasn't so carefully hidden after all. Will loved Jarred. That was clear. Kelsey, who generally didn't exactly know what she felt for Will, was swamped by a flood of affection for him. At least his motivation was pure. His familial motivation, at any rate. As far as the business part of it went, she wouldn't trust anyone inside or out of Bryant Industries. They were all too focused on the making of money, money, money.

Glancing at his watch, Will muttered impatiently, "I've got to go back to the office tonight. I really wanted to talk to him. If he wakes up, what are you going to say?"

"I'm not supposed to say anything. Dr. Alastair wants Jarred to remember on his own."

Jarred stirred, exhaling in a deep breath. Kelsey glanced around sharply, her pulse leaping skyward. Walking over to his bed, Will stared down at his brother, and Kelsey took a place by his side. Only when Jarred remained asleep did she relax again. She wanted him to wake up, too, but she didn't relish what the future had in store for any of them.

Disappointment clouded Will's face. He leaned toward Kelsey, as if to give her a brotherly kiss, thought better of it, and managed a brief hug instead. "Keep in touch."

"I will. Good-bye."

He nodded, then left. Kelsey sat in the chair next to Jarred's bed, feeling the effects of the day. She should make an appearance at work as well, but she was just too tired. Trevor, though sympathetic to Jarred's plight, didn't spend a lot of time dwelling on things. He was a man in constant motion. She knew he was about finished with feeling generous about the time she'd taken for this accident. They were in the middle of a project that required her attention, and she could visualize him pacing the floor, struggling to hide his impatience at her lengthy disappearance.

But too bad. She wasn't ready to face her other obligations yet. She was, whether she liked it or not, Jarred's wife, and she needed to be by his side during this terrible time.

Not exactly knowing why, Kelsey moved her chair a bit closer, gazing at the contours of Jarred's face and the dark wave of his hair, staring at him as if she'd never seen him before. So much of their life together she'd been uncomfortable in his presence. He'd been so — he *was* so — piercingly intent. If he were awake she could never have just looked at him like this. His eyes would have been staring right back at her, daring her to explain what she thought she was doing, silently mocking her unrequited love for him.

So now *her* eyes drank in the sight of him. She pored over the smallest details from the shape of his hairline to the small white half-moons on his fingernails. The ugly bruises that marred his skin, yet couldn't disguise his handsome profile. His strong jaw. The arch of his throat and Adams's apple. Spiky dark lashes and the curl of his hair at the base of his ear.

When she was finished, her brow furrowed in puzzlement and loss. Why? Why had things come to pass as they had? Why had he married her?

Glancing down at his hands, she felt a lump grow in her throat at the sight of the thin gold band she'd purchased for him. It wasn't horribly expensive, but it had been for her in those days. He'd never taken it off, even when he'd been unfaithful to her after that night of their worst fight. She'd accused him of that unfaithfulness — with Sarah Ackerman, no less! — and he'd furiously snarled that he *should* be sleeping with other women since Kelsey had set the rules.

With a careful finger, she touched the gold band, lightly tracing her fingers over his. When she glanced up again at his face, she got a cold jolt.

Jarred's blue eyes were open and staring at her. In that smooth drawl that so unnerved her, he said, "Hello, Kelsey."

Chapter Two

"You — you know me?" Surprised, Kelsey leaned backward. "You recognize me?"

The way he was looking at her unraveled Kelsey's nerves. He seemed so . . . so . . . so *happy* to see her!

He's medicated for the pain, she reminded herself. *Don't confuse drug-induced euphoria with something else.*

"I heard him call you by name," Jarred rasped out, as if the words were scratching his throat as they passed through. "Will."

Kelsey fought back some very strange feelings. It was odd, this loss of his memory. And the way he seemed now . . . Good grief, it was almost as if he *wanted* her here! But Jarred hadn't wanted her in years.

"I thought you remembered me," she said. "But you don't remember then?"

"Not much. Who's Will?"

Kelsey exhaled a pent-up breath. "Will is . . ." Collecting herself, she shook her head. "I'm not supposed to be your memory for you, Jarred. You're supposed to recall everything yourself."

"Why?"

"I don't know. I guess it's a function of your getting better. Some kind of yardstick maybe? All I know is that I don't want to get in the way of what Dr. Alastair feels is best for you."

Jarred seemed to think that over. "Dr. Alastair," he repeated after a long moment. "The one with the small beard and big ears."

Kelsey's lips parted in surprise. Jarred was many things, but rarely was he the observer of small things such as the appearance of others. He was just moving too fast. "That sounds like Dr. Alastair," she admitted.

"Well, I think he's dead wrong in his diagnosis. I've tried to remember what happened and it's all just a fog, which frustrates the hell out of me. I can't see any reason not to be told my own history. I want you to clue me in."

Now *that* sounded like the old Jarred. "I can't. He'll have to make that decision."

"I don't want him. I want you," Jarred said in a way that warmed Kelsey's blood even while she recognized he did not mean those words the way they sounded.

Still, she couldn't prevent a soft smile. "You don't want me, Jarred." Regret tinged her tone, and hearing it, Kelsey cleared her throat and moved toward the bank of windows, away from him and the strange feelings he evoked inside her.

"You're my wife."

Silence fell between them. Kelsey couldn't find anything to say to him.

"Aren't you?"

She inhaled through her teeth, wishing some flip comment would come to mind, as it so often did during their conversations together. But for once, her quick wit failed her completely.

"Well, aren't you?" he demanded with less patience.

"Yes."

"Then, come here."

Come here? Come *here?* Kelsey instantly bristled, hearing the request as if it were an order. But when she met his gaze, she saw nothing in his blue eyes except an emotion she might classify as need in another person.

This is Jarred, she reminded herself. *Jarred Bryant. Don't forget it. . . .*

A shade reluctantly, Kelsey returned to his bedside, but when his hand reached for hers, she couldn't meet the searching questions in his eyes. Her own hand lay limp within the warmth of his palm. Her heart thudded unevenly. His fingers tightened around hers.

"What is it?" he asked in genuine confusion.

Her breath came out in a half laugh. She shook her head.

"Something's wrong. Can't you tell me?"

"The doctor said to wait."

"I don't want to wait. You're using that as an excuse," he added with sudden insight.

"No. I told you. You're supposed to remember on your own."

"Why are you afraid to be next to me?"

Kelsey jerked. She dared to meet his gaze and those soul-searching eyes of his were glued to her face, gauging her response. "Because you're kind of scary," she said lightly.

"Am I?"

"Yes."

"Are *you* scared of me?"

A beat passed. "No."

This was true, though she'd never thought of it in these particular terms before. Jarred had never frightened her, even at his worst moments. There had been times when she'd wanted to throw a drink in his face or beat her fists against his chest or kick him in the shins or do something equally as infantile, but she'd never felt actual fear. He'd angered her and hurt her and made her feel inadequate, but she knew he would never do anything to her that would cause her true harm.

"What are you thinking?" he asked, watching the play of emotions cross her mobile face.

"I'm thinking that we should have this conversation when you're better. It's a little unfair with you in a hospital bed."

"You mean you've got the advantage?"

"I guess so."

He paused a moment. "Is our life together such a battle?"

"Mmm . . ." Kelsey refused to even go there. Yes, it was a battle. Almost from the get-go. Almost from the moment they had met and fallen in love. Or at least from when *she* had fallen in love.

"How did it end up like this?" he asked.

"Please don't make me say something I shouldn't."

"Was it an accident? It must have been. What happened?"

"You're alive," she answered, throwing a glance toward the partially opened doorway. "That's what matters."

"I'm alive," he repeated softly. "That's good, right?"

"Well, of course it is."

"Don't lie to me. I might not be in top form right now, but I can see you don't feel comfortable with me. Why? Did I do something to you? What happened to me? No, wait!" he ordered with some urgency when Kelsey automatically jerked her hand away. "Please don't let go."

It took all her might to clasp his hand again. Considering everything, his grip was incredibly strong. She felt slightly faint and wondered if she were getting sick.

"A police detective tried to talk to me but the doctor kept him away. What happened?"

Detective Newcastle had called and left a message at her office as well. Kelsey knew it must be related to Jarred's plane crash, but she hadn't called him back yet. She knew nothing about the accident — almost as little as Jarred himself — and she didn't want to consider the whys and wherefores of that tragedy and the re-sultant death of a longtime friend.

"Jarred, don't do this. I want to do what's right."

"Are we still in love?"

"Oh, for God's sake, Jarred!"

"Kelsey . . ."

A shiver slipped down her back at the soft use of her name. How long had it been since he'd sounded so tender? How long — if ever — since he'd needed her for something?

The air in her lungs had been held captive. Slowly releasing it, she said, "We're not living together right now. I've moved out."

His lids lowered and his jaw tautened. "Oh."

"It was a mutual decision. We just couldn't make it work."

"How long ago?"

"Three years."

"Three years?"

She flinched at his shocked whisper. "Yes, well, neither of us ever took that next step."

"You mean divorce?"

Kelsey nodded.

"So what happens now?" he asked. "Are you going to move back in?"

"What do you mean?"

"I'm" — he licked dry lips, pausing for a mo-ment before stating the obvious — "I'm going to need some help when I get out of the hos-pital. I was wondering if you would be there."

Be there? *Be there?* Kelsey couldn't even

44

imagine living under the same roof with him, let alone actually caring for him. "Well, you'll have a nurse, I'm sure. I mean, your mother will make certain of it. You can't just be left on your own. I can see that. It's bound to be a while before you're back to your old self."

His eyelids slowly closed and his mouth twisted. "I'm not sure I want to be my old self."

Kelsey regarded him soberly, realizing at some stronger level the depth of his injuries and the ensuing pain that had to accompany them. She wanted to reach out and embrace him and whisper that it would all be okay, but then she caught herself up short. Jarred would never allow such an open display of pure warmth and affection. "Why not?" she asked curiously.

He reopened his eyes, staring at her. "I don't think you like my old self."

Kelsey fought hard not to react. Some part of her wanted him still, and that small part seemed to heat her blood and course through her veins, infecting every inch of her being, making it nearly impossible for her to stoke the hate she'd learned to rely on instead of his love.

"Jarred . . ." She licked her lips.

"Yes?" His hand squeezed hers encouragingly. He almost seemed to lean forward, he regarded her so intently.

"Jarred, I want to —"

"Jarred!"

Kelsey nearly leaped out of her skin when Nola Bryant suddenly screeched out her son's name. Jarred jerked, too. Kelsey guiltily yanked her hand away, as if she were afraid Nola would catch them in some nefarious act.

Jarred's mother swept forward in a rush, practically pushing Kelsey out of the way. "Oh, darling, I've been waiting to find you awake! We've been downstairs talking to your doctor, but I couldn't just leave. Your father's still downstairs, but I just knew you would wake up as soon as I left, so I decided to hurry back. Oh, Jarred." She grabbed the hand Kelsey had just been holding, but this time it was Jarred's palm that lay limp.

Jarred's gaze was on his mother's thin, cosmetically perfect face. Recognizing his weariness in the lines by his mouth, Kelsey leaned closer to him, instinctively protective.

"Did you talk to Will?" Nola asked tightly.

Surprised, Kelsey slid her mother-in-law a look. Nola couldn't stand Will. He was the physical reminder of one of her husband's trysts, and Nola made no secret of her feelings toward him. It frustrated her to no end that she had to put up with him at all, but Jarred had swept Will into the family business and Will was now in a position second only to Jarred himself.

"Will?" Jarred repeated.

"He was here." Nola glanced around, as if expecting him to materialize. "Your half brother. Where is he? Surely you remember him. He works with you at Bryant Industries."

"Nola, we're not supposed to tell Jarred everything," Kelsey pointed out. "Dr. Alastair wants him to remember on his own."

"Oh, honestly, Kelsey." She kept her gaze on her son, turning one shoulder toward Kelsey in an effort to ostracize her daughter-in-law even while she spoke to her. "Dr. Alastair only wanted to make certain Jarred was ready for all the information."

"He told me to let Jarred recall everything by himself."

"You're taking him too literally," Nola argued crisply.

Kelsey had half a mind to search out Dr. Alastair herself and drag him to Jarred's room. She turned with that intention, but Jarred suddenly spoke up.

"What happened to me?" Jarred asked Nola.

His mother didn't even hesitate. With no regard for anyone's orders but her own, she said, "Well, you crashed a plane on the banks of the Columbia River."

"Nola!" Kelsey gazed at her in frustration. She wanted to kill her mother-in-law.

"*I* crashed a plane?" Jarred demanded, visibly shocked. "You mean . . . I was the pilot?"

"Yes, your Cessna." Her impatience magnified at Jarred's slow absorption of these facts. "I guess you were heading for Oregon, though God knows why. The flight plan was to Portland, but you never made it there. Something to do with the gas-feed line, I think."

"Where's Jonathan?" Kelsey asked. "Is he coming up?"

"He's meeting me at the car. He didn't think Jarred would be awake." She leaned closer to her son. "Darling, there are serious decisions to make regarding the company. We need your approval and signature."

"Nola, I believe your time is up. I'm sorry." Kelsey gently but firmly linked her arm through her mother-in-law's and steered her toward the door.

Nola yanked her arm away and gave Kelsey a scorching look.

Behind them, Jarred said in a slow drawl, "I don't think I can sign anything at the moment."

Kelsey shot him a look. He lifted one puffy, bandaged hand and Kelsey couldn't decide whether she wanted to laugh or cry. She did share a twinkling moment of repressed humor with Jarred, however, until Nola glanced swiftly from her son to Kelsey and then back again, a frown forming between her perfect brows.

"The signature is going to have to wait," Kelsey told Nola, who gazed down her nose at her daughter-in-law.

"My dear, you don't know anything about our company. You never have and you never will, and you have no right to tell me what to do with *my son.*"

"He's my husband," she pointed out.

Behind Nola, Jarred's mouth slanted into a smile. *He's enjoying this,* Kelsey thought with amazement.

"You know where I stand on this," Nola stated

tautly. "You're no kind of wife if you can't even share your husband's bed."

Jarred made a protesting sound and seemed to want to jump to his feet. Kelsey moved to stop him, automatically touching one leg still tented beneath the blankets.

"I'm sorry, darling," Nola said, as if belatedly recognizing how badly she was behaving. "I'm kind of undone, you know. I've been so worried about you. So awfully worried." She smiled down at him indulgently. "But you're going to be all right now. It's all okay."

Jarred stared back at his mother, as if he were taking stock of her. "Kelsey's my wife," he said.

Appreciating his effort, Kelsey minded her own tongue, stopping herself from delivering the furious rejoinder she wanted to hurl at Nola. She actually had to press her lips together to keep from smiling.

Nola's nostrils flared in defiance. She drew herself up to her full height, which was still several inches shorter than Kelsey's five foot ten. Kelsey's height, which had been a source of concern when she was in junior high, was a welcome bit of arsenal in the war between her and her mother-in-law.

"His memory will come back, you know," Nola pointed out. "And when it does, nothing you can say will make things the way you obviously think they are."

"I don't want to fight with you, Nola."

"Oh, honestly, Kelsey. You always want to

fight me." She glanced toward the bed. "I'll be back later, darling. Get some rest."

Her heels tip-tapped away. Kelsey felt a familiar, long-nursed frustration boil up inside her. Her mother-in-law brought out the worst in her. Just as Jarred did. There was no escaping the past no matter how much she wanted it to evaporate.

"Plane crash?" Jarred asked from behind her.

Slowly she turned around, steeling herself. "Yes," she said wearily. "It's a miracle you survived."

"I was piloting the plane."

She nodded.

"Was I . . . alone?"

A heartbeat passed. She thought back to the grave site and the last glimpse of Chance's coffin. For a moment she simply couldn't move.

"Kelsey . . . ?"

She opened her mouth and shut it several times without speaking. Her throat had mysteriously closed up. No amount of effort could bring forth words.

"Oh, God," Jarred murmured.

Tears jumped to her eyes. Her head swam.

"Are they all right?" he asked urgently. "Please tell me. Please, please tell me. Are they all right?"

"Jarred . . ." she said achingly.

"Kelsey." Guilt lay like a ton weight on her name. "You've got to tell me now. I have to know."

She struggled, unable to look at him. "A man died," she said. "Chance Rowden. A friend. I just came from the funeral. . . ."

There was something distinctly unrestful about a hospital at night. Even when the staff came and turned down the lights, Jarred remained awake, the intensity of his pain and emotions flipped onto high. Now he lay perfectly still, weary and restless and wishing for some kind of absolution, which he feared he might not quite deserve.

Tonight had been pure hell. First, Kelsey's blurted-out truth, a shock wave that still sent ripples through his whole body and tightened his chest. Chance Rowden was dead.

Because of me!

He'd heard the unspoken accusation even though she hadn't meant to say it. She'd tried so hard to let him rediscover his own memory, and he felt like a heel because he already knew a great deal of it. But he hadn't remembered the plane crash, and her revelations had left him with a strong sensation of falling down a deep, endless spiral.

And Chance Rowden. Kelsey's lover. He certainly remembered that. He'd killed the one man his wife loved most in the world.

And that wasn't even the whole of it: He still couldn't remember one damn thing about the accident. Nor could he remember the events that had led up to it. How had he come to be

51

with Chance? When he racked his brain for information, his last available memory before he awakened in the hospital was of the fight between Kelsey and him, which must have occurred about two days before the plane went down.

They were in his office and he was deeply annoyed with her, almost hurt, he recalled.

And she was standing in the center of the office, her hands on her hips, eyes flashing, lips quivering with emotion, equally as furious at him. "It's not like I was *asked* here. I was ordered! So don't go telling me that I need to change my attitude, because I'm not the one who treats people as if they're pawns!"

"Drop it," he snarled. "We've got things to discuss."

"Really. Well, I'm not interested in discussing anything. I've got work to do."

"This concerns a friend of yours."

She shook her head at him as if he were completely dense. "Because of you, Jarred, I don't have any friends. Good-bye."

"Kelsey, don't walk out until you've heard what I have to say," he called to her retreating back.

At the door, she gave him one last long look. "You don't know how to treat people. You never have and you never will, and if I stay here and put up with more of your verbal abuse, then I'm as guilty as you are of social incompetence that borders on pathology."

"Did you stay up nights practicing that line?" he demanded harshly.

"Yes, as a matter of fact. Good-bye."

"Damn it, Kelsey!" But she was gone, leaving him staring after her in frustration.

Now, as he thought back on it, his head literally throbbed. Was Chance Rowden the friend that he'd mentioned to Kelsey? He could scarcely recall what the man looked like, but he knew the man as his own personal nemesis: the man who'd stolen Kelsey's heart when she was still a girl and had never relinquished it. Oh, sure, Kelsey was adamant that Chance was a long-ago lover who held no place in her heart, but Jarred hadn't forgotten how close Chance and she had been at the beginning of their marriage, and he certainly always heard the affectionate turn of her voice whenever any of the Rowden clan were mentioned at all. From that, he'd been forced to draw his own conclusions.

Why had Chance been in the plane with him? He knew Kelsey hadn't meant to blurt that out, but she was consumed with emotion herself and she'd wanted him to know, doctors orders or no. And *he* wanted to know. Thinking, these days, was like dragging the ideas through quicksand. He pulled every thought through a thick mire just to examine it. Nothing was easy, and nothing made sense anyway. He felt too damned exhausted to even really try.

But Kelsey hadn't been his only visitor tonight. As he lay half dozing and turning over all the information he'd learned, his half brother stuck his head in the doorway, then entered the room.

Will grinned at him. "Hey, there, brother. Glad you're finally awake. All this sleeping around, and nothing to show for it but some scars and a plaster cast or two. You're going to ruin your reputation."

"My reputation?"

"That's a joke." Will's grin slowly faded. "You know, because women find you so attractive." He hesitated. "You really don't remember anything?"

"Nothing useful," Jarred responded, hating himself for fostering the lie. But the need to protect himself felt strong, and he was a man who trusted his instincts.

"God, it's good to see you again," Will stated fervently, looking for all the world as if he wanted to hug Jarred but was uncertain of how to go about it. "Man, do we have a lot to talk about. I just hope that doctor of yours stays away long enough for me to do some real damage."

Jarred smiled faintly. "I think we're safe for a while."

Will, like Nola, wasn't nearly as reticent as Kelsey about delivering news. In fact he was practically bursting at the seams with information. "The place is in an uproar. Everything's a mess. I sure wish you were there to put it all back together."

Jarred's sluggish thinking couldn't drag up

any information about work. "What's wrong?"

"Are you sure you want to hear this? I mean, can you?"

"I'm listening."

"Well, thank God!" Will said in relief. "I've been up for days, trying to figure out the right thing to do." He drew a breath and collected himself. "We still don't know who our spy is. I know you don't want to believe that it's Kelsey, but she has access. And let's face it" — he shrugged — "she's got motive. She's not your biggest fan," he added with a grimace.

Spy?

A flash of recognition. Someone working for, or associated with, Bryant Industries was systematically passing information about the development branch of the company to its most head-to-head competitor: Taggart Inc.

Kelsey works for Trevor Taggart of Taggart Inc.

"You really don't remember any of this, do you?"

Jarred focused on his half brother. He couldn't tell how Will really felt about his condition. "Could you fill me in?"

"I'm not supposed to."

"But you will."

Will nodded slowly. "I suppose I shouldn't, but I don't really care. You wouldn't either if you were in my shoes."

"Somehow I know that's right," Jarred said dryly. He was getting a picture of himself that he didn't much like.

"Well, let's start with Taggart Inc. Do you remember them?" When Jarred frowned, Will made an impatient gesture. "Look, I'll stop asking, okay? I'll just start at the beginning, and if you remember or you want me to stop and go over something again, you let me know."

"Okay."

"And if you get tired, speak up. I can come back tomorrow around lunchtime. I've got a couple of meetings in the morning — meetings with the City of Seattle over those setback requirements — but I think I can sneak out early if I have to and let Sarah take over."

"Sarah?"

"Sarah Ackerman." Will's face shuttered. "She's worked for us for years. Came on about the same time you got married. A little earlier actually."

"I don't remember," Jarred said truthfully.

"Yeah, well, she does." Will rubbed his hands together and paced the room, leaving that cryptic remark for Jarred to mull over later. "Anyway, the big problem is in the development department. Taggart's underbidding us on every job, and the bigger problem is who's giving Taggart the information in the first place. You've never wanted to believe it's Kelsey, but it makes too much sense. Anyway" — Will raised conciliatory hands — "I don't want to go over that territory again right now. You know how I feel about Kelsey. If we could take care of that leak, most everything else can wait until you're better."

"You don't like Kelsey?"

Will sighed. "I don't trust her. It's not the same."

"She's my wife."

Will regarded him sympathetically. "You've got no one but yourself to blame for that one, buddy. She swept you off your feet, and you're paying the price."

Jarred absorbed that information in silence. It was funny. He knew so little of what had happened in the past but his gut instinct was to trust Kelsey and no one else. Yet Will was acting as if she were a spy for Trevor Taggart. Though he remembered that she worked for Taggart, for the life of him, he couldn't place her in the role of Mata Hari. She was just too straightforward.

"Why was I in that airplane with Chance Rowden?"

Will started. "Who told you about that?" A heartbeat. "Kelsey?"

"Do you know?"

"No. And I sure as hell wish I did. It would help a lot."

"A detective wants to talk to me, but the doctor's keeping him away."

Will nodded. "Detective Newcastle. He's talked to me, but I sure as hell don't know what you were doing with Rowden. I mean — *Rowden!* We were all hoping you could explain." Will's eyes probed Jarred's. "Do you really not remember anything?"

. . . has to remember . . . has to recover . . . Oh,

God what if he doesn't . . .

. . . Forget it. We could never be that lucky . . .

Jarred outwaited Will, who shook his head, then ran his fingers through his hair. For a strange moment, Jarred got the impression Will was relieved that he couldn't recall anything. Was that true?

"Does the detective think the accident wasn't an accident?" Jarred asked.

"The detective's so closemouthed it's incredible that words actually make it past his lips. I swear he doesn't move his lips. But, yeah, there's got to be something going on or he wouldn't be so anxious to talk to you."

Will sounded more annoyed than threatened. Jarred relaxed a bit. Maybe his fears were unfounded.

He suddenly recalled one his own axioms: Never trust anyone. Especially family . . .

What a sorry, cynical son of a bitch you are, he thought, hating a part of himself that he recognized now as insecurity.

"At least you're going to be okay," Will said, giving Jarred a quick smile. "When we first heard it was god-awful. Sarah damn near fainted, and you know that's not like her."

Sarah Ackerman . . . Jarred recalled what he knew about her and decided that much was true. From what he remembered, she was tough and unrelenting, and though she wore skirts rather than pants, there was something almost masculine about her that had never appealed to him, no matter how many times she came on to him and let him know she wanted more than a business relationship.

He realized Will knew nothing about that either. Nor did Kelsey, he thought with a sudden pang of guilt. He'd never explained about Sarah. Undoubtedly she believed they'd been having an affair.

His heart jumped. Had they? Searching the memory that he didn't quite trust yet, he felt a few pulse-pounding moments of indecision. It was his own intense reaction that convinced him he'd never found his way to Sarah's bed. All he felt was uninterest when it came to her as a woman. Uninterest tinged with a bit of revulsion . . .

But he remembered he'd let Kelsey think the worst — a thought that haunted him now and made him desperate to undo the past.

"Dad was upset, too," Will went on. "Oh, and Nola, of course, but Dad just collapsed. I was really worried about him for a while, but he's doing better. The whole thing's been . . . well . . . hard." Flexing his shoulders, he added on an afterthought, "Sarah will be here later. We've got business issues that can't wait."

Jarred nearly groaned aloud. The only person he wanted to visit him again was Kelsey, and he knew that wasn't going to happen. He already looked forward to seeing her again tomorrow. *That is, if she decides to come,* he thought with a cold jolt of his heart. After all, Chance Rowden had died while he was piloting the plane.

"What?" Will asked, seeing Jarred's tense expression.

"Nothing. Nola brought up the business issues earlier."

Will gazed at him in surprise. "You said *Nola!*"

Jarred frowned.

"You've always referred to her as *Mother.* She wouldn't have it any other way."

Jarred thought of the perfectly dressed woman he'd encountered earlier and couldn't imagine calling her anything even remotely maternal. What was happening to him? He knew certain information as fact, but bits and pieces floated around without direction inside his head — the flotsam and jetsam of an unwanted past.

"Did you know I was taking that flight that day?" Jarred asked.

Will shook his head. "It was a Sunday, and you'd said something on Thursday about leaving for the weekend, but apparently you didn't leave till Sunday afternoon."

"I changed my flight plan?"

"Uh-uh. It was always set for Sunday afternoon. At least that's what the official report says. And Mary Hennessy said you seemed normal, so . . ." He shrugged.

"Mary Hennessy?" Jarred asked, honestly confused.

"Damn." Will exhaled on a soft breath. "Your cook. The family's cook for all the years you've been alive on this planet. Don't tell me you don't remember her, Jarred. She's like an institution!"

Memory arrived like a bullet — and with a certain amount of pain attached, as if it had actually blasted into his brain. *Mary Hennessy. Late fifties. No sense of humor. Dour and solid and honest as the day was long. His sometime cook and housekeeper since she'd semiretired after leaving Nola's employ.*

He suddenly felt extremely weary. As if on cue, Dr. Alastair stepped into the room. Glancing toward Jarred, he said rather sharply to Will, "Excuse me please while I examine the patient."

Will's brows lifted. "When Sarah arrives, tell her I'll be at the office late. I want to talk to her."

Alastair's lips thinned in disapproval as he waited for Will to exit. Jarred almost smiled, but the effort was too great. Instead he resigned himself for another brain probe from the well-meaning, but far too serious Dr. Alastair.

"I've contacted a specialist from New York. He's interested in your case."

Now Jarred really wanted to laugh. He closed his eyes and counted to five. "Because I'm an amnesiac?"

Alastair nodded. "It appears that against my direct orders, members of your family have been filling in the blanks for you."

Jarred sighed. "Don't worry about it. I've got a few memories of my own."

"Oh?"

"I just need time." He lifted his lids and gave

the doctor a long look. "I just don't feel like jumping into my old life without a net. Do you understand?"

"Not entirely."

"Let them all talk to me," Jarred directed. "It's not going to hurt. Take care of the physical side of things, Doc, and let me do the rest."

"Are you saying your memory has returned?"

"Yes — at least partially."

"But you want to keep this information from members of your family and your business associates?"

"I'm saying there's a Detective Newcastle who wants to talk to me about a plane crash, and I've got a feeling it's not because we simply ran out of gas. I'm not a trusting man, and I don't trust anyone here."

"I'm not going to lie for you, Mr. Bryant." The doctor was stiff.

"I've got gaps in my memory. The accident's still a complete loss. Maybe it'll come back. Maybe it won't. You'll be telling the truth if you say I can't remember anything about the plane crash."

Alastair considered. "Detective Newcastle wants to see you as soon as you're able."

"Fine." Jarred sighed. "He won't learn anything, but I'll see him."

Dr. Alastair nodded. He seemed slightly disappointed, and Jarred could well imagine how unhappy he would feel to have to tell the eminent specialist that his star amnesiac's memory had partially returned.

"Oh, and I'd like my wife to be here, too, when the detective comes," Jarred added as the doctor turned to leave. "Could you arrange that? I don't want anyone else."

"I'll call her."

"Jarred?"

A tall woman with short, styled blond hair and a strong chin stepped into the room. She gave the doctor a brief, cold smile. Warm, she was not, and Jarred knew instantly that this was Sarah Ackerman.

Dr. Alastair sent Jarred an askance look. Jarred's own weariness must have transmitted itself to him because he said, "Mr. Bryant just asked that he be given some uninterrupted rest. He's already been severely overtaxed."

"I won't stay long."

No amount of hinting affected the Sarah Ackermans of the world. Jarred suddenly remembered a time when she literally stood between him and Kelsey at a party, as if believing that would somehow bring him to heel. He wondered why he'd put up with her for so long. The answer followed instantly: He'd wanted to make Kelsey jealous.

Jarred physically jerked at the stinging memory. "I feel . . . fuzzy," he murmured.

"I'll be quick," she pressed.

"I think tomorrow's a better time," Dr. Alastair said, taking the initiative, and against Sarah's protests, he led her into the hall.

"I'll be there," Kelsey said. "Two o'clock tomorrow. Thanks." She hung up the phone and stared at it as if it were some poisonous snake. Jarred had requested she be at the meeting between him and Detective Newcastle?

She sank down on the bed in her tiny condominium and stared at the blank cream walls. She'd never decorated. She'd never had the time. She'd spent every moment of the last three years either working or sleeping. She hadn't been able to make a complete life for herself away from Jarred.

And now he was pulling her back into his life.

Felix, her yellow tabby, curled himself around her legs and purred and meowed for attention. Absently, she fondled his ears, her thoughts traveling long unused pathways to very exciting possibilities.

Jarred wanted her, and it was shocking how good that felt.

Chapter Three

Brrrinng! Brrrinng!

The phone rang insistently from inside Kelsey's office. Grabbing the handle of the sliding door that led into her converted loft, she heaved with all her might. The forest green metal door eased backward with a protesting squeak and rattle, part of the charm of these redone warehouse units two blocks off Elliott Bay.

Brrrinng!

"Don't hang up," she yelled across the room.

After running across the scarred oak floor, she snatched up the receiver on the fly. "Taggart Interiors," she answered breathlessly.

"There you are. I'd about given up on you."

"Oh, hi, Trevor." She groped blindly among the papers on her desk for a buried pen. Her coffee sat where she'd left it before her morning meeting with the decorative hardware people who were trying to squeeze an additional dollar out of each and every cabinet knob. Considering that Phase One of Trevor's current condominium project required about 200 knobs per unit, and there were 800 units to eventually complete, that was a lot of dollars. Kelsey wasn't about to give in without a fight.

Eyeing her coffee, she wrinkled her nose, then grabbed the paper cup anyway and swallowed a huge gulp, closing her mind to the fact that it was cold and bitter and downright awful.

"I've left ten messages already," Trevor grumbled.

"You're such an exaggerator." She glanced at her answering machine and saw that there were actually two messages waiting for her. "I had a meeting with Puget Sound Hardware this morning, those rapists, but I'm making some progress." She thought about mentioning her pending afternoon appointment with Jarred and Detective Newcastle but immediately rejected the idea. Trevor wasn't known for being close-mouthed.

"Good. Good. At least you're back on the job."

Kelsey's mouth quirked. "Jarred's better, thanks. Really improving. Nice of you to ask."

Trevor snorted in embarrassment, momentarily chastised. Still Trevor Taggart, Kelsey's boss, wasn't known for being the understanding type either. Since the accident, he hadn't expressed any emotion except impatience at the time off Kelsey had needed to take. A round man with a dapper sense of style that somehow always appeared slightly comical on his rotund figure, Trevor could be exacting and temperamental and bullish. Kelsey had gone to work for him after a short stint as an assistant to an even more exacting, temperamental, and bullish interior designer. She had been almost grateful when Trevor rescued her. Of course, that was before she'd met and married Jarred Bryant and found she was working for Jarred's most head-to-head competitor in the race to purchase prime real estate around the Seattle area and convert tired, run-down, and outdated properties into aesthetically beautiful and practical new offices, condominiums, apartments, and town houses. She'd half expected Jarred to insist that she give up her position, but in those days, Jarred had seemed more amused by his young wife's position than threatened by it. In the long run, Kelsey's job had proved to be her lifeline and had offered far more permanence and satisfaction than her crumbling marriage.

Taggart Inc., parent company of her small division, Taggart Interiors — if you could seriously call her one-person office a division — was a varied business with tentacles reaching into all aspects of real estate development. It wasn't quite as large as Bryant Industries nor as diverse as Jarred's company, which over the years had bought and sold divisions as dissimilar as art galleries and sanitation companies along with the ongoing real estate development. Kelsey had once toyed with the idea of working for her husband's business, but Jarred hadn't seemed all that keen on hiring her, and she'd thanked her lucky stars later when she learned that her career, not her husband, would turn out to be the most important aspect in her life.

"So what's the prognosis?" Trevor asked now.

"I'm not sure. It's a day-by-day thing."

"But he will be all right, won't he?"

"I think so. All his physical injuries appear to be on the mend, and there doesn't seem to be any reason that he won't be on his feet again in the next few weeks or months. I don't know. Sometime anyway."

"You sound . . . unsure how to feel."

"I just want him to recover."

"Well, of course you do. I wasn't saying *that!*"

"I know what you were saying."

"What? What was I saying?" Trevor demanded.

"Never mind."

"Kelsey, just get over here. I want you to come down to the condos. Mitch is going to be there with plans for Phase Two, and I want to get some ideas percolating."

"Trevor, I'm fighting with the hardware people and it's difficult enough right now for me to stay on task. Needless to say, my brain is not in full gear. I just feel . . ." She let her voice drift off as his words sank in. "We're going ahead with Phase *Two?*" she asked in surprise. "When did that happen?"

"Last night!" he crowed. "Score one for the good guys. I'm sorry about Jarred, but I can't say I'm sorry about Bryant Industries losing out to us again."

"But I thought Bryant Industries had that property wrapped up!"

"I know, I know." It was all he could do to not sound gleeful.

"I'm sure Jarred thought that property was his." Kelsey's brows puckered. For all her declarations about her husband and his business, she didn't like to hear that he'd actually been beaten out of something as important as this particular piece of real estate. Especially now. It was so *wrong*.

But the worst of it was that Jarred probably couldn't remember one thing about the project anyway.

"I'm sure we'll hear some repercussions and the obligatory whining out of some folks from Bryant Industries, but it won't change anything. I've been meeting with the owners of that property for months, Kelsey, and they just weren't happy with the terms of Bryant Industries' offer."

"But they signed, didn't they? I mean, there's bound to be a law suit."

"Some conditions weren't completely ironed out," he said breezily. "It's ours now."

Ours . . . Kelsey didn't like the sound of that. What Trevor called Phase Two was actually a section of prime real estate that overlooked Elliott Bay and had been bid on and bargained over for years. The last she'd heard, Bryant Industries had sewn up the deal, promising to keep with the facades of the decaying buildings that stood on the grounds, stripping the interiors to the steel beams but maintaining the architecture and general feel. Even the Historical Society had okayed and applauded Jarred's efforts. When Trevor had made noise about trying to scoop up the property, Kelsey had just assumed it was too late.

And Trevor had a tendency to slash and burn when it came to saving historical buildings rather than spending the extra effort to restore their original beauty. Kelsey, in the years she'd spent working for Trevor, had tried hard to get him to keep from throwing out the baby with the bathwater.

Also she knew Jarred had been working on the deal for over two years. Kelsey might have been having her own problems with Jarred, but she very much wanted his company to be the developers of what Trevor had tagged his Phase Two.

"I don't know what to say, Trevor."

"Hey, I'm not trying to sound like a ghoul. You did just say Jarred's recovering, didn't you?"

"Yes."

"Then . . . ?"

"It's just going to take time, Trevor. Jarred needs time and so do I. But I'll come to the condos. I need to do something anyway, and after all, I'm employed by Taggart Inc."

"That's right. Get on down here and stop thinking about Jarred for a while."

"Okay . . ."

"I mean it, you know." Trevor's voice was a

tad less brusque than usual.

"I'll be there," she said through a thick throat. Good Lord, she was on emotional burnout. With Chance dead and Jarred in the hospital, she felt unstable and weak and totally unlike herself.

Pull yourself together, Kelsey.

Grabbing her purse, she hurried to the warehouse elevator — a wrought-iron contraption with its own sliding, collapsible door and rickety, jerking movements. Her thoughts touched on Jarred and the two o'clock meeting. She could just pop in on Trevor and placate him, then she was off to the hospital again.

Still consumed by a feeling of unreality, she pushed the button to descend. The elevator groaned and bucked before moving at a snail's pace to the lower floor. To the uninitiated it was a heart-in-the-throat ride, but Kelsey was so inured to the elevator's series of jolts and rattles that she scarcely noticed any longer. And today her thoughts were full of Jarred and Chance and a lot of jumbled emotions she was pretty sure she didn't even want to touch.

The condos were a hefty walk from Kelsey's warehouse office — a rented space that Taggart Inc. paid for because it was closer to the work site than the company's headquarters just north of Seattle proper. Trevor also rented a second office nearer to the site, but his suite of rooms was on the fourteenth floor of a rather ugly modern building on the next block. In his quest to keep up with Jarred, he was in negotiations to purchase that building, as well, but so far no deal had been inked. Trevor only wanted it because it was near Bryant Industries' headquarters and Jarred's company owned the building that housed their corporate headquarters. Trevor just hated being behind in any race with Jarred.

Kelsey passed Bryant Industries' headquarters on the walk and glanced skyward. Trevor lusted after Jarred's building as well. It was only six floors — a relic from the early part of the century surrounded by newer, taller additions to the skyline — but its brick Georgian facade and stately columns were a pleasant diversion from the steel-and-glass architecture surrounding it. Apart from a bank and a restaurant on the street floor and several attorneys' offices on the third and fourth, Bryant Industries occupied most of the available space, and its very existence was a source of envy for Trevor. Kelsey knew her boss's eccentricities and insecurities, and she also understood her own role in his overall plan. But he paid well and appreciated her, and he gave her the independence that had helped her survive her marriage.

Still, Trevor wasn't exactly Mr. Aesthetic and it was lucky he hadn't been able to get his hands on Jarred's building. With his tastes, he would likely strip the place of all its natural beauty and history in his quest for renovation and modernization. Sometimes, with Trevor, she felt as if she were the lone soldier fighting an entire army bent on demolition. However, he wasn't really about destroying the old to make room for the new. He just didn't get it.

"Oh, shoot," Kelsey muttered, bending her head against a gust of sudden rain. She'd forgotten her umbrella. Scurrying bareheaded through the misting precipitation, she reached the condos half an hour later. Trevor was pacing back and forth in the open model unit. "There you are!" he declared. "My God, Kelsey. Learn to use an umbrella. Or bring a hat. You'll drip over everything."

Tara, one of Trevor's employees who was currently *sitting* the model, shot Kelsey a sympathetic look. They both knew how fussy Trevor could be, and they both gave him a certain amount of lip service before doing exactly as they pleased.

"You're right," Kelsey told him now, finger combing her curling tresses. "Where's Mitch?"

"He'll be right along." Trevor instantly forgot Kelsey's appearance. Though short and round, Trevor nevertheless possessed a natural bearing and leadership that made others respond with deference. "You said Jarred's physical injuries were on the mend. What about the rest of him?"

"Pardon?"

"Is he still the same bastard you married?"

"Trevor, that is a truly rotten thing to say," Kelsey said softly.

He grimaced at his own tastelessness. "You're right," he said, sounding almost contrite. "I'm sorry." Then he added with a sly grin, "But is he?"

"Oh, for the love of Pete," Kelsey muttered.

"Trevor." Tara sighed. "You really are the limit."

"People don't change overnight. I was just asking. Anyway, it sounds like he's going to be his old self again. That's good."

Kelsey didn't respond. Even Jarred didn't want to be his old self again, and she sure as heck didn't want him to be.

A few minutes later, Mitch appeared with plans in hand. By the obvious amount of effort and time he'd put into the project, Kelsey could tell Trevor had been seriously working on this acquisition for some time.

It was difficult for her to keep her mind on the work in front of her, and by the time she'd listened to both Mitch and Trevor discuss what the overall plan should be from ten different directions, she felt slightly depressed.

After glancing at her watch, she decided it was time to go. "Trevor, I've got to get to the hospital. I'll be at work right on time tomorrow."

"The hospital? Now?" He looked up from the drawings.

"He is my husband," she pointed out. Without another word she headed back toward her office.

Detective Newcastle wore the bland expression of a man who'd either seen too much or

74

who simply was too tired to muster up enthusiasm over anything. His tie hung too short, leaving an expanse of belly stretched tight between a white shirt and navy blue jacket. He sat in a chair with his hands on his thighs and regarded Jarred.

"I would prefer to talk to you alone, Mr. Bryant."

"I would prefer that my wife stay," Jarred responded, ignoring the rustle of Kelsey's skirt as she tried to rise from her own chair. He threw her a look. *Don't go,* he pleaded silently.

Slowly she sat back down, crossing her legs and hugging her arms around her chest. Today she wore a black skirt and a jacket, but the drape-collared, cinnamon-shaded blouse beneath that ensemble added life and a much needed dash of pure color to the room. Her rain-tinged hair looked tousled and luscious, and as if divining his thoughts, she self-consciously finger combed the tresses.

"I understand you don't remember anything about the accident," Newcastle said.

"That's right."

"You don't remember setting up a date with Mr. Rowden to go flying?"

"No."

"You were friends with Mr. Rowden?"

Jarred looked to Kelsey for help. "I don't think so."

"No, they weren't friends," she said a bit tightly. "Just acquaintances."

The detective turned to Kelsey. "I understand you are close to the Rowden family."

"When my parents died, they became my family," she said simply.

"You were a friend of Mr. Chance Rowden's then."

"Yes . . ."

"What is your investigation focusing on?" Jarred interrupted. It made him uncomfortable to talk about Kelsey's relationship with the Rowdens. There was something else there. Some furtive memory that kept slipping in and out of range.

Suddenly he made the connection. A conversation between Will and himself. Not long ago. In his office. Will pacing to and fro enough to cause the newly installed carpet to fuzz up in clumps.

"And along with everything else, she's been stealing money for years. Giving it to that druggie friend of hers, Rowden. Thousands of dollars, Jarred. You can't just sit by and say nothing. Call her on it. Damn it all! The woman's a thief. Your wife is a thief!"

Newcastle took his time answering. Eventually, as if coming to some carefully thought-out decision, he said, "The fuel line of your Cessna was tampered with. The engine eventually starved and you dropped out of the sky."

Silence followed those cold, careful words. Jarred inwardly shuddered at the mental vision, but he still possessed no memory of those awful

76

moments before the plane crashed. It could have happened to someone else for all he knew, except for the injuries that kept him bedridden.

"You're saying someone purposely did it," Kelsey said in a low voice. Her eyes were huge as they regarded Newcastle, her mouth grim.

"Undoubtedly." He turned back to Jarred. "We're talking to people who saw you at the airport that day. And we're checking who had access to the plane. I was hoping you could help in some way. Remember . . . anything."

"I wish I could," Jarred muttered with feeling.

"Is there anything you recall that might have some bearing on this?"

The detective's tone clearly said he didn't believe Jarred suffered from amnesia. But ironically, when it came to the accident, Jarred did. And he could only recall bits and pieces of his past — they came to him in blocks of information — and most of them revolved around his relationship with Kelsey and their own marital problems.

"Any enemies?" Newcastle asked.

"I'm afraid you'll have better luck interrogating my family and business associates." Jarred's voice was dry. "I seem to be kind of vague on any of that."

"Mrs. Bryant?" He turned to Kelsey.

"Yes?"

"Does your husband have any enemies?"

Kelsey blinked rapidly, a sign that she was thinking fast. Jarred knew these little tricks, these signs, these idiosyncrasies, but he'd be damned if he could remember anything else.

I want her back, he thought suddenly, fiercely. *I want my wife back.*

"Maybe business rivals? I don't know. No one who would really want to harm him. Could . . ." She hesitated.

The detective leaned toward her encouragingly.

"Could they have been after Chance instead? He was — um — involved in drugs. A user mostly, but he might have sold some? I don't really know."

"We know about Mr. Rowden," the detective said.

"I just thought he might be a more likely target. I guess that doesn't really make sense. This crime is too huge."

"No, Mrs. Bryant. Anything's possible. Mr. Rowden's background is being checked out, too." Newcastle hesitated a moment, rubbed his palms together, then laid them on his thighs once more. "Is there anything you remember in the days prior to the accident?" he asked Kelsey. "Something you noticed?"

"I . . . no. I don't . . . live with Jarred. I didn't see him . . . much."

"Did you see Mr. Rowden?"

When Kelsey blushed to the roots of her hair, Jarred instantly panicked. She'd seen Chance? She'd met with him? What? *What?* It was all he could do to keep from screaming out the questions.

Kelsey managed to meet the detective's gaze and say in a calm voice, "Chance came to see me the night before the accident. He seemed to want to tell me something, but I thought it had to do with my marriage. He knew that . . . it wasn't going well. I told him I didn't want to talk about it and he . . . hugged me." Her voice broke off. "And then he told me good-bye."

Jarred's confidence melted at the tender longing in her voice. She loved him. She still loved him. His wife loved Chance Rowden and even the man's death hadn't altered that fact.

She probably hates you, old buddy. You killed her lover. It's your fault.

"He didn't give you any indication that he was meeting your husband on Sunday for a plane trip? Nothing?" The detective sounded skeptical.

"No." Kelsey shook her head. "He was just really anxious about me. Or at least I thought it was about me. I don't know anymore."

Jarred listened, detached, as the detective asked Kelsey a few more questions along the same line, but she continually shook her head in bafflement. Jarred felt old and used up. He wanted Detective Newcastle to leave and Kelsey to stay.

When the detective rolled to his feet, Kelsey stood also. Jarred shot her a look. "Are you leaving?" he asked.

Thinking Jarred was addressing him, Detective Newcastle nodded. "If anything comes up,

79

I'll let you know." He rambled toward the door.

"Kelsey?" Jarred demanded, seeing her reach for her purse.

"Mmm-hmm?" She wouldn't meet his eyes.

"You have to leave?"

"Yes, I have some things to do. I'm sure your parents will be stopping by soon anyway and probably Will, too." Now she shot him a quick, faint smile. "You'll be well taken care of."

"Don't leave. Please."

He hated begging. It didn't sit well with him and he was pretty sure it never had. But he couldn't let her go. He couldn't.

Kelsey gazed at him in consternation. "Oh, Jarred," she sighed.

"I just want you to stay."

He could see the internal battle she waged, and he sensed it all had to do with their past history. "You look exhausted," she finally told him. "I feel guilty keeping you awake."

"I couldn't sleep now if I wanted to. Too much information."

"I guess Dr. Alastair lifted the ban on your being kept in the dark. I'm surprised."

"Well, I just think that was an experiment that failed." Jarred wished he could find a way to draw her closer to the bed. "What difference does it make? If I can't remember, someone will have to tell me eventually. And if I do remember, so what? It's still the same outcome."

Kelsey almost smiled. "Your practicality hasn't changed, I see. You've still got that in spades."

"You make it sound like a bad thing."

"No. It's just . . . a thing."

He could feel weariness entering his system like some kind of relentless virus. Soon it would overtake him, and the thought infuriated him. He needed this time with Kelsey. Before his parents and his half brother and anyone else descended upon him, talking and demanding and secretly seeking to override him. He might not remember everything, but emotions, sensations, and hidden agendas were as clear to him as Lucite.

"Have you thought about what I asked?"

"Umm . . ." Her hands tightened on the strap of her purse. "And that was?"

"Moving back in with me."

"No."

"No?"

"No, I haven't thought about it." She bent her head, then eyed him directly. "Okay, that's a lie. Yes, I've thought about it, but no, I don't think it's possible."

Her eyes were so expressive he felt lost in them. "Could you try?" he asked, his jaw tightening in spite of himself at the effort to cajole.

"Jarred, you just don't know what you're asking! We don't even . . . talk to each other anymore. You don't like me."

"I think I like you very much."

Kelsey choked in disbelief. "I don't know who the hell you are, but you're not my husband. And I don't mean that just because of this accident. You're just not you, and I never knew who you were anyway!"

Emotion radiated from her in waves. Jarred felt that insidious weakness flooding his system and silently pleaded with the powers that be for more time. "Then why did you marry me in the first place?"

"Because" — Kelsey swallowed hard, fighting sensations that threatened to rob her of her strength — "I loved you."

It was all Jarred needed to hear. His lips faintly smiled and he closed his eyes. "Don't leave," he whispered again, then fell instantly asleep.

Kelsey gazed down at his unconscious form, her gut churning and her foolish heart singing. Looking at her, one would only have seen a grim countenance and never imagined the emotions bubbling inside. She felt so weird! Almost maternal, yet there were thoughts scampering around the circle of her reason that were darn close to X-rated — and those thoughts filled her with hope and a sudden surge of joy and a flood of desire that made her knees go weak.

Oh, my God, she thought, afraid.

She shouldn't have been so honest. She should have hidden the truth and never admitted why she'd married him. She should have lied for all she was worth. But he'd been so open and straightforward and interested in her that she'd been unable to *think!*

"He's medicated," she reminded herself beneath her breath. Feeling stifled, she walked from the room, hesitating in the hallway outside. She could hear the faint sound of a television somewhere down the floor. Some talk show on which a man and a woman were screaming at each other. The woman accused the man of cheating on her, and he smugly told her that she was not enough woman for him. The audience reacted in gleeful horror.

Kelsey pressed her palms to her cheeks. She was hot all over. Sick with a kind of poisonous hope that was somehow eating away at her own common sense. *No, no, no!* Jarred Bryant did not want her. He never would — or could — the way she needed to be wanted. She hated what he stood for. Hated that he was a corporate monster who gobbled up family businesses and shared the spoils with his ungrateful, spoiled, and avid family.

And he'd killed Chance. . . .

That wasn't fair. Instantly, her own sense of fair play jumped forward, refusing to let her throw the dreadful blame on him. Hadn't Detective Newcastle explained about the tampering?

Suddenly she went cold. Maybe they *were* after Jarred. She'd said herself that Chance's problems were too small to warrant that kind of malicious and deadly response. But Jarred — or more accurately Jarred's company, Bryant Industries — was an ugly blot on the soul of corporate America. Someone might easily want to take out its president and majority stockholder.

Well, it's not exactly a blot, she reminded herself. *That's just something you told him when you were hurt and angry. One of your more impassioned moments, Kelsey, my girl.*

Kelsey pushed her hands through her hair and groaned. It was a killer to think back on certain moments in their embattled marriage. She couldn't blame all the problems on Jarred, much as she'd like to.

Glancing back inside the room, she recognized how deep Jarred's sleep was. *Don't leave,* he'd begged, but she had a few errands to run. Besides, she couldn't stay here any longer. The hair on the back of her arms stood up straight from strange emotions, and she just couldn't stand it one more minute.

Feeling like a traitor, she hurried down the hallway and away from the stranger who was her husband. But as soon as she stepped outside and gulped rain-choked air, she abruptly twisted around and sped back upstairs, where she stationed herself like a guard at Jarred's bedside, all the while asking herself what she really thought she was doing, but unable to come up with any clear answers.

Outside Silverlake, inside a small, slightly dilapidated home with a long, weed-choked, fir-draped driveway, a man examined the fruits of his so-called baking labors. A thin layer of crystals grew from thick goo spread across a remarkably clean countertop. The smell was beyond pungent — a dead giveaway to anyone who'd ever had experience with making crystal methamphetamine. A meth lab, as quoted in the papers, was generally little more than an ordinary kitchen with a few extraordinary ingredients. The risk was that the chemicals sometimes collided and exploded. One had to be careful. Very, very careful.

The man gazed on in satisfaction, but his thoughts touched on Chance Rowden. Chance — his friend, his compadre, his partner in crime and best buddy when they had still both been normal college students at the University of Washington. Ah, but that was a long time ago and now there wasn't much to think about but the joy of shrieking along on a crystal meth ride. Except Chance was gone. Killed. Murdered.

The man shuddered from the roots of his hair to the soles of his feet. He'd heard once that fear was the most powerful of human emotions. Hatred, rage, love, desire, envy . . . Nothing compared to fear. And fear was what he felt these days. Ever since that corporate suit had walked through the front door and scared the bejesus out of him and Chance.

It really pissed him off, too. He really wanted to wring the bastard's corporate neck.

The shuddering worsened, and he sat down hard on a worn ottoman, which was black leather with tufts of stuffing sticking out around ripped stitching. He chewed his thumbnail furiously. Chance had stared at the stranger through eyes the size of full moons, and the damned suit had smelled the distinctive odor in the room and done the addition.

"This is where the money goes?" he'd said in a deadly voice.

Chance had shuffled him out of the place, and the next thing you know, he was dead and gone.

And that was when the phone calls had started.

Glancing at the instrument that lay unplugged on the floor, he chewed even more desperately on his nail until his thumb bled. He was sure to end up dead, too, if he didn't think of what to do.

What to do . . . what to do . . . what to do . . .

Kelsey. Chance's girl. She was the one to help.

With sudden energy he leaped to his feet, ran to the bedroom, and threw dirty clothes and sneakers into an army surplus duffel bag. Then he hurried to the kitchen, scraped the precious crystals from their bed, and placed them in a Ziploc bag.

Hearing an engine, he dashed to the window, his own eyes wide and staring. He could feel them jutting out of his head.

Coming toward the house was a slow-moving black sedan. God almighty. Or was it a police cruiser? No. No. It was all black. All black.

Oh, shit. Oh, shit. Oh, shit!

Slipping out the back door, he sped into the dusky woods that crept right to the back of his house and he was gone.

Chapter Four

The space between memories and dreams was infinitesimally small, Jarred decided, drifting in a twilight world where all he sensed was Kelsey's presence somewhere in the dim recesses of the room. A blurred line separated memories from dreams and that line seemed to fade in and out. But he was dreaming, wasn't he? *Wasn't he?* Still, it felt as if Chance Rowden were close enough to touch.

No, it *was* a dream because Jarred was standing in his office, staring down at the scruffy, nervous man, feeling disdain and anger and even jealousy. Jealousy because this man was his wife's friend and lover. And Chance was talking, rattling on with ever increasing speed. Jarred concentrated on the man's mouth, intrigued. He was confessing, and it was as if confession were some kind of fuel for his voice. Truths fell from his lips, tumbling one upon another until Jarred's brain actually hurt from the effort of filing them away.

" *. . none of it was true. I never slept with Kelsey*

before the wedding. I never even slept with her at all. It wasn't that kind of relationship. And Kelsey was never, ever a user. You know that. All of it was a lie and Sarah let you think it because she wanted to break you and Kelsey up. I'm sorry. I'm sorry. You've got big problems of your own, but they're not Kelsey. Never Kelsey. But you can smell the problems, can't you? You can smell *them! And they're here.* Right here!"

"What do you mean 'here'?"

Chance glanced around fearfully, like a rabbit sensing a trap. "In these offices. Right under your nose. Don't you feel it? It's eating away at everything you have. Eroding like acid. It's killing you and Kelsey, and I'm sorry because I think she loves you. You bastard. You just don't deserve it. And now you hold it in your hands and all you can think about is bringing me down! Look around you."

Jarred craned his head. He looked and looked, but he couldn't see anything but gray light. Then the door to his office cracked open. A light shone through. A dark silhouette.

And Chance crying somewhere in the gloom.

Jarred's eyes suddenly jerked open. Sweat poured down his face. His heart raced.

The hospital room was quiet. Kelsey sat in a chair near his bed, her head nodding, her breath soft and steady. Relief flooded Jarred and he slowly calmed down. The vision faded away almost instantly, reminding him how strangely sinister dreams could be. But they were, after all, only dreams.

"Hey, there, Kelsey."

Kelsey's head snapped up. Instantly awake, she glanced around to see who'd spoken, her pulse lifting in spite of herself. Will was just entering Jarred's room. Disoriented, she didn't realize for a moment she'd fallen asleep in the chair near Jarred's bed.

Will looked down at her.

"He asked me to stay," she said, feeling compelled to explain. "He's been asleep awhile."

"I talked to him last night. How's he been today?"

"Better," she said, considering. "He's alert when he's awake."

"Think he's able to make some business decisions yet?" he half joked.

"You're asking the wrong person." She looked toward the windows, as much to avoid his gaze as to gather her strength for another round with one of the Bryants. Night had fallen and there was no moon. Only the glow from the fluorescent lights flooding the parking lot left any illumination. The room, too, was dim because Kelsey hadn't wanted to disturb Jarred's sleep.

Will stood at the foot of the bed and regarded the sleeping form of his older brother. "Dr. Alastair seems to think he's healing very rapidly, but I sure as hell don't notice much of a change."

"No, he's definitely better," Kelsey said again, recalling their conversation.

Footsteps approached. Automatically, Kelsey steeled herself anew, expecting Nola to march in like an avenging angel.

But it was Sarah Ackerman who walked through the door this time, and Kelsey mentally groaned at the intrusion. The blond woman flicked a look her way, then otherwise ignored her. Taking a place beside Will, who greeted her amiably, Sarah stared down at Jarred, too, and her whole attitude needled Kelsey. She didn't like either of them gazing at him that way. He was too vulnerable.

Rising to her feet, Kelsey dusted off her skirt and said softly, "Is there something I can help you with?"

Sarah looked her up and down. "No."

Abrupt. The woman was always abrupt, and Kelsey recalled the first time she'd met Sarah. They'd been classmates at U-Dub — nickname for the University of Washington — and Sarah had been in several of the same courses as Kelsey. But Sarah's style was bold, aggressive, and in Kelsey's biased opinion, downright nervy. They'd never liked each other, and by the time Kelsey met Jarred a few years later, Sarah was already employed by his company. It felt as if Sarah had always been a part of their lives, and suffering through years of the woman's same attitude, and the knowledge that she was seemingly having an affair with *her* husband, had eroded Kelsey's own natural good manners. It was difficult to even be in the same room with her, and now, feeling emotion swamping her good sense, Kelsey clamped her jaws together to prevent herself from saying something she might well regret later.

"Has he been like this the whole time?" Sarah asked Will.

"He was awake. He fell asleep in the middle of a conversation," Kelsey informed her. "It would probably be better to conduct business in the light of day."

"I would really like to talk to him," Sarah declared flatly.

"We all would. I just don't think Jarred's up for it." Kelsey was unmoving. "Come back tomorrow." *Or never . . .*

"You're planning on staying here awhile?" Sarah asked Kelsey.

Like it's any of your business. "He asked me to. I promised I would."

Kelsey's skin prickled. She sent a look Will's way, gauging his reaction. He seemed distracted rather than provoked by their subtle sparring. But Sarah wasn't immune and Kelsey could feel the woman's growing annoyance with her. There was a certain pleasure in that, which made Kelsey inwardly smile.

Looking down her nose, Sarah said, "You can't just step in at this late date and expect any of us to believe you have Jarred's best interests at heart. You're not even living with him."

You have to hand it to Sarah, Kelsey marveled. *She doesn't pull any punches.* "Well, I will be. I'm

91

moving back into the house to help take care of him while he recovers."

A pause. "Really?"

"Yes, really." The idea was firmly taking root even as they spoke. "Jarred asked me to."

"Jarred asked a lot of you, didn't he?"

"Not any more than would be expected of his wife."

"When Jarred is himself again, I'm sure things will be different," Sarah declared.

"And how's that?" Kelsey asked. Just what did Sarah expect Jarred to do? Leap out of bed and drag her into his arms, promising all kinds of things he couldn't deliver? For all their supposed mattress thumping, Kelsey had never heard that Jarred wanted anything permanent with the aggressive Sarah, and even if that were a small victory, it was one Kelsey hung on to with an iron will. Jarred was still her husband and Sarah could just stew about that.

Sarah said in her curious flat way, "He's in recovery, and from all reports, it's close to miraculous. Soon, he'll be back to normal and we can all get on with our lives."

Her supercilious words were hushed, but the staccato whispering took nothing away from the intensity of the conversation. Kelsey, who never before had actually argued points with Sarah — it had all seemed so gauche and self-defeating — felt a certain sense of liberation. She was through hearing about Sarah Ackerman and Jarred and feeling powerless to do anything about their supposed affair. And now that she'd started to project her feelings, she really didn't know if she could stop. She wanted to tell Sarah to get the hell out of her and Jarred's life, and for a moment, her lips actually quivered in readiness.

Will came to the rescue. "Okay, okay," he muttered. "Come on, Sarah. We'll come back tomorrow morning. He just needs a little more time."

"Exactly," Kelsey agreed.

Sarah opened and shut her mouth, then pursed her lips together with an effort. Her eyes glittered. It was like watching angry thoughts collide inside her head. Turning on stiff legs, Sarah marched after Will toward the door. Kelsey watched her leave. Shoulders tense, back rigid, Sarah Ackerman was an unhappy, demanding woman who only acted on her own self-serving impulses.

But she was a force to be reckoned with nonetheless.

After the fact, Kelsey's heart thumped hard several times before settling back into its natural rhythm. She hated confrontation with anyone, but it was high time Sarah learned that Kelsey possessed a backbone. Jarred was still her husband. *Her* husband.

Alone with Jarred again, Kelsey reseated herself, examining her husband's face. What was it about him that had drawn her in so completely? Was it his looks, his sense of barely leashed power, his *wealth?* No, she knew that wasn't true. Money had never interested her, at least money she hadn't earned herself and therefore felt she had no right to. But Jarred had definitely had an effect on her, straight from the start, and when she thought back to that first inauspicious meeting at the Four Seasons Olympic Hotel, she knew she'd been hooked from the moment he'd first spoken to her.

I understand you work for Trevor. Can you get him to stop designing those milk cartons and littering up the waterfront . . . ?

She'd fallen in love with him that quickly, though she hadn't realized it at the time, of course. No, it was several days after that first meeting when she was back at her office that she felt the first stirrings of love. He'd called her, intending to take her up on her offer to show him around the boxy white town houses Trever was erecting, but Kelsey, distracted by a series of misadventures at work, hadn't immediately recognized his voice. "Ms. Bennett?" he'd inquired in that slow drawl she would later come to know so well.

"Yes?"

"Kelsey Bennett?"

"Yes," she said with more emphasis. She'd been lost in an order that had gone completely sideways and had left her wanting to rip her hair out at the way the subcontractors had tiled the bathrooms of Trevor's "milk cartons." They'd installed the blue and white tiles meant for the kitchen instead of the cream faux-marble bathroom tiles, and vice versa. Furious and sure that Trevor would blame her entirely, she just wanted to scream — and her cool voice warned the caller that he was about to be first in line.

"Can I help you?" she clipped out, her voice daring him to continue.

With amusement heavy in his voice, he said, "Well, you sound a little out of sorts."

"I am. Who's this? Make it quick. It's not that kind of day."

He abruptly broke into laughter, which only irritated Kelsey further. She knew she was being rude but she didn't much care. She was about to hang up on him when he introduced himself. "It's Jarred Bryant." She could hear the smile in his voice. "I was hoping for that tour, but maybe this isn't the time."

"Tour," she repeated, jolted. "Oh, you want to see the condos?"

"I'd like to. Is there a time today that you can get away and show me around? Or is that out of the question?"

Her mind raced. She had so much to do. And Trevor would not be pleased to have Jarred Bryant poking around his property, no matter how much Kelsey might try to act as if it didn't matter. "Well, I could go . . . now," she suggested.

"Then how about I meet you over there and maybe we could do lunch afterward."

Kelsey hesitated the merest fraction of a second. "That would be great."

"Good. See you there."

It was September. One of the warmest days of the year. Kelsey instantly glanced down at her blue shift and wished for all the world she'd worn something a little newer today. A little more glamorous. A little more formfitting.

As soon as the thought crossed her mind she uttered a sound of self-disgust. He wasn't interested in *her*. He'd been photographed with every beautiful woman in Seattle, in the state of Washington, and on the entire West Coast. How, in God's name, could she even think he would look at her? Jarred Bryant was out of her league, and that was just fine and dandy because he was undoubtedly a heartbreaker, a jerk, and a self-absorbed autocrat used to having his own way. So thinking, she tried to banish thoughts of her own apparel out of her head, succeeding not at all. Consequently, by the time she arrived to meet him, she was in a complete mental dither over everything and anything — all the things that couldn't possibly matter.

He was waiting next to a dark blue Mercedes when she pulled up in her own rather dilapidated compact Chevy. In a black Polo shirt and tan chinos, he looked ready to hit the links, although she learned later that golf was not his sport. Flying was his passion, and on many weekends, he would take out the Cessna and Kelsey would accompany him to Portland, Vancouver, British Columbia, or San Francisco. But on that day, the world was new and all Kelsey could think about was the disparity in how she felt about her appearance against Jarred Bryant's cool composure.

"Hi," she said and, to her horror, felt the beginnings of a blush. She wasn't prone to blushing. Not at all! So why now? Why with him? It was practically beyond bearing.

"Hello." He stepped away from the car and walked toward her, and Kelsey struggled hard to remember that he was just a man, after all, and acting as if he were some kind of celebrity or lesser god was very bad form indeed.

She took a calming breath. "I've got the keys to one of the units with a view and another without a view. They're priced accordingly, and the viewless units are a steal of a deal."

She realized he was staring at her, and she wondered if she was rambling. She hurried up the short walkway to the unit, unlocked the door, then stepped aside and waited for him to follow.

He glanced around and his brows lifted. "They are nice inside," he agreed.

Kelsey walked toward the kitchen, where a small island, painted white and then antiqued to look "distressed," was the focal point. The rest of the cabinets were just touched across the crown molding with the antiquing. Noticing the way Jarred examined them, she said, "We did that to save money. Less time-consuming for the painters and therefore a better deal."

"Your idea?"

"Well, yes. But Trevor approved."

"I'm sure." He shot her a sideways grin, for Trevor was notorious for being cheap in his personal life. The man could certainly build a quality product, but Kelsey knew from experience that it killed Trevor to part with an extra nickel here or there. Not that he couldn't waste money on the most god-awful decisions; she'd had to explain more than a few terrible architectural blunders away as Trevor's "unique vision," a euphemism that fooled no one.

Jarred wandered through the unit, and then Kelsey took him to another one, which she'd had painted in warm yellows to brighten the rooms, thereby keeping the attention within the town house rather than at the dismal view outside of rooftops and nearby buildings.

"These really are a surprise inside," Jarred said. "Trevor must be happy with what you've done."

"He won't be as thrilled with what happened today," she said, making a face. Then she found herself telling Taggert Inc.'s most serious competitor about the tile mishap and her battle with the subcontractor to fix the problem. Jarred listened intently as they walked back to their cars, and when Kelsey finished, she suddenly worried that she'd said too much.

But he didn't comment. He just opened the passenger door of the Mercedes and motioned for Kelsey to slide in. She hesitated briefly, but what was she supposed to do? Demand to follow him in her car to their chosen lunch locale? There was nothing wrong with going on a "date" with Jarred Bryant.

In the close confines of the vehicle she was supremely aware of him next to her. His long legs stretched out in front of him and his scent — something masculine and deep and musky — seemed to reach over and pull her in. It was unfair that he was so supremely male, she thought, as they headed into traffic.

"Where would you like to go?" he asked.

"Anywhere."

They ended up at an Irish pub called McNaughton's. Kelsey ordered Irish stew at Jarred's suggestion, and when the owner of the establishment came by and clapped Jarred on the back like an old friend, Kelsey looked up to realize that faces were turned and staring at them. Even within the confines of their wooden booth, they were noticed. Jarred was well known here, and the knowledge bothered her in ways she couldn't quite define.

"And who is this?" the owner asked, giving Kelsey a wink.

"Kelsey Bennett, meet Mac. An old friend."

"Mac?" she inquired.

"Everybody calls me Mac. Short for McNaughton, y'understand."

"He doesn't possess a first name," Jarred said.

"Don't need one," the man agreed with a certain amount of pride. "Now Kelsey's a good name. You Irish?"

"More like a mutt. A little bit of this, a little bit of that."

He grinned at her. "For today, a little more Irish than the rest!"

She couldn't remember the rest of the meal. The food was good — delicious really — but it could have been ashes for all she really tasted it. Jarred discussed the waterfront and his plans to redevelop some of the older warehouses and demolish some of the worst of them. She mentioned that Trevor was doing much the same thing.

By the time he drove her back to her car, it was nearly three o'clock, and she knew Trevor would be having a cow. Jumping from the vehicle, she leaned back inside. "Thanks so much. I had a great time this afternoon."

"So did I."

"And you're not the evil foe I've heard so much about," she added with sudden candor.

It intrigued Jarred. "Oh, Trevor has nice things to say about me?"

"The best. You have no idea."

"Well, it's all true," he drawled. "Beware. You've been forewarned."

"I'll take my chances."

"I'd like to see you again," he said, and the intensity of his gaze caused her breath to catch in her throat.

"That would be . . . acceptable," she managed.

He smiled at her choice of word and said, "I'll call."

And he did. The very next day. And they went to dinner. Then to a play. Then to a social event that required Kelsey to rifle through her clothes to find a dress nice enough for the evening. And then they ended up at the house he was building on Lake Washington, the one they moved into after their wedding. It was framed, and that was about it. Jarred spread a blanket on the plywood floor of what would be the master bedroom and they made love for the first time, whispering and touching, laughing like schoolchildren, reveling in the moment as a white moon sailed in the sky and poured bright light through the window frames to illuminate their tossing bodies.

It was a moment forever captured in her memory. She could still see their pale skin, hear the cadence of their quickened breathing, feel the hot desire that melted them together.

Kelsey shook herself out of her reverie, feeling heat climb up her neck. Good Lord, she was susceptible! How could that be? How could she still feel this way when she'd learned to hate him.

Why? When did things change?

From the moment I met his family, she answered herself.

She thought of Nola and Jonathan and Will. Her relationships with all of them were difficult at best. Adding Sarah to the mix was nearly more than she could bear to think about. And apart from Jarred's personal secretary, Gwen, who seemed to at least recognize that Kelsey was Jarred's wife, no one at Bryant Industries could be considered more than a chilly acquaintance.

No wonder the marriage had collapsed. It had no foundations. No pilings. No support. Even the Rowdens, Kelsey's "parents," weren't a part of the family structure. It had only been Kelsey and Jarred, and it hadn't been enough.

Jarred stirred in the bed, his breath exhaling on a sigh. Kelsey pulled her gaze away automatically, afraid he might awaken and catch her staring at him. Climbing from her chair, she stretched her back, then pulled the chair to the side of the room. Thinking about the past made her feel anxious and unhappy; there were just so many things she would like to change, even now.

You told Sarah you were moving back in with Jarred. . . .

Chewing on her lower lip, Kelsey considered those bold words. She realized she'd made the choice even before she threw the words in Sarah's face: She was going to move back in with her husband.

"I might as well start tonight," she said aloud.

After another hour had passed and Jarred slept on, she brushed her fingers lightly across his forehead in a soft good-bye and headed for the cold comfort of her condominium.

"Here, Felix, kitty kitty kitty," Kelsey called, closing the front door behind her. The condo's entry was really just an extension of the living room; an S-shaped section cut from the carpet and filled with gold-veined cream marble. To her right lay the kitchen, a utilitarian U whose outside counter was free of upper cabinets and flanked by three maple bar stools. When she stepped around the corner to the narrow hallway that led to two bedrooms and two baths, she discovered Felix sitting on top of the toilet, his tail switching back and forth.

"Well, what are you doing?" she asked, picking up the yellow tabby, who melted limply over her arm and started purring. "We're moving, you and I. You won't like it because Jarred has a big, big dog, but we're moving just the same. I'm certain this is bound to be a huge problem, but then what isn't?"

Unconcerned, Felix butted his head into Kelsey's stomach as she sank down on her tiny love seat and arranged the cat on her lap. "Mr. Dog is a golden retriever whose loyalty to his master is totally undeserved. You're going to hate him, though I must admit he's a sweetheart. I haven't seen him in a while."

Feeling unexpected melancholy, she gave Felix a hard hug. He yowled and jumped off her lap and Kelsey decided it was high time to pour herself a glass of white wine.

She was in the process of doing just that when the phone rang. Glancing at Caller ID, she noticed she'd already had ten phone calls, none of which had left a message on her answering machine. All of them were from different numbers around the Seattle area. Strange. But the current call was listed as private.

"Hello?"

"Kelsey?"

"Jarred?" she responded, surprised. "How did you get my number?" she asked, blurting out the first thing that came to mind.

"I know your number."

"You know my number," she repeated dumbly. This, in itself, was a revelation, since he'd never called her more than once or twice at the condominium in the three years that she'd lived there. Add the fact that his memory only seemed to work in fits and starts, and the odds of him recalling this unimportant bit of information were astronomical.

He paused, then replied, sounding somewhat surprised himself, "Yes, I do."

"What . . . did you want?" she asked, gulping her wine by mistake and bringing tiny tears to her eyes.

"My dog. I have a dog. Who's been taking care of him?"

His memory was definitely returning. "Mary Hennessy, I think."

"What's his name?"

"Mr. Dog."

He muttered in frustration. "That's right. Mr. Dog. A golden retriever. I can't believe I couldn't remember him. And Mary Hennessey's been with my family for years. I didn't remember her either until Will mentioned her earlier. God, I hate this."

"You're doing as well as can be expected, Jarred. Just don't fight it. It'll come."

"How do you know that?"

"Well, I don't really," she admitted. "But you always overanalyze everything and it never works."

"I overanalyze everything?"

"Always."

"Well, I don't appear to have the brain capacity to do it anymore," he said, sounding more like a thwarted schoolboy than the owner of a multi-million dollar corporation.

Kelsey almost smiled. "Maybe that's a good thing," she stated lightly.

"What did you decide about moving back in with me?"

Realizing that this was the crux of his call, Kelsey felt herself tighten up a bit. "I'll be at the house when they spring you out of that place. And I'm bringing my cat with me."

"Good." Relief flooded his voice. Then after a moment, he asked, "What made you change your mind?"

A vision of Sarah Ackerman's cold face swam before Kelsey's eyes. "Let's just say I had an epiphany of sorts."

"Now you've got me intrigued," he said, sounding more like the old Jarred than she'd heard thus far.

"I don't think Mr. Dog is going to be happy about meeting Felix, and vice versa," she said, lithely sidestepping the issue.

"Felix is your cat? Original."

"Don't be so quick to criticize. He came with that name. I saved him from death row at the Humane Society, and I just couldn't come up with anything else. Besides, you have no room to talk with a golden retriever named Mr. Dog."

"Point taken," he said good-humoredly. "Will I see you tomorrow?"

"I'll stop by."

"Good-bye then."

"Good-bye, Jarred."

She hung up the phone, her hand resting lightly on the receiver for several long moments. When was the last time she'd talked to him over the phone without him ordering her around or her complaining about some aspect of their relationship? In their last conversation the day before the accident, Jarred had ordered her to his office. And the time before that, she'd called and coolly announced she'd hired a divorce attorney, mostly because she was feeling angry and had chanced upon a meeting with Seattle's most accomplished divorce attorney, a piranha named Jacqueline, referred to as Black Jack by the many ex-husbands whose wives had reamed out their bank accounts with Jacqueline representing them. Neither call had been what one might term a success.

How odd that now she found herself feeling so differently. So hopeful. So belatedly *thrilled* that he'd called her just to check in.

"Oh, Felix," she said aloud to the tabby, who now sat on the floor beside her feet, looking up at her. "I'm in deep, deep trouble."

The phone chimed again. Kelsey answered it on the second ring. "Hello?" She could hear someone breathing on the other end and the hairs on her forearms stood up. "Hello," she said again, more cautiously.

"Kelsey Bennett?" a male voice inquired.

"Speaking."

"You don't know me. Not really. I . . ." His voice trailed off but she could still hear him on the other end of the line.

"What do you want?" she asked, sensing her pulse rise in tandem with sudden, inexplicable fear.

"I need something," he said, his voice a near whisper. "You've got to help me."

A moment later the line went dead. Reading the number on Caller ID, Kelsey instantly phoned back. The line rang so many times she was about to hang up when someone answered: a woman.

"Who is this?" Kelsey demanded.

"Hey, I just picked up the phone 'cause it was ringin' and ringin'. Who ya tryin' to call?"

"Someone just called me from this number. I'm trying to reach him."

"Oh, yeah? Well, this is a pay phone down on Fifth, honey. Wha'dya want me to tell ya? There ain't nobody here."

"Oh . . . I see. Thank you."

Kelsey replaced the receiver. Not liking what she was feeling, she rechecked all the doors and windows and then set about packing up her belongings as fast as she could.

Chapter Five

Backing her Ford Explorer out of its tiny, exorbitantly priced parking spot on a lot outside her office building, Kelsey shook off the weight of depression that had descended upon her as soon as she'd packed the last box into the back of her SUV. She's spent half the night shoving her meager belongings in the boxes she'd never thrown away from her original move to the condo. Then she'd spent the early morning packing the car. The rest of the day she had been at the office, fighting off Trevor's furious hysteria at the ineptitude of his own subcontractors.

No wonder a headache had formed at the base of her skull. She wanted nothing more than a hot bath and a cup of tea. But she was moving. Once decided, she'd been in constant motion, more as a way to outrun her own demons than any serious need to move back. After all, Jarred wasn't even out of the hospital yet, but she needed this change and pronto. The voice on the phone had been the final impetus.

"It's not going to be the same as that old life," she muttered, heading out of Seattle city center through a hard rain that kept her wipers slapping double time as she drove toward Jarred's home.

Your home, too, she reminded herself.

But she couldn't help feeling like a returning guest. When she'd left Jarred, she'd practically run for her life and her sanity. She'd been going quietly mad inside a house that had been slowly invaded by Sarah Ackerman's presence while her own seemed to fade away.

Traffic was a mess, and by the time she'd crossed the I-90 bridge over Mercer Island to Medina and the house on Lake Washington, she was hot, tired, and sick to the back teeth of this incessant rain. Pulling into the drive of the lodgelike shingled house with white trim, she hit the garage-door button — a souvenir she'd never managed to part with, which was another point she didn't want to examine too closely — with her right hand. The house was massive with an east and west wing and two garages that could house five vehicles. A white elephant. A wedding gift.

And he'd given her a sapphire-and-diamond pendant for an engagement gift, broken now, from the time Jarred had yanked it from her throat in a moment of rage. While packing this morning, she'd seen it within the velvet prison of her jewelry box.

Shivering, Kelsey gathered up an awkward box, stuffed to the gills, and balanced it gingerly, her purse dangling from her arm and thunking against her thigh. Shifting the box's weight, she tried to twist the knob to the back door. Her hair, banded into a loose ponytail, was coming free, and mist from the rain swept into the garage on the tails of a gust of wind, coalescing on the errant tendrils and sticking them wetly against her neck.

She shivered harder.

By the time she negotiated her way through the door, trekked across the walk-through pantry, and bypassed the double glass-paned doors to the solarium, she felt anxious and uneasy and certain she'd made a terrible mistake.

From the center of the kitchen she called, "Mary?" thinking the housekeeper-cum-cook might still be at the house.

A sharp, delighted *woof* sounded. Mr. Dog suddenly slid around the corner, tongue flapping happily in his smiling mouth, tail wagging, feet churning on the slippery hardwood floors.

"Whoa, boy!" Kelsey called to the golden retriever, sensing disaster. "Stop! Stop!"

He burst toward her. Kelsey half turned. "No. *Stop!* Slow down. I've got —"

The dog leaped. Paws knocked the load from her arms. Shoes and belts and her jewelry box fell from the box. Her purse slid down her arm, slapped against Mr. Dog's face, dropped to the floor, upended, and spilled its contents on the polished American cherry floor. Mr. Dog jumped again, and this time Kelsey sighed, patted his silky head, then embraced him for all she was worth until his frenzied licking tongue washed half her face.

"Ugh." She pushed him away, but he barked in excitement and eagerness and jumped up on her again. "You moron," she said fondly, scratching his ears. Leaning his big head against her, he gazed up with solemn loyalty. Kelsey laughed. "Oh, sure, you fickle male. If Jarred were here, you wouldn't even know I exist. Now get down," she added, giving his head a slight push so that he dropped to his toes, his nails clicking softly as he nosed through the mess of Kelsey's belongings.

The sapphire-and-diamond necklace lay scattered on the floor, its brilliance dulled a bit in the gray light streaming through the solarium windows from the overcast skies beyond. Picking up the necklace, Kelsey slid its gold chain over her fingers.

"It was my grandmother's," Jarred had told her, lifting it from its original box and sliding it around her neck. His fingers had lingered against her skin. She remembered their electric touch and the breath-stopping moment when he'd presented her with such a lovely gift.

"I can't," she choked.

"I want you to be my wife," he whispered in her ear, his hands sliding down her arms. They were in the restaurant at Seattle's Four Seasons

112

Olympic Hotel and she could see their twin reflections in the white china plate that gleamed beneath the crystalline lights.

"Jarred," she whispered, speechless.

"Say yes," he ordered softly, his breath hot on her ear.

"Yes . . ."

Kelsey shook herself back to the moment. After laying the necklace on the black granite countertop, she bent down. With jerky motions, she gathered up all her spilled belongings, shoving them back in the box. Snatching up her purse by the handle, she hefted the box on the island counter, leaving it next to the necklace, which lay twisted and seductive against the cold black stone.

Feeling like an intruder, she slowly climbed one of the two fir stairways that rose upward as it jogged inward around several landings, then rose again to a gallery above the main entry hall. She turned left, toward the east wing and the guest apartments. She'd lived with Jarred in the west wing but there was no way she would invade his rooms now. Besides, he would be convalescing for a while, and she would be in the way.

Not that she *wanted* to be with him, she reminded herself quickly. Jarred Bryant had been an autocrat when she'd first met him and he was no better now, accident or no accident. He was just different — that was all. And she couldn't let her own foolish fantasies keep her from that truth. This was just a temporary situation. She wasn't giving up her condo just yet.

"How depressing," she said as she entered the guest bedroom, alluding to her thoughts rather than the beautiful appointments of the suite. The faintest peach color covered the walls and was complemented by various shades of taupe and cream in the lush downy comforter and flowered valance. The furniture was a funky bamboo she'd collected on sale in an equally funky furniture shop. She'd had fun putting the rooms together, she recalled, and Jarred had let her do whatever she wanted. That was in the first days of their marriage when she'd felt as if she was playing house. Later, nothing had been fun, and Sarah Ackerman had haunted the halls like an evil spirit.

Gazing rather grimly through the broad windows to the dark water of Lake Washington and the glimmering lights that surrounded it, Kelsey wondered how long she would be living here alone. Reminding herself to check with Dr. Alastair, she rubbed her arms briskly, trying to shake off the unpleasant sense of not quite belonging in Jarred's life and world.

The phone rang, causing her to jump. She stood stock-still and heard the answering machine in the kitchen pick up. Kelsey walked to the gallery and leaned over to hear. A feminine voice was leaving a message. With surprise, Kelsey realized it was Nola, her rather brittle voice welcoming Kelsey back to Jarred's home.

Walking slowly downstairs, she stared at the machine as a computer voice declared flatly, "End of message."

Grabbing up a box of clothes, she headed back upstairs. Dumping the box on the bed she headed for the bathroom. Closing the door, she ran a hot bath in the heart-shaped "double" tub that she and Jarred had never used together. She'd wanted to share it, she remembered. That had definitely been her original intention. But things happened, and by the time the guest wing renovation was completed, she and Jarred never found the time.

The phone rang a second time just as Kelsey sank into the hot water. "Mr. Dog can answer it," she muttered, closing her eyes and thrusting all her worries aside for the moment.

"I don't think she's there yet," Jarred said, replacing the receiver. He moved his shoulder and the arm that lay heavily in its cast, feeling everything itch and nag.

"You're sure she's moving in today?" Will asked. He sat comfortably in the hospital chair as best he could, an ankle propped on his opposite knee.

"Pretty sure,"

"You sound frustrated."

Jarred gave his half brother a wry look. "Do I? I wonder why."

Tugging on his ear, Will made a face. "Look, whatever you want, it's okay by me. I just don't want to see you get taken in by her. You *know* what she's like better than anyone, and if this crash has destroyed your memory and you need help putting the pieces back together, I'm here to help. Just like always," he added a bit tightly.

Jarred's first reaction was to argue with Will about Kelsey. He damn near told his half brother that he trusted Kelsey a hell of a lot more than he trusted *him*. But then another memory assailed him: the day eleven-year-old Will was dumped on the Bryant doorstep by his uncaring and unhappy mother.

"I don't want him anymore," were the words that hit Jarred's ears as he opened the door to find the two of them standing on the porch. Shy, scared, and uncomfortable as hell, Will brushed the toe of his shoe around in the imaginary dirt on Nola's brick entry porch, his eyes downcast. A very sore point, he was, between Nola and Jonathan since Will was the result of Jonathan's romantic tryst with an employee of Bryant Industries when Jonathan was at its helm. Nola made certain Will's mother was fired *tout de suite,* and the woman left the company and Jonathan with bad feelings all around. But that sunny Sunday afternoon when she dumped him on the Bryant doorstep was the first Jarred knew any of it.

"I'm through with living on nothing while you all dine on caviar," she said to Jarred while Will stood soberly at his mother's side. "Tell your father that Will is his responsibility now. He's a

116

good boy, but I have no money and I'm done."

She said it with utter finality. Shocked by her words, Jarred turned to Will. Jarred was fifteen at the time, and though Nola certainly wasn't up for "mother of the year" she was not nearly as heartless as this woman. "Come on then," Jarred told Will, indicating with his head that the boy was to follow him inside the house. Will complied and Jarred closed the door on the other boy's mother, who had already turned away.

That was the last anyone had seen of her.

Nola had not welcomed the newcomer with open arms, but Jonathan and Jarred were delighted to have him, frustrating Nola to no end. Will, for his part, seemed content and relieved to be part of the Bryant household. He followed Jarred through the University of Washington, eventually earning an MBA and becoming Jarred's right-hand man at Bryant Industries after Jonathan, in the wake of a very disappointing decade for the company, bowed out, leaving the business to Jarred.

Will was not in line to inherit. Even though he now used the Bryant name, he was not a legitimate heir to Hugh Bryant. So while Jarred inherited the company stock, Will was currently only a Bryant Industries' employee. This stipulation was written in stone, as far as Nola was concerned anyway, but with his father's unspoken blessing, Jarred was planning to change all that as soon as possible.

"What are you thinking about?" Will asked now, eyeing Jarred intently. "Your mind is elsewhere."

"I'm thinking about how uncomfortable I am. I can't wait to get out of here."

"No, you're not. You're thinking about Kelsey, and you don't like it that I don't trust her."

Jarred wasn't about to enlighten Will about the extent of his memory just yet. There was no way Will was going to understand about Kelsey, and Jarred didn't feel like arguing about it.

"We've lost a big section of waterfront property to Taggart Inc.," Will said soberly. "The Brunswick property was ours, and now it's not. Kelsey's been giving Taggart information on every piece we've wanted, feeding him all the facts and figures and it's child's play for him to outbid us."

"The Brunswick property . . . ?"

"Oh, God," Will sighed, sounding defeated. "You really don't remember? What do you think we've all been in such a fuss over? Your mother, Sarah, even Dad — we've all been going crazy. We've been trying to get you to sign the original papers. They were just sitting on your desk, for God's sake. Unfinished. Just needing your signature, but no one would let us get close to you. And then today we heard that Taggart's got the property, and it's too late. And we know who to blame."

Jarred mulled that over. It was all a blank.

"Why did you say, 'Even Dad,' as if he wouldn't care?"

Will stared at him in consternation. "Jarred, please. I really need you to stay on track on this. You're the only one who really knows — knew — why you never signed the deal. Think, man. *Think*."

"I wish I could help you," Jarred offered sincerely, "but I can't. What's the deal with Dad?"

"He just doesn't pay any attention to the business these days," Will responded shortly.

"Why not?"

"I don't know. And that's one thing you don't know either, so stop worrying about trying to remember it. We talked about Dad before the accident, you and I, and you said you thought his health was failing. Neither one of us knows why he's so distracted these days." Will shrugged.

Jarred dimly recalled worrying about his father. It was just one of those thoughts that swam in and out of his consciousness and seemed disconnected to anything tangible.

"All I'm saying, Jarred, is be careful around Kelsey. Okay, I grant you that we don't know for sure that she's the one funneling information to Taggart, but she's our best bet. Information's getting to him that no one, except you and me, knows anything about."

"That would make one of us the spy," Jarred pointed out with faint humor.

Will managed a laugh. "All right, someone else knows. The Brunswick property hasn't been much of a secret, but the *details* have been, the *negotiations,* and that's what's getting to Taggart's ears." He spread his hands. "Kelsey's the most likely candidate."

"Sometimes the most likely candidate is the least likely candidate. She doesn't work for us. How would she know the ins and outs of that deal?"

Will looked impressed and relieved. "Glad to see you haven't lost your cognitive skills, old boy. I was beginning to wonder."

"I just want to know how she would transfer sensitive information that she doesn't have in her possession."

"She works for Taggart," Will explained as if Jarred could have forgotten.

"But she doesn't work for Bryant Industries."

"No."

"She's not your spy, Will."

"How do you know that?" he demanded in frustration.

"I just know it," Jarred responded with growing annoyance. He was tired. Tired of arguing and tired of thinking about Bryant Industries. He realized how naive he must sound, but he couldn't come up with a better explanation at this time. "Look, I trust her. It's just something I woke up with. She's not made the way you think she is."

"You are wrong, brother," Will said with true sympathy. "And I'm sorry."

"I'm sorry, too."

Sighing, Will climbed to his feet. "Your memory will come back. Then we'll talk."

Jarred almost told him that it had damn near returned in full already, but he checked himself. Instead he asked, "If Kelsey didn't work for Taggart anymore, do you think the leak would stop?"

"I . . . don't know. She could still certainly call him or meet him and pass on our bidding information."

"But she'd have to get that information from someone from the company," Jarred pointed out. "That's who you need to find. Whoever at Bryant Industries is *taking* the information. That's your spy."

"*Our* spy," Will responded, but he looked more thoughtful.

"Ask yourself who else has access to that information. Someone must."

"No, it was all in your office."

"Then who has access to my office?"

"You mean besides me — and Gwen, of course?"

"Gwen . . . ?"

"Your personal secretary who's been with the company for forty years? The longest, most loyal employee of the bunch whose only crime is that she gets a bit flustered when the phones are ringing like crazy and who suffers from migraine attacks now and again? Gwen, whom Dad trusted like a saint and who hung in there during some hard years when profits were sinking off the charts and the whole corporation nearly sank with it?"

"I know Gwen," Jarred said shortly, recalling the thin woman with the soulful blue eyes and the gray roots showing beneath dyed black hair. He didn't disillusion Will by saying he'd wished, upon occasion, that he could find a way to either fire her or shuffle her off to someone else. She might have been one stellar secretary during his father's day, but her skills had slipped with age, and he hadn't wanted to have to rely on her. She was sweet, but unreliable.

You really were a heartless bastard, he thought with an inward wince.

"Someone's getting access to the material," Jarred said doggedly. "And that someone isn't Kelsey."

"Okay, maybe she hasn't been the one to actually lift the information," Will conceded reluctantly.

"Then, logically, someone else has been reading our sensitive information."

"Taggart has a spy," Will agreed. "That's the bottom line. And okay, maybe I don't know how Kelsey's doing it, but I can't help thinking she's involved somehow. At the risk of really pissing you off, let me say that no one else detests you as much as your lovely wife. Not even Trevor Taggart. So watch your back."

Silence fell like a lead curtain. Weariness invaded every blasted pore, and Jarred closed his eyes. He'd been told more than once that he was known for being a cold character, that ice ran through his veins instead of blood, that he could flirt with a woman, maybe even get her into bed, learn all her secrets, and then expose them without turning a hair. Maybe he'd had those capabilities once but they were gone forever. They'd been gone from the moment Kelsey Bennett entered his life.

"She is a beautiful woman," Will said after a long moment. "And she is trying to stick by you now."

"So she's not evil incarnate?"

"She's just not trustworthy, Jarred. That's all."

Will left and Jarred lay quietly in the hospital bed. Could his brother be right? Maybe Kelsey wasn't trustworthy. Maybe she was the spy who had helped leak information to Taggart. He now remembered that of the last five major real estate deals, three had gone sour at the eleventh hour — all to Taggart Inc.'s benefit.

Jarred thought of Kelsey's mobile face and lovely amber eyes. Her honesty and humor and wit — qualities he'd always found so entrancing, even when he was angry or away from her. *Could she be a traitor?* Someone who hated him so much that she would undermine his business, all that he and his family had worked for all of their lives? *Could she?*

"No," he said aloud to the empty room. Though he'd certainly entertained dark thoughts like that in the past, he knew now he'd only blamed her because he'd been hurt. It wasn't any real belief in her culpability. She didn't work that way.

Moments later, exhaustion crept in again and Jarred let himself succumb. All he wanted now was to get the hell out of this hospital bed and begin his life anew.

With Kelsey.

Wiping off the steam-fogged mirror with a towel, Kelsey examined her face. "What are you doing?" she whispered to her own reflection. "What are you doing?"

Mr. Dog scratched and whined at the bathroom door. Wrapping a fluffy lemon-colored towel around her damp skin, Kelsey yelled, "Go away. I'll be out in a minute." The whining and scratching increased. Unlocking the door, she cracked it just enough for the retriever to get his nose inside. "You're a pest — you know that?" Mr. Dog squeezed his whole head through and barked excitedly. Kelsey threw open the door, holding out her arm and commanding sharply, "Sit! Right now. Sit! Don't you dare jump up on me now and wound me. I need more armor on. Don't think I don't know that you're a spy from the other camp! And don't give me that innocent look. *Sit!*"

Mr. Dog's whole body wriggled as he sat down. He tried to scoot across the floor toward her, which broke Kelsey into laughter. The dog leaped and she screeched and laughed, pushing him away. "Oh, for Pete's sake, go away!" she cried, heading out of the bathroom, the dog at her heels. She grabbed his collar and dragged him into the hall, losing her towel in the process. Then she scurried back across the threshold, pointing her finger at him. "No! No! Stay there!"

Lifting one paw at her in a silly doggy wave, he whined and wriggled. She felt guilty, closing the door on him. Normally he wasn't so persistent, but Jarred had been gone for nearly a week and the poor thing was desperate for company. Though Kelsey suspected she was a poor substitute, she appreciated the attention.

"When I'm dressed," she called through the door to the canine. Mr. Dog barked wildly in response. "Yeah, you're happy now. Just wait until I bring Felix over."

Padding across the lush cream carpet to the bed, she snatched up her jeans and a tailored, blue cotton shirt, which she left unbuttoned at the throat. She yanked on a pair of black ankle boots, then threw on a black wool jacket to complete the outfit. Returning to the bathroom she brushed out her unruly reddish brown locks, letting them fall to her shoulders. A slap of lipstick and a touch of blush and she felt armored and ready for another trip to the hospital.

"Get out of my way," she mock growled at Mr. Dog as she ran down the back stairs to the kitchen. The dog jumped, barked, and bounded, nearly knocking her over before she reached the bottom step and the archway to the kitchen.

The pendant lay on the granite counter where she'd left it earlier. She stared at it rather grimly for a few moments, almost loath to touch it. There was so much history in that necklace, none of it good.

Mr. Dog snuffled her boots and the hem of her jeans. Absently scratching his head, she picked up the pendant. Straightening, she opened the clasp, then slowly placed the necklace around her neck, lightly touching the sapphire pendant at her throat, dry mouthed at the message she would be sending her husband when he saw her wearing it.

More dreams. Jarred thrashed against them even while he didn't actually move in the hospital bed. Visions of water. Great expanses of it. And even while fitfully asleep, he understood that he was dreaming, yet he couldn't stop himself. His mind kept traveling through the same channels.

Now he was standing on grass. He looked down at his shoes and noticed there were huge dandelions and crabgrass making up this lawn. He was worried about the grass. Whose place was so neglected? Shouldn't he tell someone?

Then there was a man in front of him. He said his name was Charlie. But abruptly Jarred was in a dirty kitchen of some sort with crusted dirt in the corners of the linoleum floor and chipped Formica counters, where Petrie dishes, filled with growing lines of microorganisms, lay jumbled up against metal pans packed with purple rock salt.

Drugs, he thought, and then he was back in the water. He was drowning! Choking! His throat clogged. Couldn't talk. He fought. A rasp. A rale!

"Jarred!" Kelsey called in his ear and he woke with a start. Her hand was on his shoulder and she gazed at him worriedly, her pink lips scant inches from his own. "I'm sorry. You were dreaming and making terrible sounds. I thought you were having a nightmare. Are you okay?"

"Fine . . ." He cleared his throat. The dream was already fading, sinking into oblivion. Frowning, he dragged it back into his consciousness, needing to examine it. "I was dreaming about . . . drugs."

"Drugs?" Kelsey leaned away from him and he instantly wished she would stay close. "You mean, recreational drugs?"

"And water." He licked dry lips. "Speaking of which, could you hand me my glass?"

"Sure." She poured water into a plastic cup, adjusted a Flex-straw, and placed the glass in his good hand.

Jarred sucked hard on the straw. "Maybe I was just thirsty."

"Why were you dreaming about drugs?" she asked.

"I don't know. I was in a room, like a kitchen or a lab," he said. "But it was more like a kitchen, and there was all this stuff. They were

127

making something."

"They?"

"The drug guys," Jarred said for lack of any better explanation. "I've seen that before," he added, thinking hard. "I mean, I feel like I have. Maybe it was on TV."

Kelsey regarded him seriously. "What were they making?"

"I don't know. What can you make?"

"I know you can grow marijuana," she said.

"No," he said, disagreeing with the image, not the statement. "That wasn't it. It was . . ."

Crystal methamphetamine.

The answer came like a bolt from the blue, and something must have showed on his face because Kelsey said, "What? What's wrong?"

"Nothing. I'm just trying to figure it out."

"Does this all have to do with Chance?" Kelsey suggested lightly, uncomfortably. "Maybe the water and the drugs. The plane crashed into the Columbia River and Chance was a . . . dabbler."

Jarred just looked at her. A dabbler? By all accounts, the man was an out-and-out user and abuser. Kelsey dropped her gaze, and it killed him to think she still had deep feelings for the man.

And then he noticed the pendant. His grandmother's sapphire-and-diamond necklace lay softly against her throat, just visible in the opened neckline of her blue shirt. She'd repaired it, he realized, and emotion swept over him, humbled him, left him mute.

"Have you moved into the house?" Jarred asked after a long moment.

"Yes . . . I'm in the process anyway." She linked her hands together, as if afraid they might betray her in some way.

"I can't wait to get out of here."

"You seem . . . stronger every time I see you."

"I have a feeling I'm going to have a fight on my hands with Dr. Alastair," Jarred complained, sounding sulky.

Kelsey smiled, relaxing just a tiny bit. He still made her so uncomfortable, and she inwardly marveled at his power. "Jarred Bryant generally wins a fight," she said with gentle humor. "I almost feel sorry for Dr. Alastair if he tries to keep you in here too long."

"You're wearing the necklace."

He gazed at her directly and it was all she could do to keep from covering the telltale piece of jewelry with one hand. "Yes. You remember it then."

"I remember a lot of things."

"Do you?" She regarded him intently.

"Most things," he admitted, and he watched the changes cross her face as she realized his memory was practically intact. "Not everything. Not the accident. And I'd rather not publicize my returning memory just yet, if you don't mind."

"No." She shook her head. "I . . . think you're probably wise."

"You don't trust my family either?"

"Not much," she admitted with a shaky laugh. "But you always have."

"Well, I don't anymore." He paused, then added gruffly, "I'm sorry about the necklace."

The scene where he pulled it from her neck replayed itself across the screen of her mind. She'd always cast him as the villain, yanking the fragile chain from her neck in a fit of anger. But with his apology, she could finally admit the truth, and she said in a voice that was not quite steady, "You had your hand on it. You were angry with me because I wanted to take it off. You liked me to wear it and I wanted to thwart you, so I leaned my head back." She swallowed hard. "And the chain just snapped . . . and I blamed you for it . . . and I was wrong."

His blue eyes regarded her for long, uncomfortable moments. Finally, he said intensely, "I want a second chance, Kelsey."

Her own eyes felt unnaturally bright. "I think I would like that."

His right hand reached for her and Kelsey slipped her left hand in its warmth.

"I need to ask you a favor," Jarred said. She gazed at him silently. "I need you to work for Bryant Industries."

"What?" she asked faintly. He'd never wanted her to work for him! There had been a time when she'd desperately wished for it to be true, but Jarred had apparently felt very strongly that she stay out of his business.

"There's a spy within the company," he said now, and very succinctly he told her about all the times Trevor had succeeded in stealing projects from his company. Kelsey listened with growing dread and a terrible sense of the inevitable. It made so much sense. Trevor hadn't scooped property from Jarred's hands through honorable means; he had someone on the inside.

"Who is it?" Kelsey asked when Jarred stopped explaining.

"We don't know."

"We?"

"Will and I talked about it." After a moment's pause, Jarred admitted, "He'd like me to think you were behind it."

Kelsey's brows shot up. "Me? How? Why?"

"He thinks you loathe me."

Kelsey flinched at the word. Until recently, she had thought just those kind of thoughts. "I don't loathe you," she responded.

Was it her imagination or had he relaxed a bit at her words? Was the all and powerful Jarred Bryant actually afraid she might still detest him? Even now, when she felt she was being painfully obvious about her feelings?

"Will you do it?" he asked.

"I don't know how I can just turn around and quit working for Trevor and start working for Bryant Industries. No one will believe I'm sincere about it. They'll think I talked you into it or worse. They'll think you're incapable of making those decisions, and they'll make my life a living hell!"

"Is that a no?"

Kelsey felt the warmth of her husband's hand, witnessed the tenseness of his expression, considered the impotence he must have felt at not being able to handle all the problems of the company on his own. "I'd love to work for Bryant. I just won't have a friend to turn to — if you know what I mean."

"You've got me," he said simply.

And with a burst of shocking clarity, Kelsey knew it was true.

Chapter Six

"We're putting you in my office for the moment," Will told Kelsey as he walked with her down the silvery-carpeted hallways of the upper floors of Bryant Industries. "I'll be pinch-hitting between my office and Jarred's. If you need anything, check with Meghan. She assists me and Sarah Ackerman. Or there's Jarred's personal secretary, Gwen, whom you know, although she's not here today. Migraines," he explained unnecessarily. Kelsey knew all about Gwen's condition.

"Thank you," she said.

"No problem."

He opened the mahogany-stained cherry door to his own spacious office, where two desks resided with expanses of gray carpet to spare. Will's desk was mahogany and placed in a commanding spot in the middle of the room. The other one — clearly a new addition — was a smaller black Techline model with a matching credenza.

Shocked as they had to be by this new arrangement, Kelsey appreciated how quickly Jarred's employees had responded to the news that she would be working for them. And though she sensed that Will was bemused by the turn of events, he had graciously welcomed her to the offices and had obviously done everything he could to accommodate her. So far, her predictions of being a pariah hadn't come true, although she suspected this acceptance was a mere facade covering a deep, underlying worry.

Still, it was better than being barred from entry, which in her wilder fantasies she'd believed might actually occur. There was no way anyone at Bryant would be happy about the new employee.

And later today, she was going to have to go to her office at Taggart Inc. and finalize a few things there. The daunting task of telling Trevor of her new employment lay ahead of her.

I hope I'm not making a terrible mistake, she told herself. She was giving up her job — the one aspect of her life these past few years that had helped get her through the pain of her dying marriage.

"This'll work great," she said. "I really appreciate it, Will. I know this has got to be strange for you. It's strange for me, too, but I think Jarred and I have turned a corner in our relationship."

"I just hope you have his best interests at heart," Will said soberly, checking his watch.

"I do. I know it may take a while for you to believe that, but I've been given a second chance and I refuse to squander it."

"Good, good. I've got to get to a meeting. Are you okay here? We can go over some of the deals in progress later, but I'm a little busy at the moment."

She could feel his reluctance about including her. She couldn't blame him. Jarred really must have put the squeeze on Will to get him to even mention the fact that she was to have *carte blanche* with the most intimate of Bryant Industries's secrets.

"I've got some ends to tie up, too," she said. "Let's start in the morning then."

"I'll be in at seven. Show up whenever you're ready."

"Seven it is," she said evenly, not to be intimidated.

With a nod, Will left her to her own devices, and Kelsey seized the opportunity to collapse in her new desk chair, her brain running in wild, frazzled circles. What was she doing? Why had she agreed to this? Did Jarred really trust her so much, or was this some kind of Machiavellian test?

And was she right to tell Will that she wanted a second chance? What if *he* were the one passing sensitive information to Trevor?

Kelsey pulled herself up sharp. Though she had quickly accepted that Trevor was taking, or even buying, information about Bryant Industries, it still bothered her that she could think so little of her soon-to-be ex-employer. With a deep search of her own soul, she realized she had never fully trusted Trevor, whose self-involved ways revealed so much more than she'd ever credited. She'd been so wrapped up in her own marital woes that she'd just thanked the heavens for her job and career. She hadn't cared to look at Trevor's faults, though now, armed with this new information from Jarred, she saw they were extremely glaring.

Shaking herself, she jumped to her feet. No time like the present to go to her office, put things in some semblance of order, then tell Trevor of her intentions. If he wanted her to stay on longer she was more than willing to, but in her heart of hearts she knew that as soon as he heard she was moving to Bryant Industries, he would show her the door and dust his hands after she left.

A moment later there was a knock on her door.

"Come in," she called.

A young woman peeked her head around the doorjamb. "Hi, I'm Meghan. Did Will tell you about me? Anything you need, just ask."

"Thanks, Meghan. I'm okay for the moment."

"It's nice to have you on board, Mrs. Bryant."

"It's nice to be here," Kelsey responded with an inward smile at the girl's rather obvious attempts to work office politics. "And it's Kelsey. Please. I don't respond well to Mrs. Bryant."

"It's nice to have you on board, Kelsey,"

Meghan said with a spreading grin. "I'm right down the hall when you need me."

"I'm sure I'll be looking for you soon."

As the door closed behind Meghan, Kelsey thought, *Maybe there are a few good souls here.*

With that encouraging idea clearly in mind, she slung the strap of her purse over her shoulder and headed for the unavoidable clash with Trevor Taggart.

"God almighty," Jarred muttered through gritted teeth as he collapsed on the bed. He'd walked. He'd *walked.* But it had damn near done him in.

Of course they would throw a hissy fit if they knew he was wandering around his room without a "spotter" in attendance. He didn't truly blame them, since he was as unsteady as a newborn lamb. But he *could* walk. If he moved really, really slowly, and if he dragged the leg that was still mending, his nerves screaming with every step.

Well, so what? He didn't have tons of time, and he recalled how often he'd been marveled over by friends, family, and physicians because he had bounced back quickly from some injury.

Still, it was an utter bitch to recover. An utter, utter bitch.

"That's a mighty frown you've got on your face, son," a familiar voice said.

From his ungainly position on the bed, Jarred snapped a look at the newcomer. His father came toward him, looking for all the world as if he'd aged a century since Jarred's accident.

Struggling upward against the pillows, Jarred said in true alarm, "Dad!"

"Are you okay? You look a little pale," Jonathan responded with a frown, ignoring Jarred's concern.

"I'm fine." He hesitated, examining his father's silver-white hair, realizing how little he'd noticed it had changed until this moment. Was it his imagination or his dicey memory? Or had his father changed from a dynamic man to a near invalid overnight? "Where's Nola — umm . . . Mother?" he said.

"Actually, she's at the offices. I decided to come see you rather than have a face-off over there."

"Face-off? Because of Kelsey?" Jarred asked.

Jonathan rubbed a hand over his face. "Why did you install her over there? You know" — he struggled for the right words — "she won't be accepted by the staff."

"I don't really care." Jarred moved his shoulder and grimaced. God, he wished he could hurry up this healing process. "I'm not going to be there for a while, obviously, and I want her to help me."

"But, Jarred, she's not the person to ask." Jonathan sighed and looked around vaguely. "You've got Will. And Sarah. You can rely on them. You always have."

"Whom do you rely on?" he asked, the question popping from some deep well of subconsciousness. It was unfair. Totally unfair. His father's reign at Bryant Industries' helm had nearly cost the family the entire company.

But I want to know. And they think I have amnesia. I can ask this.

Jonathan blinked. "Your grandfather had everything in place. It was as complicated in those days as it is now."

"That sounds like a rehearsed line," Jarred said carefully.

Glancing around for a chair, Jonathan half fell in the one currently pressed against the wall parallel to Jarred's bed. Jarred instantly tried to stand to help his father, but he was yanked up short by a stab of pain.

"Don't do that," Jonathan declared, lifting a palm that trembled ever so slightly. "Don't overtax yourself."

"I'm just worried about you."

"Do you even remember me?" Jonathan asked with uncharacteristic bitterness.

"Yes." Jarred eyed him with concern. "What do you mean? I know who I am and I know Will and Sarah and Nola and you and Gwen." He stopped when a shudder swept his father's shrinking frame. "And Mary," he added. "And Kelsey."

"You've been told about us all."

"Yes," he admitted. "But hearing it resonated within me. I knew it as truth. My memory will come back," he said, feeling like a traitor himself. The lie tasted like ashes on his tongue.

"Yes, yes. Good. I want you back, son," Jonathan declared in a voice grown husky with emotion.

A long moment passed between them. Jarred could sense his father had something on his mind, but it appeared he couldn't bring himself to say it. "What is Nola doing at the company? I don't want to sound ungrateful, but I have a feeling she won't help Kelsey's transition."

"She called Kelsey to welcome her back in the family," Jonathan revealed. "She's trying, Jarred. She wants what's best for you. That's all she ever wanted."

"She wants what she *thinks* is best for me," Jarred contradicted. "It's not the same thing."

His father's silver brows shot up and he looked, for a moment, like the man Jarred suddenly recalled from his past: amused, gentle, a bit of a dilettante, but a man whom people responded to and enjoyed. A ladies' man. One whose roving eye landed on Will's mother and whose affair with the same woman nearly cost him his marriage.

Except Nola Bryant was as strong a force as any category four hurricane. Nothing could divert her from a path once she'd chosen it, and after she'd cast her eye on Jonathan Bryant, the outcome was predictable. And she also wanted Bryant Industries for her son, which meant keeping her husband on as tight a leash as she could handle while the reins of the company passed. Since then she'd held on to him for appearances' sake, and because Jonathan Bryant's philandering ways had diminished with age.

"I'm glad you're pulling through this," Jonathan stated now in a voice that sounded alternately frail and emotional. "These past few weeks, I've suffered through the worst moments of my life, and I've spent time on my knees praying to God that my own mistakes hadn't caused me to lose my son, and then thanking Him for your life. I don't deserve His forgiveness for what I've done, but I'll take this and save it close to my heart. Thank You, Lord." He raised his eyes skyward, his fists clenched together in a zealot's prayer of gratitude. *"Thank You."*

Jarred felt a quiver of real fear. His father had never been fervent, had never shown the merest trace of religious belief, had never mentioned God in Jarred's hearing. It had been Nola who had taken her son to church when he was young, though that was more for appearances' sake than for any grand devotion. Still, Jonathan Bryant had never, ever, *ever* mentioned the Lord in anything but a passing allusion.

"Dad . . . ?"

Jonathan had closed his eyes, his body swaying a bit until Jarred suffered real concern that he would fall out of the chair. But then he came to himself, smiling a bit at his son's alarm. "Don't worry about me. I'm making my peace with God. He gave me an extra chance." With that, he climbed to his feet and shuffled over to give Jarred a kiss on his forehead.

In the wake of his father's departure, Jarred realized that every muscle he possessed was tense and stiff. This was not his father. This was not the man he'd known his entire life. Somewhere in their conversation he'd switched from being concerned about Kelsey working at the company to reveling in the joy of God's ultimate forgiveness.

Forgiveness for what?

He was still pondering that when Sarah Ackerman strode into his room. Her expression softened a bit upon seeing him awake. "There you are," she said. "You look much better. Really. It's incredible."

"I feel . . . stronger."

"Good," she said with feeling. "I was worried. We were all worried. Things have been in an uproar. We've lost deals because your signature wasn't available, and we've been putting off other documents, waiting for you. You could appoint Will as your proxy, just until you're back at work. We need to keep going. Deals are churning and churning, but they'll never get finished without some direction in the company." Hearing herself, she added diffidently, "I'm sure I'm not telling you anything you don't already know, but there've been some concerns, of course, especially today, since we have a new member on our staff."

"Kelsey isn't going to sell us out," Jarred said evenly.

"I wish I had your confidence. She was only at the office a matter of minutes before she left for Taggart Inc. I wonder what she's telling him now."

"She's turning in her resignation," Jarred said wearily. "She's got to meet him face-to-face."

"I'm sure." Sarah's sarcasm didn't register on her face, which could have been cut from stone. Not a lighthearted being. This woman was really not a hell of a lot of fun. Jarred couldn't imagine why people felt he'd ever been interested in her, unless . . .

Unless you let them think the worst because it suited your purposes.

"I'm counting on you to help her make this transition," Jarred told Sarah. "It'll be okay."

"I'm sorry, Jarred. I disagree. I think you've made your first emotional decision, and you're the one who's always said you can't run a business on emotion."

"I said that?" To her nod, he added, "There might be some truth in that, but I don't know if anything's that black and white."

She stared at him as if he'd grown antlers. "I see. Well . . . are you going to give Will the power to sign for you?"

With a feeling of near childish delight, Jarred said, "Actually, I'm thinking of turning that task over to Kelsey."

Felix meowed plaintively from his carrier as Kelsey tucked his small cage under her arm, then closed and locked the door to her condominium. "Don't think I don't know how you feel," she said to the anxious feline. "It's been one hell of a day, and it isn't over yet."

She drove straight from the city, her eyes glued to the road, her thoughts as fretful and anxious as Felix's. Her meeting with Trevor had *not* gone well, and that was the understatement of the year. She'd met him at his office with all Taggart Design's pending invoices, her appointment calendar, and her book containing the phone numbers and addresses of all the people her division dealt with. Everything else was in files in her office, but knowing Trevor, he could leave everything for months before it occurred to him that *he* might actually have to do something about it.

"What's this?" he demanded, when she appeared lugging a heavy briefcase — damn near a suitcase — of her most pressing work.

"I'm quitting," she said gently. "If you want me to, I'll come in afternoons to finish works in progress, but I have a feeling you won't want that."

"Quitting!" he practically shouted. "Is this some kind of joke? No, wait. Does this have to do with Jarred? He hasn't taken a turn for the worse, has he?"

"Jarred is recovering remarkably fast."

"Oh." Trevor swept a hand over his balding pate, then readjusted his tie, a move made out of habit more than necessity. "What do you mean,

144

quitting? You can't quit."

"I am, Trevor." Kelsey thought about what she wanted to say for the space of ten heartbeats, then took the plunge. "I'm going to work for Bryant Industries."

"*What?*"

"This job has meant so much to me, and I want you to know that, without it, I don't know if I could have survived these last few years. You've been good to me. I'm sorry that things turned out this —"

"You're joking! Kelsey. You're joking."

"No."

"*Why?*"

"Jarred asked me to."

Trevor looked as if he wanted to grab her by the shoulders and shake her. Instead he paced his office in jerky strides. The color departed his normally ruddy face, and he looked for all the world as if he might break down emotionally.

She should have known better. Less than three minutes later, he stopped short, glared at her, and said succinctly, "You were right. I don't want you to stay on."

Stung even though she'd expected his response, Kelsey nodded in curt understanding. She turned on her heel and left before tears, forming precariously in the corners of her eyes, dampened her lashes. Blinking madly, she entered the elevator, glad to find herself its only occupant.

And that was when anger replaced her sense

of hurt. As the elevator doors closed, she stuck her arm out to stop them. She backtracked to Trevor's office, sweeping in a breath of air the better to blast him with for being such a controlling, meddling, and insensitive jerk!

Arm stiff to punch open his partially opened door, she stopped short upon hearing his voice filter through, its message lifting the hairs on her now frozen outstretched arm.

". . . so you'd better fix things," he was muttering sharply into the telephone. "She's just left. And she's working over there with you now, you know. *He* put her there." He paused while the person on the other end of the line responded. Then he said, "I don't really care! But I've got a lot at stake and so do you! This isn't magic, you know. Phase Two didn't happen because I was *lucky!* It doesn't take brain surgery to figure this out. I need to know what's going on at Bryant, or we don't get the edge on those properties!" After another pause, Trevor sighed dramatically. "All I know is you've lost your scapegoat. So what the hell do you plan to do about it?"

At that point, Kelsey tiptoed backward, away from the door. Rather than wait for the elevator a second time, she hurried toward the stairs, half running down to the first floor and bursting through the lobby into the gray, cloud-scattered afternoon.

She hadn't returned to Bryant Industries. She'd headed straight for the condo, tried to out wait a deluge of rain, given up, grabbed Felix, and bolted. But now, with the miles clocking beneath her wheels on the way to Jarred's house — *her* house — she felt drained and exhausted. What had Trevor meant? What was he doing? It was dreadful to think that while she'd been grateful for her job, and guilt stricken over quitting it, he'd been using her as a scapegoat for his spying!

And who was on the other end of the phone line?

Jarred was right. There was a spy at Bryant Industries. Someone who, along with Trevor, had quietly sown the seeds of distrust whenever Kelsey's name had come into the conversation.

By the time she pulled in the driveway, her spirits were so low she damn near turned the Explorer around and headed back to her condo. Instead, she hit the button for the garage door, pulled into the same spot she'd occupied as Jarred's wife, then hauled Felix's carrier out and toted him inside to the kitchen.

Mr. Dog wasn't in immediate range. *Upstairs in Jarred's suite, no doubt,* Kelsey decided as she sat Felix, still safely in his carrier, on the floor beside the island. Though she'd just been here, her restless eye examined the kitchen as if seeing it for the first time. Stainless steel appliances gleamed lustrously beneath tastefully dimmed can lights. The counters were black granite and the floor was a rich, natural cherry, which added warmth to an otherwise stark room. Kelsey fingered the mesh bowl that sat square in the center of the island. It was filled with red Delicious apples grown in the state of Washington. She hadn't noticed any of this before. She'd been too immersed in the moment, the move, Mr. Dog, or her own perilous emotions.

Those same emotions weren't doing too well today either. Struggling to forget them, she gazed hard at the cold silver surfaces of the oven range top and refrigerator. Without warning a memory surfaced: the time toward the end of her cohabitation with Jarred when she'd decided maybe she could cook her way into the role of happy wife.

What a joke. She'd attempted several home-cooked meals, a different state of affairs since Jarred had always had Mary Hennessy take care of those duties. Mary had been with the Bryant family for most of Jarred's life, and though Kelsey felt a full-time cook and housekeeper was rather excessive, it hadn't been her place to question Jarred's domestic arrangements since Kelsey had been the later addition to the household, not Mary.

So Mary had stayed on and become a grudging friend. Grudging because the older woman had suffered serious doubts about Jarred's young bride. She was loyal to the Bryants, and Kelsey learned she would have to earn the woman's trust and respect and vice versa. That miracle was accomplished toward the end of Kelsey's tenure, a bittersweet irony.

But during those weeks, when Kelsey had experimented with a few entrees to entice her ever more distant husband, Mary hadn't been too enthusiastic. The kitchen was, after all, her domain, and she was loath to let anyone take control of it.

So, under the hawk eyes of Jarred's cook and maid, Kelsey had tried out several meals on her husband. To his credit Jarred had acted as if everything she'd concocted was wonderful even while he eyed her in that speculative way, as if working out her newest motivation. Mary, feeling no compunction about speaking her mind as Kelsey prepared her first meal, said in her rather imperative way, "You don't want to mess up my kitchen now."

"I'm just trying out a couple of recipes," Kelsey said. "As we both know, I'm no cook, Mary. I'll try to remember to put everything back where I find it."

"It's no problem, ma'am. I can always find it again," she said rather hurriedly as if hearing her own suspicious tone.

"Still, I'll be careful. I wouldn't want anyone disturbing my things."

With a smile to cover up her actual thoughts, Kelsey had managed to keep the older woman at bay. Though Mary regarded her with a deepening frown, she gave up the fight and let her young mistress do as she wished. Kelsey had then actually turned to a very plain cooking — a pot roast with tiny red potatoes, carrots, and mushrooms — because she knew Jarred's tastes.

Although he was a man used to the lap of luxury, he'd never been able to handle the folderol of the exotic meals foisted on him first by Nola and then by Mary, who'd learned from example. Though Mary had slowly changed her ways, she'd never quite given up the idea that Jarred was too important to simply cook for. He needed a chef and gourmet meals, and though Mary herself held no such claim to fame, she'd certainly over the years slipped some rather exotic food both Jarred and Kelsey's way.

So, when Kelsey managed a simple meal with mouth-watering results, Jarred had praised her attempts, at least until he'd fallen into his usual mode of needling her, which began almost the moment they sat down opposite each other at the dining room table.

"How very domestic of you," he said, twisting his fork between his thumb and forefinger as if he were reluctant to actually dig in. Indirect lighting touched the corners of the dining room ceiling and only the flicker of two gold candles actually illuminated Jarred's face.

"A moment ago you praised my efforts."

"It's great," he agreed. "I'm just wondering what it means."

"It doesn't mean anything. Can't I just feel like cooking you a meal?"

He eyed her in that ironic way that always made her feel so small and naive. Irked, Kelsey tucked into her own pot roast and was rewarded when the flavors from the wine and bay leaf and garlic created their own kind of heaven.

Spying her smile, Jarred tasted his own meal, chewing slowly, his gaze centering on her pleased face. "It's good."

"It's damn good," she declared.

His lips twitched. "Yes, it's damn good," he agreed, disconcerting Kelsey once again. She almost preferred it when he was mean to her or put her on the hot seat. At least at those times she understood him — or part of him anyway.

"I think I'll cook tomorrow night, too."

He lifted his glass of cabernet and eyed her thoughtfully. Red light refracted through the crystal goblet. "No one told me hell had frozen over."

"Just shows you that you should pay more attention to the news."

He grinned, bestowing on her a dazzling smile that was all too rare and way too attractive. Kelsey finished the rest of her meal in silence though Jarred attempted to provoke her into further conversation. In any event, she followed through on her cooking the next evening, but her second attempt was little more than a vat of soup that she left to simmer on the stove. At the last moment she scratched out a note that said she'd be out, and she made certain she was gone for all the hours that could be construed as dinnertime.

Returning late after wandering a nearby mall and then standing on a pier above Lake Washington, Kelsey was glad the lights were dimmed and no one was about. Jarred had left her a note on the kitchen counter. Picking it up, she was disconcerted by the words, "It was good," written in his distinctive scrawl. For reasons too odd to contemplate she'd wanted to sit down in the middle of the floor and bawl her eyes out, though she chose instead to head up to the guest room and bury herself between the sheets.

She'd given up then, both cooking and battling Mary Hennessy. And though Mary came to sympathize with Kelsey, she couldn't quite embrace the cook or find a way to rekindle the flames of her dying marriage. What was the point? Shortly thereafter she'd moved into her condominium, and now, she was moving back in with Jarred.

The telephone suddenly shrilled into the silent room. Figuring it was meant for Jarred, she waited for the answering machine to pick up, then was pleasantly surprised to hear Marlena Rowden's voice.

"Hi, Kelsey. It's Marlena. Sorry I missed you, honey. I just wanted to say thank you for the —"

"Marlena?" Kelsey snagged the receiver.

"Oh, you're already there. I wasn't sure if you'd left the comdominium yet, but it just rang and rang when I called there earlier."

Kelsey had left the message with Robert Rowden that she was moving back in with Jarred. Robert had stoically taken the news. He loved Kelsey like a daughter and wouldn't offer his opinion unless it was asked for. What the Rowdens truly thought of Kelsey's sudden desire to move in with Jarred was a mystery — one she didn't even want to try to solve.

"I want to thank you for your generous gift. Ted's pretty much moved in with us now, and you know we couldn't make it without your help."

"You are so welcome, Marlena," Kelsey responded warmly. "I'm just glad Ted's working out."

Ted was a caregiver who'd stepped in when Marlena couldn't handle the daily chores of taking care of her husband by herself. Ted kept Robert from facing a nursing home, and Marlena from trying to do more than she was capable of. Kelsey had helped fund both Robert's care and Chance's treatment as the Rowdens simply couldn't afford all the expenses.

"How's Jarred doing?" Marlena asked.

"Better. He'll be home soon."

"He called us, you know," she said softly.

Kelsey's clutched the receiver hard. "He did?"

"To talk to us about Chance."

"He . . . he didn't mention it," Kelsey answered softly.

"He doesn't remember the accident, but he feels terribly guilty, I think," Marlena said, her own voice deepening with emotion. "I broke down on the phone, honey, and I think I made it worse. Could you tell him that we know it's not his fault? I mean, whatever reason they were together, the accident was an accident and that's all there is to say."

Or a criminal act, Kelsey thought, recalling Detective Newcastle's words. Apparently the detective was still keeping Chance's parents in the dark, and that was just fine with her.

"I'll tell him," she responded softly.

"We do miss him a lot," she added sadly, and Kelsey knew she'd jumped to thoughts of Chance.

"So do I."

"I'd better go now." Her voice shook a bit, ripping at Kelsey's heartstrings.

"Let me know if you need anything else," Kelsey said before she hung up the phone.

A moment later Mr. Dog rounded the corner, smelled Felix, and ran pell-mell to the cat carrier, barking his fool head off. Felix screeched and spit and generally had a fit, and Kelsey spent the next half hour soothing both animals' jangled nerves. By the time Dr. Alastair called and informed her that, barring any unforeseen circumstances, Jarred would be released in the next several days, Kelsey was halfway through her store of boxes and well on her way to moving back home.

Chapter Seven

December

"You know we have a virtual reality setup at the hospital that helps distract patients from the pain of physical therapy," Joanna Wirth said as she watched Jarred rotate his left arm.

Sweating and aching, Jarred was in no mood to chat with his physical therapist. He grunted instead and kept rotating the arm and bending his elbow. It was out of its cast and weak and puny looking. Frightening how quickly muscles atrophied.

He didn't even want to think about his right leg.

"We use it mostly for our burn patients. Their pain is excruciating. They put on the headset and chase a virtual spider all around. Keeps their mind off the pain." She smiled. "Really quite effective."

They were in Jarred's master suite, which was currently filled with exercise equipment that he had mostly yet to use. Joanna came in daily to check on his progress. It was a routine that left Jarred exhausted, cranky, and impatient because he wanted complete recovery and he wanted it now. He felt as useless as a kitten and his mood reflected his current dissatisfaction, and for that reason, he kept his mouth firmly shut.

"You can try it when you're next at the hospital. See what you think."

Jarred just looked at her. Joanna was infuriatingly cheerful. Sometimes he wanted to blast her with a meteor of white-hot fury. Only years of Nola's behavior training in manners kept him from roaring out his frustrations at her now.

Truth be told, it wasn't just the physical therapy and snail-slow mending of every broken bone and torn muscle. Sure, that was a huge part of it, but there was also Kelsey.

Kelsey.

Gritting his teeth, Jarred felt frustration boil like a live volcano inside him. She lived right down the hall but he saw even less of her than when she lived at the condo. Okay, that wasn't completely true. But she was gone at the crack of dawn and by the time she returned at night he was practically in a coma of exhaustion. Like an automaton, she would report on what had happened at work that day, but then she would leave him alone to get his rest. It felt as if they never, ever saw each other.

"Let's see you walk," Joanna suggested.

156

All he wanted to do was throw himself on the bed and groan. Every muscle seemed to be quivering from overuse. With a supreme effort of will, he rose from the chair, ignored the walker, and reached for the crutches propped against the opposite wall. Joanna opened her mouth to protest, but after one scalding glance from Jarred, she reluctantly kept her thoughts to herself. Hurting at every step, he managed a piss-poor job of thumping from one side of the room to the other. He winced every time his right leg bore even a modicum of his weight. Raw nerves screamed. He sweated and panted. Still, it was better than yesterday. And yesterday had been a little better than the day before.

"Very good," Joanna decreed with a slow clap of approval. "*Very* good."

Jarred sank back into the chair as she gathered together her things. He tried not to reveal his complete physical exhaustion. He waited for her to leave, but she was damn fussy about collecting all her belongings, and by the time she was at the door and throwing out more words of encouragement and advice for further rehabilitation, Jarred felt himself melting toward inexorable, physically driven sleep.

"You okay?" Joanna asked, hovering by the outer door to his suite.

"Never better."

"Rest. You need it."

The door closed behind her. Jarred stared at it. He lay back on the bed and stared at the ceiling. Turning on his side, he stared at the wall.

I want my wife, he thought, feeling welcome, if unrequited, stirrings of lust. Thank God that apparatus seemed to be in functioning order. Now if he only had a chance to use it. For the time being, he couldn't even get his wife to kiss him, and that knowledge had worn his patience too thin to measure without micron precision.

She was avoiding him on purpose. There was no other explanation. A quick recitation of the events of the day and she was gone. *Poof.* And he just didn't have the strength to go after her.

During those initial days of his recovery she'd seemed a willing partner, but now she'd retreated from him in a way that baffled, annoyed, and exasperated him. Add to that, she'd befriended Mary Hennessy, who seemed to have switched allegiance entirely, being more accommodating to Kelsey than she'd ever been to Jarred. He was *persona non grata* while Kelsey appeared to be the flavor of the month. Not that that bothered him, particularly. He was glad they'd found a level of respect and cooperation and maybe even friendship. Anything that kept Kelsey close was all right by Jarred.

Still, he couldn't help feel like the interloper at his own party. Mary, apart from cleaning his rooms and complaining a bit that his prescribed diet was playing havoc with her culinary skills, paid him scant attention. And if he should ever ask about Kelsey, heaven help him! The woman would scowl and glare as if he'd asked about her own personal sex life. His frustration had a tendency to surface at those times, and more than once he'd barked and growled at Mary like a chained pit bull. Her response was to avoid him even more, and the trickle-down effect was that Kelsey responded in the exact same way.

"Damn it all," he muttered aloud, to which Mr. Dog, who'd ignored both him and Joanna during the rehab session, suddenly thumped his tail against the plaid pillow of his wicker dog bed.

Jarred's eyelids, weighted down, closed and he fell asleep as quick as a thought. When his eyes snapped open again, dusk had fallen, infusing the room with dim gray light. Stretching, he caught his breath as pain shot up his leg. He groaned and stayed perfectly still until the moment passed. Pulling himself carefully to his feet, he reached for the nearest crutch and hobbled slowly toward the windows, gazing at the darkening skies and windfeathered water of Lake Washington. There was no drizzling rain tonight, but a cold Alaskan front had dropped the temperature so that this December was hovering at the record-breaking mark for an all-time low.

Itchy and frustrated beyond bearing, Jarred sought some inner peace. He was hot. It might be frigid outside, but the temperature inside the house felt as if it had been cranked to the max. In a fit of pique he ripped off his shirt and leaned bare chested against the rubber padded top of the crutch. A scar curved over his left shoulder like a crescent moon. Surgery had pulled ligaments back together and redirected bones that had been snapped, but nothing was quite working the way he wanted it to . . . yet.

But then there were things to be thankful for, too. His right arm and hand, miraculously, had basically been untouched. All organs, though jarred and generally maltreated by the crash, seemed to be working perfectly, and his head injuries had turned out to be less serious than anyone would have believed. He was unbandaged, and though his scalp had been zipper stitched in a few places, the hair had filled in so he looked almost normal.

Except for his right leg, everything was better than he could have hoped for. Glancing down, he examined his still mending limb. His exercise shorts stopped about three inches above the knee and stitching radiated downward and around in an ugly reddish embrace. This was where the real damage had occurred and the bones were healing with painful slowness. The swelling hadn't quite gone away either, and the leg felt fat and unwieldy.

You are so goddamn lucky, he reminded himself with a hard swallow.

His ankle was a source of concern. He wasn't going to be playing any tennis in the near future. He wasn't even going to be walking around without support. The word *pulverized* seemed stuck in his head, though he knew no one had used it to describe his injuries, at least in his presence.

Chance Rowden wasn't so lucky.

Closing his eyes, Jarred struggled to remember anything — anything at all — about the time directly preceding the plane crash. He'd tried so many times. Hour upon hour of reflection without a glimmer of remembrance. But all he really had to show for those intense spates of reflection were dim memories of voices wishing he wouldn't recover, the sense of drowning underwater, and a recollection of drug paraphernalia scattered across a scarred and squalid countertop in a shack that seemed to have no bearing on anything at all.

Mentally flailing his wretched memory for its capriciousness, Jarred thumped his way toward the inner doorway that led to the sitting room. It didn't help that Detective Newcastle kept hoping he'd drag something from the blank depths of his recall, but to date, his memory was still a black enigma, impenetrable and unrelenting. Jarred's inability to help seemed to create its own set of problems since Newcastle tersely explained that nothing had developed further other than the absolute certainty that the accident had been no accident. The detective seemed to feel that Jarred had let him down. As if Jarred were purposely holding back that one tile that would arrange all the pieces into a readable mosaic.

Oh, sure.

As if that weren't enough to tax his body and brain, events were happening at work as well. His absence and lack of direction at the helm had created its own turmoil within the company. He'd heard from Will and Sarah and Gwen and even some members of lower management whom he honestly couldn't remember at all. Kelsey's transition had not, apparently, been a smooth one. No one liked her being privy to the inner workings of the company, and she'd been deliberately left out of meeting after meeting. They'd put her in charge of interior design of their latest project, bumping a woman who'd worked for the company for ten years. And though Will had bumped that woman into a higher position, she'd quit in a fit of pique. Jarred could scarcely blame her, but he was bugged that Kelsey allowed herself to be shuttled to whatever position they decided to put her in. He wanted her in the thick of it, and though he knew that she was meeting continual resistance, he didn't have to like or accept it!

Mr. Dog suddenly lifted his head, barked in delight, and scrambled for the door, nearly knocking Jarred over in the process. Muttering furiously, Jarred clung to the jamb of the archway between his bedroom and sitting room. For inexplicable reasons, Felix chose that moment to enter through the hallway door, which Joanna had left ajar. Since the cat nearly always avoided Jarred's suite, out of respect for Mr. Dog's territory, this sudden reversal of behavior caused a minor sensation. Mr. Dog zipped toward the door and Felix arched his furry yellow back and spit fire. The golden retriever, who'd grown bored with this measly intruder, snuffled Felix's side as he cruised by, sending the cat into paroxysms of yowling fury.

Jarred muttered, "Oh, relax," as Felix streaked past him to hide beneath the bed, alternately growling low in his throat and cranking up to a wail of utter indignation that sounded like a feline siren.

The soft closing of the kitchen door to the garage reached Jarred's ears. Beneath the racket of the dog and cat, he'd missed the hum of the garage door being electronically lifted. Kelsey was home. Mr. Dog's reaction had been in answer to her arrival.

Moving like the cripple he currently was, Jarred inched his way to the stairs and the long descent in front of him. He gazed downstairs, wondering if he dared attempt to corral his wife. Gritting his teeth and grabbing the rail, he half hopped, half slid down to the first landing.

"Hello, there," Kelsey greeted the golden retriever fondly as she entered the room. Mr. Dog politely waited inside the kitchen, tail frantically sweeping the wooden floor. Since his first overanxious greeting, the dog had learned a bit of restraint. He was excited to greet Kelsey, but not nearly so enthusiasticaly. Jarred's return had calmed him down considerably, but he was still nice enough to mark her arrival, waiting for her inside the door like a butler.

Felix, on the other hand, having adjusted poorly to the change, hid in Kelsey's closet for most hours of the day. Sometimes, Kelsey wished she could join him.

Not that Jarred had been a problem — far from it. He'd been confined to his rooms and that was just as well because she *hated* working at Bryant Industries and pretty much felt the same way about *all* of his employees! They treated her like a spy, a thief, and a poor relation, and they wanted nothing to do with her at all. The only one who'd shown a modicum of empathy and interest was Jarred's personal secretary, Gwen, and that was why Kelsey had gratefully agreed to meet her for a drink and dinner later tonight. Sure, she should have stayed in the city to make that meeting, but Kelsey felt anxious about Jarred these days. He was making great progress, according to his physical therapist, but it was a long road. She felt compelled to check up on him. Then, feeling as if she were overburdening him, she would slip away quickly after reporting on the doings at Bryant Industries.

And his personality had tanked during the process! He was, in a word, a grouch. Half the time, Kelsey had to smother a smile at his grumbling. She felt like a little mother hen, and she knew, if Jarred suspected her maternal leanings, he would have a fit. He'd been too supremely male for too long to appreciate the reversal of roles.

But that's not the only reason, is it, Kelsey? You're afraid Sarah will be with him. . . .

Grabbing an apple from the basket, she polished it on her blouse, not liking her own thoughts one iota. She'd caught Sarah lurking around the house a time or two — once with Will, once without. It had bugged her to no end, and though she knew Sarah's presence undoubtedly had to do with business, she could just imagine the blond amazon stroking Jarred's injured limbs along with his pride. The image was enough to make her crazy.

But it was partly her own fault. She'd absolutely refused to become a signer at Bryant, thinking Jarred really had lost his mind. So since Jarred hadn't abdicated that responsibility to anyone else, Will and Sarah trooped over to the house and went over documents with Jarred himself. Which was fine with Kelsey. She could be his eyes and ears, but she sure as hell didn't want to make any decisions when she *knew* she was only being given half the information. It wouldn't be beneath Sarah to set her up and watch her fall.

There was no Sarah here tonight, however, unless she'd arrived by taxi. She'd apparently gone home after work after all. Kelsey had been suspicious when Sarah left a bit early, and as soon as she dared, she'd torn out after her nemesis, driving like a maniac through the burgeoning traffic. But she'd been greeted by an innocent-faced dog and nobody else. Not even Mary, as evidenced by the note left on the kitchen island. So her race home had all been for naught.

"You're ridiculous," she muttered to herself, biting into the apple.

Footsteps on the stairs. Instantly she froze and glanced at the ceiling. Maybe Sarah was here. Upstairs. With Jarred.

Striding to the foyer, she looked up to see her husband clinging to the rail on the upper landing. "Jarred!" she cried, in alarm. "What are you doing? My God! Don't move. Don't . . . move. . . ."

His lips were white, his jaw set. She walked to the bottom of the stairs and looked up. "Jarred?" she asked carefully.

"I'm . . . coming . . . down. . . ."

The words were a pant. She instantly had visions of soft bones buckling under the strain. Tossing down the apple she hurried upward and wrapped her arms around his chest to support him without a second thought.

The touch of his bare skin shocked her. It shocked him, too, apparently, because he flinched, and for a moment she was afraid they were both going to tumble downward.

"Jarred," she whispered softly, her voice breathless with fear and dismay.

For an answer he turned his lips into her hair, by design or mistake she wasn't sure, and said simply, "Shh."

One hand was around his back; the other was placed on his chest. His heart beat heavily beneath her palm. His skin was hot and smooth apart from the V of crisp chest hair that invited her fingers to curl into it. She remained ultra-still, scarcely daring to breathe. She wanted to drag him back to safety. She wanted to wrap herself around him like a cloak. She wanted to keep on touching him.

"Can you take a step back?" she whispered.

"No."

"If you keep going downstairs, you'll have to stay there. I can't carry you upstairs."

"I hate this."

"Take a step back, Jarred. I'll help you."

It was all she could do. His arm was over her shoulders, his weight nearly crushing her as he shifted against her for support. They took one step backward, then another. Then they bumped across the upper gallery landing and managed the five stairs to the upper floor. She kept hold of him through the outer door of his sitting room, and he indicated with a grunt that he wanted to sit on the sofa in front of the windows.

"Maybe you should go back to the bedroom while you have the chance?" Kelsey suggested.

"I can get there," he bit out. Sweat beaded on his forehead as he aimed for the gray-and-white-striped couch flanked by two black leather chairs. Collapsing onto the couch and out of her arms, he sat white faced and silent for several moments.

"You okay?" she asked.

"Don't leave."

"I'm not. I'm just . . . looking for a place to sit," she lied, seating herself on a black leather ottoman.

He lay slumped to one side, favoring the bad leg and straining the opposite arm, his injured one. Though he fought it, his breath came in hard pants, which he tried to disguise. Kelsey clasped her hands between her knees and asked, "What exactly were you trying to do?"

"Go downstairs."

His terse response forced her to smile in spite of herself. He looked so vulnerable and attractive and annoyed at himself. The semicircular scar around his shoulder was smooth and already fading, noticeable for the moment, but soon it would blend in and be a memory. The scars on his leg told another story, but Kelsey wasn't put off by them at all. Jarred, however, appeared to be having second thoughts about this appearance, for he frowned down at the offending leg and his right hand dropped protectively to his knee.

"Could I get you something to —"

"No."

" — drink?"

"No." A pause. "Thank you."

"You sure you don't want help to your room? I don't want to leave you here and find out tomorrow that you couldn't get to bed."

"I'm fine."

"What was so all fired important about going downstairs?"

His jaw tightened. "I just . . . wanted to."

Silence pooled in the space between them. Kelsey felt useless and incredibly healthy and strong, and she knew he sensed the disparity between them and hated it. She tried to figure out how to tell him she was on her way out, wondering why it mattered so much, wishing she'd stayed in the city instead of driving all the way home just to — what? Confront Sarah Ackerman?

She couldn't know that Jarred was suffering all kinds of indignities and defeat when it came to his wife. Her unconscious beauty knocked him over. How could he not have noticed all those years before the accident? How could he have nursed such a hurt and anger that the very things that had attracted him to her in the first place were forgotten, lost, and overlooked? Now he felt their power as never before. Her amber eyes and delicately winged brows, her brown hair, shot with red, her soft lips and the tiny lines of amusement that deepened around her mouth when she smiled — every aspect of her face entranced him. And he felt ugly and awkward before her fresh beauty.

"Is something else wrong?" she suddenly asked, her gaze sweeping over him.

Her concern irked him. "You mean, beyond the obvious."

169

"Did you reinjure yourself?"

"No."

"You're sure."

"Yes! I'm not an invalid, Kelsey!"

"I know."

He closed his eyes, his mouth grim. "Do you?"

"I know very well what you are," she said, smoothing her palms down the thighs of her taupe slacks. Climbing to her feet, she said, "I have an appointment in town tonight."

His eyes flew open, narrowing on her face. "Appointment?"

"With Gwen, actually. I think she feels sorry for me," Kelsey admitted with that enticing quirk of her lips. "Everyone else at the company just wishes I would evaporate."

Jarred shook his head. "Don't let them do that to you."

"Let them," she repeated with a snort. "It's not like I have much of a choice. I know you want me to help ferret out what's going on, but so far I've been less than effective. They don't want me around. Maybe it's to cover up their nefarious doings, maybe not. I think they're worried you've lost your mind and I've taken advantage of you."

"I have lost my mind," he pointed out.

"Not that much," Kelsey disagreed. "Maybe if they knew how clear your thinking really is — I mean, it must scare them to death to depend on your signature, thinking you're an amnesiac."

"They know I can reason just fine. I just don't want to rehash some of the past with any of

170

them," he admitted, frowning. "It's easier to keep them in the dark, and besides, somebody tried to kill me."

His bald words silenced Kelsey for a moment. "You still can't remember anything about Chance?"

"No."

Kelsey had thanked Jarred for calling the Rowdens and offering his condolences, but he'd dismissed her gratitude. He'd needed to talk to them, and he'd told her he planned to visit them when he was mobile again. He'd admitted that he felt somehow bonded with them, and he hoped — as did Marlena and Robert — that somehow, someday his memory would flood back and offer an explanation, and therefore closure, for everyone.

"I remember our marriage," Jarred said into the silence.

Kelsey tried not to overreact. There were so many aspects of their marriage that she herself would like to forget. "Oh."

"I'm sorry for being such a bastard. It won't happen again." He paused, then asked, "Do you believe me?"

"Yes," she said. Shooting him a sideways look, she said, "I'm probably the biggest fool on earth, but yes, I believe you."

Relieved, Jarred grinned. "You probably are. Thank God."

Kelsey shot him a quick smile. "I've got to go."

"Wait!"

He struggled to sit up, silently cursing his inability to make even the slightest move without turning it into an amazing feat of physical strength. Kelsey rushed to his side and reached around Jarred's chest just as his bad leg jarred and he let out an inadvertent grunt of pain.

"Are you okay? Jarred? Tell me, are you all right?"

No. His face was buried into the cushions of the couch. He felt tangled and wrenched and angry, and somewhere, in the midst of all that feeling, he also felt new stirrings of desire. It was the seductive smell of her hair and heat of her body. Her breath and the tone of her voice. The curve of her cheek. The downy softness of skin, bare millimeters from his view. The pressure of soft breasts against his chest.

"Jarred?"

"I'm fine," he bit out gruffly.

"You're lying."

"I'm not lying." He forced the words through clenched teeth.

And then Kelsey made a fatal mistake. She pulled back just far enough to look directly into his eyes. He could feel desire swarming through his blood, affecting his senses, turning his manhood hard, increasing the tempo of his pulse. Whether she could read that in his expression, he wasn't quite sure, but then her brows drew together in a slight frown and those lovely amber eyes glanced toward his lips. It was enough for Jarred. His hand curved around her nape and he brought her mouth to the heat of his.

The shock of his hard lips pressed to hers froze Kelsey in place. She nearly gasped in surprise, but she managed to remain still. When she didn't resist, he deepened the kiss and Kelsey's nerves suddenly went into overdrive. Dimly she noticed the warmth and smoothness of his skin, the hardness of tensed muscles on his back, his "Jarred" smell, which she'd once giddly described to a friend as sexy. She wanted to dig her hands into those muscles and press herself against him, wanton and a little desperate. How long had it been? *How long?*

When his mouth released hers, it followed a path down her throat and Kelsey couldn't control the soft moan that squeezed past her lips. Her head lolled back, allowing more access, and Jarred took instant advantage of her abandonment. He pulled her closer, half beneath him, and kissed her ear and neck and downward, pulling at her blouse until the buttons gave and he was suddenly sucking on her breast through the sheer ecru lace of her bra.

The heat, the feel of his marauding tongue, the sound of mouth sucking against her skin sent Kelsey trembling wildly. It was wonderful. *Too wonderful!* She felt like she'd withered and died and he'd brought her to life. She pulled his head back to her mouth, her wondering gaze reading the slumberous desire that burned in his eyes like a blue flame.

And then she kissed him, helplessly, deeply,

desperately. He groaned. "Kelsey," he murmered in a shaken voice. "Kelsey."

It emboldened her. Her hands slid downward, to the band of his exercise trunks. She slipped a hand inside, down the curve of his buttocks, and it was Jarred's turn to tremble. His own hands swept down the curve of her hip, dragging her close until there was no doubt — if there ever had been — that Jarred's emotions were totally involved. The feel of him hard against her brought out a wantoness that Kelsey hadn't known she possessed. She wrapped a leg over his hip, eliciting another groan, but when Jarred twisted to slide her beneath him, a sharp shudder went through him that had nothing to do with desire. He swept in a breath and froze, and Kelsey whispered somewhere near his ear, "Are you all right?"

His harsh laugh was humorless. "For the thousandth time, yes!"

"The hell you are," she murmured, pulling back slightly to disentangle herself. Stupid, stupid, stupid. Her fault. She knew he was in recovery whether he did or not. She knew to tread carefully. "You're on the mend and I'm not helping."

"Believe me, you're helping."

"Helping undo all the good the surgeons managed. No," she stated firmly, laying a finger across his lips as he attempted to kiss her again. "We've got time for this later."

"No time like the present."

She grinned, loving him at that moment more than she ever had before. The thought amazed her, burned into her consciousness, silenced her tongue.

For Jarred, watching the play of emotions cross her mobile face, it was an excruciating moment of desire at war with common sense. She was right, of course; he was a fool to try to make love to her when every jar to his leg sent him into orbit. But he *wanted* her, and he did not believe that they had time for this later. The time was now. Right now.

His mouth touched hers gently. Kelsey's eyelids fluttered closed in spite of herself. His kisses were soft as whispers and she felt her bones melting at the sweet, sensual invasion.

"Don't," she whispered.

His hand swept over her hip, his fingers delving between her thighs, stroking her through her pants, creating a desire she couldn't ignore. She wriggled against him, unable to stop herself. For an answer, he unbuttoned her waistband and drew down the zipper.

She wanted to rip off her own clothes. His mouth opened over hers, his tongue sliding between her lips, delving deep inside as his fingers slid farther downward, beneath the scrap of her panties, to gently gain a different entry. The sensual onslaught was too much for Kelsey, who simply whimpered and dragged her hands through his hair, deepening the kiss, demanding more.

Sliding one leg over his, she felt the sharp jolt that ran through him, pulling him up short. His breath caught. "I'm sorry," she whispered achingly.

Jarred's whole body was tense. Realizing this couldn't go on, no matter how either of them felt about it, Kelsey gently drew away from him. This time he let her go. The ache in his leg had superceded the ache of lust and desire, and he could feel himself tightening up inside, shoring defenses against the tide of pain that would inevitably follow this twisting and pulling of muscle and bone.

With one last, lingering hold on her arms, he released her, allowing her to climb to her feet and try to put some semblance of order to the disarray of her hair and clothes. He watched as she ran fingers through her hair and smoothed her blouse and slacks, buttoning up the former, zipping the latter, and shooting him a sheepish look in the process.

"You're not ready for all that," she said with repressed humor.

"Yes, I am."

"I'm not going to be responsible for a setback. How would I explain it to Joanna? Hmm? 'We were just —' "

" 'Getting to know each other again,' " Jarred interrupted.

"More like fooling around on the couch like teenagers."

"That's okay, too."

They stared at each other. Kelsey could feel the increased tempo of her pulse, a light, fast beating that had everything to do with excitement and nothing to do with anxiety or regret.

"When you get back tonight . . ." He left the sentence unfinished.

Kelsey hesitated, then shook her head. She turned toward the hall.

"I'll be awake," he told her as her footsteps sounded along the upper gallery. Before she headed downstairs, he called, "And I want to talk when you get back. More than just the daily Bryant Industries report. In depth. Okay? Kelsey?"

"Okay," she called back, her footsteps hurrying away as if she couldn't wait to get away from him.

With that final exertion Jarred heaved a huge sigh. Now, how the hell was he going to get back to his bed when he felt as if he'd been run over by a freight train?

The Four Seasons Olympic Hotel was where Kelsey had first met Jarred. It was also the venue for their first real date, and its restaurant was where Jarred had slipped his grandmother's spectacular sapphire pendant necklace around Kelsey's neck and asked her to marry him. She'd avoided the hotel like the plague since the decay of her marriage, and now it seemed somehow fitting that she should be currently walking up the set of three marble steps that led from reception to the Georgian Room itself, intending to meet Gwen, who'd chosen the site for their meeting.

The last time she'd been here was her very least fond memory. The occasion: a Bryant Industries' Christmas party for People Who Mattered around Seattle and the entire Northwest. Kelsey arrived angry, convinced that Jarred had spent the evening before making love to his paramour Sarah Ackerman because Sarah had "innocently" asked Kelsey if she'd found her silk stockings, which had gone missing since her "business meeting" in Jarred's room the night before. Kelsey had known about the late-night meeting and had purposely stopped by Jarred's office that morning, hoping to get to the bottom of a lot of issues between them, but Sarah's intervention had stolen the wind from her sails. Instead of facing him, she'd headed into the women's room, splashed her face with cold water, then left Bryant Industries and returned to the house, where she'd brooded over the disintegration of her marriage and her paralyzed inability to do anything about it.

And in that miserable state, she'd rerun what she knew about Sarah's visit to the house the night before. She'd known Sarah was in Jarred's suite; she'd heard them together. And since Kelsey was living in the guest suite at the time — a move she'd made as a means to gather her own wits and soothe her trampled, beaten heart — the meeting had taken place without her having any reason to really complain about its venue.

When Sarah stayed on and on, Kelsey buried her head under her pillow to block out the sounds of their shared laughter and animated conversation. She told herself she didn't care. It didn't matter. Jarred could spend every moment with that Amazonian, soulless slut for all she cared. He was the one who would eventually pay the price.

But then, that morning, when Sarah slyly asked about her silk stockings, waving her hand and informing Kelsey that the only reason she cared was that they were *so* incredibly expensive, Kelsey's temper ignited. It hadn't mattered to Sarah whether Kelsey got them back to her in time for the party that evening; she'd just wanted to make a point, but she pretended that she needed them as a means to turn the knife. Would Kelsey mind looking for them?

She discovered the stockings beneath Jarred's bed. Pulling them out, Kelsey sat down hard on the mattress, holding the silken scraps in her hands. She knew it wasn't beyond Sarah to plant them there. The woman was capable of anything. And she also knew that confronting Jarred would only get her a terse "Nothing happened," even when it was clear *something* had to be going on or the stockings would have stayed on Sarah's long legs where they belonged.

It pleased her to no end that the sheer black stockings were covered with Mr. Dog's tawny fur.

She'd stuffed the offending garments in her handbag. Then she had stared at all the gowns in her closet in vain hopes of finding the perfect one for the party. Eventually, she settled on a plain black above-the-knee dress and an equally plain pair of black pumps. Combing her hair, she let it fall in restless auburn waves to her shoulders, her amber eyes staring back at her in the mirror, wide and mistrustful. When her bottom lip trembled, she bit down hard. She was not going to feel sorry for herself.

At the last minute she grabbed the sapphire pendant and clasped it around her neck. It glittered in the hollow of her throat, looking exceptionally pretty against her pale skin above the heart-shaped neckline of her dress.

She'd been too upset to realize how dramatic she looked. It was Jarred who complimented her, but she was in such a state by that time that she hadn't been able to listen. She hadn't cared anyway. Her marriage was over. She'd accepted the truth with the discovery of the stockings.

Walking across the lobby that night, Kelsey had found herself lost in memories. She'd closed her eyes, listening to the sounds of merriment from up above. The Bryant Industries Christmas party was on the mezzanine level in a private room. Kelsey mounted the stairs like a prisoner heading for the gallows. Entering through the opened paneled doors of the reception room, she was suddenly thrust into a room of around one hundred people, all dressed in semiformal cocktail attire, jewels, and perfume. A string quartet played softly, and muted laughter and the clink of glassware met her ears.

Though it was a trick of her imagination, she had the terrible impression that all conversation hushed as soon as she crossed the threshold. Gulping back her misgivings, Kelsey went in search of her husband.

It was Will who approached her first. Not exactly a knight in shining armor, he greeted her uncomfortably. "Hello there, Kelsey. We thought you weren't going to show."

"Am I late?"

"Well, a little. Jarred was asking if you were here yet."

"Oh, I'm here. You can tell him."

Will half laughed, not understanding her strange mood in the least. "Okay. Can I get you something to drink?"

"Champagne would be great."

"Sarah said you stopped by the office today."

"Yes, I did."

Will was nonplussed. Kelsey wasn't normally so taciturn in her answers. He clearly wondered what the heck was going on inside her head, but he couldn't seem to find the words to ask her.

"Did you see Jarred?"

"Nope. But I'd certainly like to see him now."

"Okay. He's around. I'm sure he'll spot you soon."

"That would be just great."

He led her toward a table draped with a white tablecloth and stacked with glass champagne flutes. A clear, cold December night lay outside the bank of windows above the street. Kelsey stepped close, gazing down to the street, where traffic sped by and crystal lights twinkled in trees like starlight. Calling over the bartender, Will stepped back and told her, "I'll get Jarred."

"Whenever he can break away," Kelsey said with a tight smile.

The bartender poured her a glass of champagne. She gulped her first drink, bringing tears to her own eyes, or was that the effect of Jarred's cheating?

To Kelsey's consternation, it was Sarah who noticed her next. Turning sharply toward Kelsey, she strode forward like a general on the march. Kelsey downed the rest of her glass and turned to the sympathetic bartender, who, with a look of understanding, refilled her glass automatically.

"Hello," Sarah said, her gaze centering on the pendant at Kelsey's throat. "Have you heard about your boss's decision to knock down those warehouses along the waterfront and build office buildings? The city gave him a thumb's down, of course. Thank God."

"Yes." Though Kelsey essentially agreed with Sarah, she didn't feel like badmouthing Trevor. "There are a lot of different styles of architecture," she pointed out.

She knew she was viewed as a turncoat amid

this group. Half the time she felt like one. But she couldn't bend even the tiniest bit around Sarah Ackerman and expect any kind of positive payback. The woman was a snake, through and through, and with a third glass of champagne in her hand, Kelsey debated telling her so.

But Sarah was going on about Trevor Taggart versus Bryant Industries, breathlessly peppering the conversation with Jarred's name. Kelsey wasn't good at being jealous, but brother, she could feel its green poison infecting her as she stood and listened to this woman who wanted to steal her husband away more than anything else in this world.

"Oh, I brought you your socks," she said, breaking into Sarah's diatribe.

"What?" Sarah blinked at Kelsey.

"I brought you your socks. Your stockings," she clarified. "They're in my purse. Do you want them now?"

"Ahhh . . ." Sarah actually managed to look embarrassed. Rubbing her nose, she glanced around for help, but the only person who noticed was Gwen. Gwen smiled. Then a line drew between her brows as she tried to read Sarah's expression. "No. I'll get them later," Sarah murmured, turning away.

"Good riddance," Kelsey said beneath her breath to no one in particular, and it was at that moment that Jarred pulled away from a group near the front of the room and headed toward her with ground-devouring strides that shattered her resolve with each closing step.

He was devastatingly handsome, she noticed in a distant corner of her mind. In a black tuxedo and crisp white shirt, he looked as if he were about to film a perfume commercial or climb atop a wedding cake or extend his arm and pull her onto the dance floor, Fred Astaire to her Ginger Rogers.

Not a chance.

"What took you so long to get here?" he demanded.

"I didn't realize I was late. I came to your office to find you today, but you weren't there."

His gaze also centered on the pendant and the annoyance in his eyes gave way to an unusual tenderness. Kelsey immediately glanced away, dragging air into lungs, which suddenly felt too small, tight, and constricted.

"Why were you looking for me?"

"I wanted to talk to you about . . . something," she said.

"Okay." He glanced up and shot a smile at one of the managers from another division, who was dragging his wife onto the dance floor against her objections. The wife's dress was the culprit: a straight sheath that left little room to move from hip to ankle. She managed to tiptoe around the floor while her husband gyrated in a manner that brought a wider smile to Jarred's lips.

When Kelsey didn't respond, Jarred returned his gaze to her trouble face. Without another word, he pulled her through the crowd, onto the mezzanine, and into a smaller room, empty save for several chairs stacked at the end of the room. "What?" he asked her straight out, his earlier humor completely vanished.

"I wanted to talk to you about Sarah," Kelsey said, lifting her chin. If this were to be the moment of their marriage's dissolution, so be it. She was tired of pussy-footing around. "I'm tired of this situation we've got."

"What situation?"

"Don't play dense, Jarred. She was in your room last night till way after midnight. And I'm tired of pretending I don't know what's going on. I'm tired of pretending period."

"I'm not interested in Sarah. She's an employee. We talk business."

"Yeah, yeah, yeah," Kelsey waved a dismissive hand.

To her shock Jarred grabbed her upper arm. "I'm tired of this, too,' he stated shortly. "I'm tired of my wife playing some game with me."

"What do you mean?" Kelsey glared at him.

"You moved into the other bedroom."

"Yes."

"Either move back or move out."

His ultimatum stunned her. It was so unexpected, yet so like him when she thought about it. And it hurt! Like a slap to her face. "I'd have to share you with Sarah."

"No, you wouldn't." His answer was hard as granite.

"Then tell me why her silk stockings were under your bed. Can you explain that one? She asked for them, and I found them."

"I don't know," he stated flatly. "She must have taken them off."

"And you *didn't notice?* Sorry, Jarred. My naivete doesn't extend that far!" Kelsey yanked her arm from his. The sapphire pendant swung at the base of her throat, catching Jarred's attention once more. He reached for it, then closed his fingers around it. Kelsey jerked backward, away from his touch. They locked glances and she could see how angry he was.

"I'm leaving you," she said in a scarcely audible voice.

"The hell you are," he grated right back.

It was her next involuntary step backward that broke the chain. The snap of the fragile links sounded loud like a gunshot, and when they both stared at the broken necklace, the symbolism was too great to ignore.

Kelsey left without another word and spent the night packing. Jarred never came home at all. She left the following morning, murmuring vague threats of divorce, and until the accident, nothing had changed.

"Kelsey?"

Gwen's voice brought her back to reality with a bang. Kelsey jumped in surprise. She was standing just outside the Georgian Room. Gwen hovered near her elbow, a fiftyish woman

186

whose once stylish appearance had changed for the worse with time and who now regarded Kelsey with a tense expression that bordered on pure anxiety.

"Oh, hi. I'm sorry. I was just thinking so hard I forgot where I was. One should never think that hard," she added with a smile. "It's bad for the brain."

"You had me wondering," Gwen revealed. "You looked like you were in a trance." She looked around herself as the maitre d' came forward to guide them to a table.

It gave Kelsey a moment to collect herself. The maitre d' pulled back Gwen's chair, then did the same for Kelsey. Seating herself, Kelsey accepted the gold-tasseled menu and struggled to put thoughts of Jarred aside. Gwen had asked her here for purpose and she wanted to hear what that purpose was.

As if divining her thoughts, Gwen suddenly lowered her menu. She fiddled with the silverware. A strand of dyed black hair dipped over her eye and she pushed it back with faintly trembling fingers. Kelsey noticed how strained her eyes looked, and suddenly she wasn't thinking about Jarred at all but about the woman across from her who looked as if she'd seen a ghost.

"What is it?" Kelsey asked.

"Oh, I don't know how to say this, so I guess I'll just jump in. I've — I've heard you on the phone to Jarred. I know you're worried something's going on at the company, and I agree."

"You do?"

"Someone wants to do Jarred harm."

Kelsey lowered her menu as well and stared at Gwen.

She lifted a hand to her head. "I've got such a headache starting. I'm sorry. It's Will, Kelsey. He's undermining the whole operation. I think it's jealousy."

"Will?" she repeated faintly. "Are you sure?"

"I'm really, really sorry. He's Jarred's brother — well, half brother," she amended, "but Jarred believes in him completely."

Kelsey's head swam from so much information. "How do you know?"

"You're not the only one I've overheard," she admitted, lowering her eyes. "I've caught him on the phone with Trevor Taggart. Maybe it's innocent. I don't know. I just thought you should know."

Kelsey didn't want to believe it. Not Will. Not to Jarred. "Well, if Will's the one giving Trevor information, then it's because of Sarah," Kelsey defended. "They're together all the time, talking over deals. I'm sure she's involved!"

Gwen pursed her lips and shook her head. "I know you don't like Sarah, but she wants the company to succeed. It's Will who wants it to fail. He'll never measure up to Jarred and he resents it. I'm telling you this in confidence. I have no proof, but I *know*. So what are you going to do?"

Kelsey shook her head.

"Don't tell Jarred. At least not yet. Not until he's better. This'll kill him for sure. Will's the only person he truly trusts." Gwen rubbed her temples with her fingers. "I just wanted you to know that I know you're not the spy who's been leaking information. You can count on me to help, Kelsey."

"Jarred wants to know what's going on," Kelsey murmured. "Did he mention to you that he believed there was a spy within the company?"

"No. Will and Sarah mentioned your name a few times. I put two and two together."

The waiter came to take their order and Kelsey realized she had absolutely no appetite. She couldn't think. Not Will. *No, no, no.*

"What are you going to do?" Gwen asked anxiously when Kelsey declined anything but a cup of coffee. "I've upset you. I'm sorry."

"No. Don't be. I've got to . . . think about this."

"Don't tell Jarred," Gwen appealed again. "Not if you want him to recover."

"I was thinking about talking to Will."

Gwen shivered. "I don't know. But promise me you won't tell Jarred yet. Oh, what do I know anyway. I'm just an old woman who meddles too much. I'm jumping at shadows."

"You're not old, Gwen."

"Promise me, Kelsey. Please."

Because she was so terribly upset, Kelsey said,

189

"I promise I won't tell Jarred anything yet. Not until there's something more concrete. I don't know how I'd ever tell Jarred anyway. He would never want to believe this about Will."

Chapter Eight

"So what's eating you?" Will asked, regarding his brother with a slight frown. "You've barely said two words all night. Oh, wait. It's not because of Kelsey, is it? Are you starting to doubt her sincerity, too?"

It was all Jarred could do to appear as if he possessed even a modicum of desire to talk to his younger brother. Almost on cue, as soon as Kelsey had pulled out of the driveway, Will had pulled in. He rang the bell and called out, but Jarred was helpless to do much more than gnash his teeth in frustration at his own immobility.

Growing concerned, Will had pushed the buttons for the garage-door code and let himself in. Upon hearing Jarred's grunt of greeting, he'd shot up the stairs and strode into the room, ready for battle. "My God, I thought you were being attacked or something!"

"I'm just fine," Jarred responded shortly.

Will's bristling health and strength were enough to lower Jarred's spirits still further, so he'd spent the last hour attempting to keep from revealing how outmatched he felt against his half brother's extreme hardiness. What a killer. He humbly realized how much he'd taken his health for granted. Faced with Will, he found it daunting to ever believe he'd be back in that kind of shape again.

"I'm actually glad Kelsey's not here," Will revealed, making himself comfortable in one of the sitting room chairs, oblivious to Jarred's darkening mood. "I know you trust her and want her at the company. Fine. We're all trying to help her out."

"Are you?"

Will inclined his head, slightly acknowledging the rebuke. "Until you're back at the company, we're walking on eggshells, and yes, we all want to make this work. It's what you want, so it's what we want. But . . ."

"But?" Jarred prodded when Will didn't seem to know how to proceed.

"There are some issues that need to be cleared up. That's all." He spread his hands.

"Such as," Jarred asked, shifting his weight. Carefully — oh, so carefully — he rose into a sitting position, conscious of the sweat pouring down his back at the effort it took to hide the jarring pain even this small movement created.

"I want to talk about the money she's been hiding."

"Hiding." Jarred snorted. "Hardly the word for it."

"Well, you uncovered it and you thought it was pretty damning before. Now, I realize you've had a change of heart, but, Jarred, just don't forget about it."

Will's logic was impossible to completely ignore even though everything Jarred believed cried out that it wasn't true. For the years of their marriage Kelsey had withdrawn sizable chunks of cash from her checking account with no explanation. Because they'd never divorced, and she'd never bothered to take his name off her accounts, Jarred had been able to keep accessing those accounts, checking the deposits and withdrawals. And those cash withdrawals had continued.

And now he felt ashamed for spying on her.

"Apparently she's been shifting some serious dollars around. You thought she was giving the money to Chance Rowden for drugs."

Jarred couldn't deny it. "It was her money," he pointed out.

"It's nice you feel that way. You didn't before."

"I didn't do a lot of things before," Jarred pointed out, losing patience.

Silence fell between them. Jarred recognized Will was right, but that recognition didn't endear him to his brother. He wanted to kill the messenger. "So what's the story with you and Danielle?" he asked, needing to shift the spotlight.

"What do you mean?"

"Oh, come on. You've been digging at me and my personal life ever since I woke up in the hospital. How come I haven't seen or heard about *your* wife?"

"I suppose because she's not likely to be my wife much longer." The quiet pain in Will's voice rang through like a chime.

"Really?"

"Really."

Jarred was sympathetic. "That bad?"

"Even worse." When Jarred waited for an answer, Will shrugged and got to his feet. "Things happen. Danielle wants different things than I do. It's been a problem for a while." To Jarred's continued silence, he added, "There's another man involved."

Jarred felt a jolt of memory. He certainly knew how that felt. "Ouch."

"Yeah, well, all I'm saying about Kelsey is maybe you should get to the bottom of this money thing. You've got her working for Bryant Industries now. You need to know what she's up to."

Jarred nodded, forced to at least acknowledge that Will had a point. Will tried to further his argument by bringing up past problems in Jarred's marriage, but a cold, quelling look from his brother kept Will from going to far. Eventually he gave Jarred a pat on the back and left.

Jarred sat in silence for what felt like an eternity. It was flat-out depressing to be faced with the fact that Kelsey might have a hidden agenda, yet it was worse to hide his head in the sand. Something was going to have to be done. Some confrontation would have to be faced. Probably tonight.

Weary to the bone, he grabbed the crutches and made his way to his bed. Inside his room, he hesitated, however, as his mind ran over all the events of the evening, lingering on those moments when he'd held Kelsey in his arms, his blood singing with desire. He might be tired, but he wasn't dead. Yet.

To hell with this invalid stuff. He wanted his wife, and he wanted her now.

Tired, worried, her head full of Gwen's accusations and her heart full of worry, Kelsey parked her Explorer next to Jarred's Porsche and let herself into the house. Tossing her keys on the counter, she headed upstairs, anxious to see her husband again. The hallway door to Jarred's suite was ajar. After pushing it open, Kelsey tiptoed into the unoccupied room. The lights were still on, creating warm pools of illumination, but a kind of dead silence reigned. Jarred had obviously gone to bed.

Her shoulders slumped and she sighed. She hadn't realized how much she'd looked forward to the "evening report" until now. Disappointed, she walked down the hallway to her own rooms, then pushed open the door to her sitting room. She'd apparently left the bamboo lamp atop her nightstand on, for a thin shaft of warm yellow light spilled from the slightly open bedroom door.

She sighed. Maybe it was just as well Jarred wasn't awake. She would hate to have to lie about what Gwen had said concerning Will. No, it was better for Jarred to learn later. Tonight wasn't the right time to make unfounded accusations.

After unbuttoning her blouse, Kelsey slipped it off her shoulders and pulled it from her slacks. Then she pushed open the door and crossed the threshold from the sitting room to her bedroom.

Dark head on her pillow. A man in her bed.

She screamed without thinking. Terror choked. Frozen. A millisecond later she realized it was Jarred propping himself up on his elbows. Jarred, whose expression changed from anticipation to sheepishness.

"My God! You scared me!" Kelsey's voice shook.

"I'm sorry."

"I thought you couldn't even make it back to your own bed!"

"I know. I'm sorry."

Kelsey narrowed her eyes at him. His voice was shaking with repressed amusement. "Not funny," she told him, crossing her arms over her chest.

"I'm not laughing."

"Oh, yeah?" She arched a brow.

"No." The shit-eating grin plastered on his face told a different story.

Kelsey fought a smile. "If I thought for a

minute that you were amused by this, your life wouldn't be worth living."

"It's not even remotely funny." His blue eyes danced with humor. His mouth curved. He fought the little chuckles of amusement that set his body shaking and lost the battle.

She laughed. "Okay, it's funny. But you scared the bejesus out of me!"

"I didn't mean to," he admitted. "I just couldn't stand being so helpless, and as soon as you left, I wanted to drag you back."

"You were exhausted," she reminded him, crossing the room.

His hand curved from the bed and circled her waist, pulling her close. "I got a second wind. After Will left, I decided to meet you on your own turf."

"Will was here?" She fought to appear normal.

"Just for a while. What did Gwen want to talk about?" he asked, trying to stifle a huge yawn.

"Nothing much." Kelsey wouldn't have been able to bring up the truth about Gwen's suspicions even if Gwen hadn't already sworn her to secrecy. There were just too many questions still, and she didn't feel like finger pointing. "She just wanted to make certain you're on the mend. I think she's worried about you."

"No need. I'm fine. So are you coming to bed?" He fought another yawn. "Better make it quick."

"Let me change."

"Just take off what you've got on and crawl in," Jarred suggested.

"I need to wash my face and do a few things first."

Kelsey escaped into the bathroom, her pulse beginning to race again in spite of herself. Was this what she really wanted? Yes! But should she? Everything was happening so fast, and so little had actually been resolved.

After scrubbing her face with more force than necessary, she patted her skin dry with a fluffy yellow towel and stared at her own reflection. "It's just sex," she whispered.

Liar.

Stripping down to her bra and panties, she ran her hands over her flat stomach. There was no way she could take off every stitch. It had been years since Jarred had touched her or seen her completely nude or shown any interest in her emotionally or physically. She felt like a schoolgirl now: inept and inexperienced and way too excited for the circumstances.

After a number of tense minutes, she softly opened the door, clicked off the switch, and let her eyes adjust to the room, which was dark because Jarred had turned off the nightstand light.

Mr. Dog barked softly. He'd entered through the open door to the hallway. Kelsey bent down to the dog and silently rubbed his silky ears; then she led him to the door and gently shoved him outside. After closing the door, she waited in tense expectation. Jarred's even breathing told a story. Her shoulders slumped. *Damn, damn, damn,* she thought without heat. She should have known.

As if sensing her indecision, Jarred half surfaced. "Kelsey?" he murmured.

"Right here."

"Climb in," he murmured. "Please . . ."

Without further ado she crossed the carpet and slipped under the covers. He was on his side but his hand reached back for her. She snuggled against the curve of his spine, loving the closeness.

Memories instantly assailed her. She recalled those times when she'd never wanted to get out of bed — how she'd begged him to sleep late with her, how they'd made love for hours.

His arm pressed her close to him. Kelsey slipped her own arm around his torso, her fingers curling in the fine hair on his chest. She closed her eyes. His hand slipped to the curve of her hip. Her eyes flew open, a warm heat rising inside her despite her own misgivings about making love to her husband again. Still, she couldn't stop herself from rubbing her lips against his back. As if the devil himself were guiding her fingers, she slid her hand downward and realized Jarred was wearing nothing at all. She should have known. Pajamas weren't his style. He was all masculine angles and taut skin, and she sighed with genuine regret that he was so done in.

He started to shake with laughter.

"You're awake!" she declared.

"Well, yes, I am." He sounded inordinately pleased with himself.

"You fooled me!"

"You were thinking about not getting into bed with me. I had to come up with something to change your mind."

"By pretending to be asleep?" Kelsey asked.

"It worked," he said simply.

With that, he carefully turned toward her. With his lips a hairbreadth from hers, his eyes open and gazing at her, and his nose nearly touching hers, Kelsey was torn between desire and nervous laughter. A soft breath escaped her. More a moan than a laugh.

But he wasn't going to have it all his way.

"So are you ready for the report, Jarred? As I recall, you wanted to know each and every little thing that's been happening at work."

For an answer, Jarred kissed the soft, shining hair at her temple, his lips warm against her skin. Kelsey swallowed and ignored the tender assault. "Let's see. . . . I've won Meghan over to my side, too. She's Sarah and Will's gofer. She's more than helpful. Sharing an office with Will makes it kind of tough to get anything really done. I keep trying to answer his phone when he's not there, which is most of the time since he's always in your office. On the other hand, when he is around, I get more information about what's going on. Sarah tends to be wherever he is, and when the two of them get talking, they seem to forget I'm listening. Or at least they act that way. Meanwhile, there's talk of clearing out one of the storage rooms for me. That would put me closer to your office, however, so I get the feeling Will and Sarah are reluctant to do that. Am I boring you?"

Her innocent question broke him into deep chuckles. "Yes!" he said.

"Good." Kelsey grinned. "Where was I?"

Jarred groaned and crushed her mouth beneath his. The curve of his lips slowly diminished as amusement turned to something else. For Kelsey, it was a sweet realization that she had such an effect on him. She'd forgotten how heady it was to make him stop and notice her. She'd been able to capture his attention once, but it seemed so long ago now.

With an effort, Kelsey fought free of his marauding mouth, only to have him slide those warm lips down the arch of her throat. "So things are progressing at work," she went on. "Gwen's worried about you. I told her you were recovering and she was glad to hear it. At least I have one friend there. Well, two if you count Meghan."

"You have more than that," he disagreed, his husky voice sending shivers down her spine.

"I don't know about that. Gwen's really the only one who's even tried to "

"Shh." The finger he placed over her lips said he was through listening to shoptalk. Kelsey's eyes met his. Even in the semidarkness she could read the stirring sensuality in his gaze. "I've been thinking of this a long, long time," he said softly, his mouth moving to capture her lips and stay her words. With a soft sigh, Kelsey's lids fluttered closed, and she gave in to her own desire. He'd read her so easily and scaled her defenses. She ought to be furious and put up some kind of fight, but there was simply no fight left within her.

"You win . . . this time," she whispered into his mouth.

His lips curved up in silent answer.

Then his mouth gently rubbed against hers, stroking the contours of her lips until she shivered. Her whole body was tense with suppressed emotion. It felt like the first time. So long ago, so long . . . She'd been living in limbo so long that she hardly knew what to do first.

But Jarred had no such qualms.

His right hand slid over her shoulder to her breast, to the front clasp of her bra. A quick twist and her breast spilled into his palm. Instantly he bent down and suckled the nipple. Kelsey simply melted. When he lifted his head, it was to allow room to remove her bra, and as soon as that was accomplished, his finger hooked into her panties and slid them down her legs.

Naked next to her husband, she marveled at how odd, and how wonderful, it felt. Nagging thoughts tried to invade her consciousness, reminders of the unhappy past and a problematic future. But for tonight she mentally slammed the door shut on the Pandora's box of memory. Tonight was for her.

Her hand slid over his smooth, taut skin and his warm muscles. She smiled.

"What?" he whispered, watching her.

"Physical therapy's been good to you."

His mouth opened over hers, his body sliding smoothly atop her, his hands curving around her buttocks. The combination of heat, musky scent, hard touch, and urgent desire made Kelsey's head swim. She dug her fingers into his lower back, unconsciously begging, her body arching against him.

Jarred's tongue invaded her mouth, stroking, testing, commanding. Kelsey answered with quickened touches, fingertips dancing over his skin in a way that had once elicited groans of pleasure from him, long forgotten now, but suddenly remembered.

"Kelsey," he muttered on an escaped breath, and warmth flushed through her as he, too, recalled how good it had once been. A slight jerk of muscle and he tensed. Pain. They'd moved too quickly.

"Are you sure you —" she began, but he cut her off with another hard kiss.

And then his fingers began a lower exploration. Kelsey swept in a breath, then writhed beneath him as the sensual exploration of his fingers was matched by a silken stroking of his tongue within her mouth. She pulled at him, forgetting his injuries, forgetting everything, in the sudden, hot, compelling need for fulfillment.

And Jarred complied, pushing against her, his heart pounding deep in his chest hard enough for her to feel against her breasts, his manhood sliding along her ready feminine parts. She pulled him tight, silently begging for possession. Everything was wet and slick, and she thought she'd scream if something didn't happen soon.

But Jarred was nothing if not thorough. That she could remember! He held her hips, poised, drawing out the moment, until Kelsey was so desperate with wanting that when he drove slowly into her she dug her fingers into his buttocks and demanded just as much. Each powerful thrust was a memory timed to drive her crazy. She pressed her mouth into the neat of his neck and arched her back, consumed with mounting waves of desire. Closer and closer to the edge . . . until the scream she felt inside her passed her lips in a moan of pleasure. Moments later she pulsed with fiery climax, and Jarred drove one more time, deeper and stronger, groaning with the climax of his own sweet pleasure as he fell forward against her, his breathing hot and fast against her shoulder.

"Kelsey," he whispered achingly.

"Yes," she sighed.

Moments later, he turned gently on his side, pulling her with him. Feeling oddly shy, she ran her fingers along the contours of his cheek, dropping a soft kiss on his lips. "Worth the wait?" she teased, and his answer was a groan of submission.

"How long has it been?" he asked after a studied moment.

"For me, years. Since you," she admitted, almost embarrassed to admit the truth.

"There's been no one but you," he responded, tracing one finger down the sculpted curve of her cheekbone.

Kelsey froze a little inside. Was this the truth? No. It couldn't be. What about Sarah? It had been years since they'd been together, and she knew from experience what a sensual creature her husband was. He could never wait that long for a woman. He hadn't during their marriage by all accounts, why would he after she left?

Feeling her withdrawal, Jarred stared at her hard. "I'm not lying," he said seriously. "Whatever you thought of me in the past, I never cheated on you. Not with anyone."

"Faulty memory," she whispered.

"No."

She shook her head ever so slightly, negating the impossible. Swallowing, she addressed the root of the problem. "Sarah Ackerman."

"Kelsey, I don't find her attractive in the least. I *never* have. I know it. But I confess that I used her aggressiveness for my own purposes. Whenever you hurt me, I let you think the worst." He drew a breath and exhaled slowly. "I'm not proud of it, but I wanted to hurt you back."

"Whenever I hurt you?" she questioned. "When did I hurt you?"

"With Chance Rowden."

"But . . . we were just friends."

"Friendly friends," he corrected.

"No." Kelsey was adamant. "High school sweethearts. That's it. We never even had a serious relationship."

Jarred stared at her through the darkness, fascinated but disbelieving. He'd heard differently. From the horse's mouth, too, and though he knew it was the time to throw his knowledge of the truth in his wife's face, he was too enamored with her right now to spoil the beauty of the moment. And anyway he didn't care anymore. The past was over and wiped clean from the accident. Chance was dead. Nothing more needed to be said.

"Jarred?" Kelsey gazed at him, a bit alarmed when his eyes closed as if he were in pain.

"Shh . . ." He kissed her gently, tenderly. "I love you. Good night."

She was still reeling from that admission when she heard his even breathing and realized this time he was definitely asleep. Either that or making a damn good representation of it.

Moments later, his arms released her and he turned over. Instinctively she nestled her body up against his. Her mind churned. Had he told her the truth about Sarah — and any other woman? Couldn't be, yet it was certainly a lovely, seductive thought, and she suddenly so wanted it to be true that it almost hurt.

But on the heels of that thought came another — one she kept locked in a distant part of her brain: the time of her short-lived pregnancy and Jarred's harsh reaction. Blinking in the dark, Kelsey gingerly explored the jabbing memory. She'd kept herself from thinking about it for so long that she'd almost believed it hadn't happened. In the wake of other problems with Jarred, it was just the worst and deepest cut, and she'd refused to dwell on it. But thinking about it earlier in her memories of Nola had twisted the lock, and with all these new feelings and discoveries pouring over her, she couldn't ignore the worst of his faults and expect any kind of long-term solution for them.

But whether Nola believed it or not, there had been a baby. A conception of their love. And Jarred's cold reaction had surfaced even before Nola suggested that Kelsey had made the whole thing up. Jarred's stony reaction had been to the *idea* that she was pregnant! He'd never said he didn't want children, but upon learning his new bride was carrying a child, he'd suddenly turned into a distant, chilly stranger. That had been the start of the ruin of their marriage. Oh, he'd expressed some sorrow when her heart was broken over the "miscarriage," but she'd known by then that it was merely lip service.

And she'd never forgiven him. Never. No other slights he'd dished out had ever bothered her so much. Not even his apparent attraction to Sarah. But his attitude during that time had crumbled Kelsey's love for him until everything between them became a simmering, angry battle.

Until now.

Pressing her cheek against the warm skin of his back, she squeezed her eyes closed. Her heart hurt. She'd wanted that baby so much, and because of Jarred's lackluster response, she'd fooled herself into believing she didn't want *him*. But she did want him. So much now that she realized how thoroughly she'd subverted her feelings all these years.

And if you were wrong about the Sarah issue, could you be wrong about this one, too? a hopeful little voice asked inside her head.

With scary, wonderful, dangerous new thoughts circling her head, Kelsey didn't fall asleep for a long time, but finally near morning she slipped into deep, dreamless slumber, where worries couldn't find her.

Jarred woke up with a start. "Kelsey?" he said into the dark December morning.

"Hmm?"

Her body was curled around his, her voice sleepy. He relaxed, inordinately pleased that she was still in bed with him. "Just checking that it was you," he admitted, sounding pleased.

"Who did you think it was?"

"I was afraid Mr. Dog or that feline of yours had found their way in here." He ran a finger down her bare arm. "Want to make love?"

"Shh. I'm tired. I'm just sleeping with you, okay? I'm not *sleeping* with you again."

"You won't hurt me," he said dryly.

"I've got to go to work."

"Call in sick. I know the boss."

She chuckled and shook her head. He ran his fingers through those reddish brown waves, then dragged them to his mouth and nose. "You're wearing Kelsey," he said, drowning in the scent of it.

"That's not its name."

"What's it called?"

"Something like Fragrance Number Eighteen."

He made a sound of utter annoyance and Kelsey started to laugh. What a wonderful way to wake up in the morning! "I do have to go."

"Not yet." Jarred kissed her and held her until she was a willing slave to passion again.

And besides, he *did* know the boss.

"I've got to leave," she protested half an hour later, refusing to let him hold her captive one moment longer. "Believe it or not, I've got a meeting this afternoon with the woman who painted the cabinets in the waterfront units. The one who painted the ivy design along the crown. Apparently she thinks her art has been compromised by the financial restrictions Bryant Industries placed on her."

Jarred closed his eyes and shuddered. "Why

are we still using that woman? I made it clear I thought she was a kook after she stormed into my office sobbing and wailing. Sarah was supposed to tell Elisabeth to get rid of her."

Elisabeth was Kelsey's predecessor — the woman who'd been upset when Will had tried to make room for Kelsey at the company. "Elisabeth quit when I came on board," she reminded him.

"You don't have to meet that woman today. She was Elisabeth's problem, not yours."

"I can do it. I've dealt with temperamental egos before." She smiled at him. "Case in point."

He gave her an innocent look, which cracked her up. "Listen, I'll take care of it," she assured him, then slipped away from his arms and dashed into the bathroom before he could raise another argument. A quick shower, brushing of her hair, and light dusting of makeup and she was ready for anything.

When she stepped back into the bedroom, the bed was empty. "Jarred?" she asked, but there was no answer. The crutches were not in their spot next to the bed, so he'd left without saying good-bye.

I love you. . . .

Had he really said those three little words? She was fairly certain she knew what she'd heard. After slipping on a gray skirt and sweater, a black wool jacket and black pumps, she headed down the hallway in search of him.

She found him back in his bedroom, clad in

210

workout gear and stretching his muscles. Mr. Dog sat to one side, wagging his tail.

"If you're going to keep leaving me, I'm going to have to get myself fit enough to chase you," he said.

"You've got a long way to go. I'm pretty fast."

He examined his right leg and ankle. "Yeah," he agreed soberly, and Kelsey stepped forward, wrapped her arms around him and kissed him hard on the mouth. "And what was that for?"

She arched one brow. "For last night."

It was as if they'd never had a break. Years had passed, yet teasing her husband was a pleasurable memory that had never fully left her, even in her worst moments of telling herself she hated him.

The phone rang before he could respond. "Do I have to get that?" he asked, his hands in her hair, his lips near her ear.

"Yes."

"Forget it." With that, he pulled her down on the bed against Kelsey's protests. Kelsey listened hard, but she couldn't hear the kitchen answering machine from inside his bedroom.

"You're making this difficult for me," she mock scolded him.

"That's what I'm here for."

Moments later the phone began a second insistent ringing. Jarred sighed and Kelsey said, "Someone wants you pretty badly." That reminded her of her prank call, and as Jarred untangled himself from her, she said, "Some guy left me a strange message on my phone at the condo."

"Some guy?" He carefully climbed to his feet and limped toward the phone. By the time he picked up the receiver, the caller had hung up. "They'll call back if they really want me," he said with an unconcerned shrug of his shoulders.

Kelsey told him about the prank call from the public phone and the scads of other calls on Caller ID that she couldn't account for. "They might have been from him, but he hung up on me before he said anything."

"He said he needed help?" Jarred frowned.

"Maybe he's got my number mixed up with someone else."

"This just makes one more reason why I'm glad you're staying here."

Seeing how concerned he seemed to be, Kelsey was both touched and sorry she'd brought the calls up. "It's probably nothing. I'd practically forgotten about it until the phone started ringing."

"I don't like it."

"I shouldn't have brought it up. I'm sure it's nothing."

"You know, if I'm not around, you can count on Will. He'll take care of things."

Will. She thought back to Gwen's concerns. "Will doesn't trust me," she reminded Jarred.

"Like everyone else, he's just being overprotective. Give him time."

She gazed at her husband, wondering if he

truly believed his words or if they were just wishful thinking. Yet when she tried to put Will in the place of the spy within the company, she just couldn't do it. He was too loyal to Jarred.

"Part of Will's problem these days is that he and Danielle are having trouble," Jarred revealed.

"Marital trouble?" Kelsey asked.

Jarred nodded. "That's why we haven't seen her around."

Gwen might not want Kelsey to relay her suspicions about Will, but there was no reason to completely exonerate him either. "Will's been pretty tight with Sarah," she said. "I wasn't kidding when I said that, whenever he's around, she's around."

"You think there's something going on between them?"

Though she knew she was being too sensitive, she couldn't help a prick of uneasiness. He'd said he didn't care about Sarah, but years of conditioning herself to believe otherwise couldn't just be brushed aside. "I have no evidence to support anything," Kelsey told him. "I just noticed how close they've become, and since I don't like her, I always think the worst," she admitted candidly.

"I never had an affair with her," Jarred said pointedly. Silence pooled between them. The only sound was their breathing. "I don't find her attractive and I never have."

Kelsey gazed at him soberly. "Do you really

remember everything?"

"All of that, yes! Sarah is an employee, period. And like I said, there were times when I used her attraction to me to my advantage. I wanted you to think the worst."

"I always think the worst with Sarah," Kelsey admitted.

"Yes, I know. I didn't have to try that hard," he said with dry humor.

Smiling, Kelsey glanced at her watch, raised her eyebrows, then turned toward the door.

"Wait!" Jarred worked his way toward her, shooting his own ankle a dark look. He reached her and held her close. Kelsey was afraid to move, considering he wasn't exactly steady on that one leg. But when he kissed her, she pulled back.

"As much as I would like to play around some more, I'm leaving," she said.

He kissed her neck, her cheek, her lips. But Kelsey stood her ground. She couldn't believe that she was suddenly going to fall back into romantic euphoria with Jarred. That was too dangerous, too soon.

Reading her stoicism, Jarred sighed. "Oh, Kelsey," he said with real suffering. "You're going to kill me."

"Later," she told him.

"I'll be here. . . ."

"This is Jarred Bryant," he said crisply into the phone. "Tell Neil I'd like to talk to him. I'm sure he's heard all about the accident, but I'm getting back to work and I'd like to straighten some things out that were unfinished."

The female voice on the other end of the phone assured him that Neil Brunswick would call him soon.

"Let me give you my home phone number." Jarred recited the numbers, then hung up the receiver. Rain pounded the windows behind him. Miserable day.

He'd spent a few hours under Joanna's careful ministrations, working muscles and making plans. Time to get back to work. Watching Kelsey leave while he was forced to stay behind was more than he could bear.

After Joanna left and he still found himself with time on his hands, he'd gone through copies of the papers Will and Sarah and Nola had brought by and asked him to sign. He'd done so with hardly a second glance. They all thought that he couldn't remember and that he was their puppet, but he'd known about each and every unfinished deal. And he'd known why they'd remained unfinished until now.

The Brunswick property, for instance. Trevor Taggart's "coup."

There was a lot more going on there than anyone knew, and he liked keeping it that way for now.

The rest of the day passed excruciatingly slowly. He thought he might go crazy if he actually had to spend one more day here with only himself and a cat and a dog for company. Even Joanna's boot camp physical therapy was preferable to twiddling his thumbs. He would have to get back to work soon, or he would go quietly out of his mind.

Kelsey came home promptly at seven. The garage door hummed upward and Mr. Dog barked and raced down the stairs. Thank God! Jarred stood at the top of the stairs and tested his ankle. He could make it down if he tried. He wasn't as weak as yesterday, not by a long shot.

Because you slept with your wife.

It was the most ridiculous thought, and the most true.

Listening to her footsteps crossing the kitchen floor, he limped and hopped his way back inside his room, stripped off every stitch of clothing, grabbed a fresh rose from the flowers in the vase on the gallery table, stuck the stem in his teeth, limped back out to the upper landing without the benefit of the crutches, and struck a pose like Michelangelo's *David* at the top of the stairs.

Moments later Mary Hennessy walked into view and stared up at her employer.

Kelsey doubled over with laughter. Tears filled her eyes and she couldn't speak. Jarred, dressed in jeans and a sweatshirt, sat on the sofa in his bedroom suite and blandly ignored her fit of hysteria. "She said, 'I thought I forgot to turn the oven on. I'll be on my way now.'"

This cracked Kelsey up all the more. "Oh, my God!" she said, swiping tears of hilarity from the corners of her eyes.

"Yes, well . . ."

"I wish I could have been a fly on the wall. Are you sure she's going to come back?"

"Not completely," he admitted, sending Kelsey into new fits of laughter.

With more love than she'd thought possible, she crossed the room and slipped down next to him on the couch. "I forgot what you could be like," she said softly. "I never realized until the accident how much I've missed you."

Her admission touched him. He pulled her close, not wanting even the smallest space between them. "I've been giving the accident a lot of thought. Turning it over in my mind. The crux of it is, I don't know why I was with Chance. It doesn't make sense."

"You still don't remember anything about the accident?"

Jarred shook his head in frustration. "I had a dream about him. I've been trying to remember, but it's not there. He looked like hell, though. Scared and upset. We were in my office," Jarred suddenly recalled.

"In your office? In the dream?"

He nodded. "But it seemed more like reality."

"Chance looked terrible the night he came to see me," Kelsey said.

"Skinny. Jittery. Unclean . . . ?"

"Well, yes," she said, hating to talk badly

about Chance. "He broke down and cried."

"Do you think he was on something?"

"He was always on something," Kelsey admitted with a sigh.

Jarred drew her close and talked into her hair. "Why would I invite him on the plane? I never even liked him. I always thought he was your lover."

"I told you he was a family friend."

"I know . . . now. . . ." Jarred struggled to make her believe something that he was just beginning to believe himself. "But for a long time I thought you were sleeping with him."

"Do you mean *during our marriage?*" Kelsey was affronted. "You thought I was sleeping with someone else?"

"You thought I was sleeping with someone else," Jarred pointed out reasonably.

"Well, yes, but that was different. Sarah was always with you. I hardly saw Chance."

Jarred inhaled deeply, weighing his words, wondering if this was the right time to bring up something he now wished he'd never believed. "I know the truth now."

"But you didn't then?"

"No."

"Why did you mistrust me?" Kelsey had never done anything the least bit suspicious or nefarious during the length of their marriage, and it bothered her that he thought she had.

Inhaling a deep breath, Jarred took the plunge. "Sarah told me she saw you coming out of his apartment the morning of our wedding. She said you'd slept with him."

Kelsey's mouth dropped open. "You can't be serious."

"And then I confronted Chance with it, and he said it was true."

"*What?* No. Chance wouldn't lie like that!"

"I'm just telling you what he said. I believed him."

"Oh, Jarred." Kelsey melted against the cushions, shocked and unhappy and recognizing things for what they really were in a new and awful way. "He didn't want me to marry you," she realized, "even though he wished me well. He didn't want me to marry you. I did go see him that morning — the morning of the wedding — but it was just to say good-bye. He wished me the best. He did." Moments later, she muttered, "*Sarah!* She pretended she was Chance's friend, but she was always stirring up trouble. And she ran right back to you with that information, just hoping you'd call off the wedding!" Kelsey could scarcely credit it. "Why didn't you tell me?"

"Because I believed her."

With a bolt of realization, Kelsey saw those first years of her marriage for what they were. "That's why you became so distant."

"I remember you pulling away from me," Jarred said, "and that was when things started to go bad."

"No." She stopped him. "You've got that backward. I pulled away from you because you were cold and uncaring."

"Only because I believed — I was told! — that you loved Chance."

"No, that's not it. That's not it."

"Kelsey . . ."

"You didn't want the baby!" she burst out, the words popping past her lips without her brain's consent.

A huge silence settled between them. Kelsey tensed. It was shocking, how easily these truths were coming out when for years — *for years!* — she'd held them all behind a wall of hurt.

In a voice full of reluctance, for he knew this was going to hurt, Jarred corrected softly, "I didn't want Chance's baby."

Kelsey flinched as if he'd struck her. The message drove into her heart like a dagger. How could he have believed it of her? Even now, she couldn't reconcile it. She tried to pull away but he held her close.

"I'm sorry," he whispered against her hair. "And for these reasons, I'm almost glad the accident happened. It gave us a second chance."

A second chance. Kelsey could scarcely grasp the meaning. A second chance. She wanted it desperately. But was it really possible? "The accident wasn't an accident," she said, drawing the conversation away from these painful embers of truth. "Someone tampered with the plane. I'm scared that this is all coming too late. What if something else happens?"

"It won't."

"How can you be sure?"

"Because we're on the same side now," he said urgently. "We won't let it. Whatever happened, it involved Chance Rowden. I'm sorry he's dead. But maybe whatever set up that plane crash died with him. The only issues we've got left are within Bryant Industries, and as soon as I'm able, I'm going to get to the bottom of everything."

She almost believed him. Touching her cheek, Jarred turned her head so she could look directly into his serious blue eyes. Kelsey gazed at him long and hard, loving him, wanting back what they'd so very nearly lost for all time.

"You're certain?" she asked, needing to hear the words even if they were a lie.

"Everything's going to be fine," he assured her. "Nothing, and no one, can hurt us now."

The last ferry to Vancouver Island ran at midnight. It was his ticket out. His way to safety. His means of escape.

He rubbed his face. He'd been going strong for three days and three nights, running on empty, a wild meth trip that would end in about the same amount of time in a near coma of complete exhaustion. The price one paid . . . the price one paid. But he'd been fooled by *them* once and he wasn't going to let it happen again. *They* didn't give up. *They* kept coming.

He'd have to leave his car behind. It wasn't his anyway. It was Chance's. But he couldn't take it

221

to Canada. *They* would trace him.

Chewing on his thumbnail, he dug in one pocket and came up with forty-two dollars and some change. Enough to get to Canada. But then what?

She should have been there when he called. She could help. She *would* help. Chance had said so.

A catch in this throat. A sob. Chance was gone forever and it was his fault.

A whistle shrilled loudly into the cold air. He shivered, started, scurried toward the ticket booth. No problem going over without a car. Get on board. A long, long line. Anger surged through him, heating his blood, pushing out remorse. Damn *them.* Damn the world. It *wasn't* his fault. The bastards.

He shuffled forward, one foot in front of the other. Gritted teeth. Hot, hot anger and a beating pulse at his temple. Would his head explode? He pressed the heels of his palms against the sides of his head, holding in a wail of repressed fury and hopelessness.

A cold hand on his shoulder.

He whipped around, and his fists came up like a boxer's. He blinked. A woman.

"Whad're you doin' here?" he slurred. Running a tongue over his dry lips, he tried again. "Good God. You lookin' for *me?*"

She was as cold as an arctic front. "I know what you did."

"Whad I do? Whad I do?" he screamed.

"You killed Chance Rowden and you damn near killed Jarred Bryant."

"Chance was a mistake! *A mistake!*" He started crying in earnest now. People turned, stared, felt revulsion. The woman drew him to one side.

"Where do you think you're going to go?" she hissed in his ear. "Canada? Not far enough, you stupid ass."

"It's not fair. He shoulda died. It was his plane. Chance wasn't supposed to be on that plane. What was Chance doin' on that plane? It was Bryant's plane!" He choked and sobbed and struck out at the crisp night air with flailing fists.

"So you were trying to kill Jarred Bryant."

"He's a fucking bastard. Everybody knows it. Chance wanted him gone." He swiped an arm across his runny nose.

"Why?"

" 'Cause of his wife. Chance loved Bryant's wife."

"No! Why were you trying to kill Jarred? Pay attention!" She shook him for all he was worth till his teeth and head rattled as if filled with loose change.

"He saw us, okay? He confronted us at the house, right in the middle of it and saw all the stuff all over the place. He *knows.*"

"When did he see this?" she demanded. *"When?"*

He gazed at her through narrowed lids. She

was better off than he was, but she was using, all right. He'd known about her. She was crafty, but he was smarter. For a moment he felt smug. "Before the accident. Sometime."

"*When?*" She shook him again and his knees buckled. Clutching her arm, he thought of shoving his fist into her face until it caved inward. His head whirled. It hurt to think. "How much time did he have?" she was shrieking at him. "Did he tell anyone? Did he?"

"You're afraid of him."

"You should have killed him! You killed your best friend, and Jarred Bryant survived!"

"But he can't remember! He can't!"

"Shut up! I have to think!" For a moment, she crumpled, pressing her fingers to her eyes, shuddering all over. "You've turned a radiation leak into a nuclear explosion. You're lucky to be alive."

The black car. *They* were in the black car. She'd sent for *them!*

Nearly choking with fear, he stumbled away from her. Away from the line. Away from everything. He ran and ran until sweat poured off his back and spittle flew from a mouth that hung open and gasped for air.

She watched him tear away, zigzagging like a drunken sailor. She was really messed up. She could feel it. Paranoia fueled her. She'd been scared straight for weeks, but tonight she'd lost control and fed her addiction. She'd gone to see him and found him backing Chance's car out of his dilapidated garage, so she'd followed him. Fear kept her mind in focus all the way to the ferry terminal in Anacortes.

The fool thought he'd be safe in Canada, but if Jarred Bryant started remembering there would be nowhere on earth safe enough for their sorry souls.

Nothing had gone right. Nothing. Not from the very beginning, and *it just wasn't fair!*

She had to think. If Jarred knew about Chance, he would eventually learn about her. Maybe he already knew and was either unable to remember or was keeping his mouth shut until the time was right. She knew Jarred. He wouldn't stop until he got to the truth. The police didn't worry her. Maybe they could catch that fleeing moron but they wouldn't link her to anything.

Could they?

Her teeth chattered as her mind skipped and jumped and reversed. Painful. But it was Jarred Bryant who would do the most damage. He would want to know everything. Everything!

She was going to have to stop him.

And she knew just the kind of people to help her.

Chapter Nine

"Could I talk to you?"

Looking up from her desk, Kelsey was surprised to see Will entering "their" office. His grim expression did not bode well, and for a wild moment, she wondered if he knew what Gwen had said about him. "What is it?" she asked.

"Nola's on line one for you."

"Oh!" She half laughed, then grimaced involuntarily. Of all the things she could have done to endear herself to Will, this, apparently, was the best. His lips twitched in shared understanding. "We're going there tonight," Kelsey told him. "Apparently she talked to Jarred into it even though he's barely mobile. He let me know a while ago."

"I know. It's a command performance for all of us."

"Really." Kelsey was surprised.

"Jarred conned her into asking me, I'm sure. He wouldn't go unless I was invited."

Not knowing quite what to say, Kelsey murmured, "I see," as she punched the button for line one. Will mouthed, "Good luck," and disappeared out the door. Kelsey's smile almost returned at this small gesture on Will's part, but she also hadn't forgotten Gwen's fears about him.

"This is Kelsey," she answered a tad briskly. Dealing with Nola was never easy.

"Hello, Kelsey. It's Nola. How are you?"

"Fine. Just fine."

"Did Jarred tell you I'm expecting you both by seven? I wanted to reconfirm."

"Yes." She hesitated. "Is Jarred certain he's up for this? He's not exactly in prime condition yet."

"He said he'd be glad to get out of the house."

It had only been three days since their first night in bed together. It was almost as if the three-year gap in their marriage hadn't occurred. Sometimes she asked herself if she was really ready for all of this. *Was* she? What if Jarred turned around and again became the suspicious, coldhearted autocrat whom she'd sworn to divorce?

But no. That was just her own fear talking. Jarred trusted her and loved her. He'd even said as much that one time. And if she wanted to hear it more and reassure herself — well, she was going to have to whisper those three little words right back to him, which she'd found herself unable to do just yet.

"Then we'll see you at seven," she told Nola lightly.

"Good. Oh, Will is going to be there, too." Her voice grew noticeably chillier.

"And Danielle?"

"He didn't mention her name. I got the feeling he was coming solo."

Kelsey murmured a good-bye, hung up the phone, and stared into space. Unwillingly, she felt Gwen's fears about Will reenter her head, and wondered if Jarred would be so ready to visit his family if he knew Gwen's concerns over his brother. She would have liked to talk to Gwen some more, but the secretary's migraines had been troubling her and she'd been out of the office since Tuesday.

Sarah had also missed a few days, but she'd been back with a vengeance today, lurking like an evil spirit. Anytime Kelsey had run into her she seemed to be orbiting around Will. With Jarred out of commission, she'd apparently gone to the next best thing.

And how about when Jarred comes back?

"I'll jump off that bridge when I get to it," she muttered aloud. Jarred professed to have no feelings for the woman. She just hoped it would stay that way.

Three hours later, she closed up her office and headed for the elevators, again running straight into Sarah Ackerman, who'd already pushed the down button. They half smiled at each other in acknowledgment, and Kelsey hoped her expression didn't look too forced. Silently, they entered the elevator and took it to the first floor. At the bottom, Sarah headed quickly for the front doors and Kelsey dawdled, waiting for the other woman to leave first.

There was just no way she was ever going to like Sarah.

By the time she arrived home, it was after six. To Kelsey's surprise, Jarred was in the kitchen. "Congratulations. You made it down here all by yourself."

"Nearly killed me," he grumbled. "And this beast tried to trip me."

Mr. Dog barked at Kelsey as if pleading his case to the opposite. He wagged his tail and wriggled. "He doesn't look too remorseful," Kelsey said.

"And they call him man's best friend."

She laughed, then inhaled in sudden surprise when he reached for her. His scent enveloped her as he placed a long, lingering kiss on her lips, reminding her very clearly of their shared evenings together. The embrace lasted long moments, and slightly breathless, Kelsey broke away first.

"You're also dressed, I see," Kelsey observed. In a black shirt and black slacks, Jarred looked like his old handsome self. His grip was strong, his lips warm and demanding. She could almost believe the accident hadn't happened, except for the crutches propped against the kitchen island. "I'm going to have to change, and I'd better be quick."

"Nola can wait," he said, unperturbed.

"She wants us there by seven. She called today. She said you said you wanted to go."

"Wanted to go?" He snorted. "She harangued me until I caved in!"

Kelsey laughed and headed upstairs. It felt so good to talk to him without all the old animosity. She wanted to pinch herself sometimes. It just didn't seem as if it could be real.

Half an hour later, she was driving Jarred toward his parents' house, which was only a few miles and a bridge away on Mercer Island. The Bryants lived in a wonderful brick home nestled within a stand of fir and cedar trees and placed to offer a sweeping view of Lake Washington. It wasn't as grand as Jarred's house, but what it lacked in space, it made up for in charm and heart. Nola had kept wonderful care of the house and grounds, and there was no question that it held its own among the newer, snappier homes that had replaced the ones in the Bryants's era.

Still, Kelsey felt a bit of a chill as she drove down the curving, fir- and maple-flanked drive. Maybe it was because the maple trees were denuded this December, their dark limbs skeletal against the gray sky. More likely it was that Nola had never been fully welcoming; it wasn't her nature, and as a result, Kelsey had always dreaded visiting Jarred's parents. One of the few pleasant byproducts of Kelsey's estrangement from Jarred was that she hadn't had to suffer through any more dinner engagements at the Bryant home with Nola residing fiercely and coldly over the festivities.

"Will's here," she said, recognizing his car. "I understand it was one of your conditions."

"She told you that?"

"He told me," she corrected. "We had a brief discussion at work today."

Jarred gave her a searching look. "He's trying harder. Good."

"I don't think Danielle's accompanying him."

Jarred made a noncommittal sound.

Kelsey hadn't seen Danielle since the night of the accident, and then Will's petite, rather serious wife had stood a distance away, lost in her own thoughts. But then they'd all naturally been upset and shocked, so it wasn't any wonder that she'd tried to stay out of emotional range.

"At least with Will here, the heat's off you and me," Jarred observed.

"That's not a very nice way to speak of your mother."

"Facts are facts," he said without the slightest shade of remorse. Reaching over, he placed a hand on her knee, warming Kelsey through and through. "She should accept Will as a member of the family, but she never will. It's just a battle she can't stop fighting."

"Why can't she?"

He shook his head. "She won't share anything with Will. He's not *hers*. She was civil to him when he was dumped on our doorstep, but she doesn't know how to really embrace anyone."

His mouth formed a grim smile. "But she's going to accept you," he added in an iron voice. "One way or another."

"Why do I believe that's wishful thinking?"

"Because you've never trusted my feelings for you."

Kelsey controlled her surprise as she pulled the Explorer to a stop and climbed from behind the wheel. He never ceased to amaze her. Slowly, she was beginning to trust that this change in him was permanent.

Jarred, who eschewed the crutches for a rather sturdy-looking cane, refused to let her help him as he walked to the front door. It took him a while to get from the car and walk the curving brick path. His right leg could accept almost no weight and the cane frustrated him in a way that was almost amusing. But the glacial look he shot her way when he saw the corners of her mouth twitching instantly wiped the smile from Kelsey's lips.

"Someday you'll pay," he whispered as she rang the bell, and her laughter died in her throat when he suddenly pressed his face against the smoothness of her hair and inhaled deeply.

Rattled, she started guiltily when Nola threw open the door herself.

"Darling!" Nola greeted Jarred, reaching out her arms and hugging him hard. Kelsey worried that Nola's enthusiastic welcome might actually topple him over, but when he saw her hovering anxiously, he mock glared at her and shook his head ever so slightly.

"Come in, come in," Nola enthused, barely offering more than a belated hello to Kelsey before fussing over Jarred. Kelsey followed after them, and when they entered the living room and she saw that Will was alone, she decided to attempt to improve their relations by taking a seat near him.

To her surprise she saw that Will wasn't alone. Danielle stood beside the cart of drinks, slowly sipping a glass of white wine, her expression as distant as one of Saturn's moons.

"So how's it going?" Kelsey asked him.

He threw a glance at his wife. "Not well," he admitted.

"Hello, Danielle," she said.

Rousing herself briefly, Danielle offered a flickering smile. One moment it was there; the next it was as if she hadn't even responded. Will regarded his wife moodily, but Kelsey got the feeling there wasn't a real desire inside him to attend to his wife. Neither one of them appeared to be making an effort, and Kelsey was asking herself why when Sarah Ackerman strolled in from the den with Jarred's father escorting her.

Kelsey managed to fight back a gasp of surprise. She shot a look at Jarred, whose own expression had darkened into a scowl.

"Well, hello, all," Jonathan greeted them. Like Jarred, he relied on a cane, but unlike Jarred, Jonathan seemed to be hovering over the three-footed chrome device as if it were all that kept him from completely collapsing into a heap.

Will got eagerly to his feet and met them. The frigid glare Nola sent Sarah spoke volumes, and for the first time, Kelsey warmed to her mother-in-law. Kelsey might not be blue-blooded enough for Nola, but Sarah Ackerman was even worse. And it didn't matter that Nola refused to consider Will a true Bryant. He was, for better or worse, her husband's flesh and blood, and she was compelled to put up with him, at least on some level.

But again, Sarah was something else.

"Let me get you a refill," Will said to Sarah, taking her empty wineglass.

"Oh, no, thanks. I'm fine." Sarah wisely moved away from the drink cart and Danielle.

Danielle seemed to surface. "I'm sorry. I can't stay. Nola, thank you for inviting me, but I've got things to do." She glanced at Will, opened her mouth to say something, changed her mind, and collected her coat from the hallway closet. The soft closing of the door marked her exit.

"Anyone else?" Will asked a trifle bitterly, gesturing to the cart.

"White wine," Kelsey jumped in, beating back the uncomfortable silence.

Nola's mouth was pinched. "Excuse me for a moment, will you?" She retreated to the kitchen.

"After you get your drinks, come on in to the den," Jonathan invited, motioning gently to Kelsey and Jarred with his other hand. "I'll have some scotch, Jarred."

"I'll get it," Kelsey said since Jarred was hardly the one to ask for help.

While Jarred and Jonathan passed through the double doors into Jonathan's private den, Kelsey searched the crystal bottles on the cart. Without being asked, Will poured Jonathan's drink, handing the cut-glass old-fashioned glass with two fingers of scotch to her. Next, he pulled a bottle of chardonnay from a sterling silver wine chiller, poured her a glass, and handed her the long-stemmed glass, meeting her gaze briefly and silently.

Sarah observed from a distance. A prickle of awareness feathered Kelsey's skin. There was much more going on here. Much, much more.

"I'll bring this one to Jarred," Will said, holding another glass of scotch.

Jonathan was seated in a bloodred wing-backed chair, his feet propped in front of a gas fire. Jarred sat in the adjoining chair. When Kelsey entered the room, he motioned for her to join him. Will handed him his drink as Kelsey gave Jonathan his; then Will left, closing the doors behind him. Thinking that climbing into a chair with Jarred might be a little over the top, considering the tensions of the evening, Kelsey signaled Jarred with a slight shake of her head, then took a place in front of the fire.

"My dear, won't you take a chair?" Jonathan asked.

"In a minute. I need to stretch a bit." She

frowned at Jarred's scotch. "Terrible stuff," she told him. "I'm sure Dr. Alastair would not approve."

Jonathan frowned. "Should you have that, son?"

"I'll survive," Jarred's voice was dry.

Jonathan looked as if he wanted to argue, but instead he said, "So how are you doing?"

"On the road to recovery," Jarred assured him. Then, very seriously, he asked, "What about yourself?"

"Me?" Jonathan was surprised. "Why, I'm the same as ever."

Since this was patently untrue, Kelsey flicked a glance at her husband. Jarred regarded his father soberly.

The door opened and Nola entered, smelling faintly of smoke. She'd been nervous enough to have to sneak away for a few minutes and rely on a cigarette. Kelsey almost envied her the vice. The white wine just wasn't cutting it in this strained atmosphere.

"I don't remember inviting her," Nola bit out. "Was that your doing?" she asked Jarred.

"If you mean Sarah, I think Will invited her for moral support," Jarred revealed.

"What do you mean?"

"Danielle isn't the warmest person on earth. Maybe he wanted someone around who shares at least some of his thoughts."

Or maybe she invited herself, Kelsey thought.

"Is there some reason they're out there and

we're all in here?" Jarred asked next.

"I'll go out." Kelsey left before anyone could disagree with her. She knew what it was to be ostracized by this family, and though she was no fan of Sarah's, and she didn't know quite what to think of Will, she could at least be polite.

But they were nowhere to be seen, and when she peeked around the corner into the nooklike room next to the kitchen, she caught them in an impassioned embrace.

Retracing her footsteps, she stood undecided in the kitchen. Her heart thudded and her head reeled.

"Kelsey?" Jarred called from the door to the den.

Feeling like a spy, she hurried to meet him.

"Where are Sarah and Will?"

"Oh, they're talking in the other room." Should she say something? Deciding it was better to keep quiet until they got home, she added, "Business, I think."

She didn't fool him for a minute, but he let the moment pass. Later, she would have to come clean about everything, including Gwen's assessment of Will's character. After all, this was exactly why Jarred had placed her in a position of trust: He wanted to know what was going on at his company while he wasn't there.

Dinner followed shortly thereafter, and nothing of import was said. Seated beside Jarred and across from Will, Kelsey began to feel the dreaded pressures that accompanied an evening with the

Bryants. She tried desperately to shake off the sensation without much success. Will and Sarah didn't seem to be particularly cautious about others knowing about their burgeoning relationship, however. They smiled and joked and generally seemed more at ease with each other and intimate than their business warranted. What it really meant was anyone's guess, and Kelsey was torn between the feeling that she should warn Will about her nemesis and a surging relief that Sarah had moved on from Jarred.

But it was still all in the family.

The maid was clearing the dishes when Nola asked, "Kelsey, could I have a word with you?"

Shooting Jarred a look of dismay, Kelsey nevertheless followed her mother-in-law into the nook that Sarah and Will had previously occupied. Wondering what this was all about, Kelsey stood next to the built-in sideboard, catching her reflection in the diamond panes of the upper cabinet. Her furrowed brow reflected her feelings, and she cleared her expression.

Nola, for once, seemed at a loss for words. She fingered a crystal glass full of port and gazed out the windows to the drooping limbs of a water-soaked fir tree. "Will's certainly surprised us all, hasn't he?"

Kelsey wasn't going to go *there*. Will was capable of making his own decisions, bad or good, and Nola's opinion really didn't matter.

"No comment?" Nola's lips pursed.

"None whatsoever," Kelsey said, meaning it.

"Well, you've grown wiser over these last few years, I see." She moved restlessly to the other side of the room, one ear cocked toward the open door to listen for unwanted eavesdroppers. "I never believed you and Jarred would stay together, but I see now that this accident has done the impossible. It's brought you back to one another again. And Jarred seems . . . happy, for lack of a better word."

Since there seemed to be no response needed, Kelsey remained quiet. But some sixth sense warned her of pending disaster, for the hair on her forearms lifted.

"I thought he would never forgive you for that pregnancy scare, but I see I was wrong."

"Forgive me?" Kelsey repeated in a warning tone. "You still think I *lied* about it?"

Nola waved her away. "Let's not argue about this again. I was told that you made it up."

"By whom? Jarred?" It nearly killed Kelsey to ask the obvious.

Nola set the crystal glass down with unsteady fingers. "No. I don't remember now. I think it was . . . something I overheard."

The hell she didn't remember! Kelsey's mind instantly sought for an answer, and she landed on Sarah once more. But at least Jarred, even believing that the baby wasn't his, hadn't repeated his fears to his mother. "I believed I was pregnant. I still do. I had an early miscarriage."

"All right." Nola conceded the battle so quickly that it took Kelsey a moment to realize this wasn't the purpose of this meeting. "I wanted to clear that up before anything else was said."

"Okay." Kelsey trod lightly, waiting.

"You know Jarred's thirty-ninth birthday is right around the corner. I know he'd like to have a child, and though I admit I felt he should divorce you and get on with his life, I see now that things have changed."

Kelsey couldn't believe her ears. Was Nola, who'd fought her at every turn, going to come full circle and beg for the grandchild *she* wanted? This had nothing to do with what Jarred wanted. Nothing!

"I really think you need to know the terms of Hugh's will and how it affects Jarred."

"Hugh's will?"

"Yes."

"Nola, I don't think I want to hear any more. Whatever it is you want to say, maybe you should say it to Jarred. I can already tell this is dangerous territory, and frankly, I'm not interested in discussing the will."

Color returned to Nola's pale cheeks. "Well, there are some things you should know if you don't already!" she snapped, recovering her starch with remarkable speed. "By the time Jarred is forty, if he doesn't have an heir, preferably male, then by the terms of his grandfather's will, the business reverts to Will. Of course Will isn't a real Bryant, but that doesn't matter according to our legal counsel. If Jarred doesn't produce an heir and Will does, Will inherits. The stipulation being that Will must produce an heir by the time *he's* forty. He'll have years to accomplish that goal whereas Jarred's running out of time!"

Kelsey absorbed that startling bit of news in disbelief. She'd never heard anything of the sort, yet she and Jarred had so rarely talked about his business and family outside of a few comments on Jonathan and Nola's health and personalities that anything was possible. "What are you saying?" she demanded, wanting Nola to baldly spell it out.

"I'm saying it's time you knew why Jarred and Jonathan and I were so upset when you said you were pregnant and then you weren't. I don't think Jarred knew you'd miscarried."

"I told him. He knew."

"Darling, he didn't believe you," she said on a sigh.

No, he didn't believe the child was his. . . .

Kelsey thought back to that terrible time and suddenly saw a whole new angle: Jarred struggling to hide his feelings about the pregnancy from Nola, who had her own agenda working. And Sarah, lying every which way, hoping to destroy Jarred's marriage for her own purposes.

No wonder Nola had made those remarks about Kelsey not sleeping in the same bed as her husband. She'd been worried sick that Jarred's fortieth birthday would come and go, and Jarred and Kelsey's marriage would still be stuck in limbo! Now Kelsey's anger with Nola and Sarah intensified. They'd meddled in her life — hers and Jarred's — and been the wedge that had nearly broken them apart.

"It seems to me you might be more concerned with your son's health than his ability to keep the family money away from Will."

"You think I don't care?" Nola's lips parted in protest. "Is that what you think?"

"I think you've got the cart before the horse."

"When I saw Jarred in the emergency room, I thought I was going to die. And then when I learned he was going to live, I broke down and cried." Nola's hands shook. "Jonathan got down on his knees and prayed."

Kelsey's anger became a low simmer. Being furious with Nola for being Nola wasn't going to help anyone. "How does Jonathan feel about the terms of Hugh's will?"

"He doesn't want Will to inherit any more than I do. You may not believe me, but that's the truth." She sighed. "He's become rather religious over this whole experience, I'm afraid. It's all been so . . . hard. But then Jarred woke up and you and he started to reach out to each other, and I thought maybe miracles do happen. You just have to realize they're miracles. But I can't sit and wait for you two to court each other all over again! Jarred's fortieth birthday is coming right up."

"He won't even be thirty-nine until January," Kelsey pointed out.

"And that's not that far away."

If Nola were anyone else, Kelsey would have laughed out loud at her fears. With all the problems facing the company and the mysteries surrounding Jarred's accident, this was the issue that ate away at her soul? This was the most important piece of her life still unfulfilled?

But this was clearly no laughing matter to Nola. She gazed at Kelsey intently, desperate for that heir, that grandchild, that permanent wall that would keep Will locked away from Bryant money.

"Do you want a baby, Kelsey? Jarred's baby?"

The thought brought Kelsey up short. Though she thought Nola was completely out of line on the issue, there was no denying the idea was more than attractive to Kelsey. She'd wanted that first baby. Nothing had changed in her heart.

Reading the series of swift expressions that crossed Kelsey's face, Nola visibly relaxed. She walked over to Kelsey and patted her arm. "That's all right then," she said. "Welcome back to the family, Kelsey."

The ride home was quiet, and Jarred fought to keep his hands off his pretty wife as she drove them through the wind-torn night. She'd withdrawn from him after her encounter with Nola, and it bothered him. Kelsey was way too adept at pulling away. *That* he remembered in spades.

"So what was that conversation with Nola all about?" he asked.

"Your mother welcomed me back into the family."

"With open arms?"

She slid him a look and a slight smile that blew his concentration. "As open as they will ever get. How did it go with your father? You looked kind of tense when I returned. What did he think of Will and Sarah?"

"I'm not sure." Jarred inhaled slowly and shook his head. He was worried sick about his father. Something was going on there that he couldn't understand. The man was deteriorating right before his eyes, and he had a tendency to want to hold on to Jarred's hand or arm, as if touching his son were some kind of lifeline. It wasn't that Jarred minded, but it was so damn weird since Jonathan Bryant had always been a standoffish individual. He wasn't as cold as Nola, for certain, but he'd never been the touchy-feely guy he was today either.

"He didn't seem to register that Will was with Sarah and not Danielle. I don't think it's on his mind. I don't know. I think my father's feeling his own mortality. Ever since my accident, it's as if he's staring death in the face."

"Nola said something about him embracing religion."

Jarred ran a hand through his hair. "He's so fervent about it, and he never was before. It's like I woke up in the hospital, and my father was somebody else."

"Does Will notice the change?"

"He has to," Jarred said, although tonight he seemed to be noticing more of Sarah than anything else."

"What do you think that's all about?" Kelsey questioned.

"I think it's directly related to Danielle. She's not exactly full of warmth and joy."

"She is a bit remote."

"No kidding."

Thinking of how remote things had been between them not so long ago, Kelsey said lightly, "Maybe neither one of them is trying hard enough."

Jarred shot her a sideways look. "Maybe they should look at what they've got and give it a second chance."

"Are you going to be the one to tell him?"

"I think he's going to have to figure that out for himself. The problem is, Will's interest in Sarah is probably a direct result of his failing marriage. When things aren't working out, you want someone to make you feel good."

"Someone like Sarah?" she said, and her tone of disbelief made Jarred chuckle.

"She's not *that* bad."

"Oh, no?"

"I'll never convince you, will I?"

"I'm sure she's good at business," Kelsey said. "But I saw the way she looked at you, and the way you looked at her, and it was tough."

"Well, it's nice to know you noticed, at least.

You were so damned impervious. I just wanted you to look at me!"

"Look at you?" Kelsey snorted. "Are you kidding? You acted as if I were invisible!"

"You weren't invisible," he sated firmly. "Your heart was with Chance."

"Never," she said softly.

Silence fell between them. Jarred remembered the time Kelsey had asked him if he would hire Chance. A business major himself, Chance Rowden had not fared well in a series of jobs after graduating college. He's been too unstable, too addicted. But Kelsey had never given up on him, and Jarred had believed that she had never stopped loving him. So he'd refused to hire Chance, and then Jarred had overheard Kelsey on the phone with Chance later that night, softly promising to keep after Jarred to give him a job.

And that was directly after he'd learned — from Sarah again — that Kelsey and Chance had been sleeping together, even after the wedding.

"It's all so stupid now," he said.

"Yes."

When they got back to the house, Kelsey pushed the button on the answering machine. Detective Newcastle's distinctive voice said he would like to meet with Jarred soon about some developments on the case. "A man was seen hanging around your plane that day, but everyone thought he was one of the mechanics.

Description is vague. About five foot ten inches, thin, dark, unkempt hair, blue jeans — pretty much describes everyone who works there. Let's talk tomorrow."

Jarred listened thoughtfully to the message. Kelsey regarded him soberly. "Does that sound like anyone you know?" she asked.

"Will?" he teased. "Except for the unkempt hair. Will's too fastidious." When Kelsey instantly tensed, he added, "Oh, come on. I was kidding."

"I know. But Will isn't acting like himself these days."

"He had nothing to do with that plane crash. You know it, Kelsey." He refused to even entertain any ideas in that direction. It was those kind of sneaking, trust-destroying thoughts that had nearly ruined his marriage.

"I agree. But . . ." She swallowed hard. "Gwen thinks Will is the leak in your office. She thinks he's been passing information to Trevor. She's heard him on the phone."

"What?" Jarred said in a deadly voice.

"Maybe it's because he doesn't feel he'll ever be a real Bryant," Kelsey said quickly. "I don't know. But Gwen really believes he's the one."

"Will doesn't think he's a real Bryant? Did my mother put that idea in your head?" Jarred demanded, sounding more like his previous self than he had thus far. "Will *is* a Bryant. My father is his father, and it doesn't matter how much Nola prefers to think otherwise."

"Talk to Gwen," she said, washing her hands of the whole thing. "She's the one who's noticed things."

"Gwen isn't the right person to make that judgment call. She's not that . . . clear about people's characters. Half the time she's not even in the office because of her migraines."

"Are you saying I shouldn't trust Gwen?"

"It's not a matter of trust," he disagreed. "It's that her insights aren't always accurate. That's as diplomatic as I can be. I know all about Gwen," he added, in case she thought this was one of those slippery memories. "She was my father's secretary and now she's mine. And she's wrong about Will."

"Fine." She lifted her hands in surrender.

Frustrated with their conversation, Jarred reached for her. After hesitating only a moment, she slipped into his arms. "Now help me upstairs and let's go to bed," he whispered against her hair. "And no more talk of any of this until morning."

An hour later, Kelsey lay beside him, her hand lightly running over his abdomen, her breath soft in his ear. He'd made love to her with a tenderness that had surprised and delighted her, and she wanted to tell him that she loved him. He'd told her, hadn't he? It was her turn, but the words still trembled on her lips, unable to be voiced.

His fingers grazed the arm she had thrown

over his chest. Glancing up, she saw that his eyes were focused on the windows, as if he were seeing something far, far out on the water. "What are you thinking about?" she asked, swallowing back her own need to confess her feelings.

"You."

"Liar. I see the way you're looking outside."

He twisted to gaze down at her, his fingers tenderly tracing her winged brows. "I was thinking about when I asked you to marry me."

"You were?" Kelsey lifted herself up on her elbows, her hair tumbling gorgeously around her bare arms.

"I used to wonder why you said yes. I thought you loved Chance, so I thought you married me for other reasons."

"What other reasons?" Kelsey demanded, thinking she should be more incensed than she was.

"Security mostly, I guess. When you wanted Chance to work for Bryant Industries, I figured it was so you could be near him. And then when you said you were pregnant, I thought the baby might be Chance's. It just seemed so coincidental, since Sarah told me she'd seen you coming out of Chance's apartment early that morning before the wedding, and then that you were still seeing him. And you were so adamant about having him come to work for Bryant."

"I just wanted him to succeed at something. I wanted him to have a break."

"I should never have listened to Sarah," he admitted.

"No, you shouldn't have," Kelsey agreed. "Look at all the trouble it caused."

"But then I went to see Chance and he confirmed that you were lovers. I realize he lied to me. Now. But I believed him then."

"I feel so bad about him," she said softly, laying her head against Jarred's warm chest once more. "I think he wanted to tell me how he felt that night before the accident. I wish I'd —"

A roaring *bang* cut Kelsey off. Her ears rang. She couldn't hear! Heat flared into the room. Timbers shuddered. Sheetrock cracked and the house trembled. Dust swirled and bits of tiny shrapnel darted around. The whole house felt as if it were caving in.

With a cry of terror, Kelsey clung to Jarred, who tumbled them both out of bed onto the floor. The house alarm *whoop-whoop-whooped.* Mr. Dog whined and snuffled their huddled bodies, his furry body trembling violently.

Felix crouched by Kelsey's head and let out a long, terror-filled wail.

"Jesus," Jarred muttered, holding Kelsey close. He waited for something worse to happen. He knew he'd wrenched his leg but the pain was eclipsed by his own wildly thundering heartbeat.

"What is it?" Kelsey whispered.

"Some kind of explosion," Jarred answered. The house stood. The alarm shrilled on. Mr.

Dog's and Felix's bodies pressed close to Kelsey and Jarred and each other, their animosity forgotten in the moment of shared fear. They lay in a tense embrace. Seconds passed. Eternities. Slowly, Jarred gently unwound himself from Kelsey.

When he reached for the discarded crutches, she said, "Where are you going? What are you doing?"

"I'm going to find out what happened. Can you cut that alarm?"

"I . . . don't know."

Jarred thumped into the gallery. Dust and debris floated in a cloud, filling up the house like fog. He worked his way downstairs, hardly even conscious of his own disability. The kitchen was white with Sheetrock dust. The door to the garage hung askew on its hinges. A hole gaped and frigid air blew into the kitchen.

Kelsey came up beside Jarred, her arms surrounding him, her body shaking uncontrollably. "Oh, my God!" she whispered, her gaze following Jarred's.

There was no south side of the garage to speak of. Jarred's Porsche lay blasted apart, a hunk of blackened, twisted metal, shards of which had embedded in and smashed against Kelsey's Explorer.

Above the still whooping alarm, in the distance, they heard the sound of an approaching police siren. Silently, wonderingly, Jarred and Kelsey settled in to wait.

Chapter Ten

Kelsey poured black coffee into three cups. Decaf. Detective Newcastle suffered heart palpitations and his doctor had ordered him off caffeine.

Jarred and the detective sat in Jarred's den — a square room at the back of the house paneled in cherry wood, which was stained a dark, beautiful mahogany and seemed to whisper "rich" when anyone crossed the threshold onto the lush green carpet. Brass knobs glinted beneath the flames of a gas fireplace. The gas lines had been left untouched by the blast, and the fireplace threw out a lot of heat. Kelsey, in fact, felt flushed and uncomfortable, though she suspected the reason was rooted in fear rather than the hissing gas flames.

Hands on his thighs, Newcastle sat broodingly in one of the black leather wing-backed chairs. He lifted one hand for the coffee mug, barely remembering to offer thanks, he was so intent on talking to Jarred.

"There's some reason this happened," he pointed out again. He seemed to feel if he covered and recovered the same territory enough times Jarred's brain would suddenly jerk into overdrive and pop out an answer. "These people want something: either to scare you into giving it to them or to remove you as an obstacle."

"I prefer the first interpretation," Kelsey murmured.

Jarred, seated behind his desk, looked grim and a bit white faced. Hearing Kelsey's soft voice he glanced at her and half smiled. She wanted to drag him away somewhere safe and make love to him for hours. Her desire must have communicated itself to him, for his expression altered slightly. For a moment, she sensed he was ready to chuck it all and go with her.

But running away would hardly solve their problems. "Who are 'these people'?" Jarred asked.

"This wasn't an amateur job. This is the kind of thing I've seen done by loosely organized groups. Not exactly organized crime as you might think of it, but a rawer, younger, more ganglike group." He paused. "The drug culture."

Kelsey's dread increased with each word Newcastle spoke.

"I've seen this kind of car bomb before. Not like the crude dismantling of your plane. I'd venture to guess that was done on the spur of the moment. You were going on the trip. Someone knew it, and they were desperate enough to take desperate measures. This, though, took some thought."

Jarred met the detective's eyes and shook his head. "I don't represent a threat to anyone."

"Somebody's pissed," Newcastle disagreed. "They took out the Porsche, not the Explorer. They either think you're up and driving or they meant this as a warning. Either way, you could have easily been killed."

Jarred seemed lost for words, so Kelsey asked. "When did they do it?"

"The explosive was planted in the last couple of days. Had a timing device. It was set to go off at midnight."

We could have taken the Porsche. If Jarred were better, or if I had some skill with that machine, we would have. And we could have come home later.

"What about your business?" Newcastle asked. "Made anybody mad at you lately?"

"I told you before, no."

"A business rival?" The detective took out a small notebook, clicked a pen, and prepared to write.

"No one who would do anything this drastic," Jarred said.

Kelsey curled into the window seat behind him, feeling the icy cold off the panes on her back and the warmth of the fire at her feet. Hammering sounded from the direction of the garage. Workmen. On the payroll at Bryant Industries' construction division. Willing to come and secure the house at night for their employer without even being asked.

"Maybe somebody's got a serious beef with you."

Jarred lifted his palms. "The man who dislikes me the most just outbid me on a piece of property. He thinks he's ahead of me. Ahead of the game."

"Thinks?" Newcastle waited for an explanation, but Jarred shrugged. "Maybe he wants the competition out of the way permanently."

"If your talking about Trevor," Kelsey inserted, "you couldn't be more wrong. He likes to win, but he likes to do it by his wits. This kind of thing is too . . . terrible, too blatant." She cleared her throat, conscious of the shaking quality of her own voice.

"What about your family? Anyone benefit from your death?"

"No." Jarred was adamant. Kelsey fleetingly thought of Will, but knew better than to throw suspicion on Jarred's half brother in front of the detective.

Newcastle clicked his pen again several times. "You seem to be in control of Bryant Industries today. Your father was before you?"

"Yes," Jarred answered cautiously, frowning.

"I understand the company never did as well under his management."

"No."

Kelsey shifted position. Jarred's clipped voice

declared his dislike for this avenue of questioning.

"And your half brother. He works for you, but does not own any portion of the corporation itself."

"That's correct."

"Mr. Bryant, we'd like to keep you alive." A long pause ensued. Then Detective Newcastle said, "It was a rather sophisticated, but small, bomb. The kind of thing you see when rival gangs reach a new level of turf war. They meant business."

"But this isn't how the plane went down?" Kelsey reiterated.

"No. I'd say that was the destructive work of a talented amateur who knew just enough."

"But you think these attacks were related," Jarred put in.

"Yes. I do. I just don't know how or, at this juncture, why. Has anything more come to you about Chance Rowden?"

"No."

"Nothing?"

Jarred hesitated. "I dreamed about him."

"What was the dream?"

Jarred reluctantly told Newcastle about Chance supposedly being in his office. He finished by saying, "Maybe I'm just trying to come up with an explanation."

Newcastle ran over a few more points a final time but he couldn't get what he wanted from Jarred, so he lumbered to his feet. Kelsey walked him to the front door. "Are you planning to stay here tonight?" Newcastle asked, referring to the hammering and pounding.

"No. We're going to the Four Seasons Olympic."

"Good idea."

When she return to Jarred, he was on his feet and staring through the windowpanes of the den to the black water of the lake far below. Firelight flickered on his jean-clad legs. He looked tense and stern.

Swallowing, Kelsey said, "I think I'll pack my overnight bag now."

He nodded. "I want to see the Rowdens. Maybe as soon as tomorrow."

"Tomorrow?" She shivered. "Are you really up for this?"

"I think I'm going to have to be," he said grimly, turning toward her. She moved forward and curved beneath the familiar warmth of his embrace, gazing up at him. He kissed her lightly, absently. "Now let's get to the Olympic and try to find a way to sleep. Starting tomorrow, I'm back at work."

They took a cab to the hotel because Kelsey's Explorer, though still able to run, was charred, skewered with bits of shrapnel, and generally unfit for the road. Being back at the Olympic Four Seasons so soon after her dinner with Gwen was a bit like coming home for Kelsey. But instead of reflecting on moments from those first, uncertain years of her marriage, this time she enjoyed the warmth and security of being held close by a husband, who seemed to love her anew. Still, in the unfamiliar room, she kept waking up, startled, heart racing, tense, and ready to bolt. Jarred, too, slept lightly, and at those times when they would both awaken, he would wrap himself around her and the moment would pass.

Fear seemed to have settled in Kelsey's bones, and when she examined the feeling, she realized it was fear for him. The fear of losing something she'd just rediscovered.

The following morning, Jarred got dressed for work. Neither of them said too much about the events of the night before. In the cab on the way to work, they sat in silence, lost to their own thoughts. Kelsey planned to walk into the office with Jarred, then head to the house and see how Felix and Mr. Dog were doing. Even though the garage had been secured in the night, she dreaded the idea of walking into the house alone. Her whole world felt as if it had been invaded.

As they headed up the elevator together, Kelsey threw Jarred a look. His expression was grim and determined. Something had happened to him. The explosion had started his engines, and he was no longer willing to wait for complete recovery. Whether this was good or bad, she couldn't say, but one glance at his hard face and she knew better than to argue.

And she realized she wanted to help him learn

the truth. She wanted to be his ally. His coinvestigator. Though he'd asked her to be his eyes and ears while he was recovering, now she wanted a more active role — one he would certainly object to. With last night's attack still so fresh in his mind, he wouldn't want to risk her safety. Still, she could be of help to him. And that was what she planned to do.

"Mr. Bryant!" Meghan called upon seeing him in the outer hallway. "Oh, my. You look wonderful. I hope this means you're back for good!" Her enthusiasm was genuine.

"I'd say so," he answered her with a smile.

Kelsey could tell how much it bothered him to use the cane, but it was still a necessity.

Gwen was the next employee they met. Seated at her desk in the anteroom outside his office, she glanced up in utter surprise, staring at him as if seeing the proverbial ghost. "Jarred!" she choked out. A hand flew to her mouth. For a moment, Kelsey thought she was going to cry. Then she pulled herself together and scrambled to her feet, giving him a self-conscious hug. "I'm so glad to see you. So glad. How are you? You look . . . great!"

"Thanks," he said. Then, recognizing her deep anxiety, he asked, "And how are you doing, Gwen?"

"Fine. Good." She bobbed her head. She half laughed. "I hope you don't mind, but with that cane — well, you're the spitting image of your father!"

"I'll take that as a compliment," he said, and Kelsey realized Gwen had not yet seen the terrible deterioration of Jonathan Bryant's health.

The word spread and the company's employees came like a horde into his office to wish him well. Sarah stood to the back of the room, surveying the group like a reigning queen. Will popped his head in, winked at his brother and left.

As soon as the crowd began to disperse, Jarred said, "So where's your office?"

"I'm sharing Will's."

"I thought they were putting you in an office near mine."

"There was talk of that, but it hasn't happened yet."

Promptly he made his first order of business finding her a new space. A small, sometime conference room down the hall from his office became hers within the hour, and Kelsey moved her belongings into the private space, appreciating Jarred's effort. *Maybe this will work out,* she thought, realizing that now she was a normal, regular employee whose boss just happened to be her husband.

It was so close to her one-time dream that a shiver of something like premonition slid down her back. Could anything like this last?

"I'm going to check on Felix and Mr. Dog as soon as I'm settled here," she said, sticking her head inside his office later that morning. "You okay?"

"Better than okay." His hand had been on the receiver of the phone, but he set it back down and motioned her over. "I should have come back last week. Too much is going on for me to just sit back and wait for it to happen."

Jarred's direct line rang. "They know you're back," Kelsey observed.

"Probably Nola again. I let her know what happened, and she's been damn near hysterical. But it's bound to hit the news."

Kelsey nodded.

"Want me to go to the house with you?"

"No, I'm fine."

He frowned. "You sure?"

"Yes," she said, giving him the benefit of a smile to prove, though it was a lie, that returning to the house was no problem at all.

"Could you wait?" she asked the taxi driver as she climbed from his cab. "I just want to check on some things. Then I'm going to need a ride to a car rental company."

"What happened here?" he asked, staring at the boarded-up garage.

"An accident," she said, beginning to hate that word.

She hurried to the front door. Fumbling with the keys, she entered the foyer and stood still. The house felt cold. Kelsey rubbed her hands together, checked the thermostat, then hugged both pets. Felix scrambled from her over-enthusiastic embrace but Mr. Dog licked her arms and face and stayed close.

I can't sleep here, she thought, hating herself for her own cowardice. Not until the garage was completely repaired. Not until the shards of metal sticking into the Explorer were removed and the SUV's charred exterior was buffed out and repainted. Not until I felt *safe.*

She knew she should hurry; nevertheless she walked outside onto the back deck and stared down the hill toward the water. A winding trail with a series of brick stairs zigzagged down to the dock. She debated for a moment on traversing her way to the lake, because she needed some time to think away from the house. But the flirty wind that caught at her hair and blouse dissuaded her. Too cold. Too slippery. Outside of her security.

And where's the brave woman who earlier vowed to help her husband solve this mystery?

After locking the doors, she returned to the taxi and gave the cabbie the car rental company's address. Once she was behind the wheel of a clean, but rather well-used dark blue sedan she drove to the site of Jarred's town houses, not far from Trevor's Phase One and only a half mile away from 'em. On an impulse she checked in at the model, hoping to find Tara, but the door was locked and no one was around. Disappointed, she retraced her steps and wandered through the Bryant Industry town houses. The units were at the Sheetrock stage, and all the decisions for fixtures, hardware, etc., had already been made. Kelsey had okayed several invoices and had changed others, but her work, until the model needed to be furnished, was basically done.

Back at Bryant Industries she stood outside Jarred's door but she could hear him talking animatedly on the telephone. Not wanting to interrupt, she turned back to her new office. She'd give him another half hour. Clearly, he was flourishing in his regular milieu — a thought that left her with a feeling of uneasiness she didn't want to explore.

Around five o'clock, there was a knock on her door. She looked up. Sarah stood there. "Hello," Kelsey greeted her, instantly on the alert.

Coming inside, Sarah closed the door behind her, sending all Kelsey's nerves into overdrive. "I know you were shocked to see me at Jarred's parents' last night. I was a little shocked to have Will invite me."

Arranging her pencils next to the leather desk pad, Kelsey said lightly, "Well, Will can certainly make his own decisions."

"Yes." Sarah frowned. "I'm sure you know that he and Danielle are having some problems. She's here right now. Talking to him. Will says they're hammering out a divorce settlement."

"Really." Kelsey was shocked. Though it was clear that Danielle and Will were having serious problems, divorce was such a final step.

"I felt that since you're a part of Bryant Industries now," Sarah went on in her flinty voice, "we should maybe lay some groundwork between us."

"Such as?"

"I'll try to give you a lot of space, and maybe you can do the same for me."

"I think that's very possible," Kelsey responded evenly.

"Good." Sarah still seemed to want to say something more, but the *thump* of Jarred's approaching cane heralded his arrival. Sarah leaned around the doorjamb and observed, "You're really moving around these days."

Jarred appeared in Kelsey's vision. "Not as fast as I'd like to," he told Sarah, who offered a few more words of encouragement, then left. Jarred's brows lifted. "Friends?" he asked Kelsey.

"Bosom buddies."

He chuckled. "She does good work around here," was his only response — not one Kelsey particularly wanted to hear.

"Are you ready to leave?" Kelsey asked, her heart sinking a bit at the thought of returning to the house.

As if reading her mind, Jarred said, "I've got some other plans before going home."

"Oh?"

"I've talked to Marlena Rowden. I'd like to stop by and see her and her husband today. Would you mind driving?"

"Oh. . . . no . . ." Kelsey was flustered. Jarred at the Rowden's was a vision she found difficult to put into focus.

"I just don't want to waste any more time," Jarred said soberly.

"I understand."

Last night's attack was an indication that Jarred's life was still in jeopardy. Waiting around in recovery was being a sitting duck, and he didn't want to do that any longer. Grabbing her coat, Kelsey impulsively kissed her husband. Then she held the door for him as they headed for the elevators.

The Rowdens' home, a modest '60s ranch with white windowpanes in diamond shapes, stood at the end of a long, weed-choked driveway. Signs of neglect were everywhere, and Kelsey realized how little of the money she'd sent them had helped with upkeep. Robert's condition took most of the cash. It was the financial hell of a long-term illness. Marlena had struggled to understand what the insurance company would and wouldn't pay, and Kelsey, upon occasion, had tried to help her. But the bottom line was coverage included major medical and that was about it. A part-time employee who spent most of his duties in caring for Robert's personal hygiene and a bit of physical therapy were outside the benefits. Medications were another issue. It was a mind-boggling mess — more stress than the family could cope with. And it was worsening by the minute.

"Robert Rowden has Parkinson's disease,"

Kelsey said as she parked the car. "I thought I should let you know."

Jarred pushed open his door. When Kelsey came around to assist him, he shook his head. "I can do this on my own. Thanks."

Kelsey led the way to the house. *Jarred is getting remarkably adept with that cane,* she thought, admiring his tenacity and natural athleticism — two qualities that were aiding his swift recovery.

Robert Rowden, on the other hand, was physically deteriorating. Still, he met them at the door and shook Jarred's hand, setting the tone of forgiveness. Kelsey bent down and gave Robert a quick kiss on his cheek. He patted her hand and invited them inside as Marlena came from the kitchen, slightly flushed.

"Hello, Kelsey . . . Mr. Bryant," she said. "It's nice of you to come, but it wasn't really necessary."

"Call me Jarred," he invited, moving toward the couch Marlena had indicated. "I know it's less than nothing, considering you've lost your son, but I'm sorry about Chance."

"Oh, I know. I know. Kelsey said so. And you were hurt, too." She gestured toward the cane. "Please sit down."

"Thank you." Jarred sank onto the couch. Marlena clasped and unclasped her hands in front of him.

"That detective came to see us."

"Newcastle?" Jarred asked.

"He asked us a lot of questions about Chance.

266

I don't think I was very much help." She looked imploringly at Kelsey, who wrapped her arm around Marlena's shoulder.

"I'm sure you were fine," Kelsey soothed.

"He wanted to know all about where Chance lived and who with," Robert added, clearing his throat.

"Have you been there?" Marlena asked Kelsey, who shook her head. "It's not all that far from here. It's . . . run-down," she said a bit lamely, needlessly explaining Chance's state of living.

"That detective called again today," Robert added. "But we were at the pharmacy. Marlena was going to call him back, but then you called." He inclined his head toward Jarred. "We decided to wait until after we'd talked to you before we called him back."

"He makes me feel like a criminal," Marlena confessed.

"You're not a criminal," Kelsey assured her with feeling. "Detective Newcastle's just kind of that way. And anyway, I suspect he might be calling for another reason. . . ." As gently as she could, she explained about the explosion that had torn off a wall of the garage and decimated Jarred's Porsche. Robert and Marlena were shocked. Robert's right hand tremored more violently, a symptom of his disease, while Marlena held a hand to her mouth.

"What is going on?" Marlena asked Kelsey, her voice quavering.

"I wish I knew," Kelsey answered fervently.

"That's one of the reasons we're here. To try to piece together what was going on with Chance right before the plane accident and see if anything's related."

"I'm obviously a target," Jarred said. "But I don't have a clue why. I wanted to talk to you about Chance, if you don't mind. See if there's anything we can come up with that would have to do with this."

"You think this has to do with Chance?" Marlena looked stricken.

"I don't know," Jarred answered truthfully.

Marlena reached over and clasped one of her husband's shaking hands. "I would love to help you if I can," she said, suppressing a shudder. "Would either of you like something to drink? Coffee, a soda, or water?"

"Maybe something stronger?" Robert said with faint humor.

Jarred and Kelsey demurred. They gently probed the Rowden's memories for some clue as to why Chance would have gone to see Jarred, but both Marlena and Robert were as baffled as Jarred and Kelsey. The last few days of Chance's life were still a mystery, and unless Jarred's memory returned, they were likely to remain as such.

"The last time I saw Chance he was here with Connor," Marlena admitted. "About two weeks before the accident."

"Connor's Chance's cousin," Kelsey explained for Jarred's benefit.

Marlena sighed. "Connor stayed with Chance sometimes. He's . . . well . . ." She cleared her throat. "He uses drugs, too, I think. He's kind of erratic."

"Where is he now?" Jarred asked.

The Rowdens shook their heads.

"Maybe he took over Chance's lease on that house Chance was renting," Kelsey suggested.

"Connor wouldn't be able to make the payments. He doesn't work." Robert didn't pull any punches. "He stopped by here looking for money. Well, you know what he's like, Kelsey. If I blame anyone for what happened to Chance, it's him!"

Jarred looked at Kelsey but she shook her head. There was no use stating the obvious to Chance's father. If it helped Robert to believe there was someone to blame other than his son, so be it. And Connor certainly was no model citizen when it came to drug abuse either.

When the conversation dwindled for lack of any further information, Jarred and Kelsey took their leave. Marlena squeezed Kelsey and made her promise to visit again soon, and Robert solemnly shook their hands.

On the way home, Jarred said thoughtfully, "I'd like to talk to Connor."

"Oh, he'd never talk to you. You're too . . . establishment."

"Would he talk to you?"

Kelsey shrugged. "I don't know him really. I think he saw me as an obstacle. I wasn't into using, and he and Chance traveled that path together."

Jarred looked thoughtful. Kelsey mentally shrugged off that avenue of investigation. Jarred's problems were bigger than those of a couple of small-time drug abusers. If she had to bet on it, she'd wager that the issue behind the attacks involved money. Big money. The kind of money generated by corporations or invested by wealthy families. The kind of money held by the Bryants.

Still, it wouldn't hurt to talk to Connor. Mulling that over in her mind, Kelsey wondered if she should try to find Connor on her own and hear what he had to say. He was close to Chance and maybe could offer up some explanation as to why Chance had been with Jarred. He might even be able to shed some light on this whole situation that none of them had ever thought of.

But she would have to visit him without Jarred. She'd been right on that: Connor would never talk to someone like him.

By the time they returned to the house it was raining in earnest, the kind of cold, December precipitation that soaked into the skin, cold and clammy. Kelsey shivered inside her coat as she stopped the car in the driveway and pulled on the emergency brake. In the dark, the plywood-covered garage seemed ominous, a thin shield against those that would try to hurt her husband.

Jarred, however, threw open his door with anticipation.

"I take it we're not spending another night at the Olympic," she observed.

"You don't want to stay here?"

"No, I guess — well . . ."

"Well?"

She didn't trust his mood, which had seemed to rise on the trip back from the Rowdens while hers had deteriorated. "I don't mind."

"Like hell you don't." He grinned, ducking his head against the rain and limping toward the front door. He was certainly in a strange mood. After locking the car, Kelsey scurried along beside him. She twisted her key in the lock and pushed open the door. She flipped on the light and was greeted by a series of barks from Mr. Dog.

"Hello, there, fella," she said, scratching his ears, but he turned to Jarred, tail wagging furiously. "Oh, yeah, show your true colors."

She straightened up, feeling that same uneasiness that had plagued her earlier. She felt silly about it, but maybe she should tell Jarred of her fears.

For his part, Jarred limped through the entry and into his den. "Come here," he called to her. Reluctantly, Kelsey wrapped her arms around her waist and walked to the edge of the room. Jarred stood at his desk. Something glinted in his eyes. Something devilish.

"What are you up to?" she demanded.

"What do you mean?"

"Oh, don't play innocent with me." She

stepped into the room and glanced around, expecting to find some clue to his strange attitude. "You're hiding something, and I have no idea what it is. Is this some game? I've gotta tell you. I'm really not in the mood, considering —" She suddenly swept in a breath, staring out the window. "Oh . . ."

"What?" Jarred asked, pretending to peer into the darkness as if blind.

"Is that *December's Wish*?"

"I believe it is," he admitted.

Soft lights twinkled from the sixty-foot boat moored at their dock. It was Jonathan Bryant's boat. A gift to Nola one Christmas, it was generally docked at a marina on Lake Union since Jonathan and Nola rarely used it. Will sometimes took it out, and Jarred upon occasion, but as far as Kelsey knew, it had never been moored at their Mercer Island home, and it certainly hadn't been here.

"You had it brought here?"

"*Her.* I had *her* brought here. Until this house is completely secure, it doesn't feel right. I know you feel it," he confessed. "But I didn't feel like staying at the hotel any longer, so I had her brought around. That's one of the reasons I wanted to see the Rowdens today: to waste a little more time while she was set up."

Kelsey gazed at him with pure relief and love. "Thank you," she said simply.

"My pleasure, Mrs. Bryant."

She swallowed, feeling a bit overwhelmed.

"How are you going to get down there?"

"With your help," he told her firmly. "So grab some things and let's move on in."

"Aye, aye, Captain."

Thirty minutes later she crossed onto the bridge, hanging tightly on to Jarred's hand even though she was undoubtedly the more stable force. But black water dimpled by rain seemed to boil and threaten all around her, and only when they were safe inside the main cabin did she feel entirely secure.

"What is it?" Jarred asked, sensing her tension.

"What isn't it?" she countered. "Jarred, this is wonderful!"

And it was. Done in shades of tan and navy blue, highlighted by glistening brass fixtures and set off with navy, yellow, and beige plaid drapes and bedspreads, it was a snug bungalow, a sea captain's dream.

"I had it redone a while back," he said.

"Love the interior design," she teased, sinking onto the bed.

"*December's Wish* has been neglected for a long time. I thought we should change that tradition before another holiday season."

"Which is just about upon us," Kelsey observed.

"The Bryant Industries Christmas party is coming right up," he said dryly.

Kelsey grimaced, remembering the last one she attended. "Can't wait."

He laughed and sank down beside her on the bed, staring into her eyes, his own dancing with wicked delight.

Kelsey, suddenly overcome by everything, said shyly, "So what do you want to do first?"

For an answer, he tilted her chin up, grinned like a devil, then kissed her all over her face and neck until she was screaming with laughter.

And after that, he showed her what he wanted to do second. . . .

Chapter Eleven

Drumming his fingers on the receiver in his office, Jarred considered the state of his business, his life, and his marriage. It had been three days since the explosion. Three days of growing certainty that whoever, or whatever, had opened Pandora's box was not about to stop now. Three days of loving his wife and recognizing fiercely that he had to do *something* or face losing everything.

He felt frozen in indecision, not a comfortable state for a man like Jarred. After a few moments, he pushed thoughts of his faceless nemesis aside and concentrated on the one area where he was completely comfortable: business.

Ducking his head into the anteroom outside his door, he told Gwen, "Put me through to Neil Brunswick."

Gwen gazed at him in consternation. "Mr. Brunswick . . . but I thought . . ."

"Neil's expecting the call. Trevor Taggart can't have everything his way," Jarred answered, cutting her off. "It's time I took back control."

Kelsey gathered up her coat, intending to check the town houses one more time and possibly drop in on Tara. Trevor had been remarkably quiet ever since her defection, and truth to tell, she felt a little bad. Oh, sure, she still believed he was working with someone inside Bryant Industries to keep a leg up on the competition, but he wasn't evil incarnate. He'd been good to her.

And he was as good a place to start as any if she wanted to unravel the threads of this mystery.

The door to her office suddenly swung inward. The handle banged into the wall. Startled by the intruder's abruptness, Kelsey clutched her coat close to her chest. "Well, hello," she said, trying to keep her tone neutral. It was no surprise that Sarah was behind this abrupt entrance.

"So are you going to tell him or am I?"

"Pardon?"

"Are you going to tell Jarred that *you* were the one spying on Bryant Industries all these years or am I?"

Kelsey's jaw dropped in surprise. She was still formulating an answer to that shocking declaration when Sarah swept on. "And now you're suddenly on *our* side. Always the heroine, aren't you? I'm sure Jarred doesn't have a clue."

"I don't have a clue either," Kelsey said, meaning it.

"You helped Jarred reacquire the Brunswick piece. I almost admire your ability to switch allegiances so fast. Must make it convenient for you, and at least this time, you're on the winning side."

Kelsey stared. *Trevor's Phase Two!* Jarred had reacquired Phase Two?

Sarah snorted. "Of course, I'm certainly happy Trevor didn't end up with it. That would have been a disaster. Still, it begs the question: How did Jarred do it? With whose help? You certainly sold Taggart out. You know he's been on the phone all morning, screaming for your head."

Kelsey shook the cobwebs out of her head, coming up to speed. "Trevor? He's always screaming for someone's head. So Jarred got the Brunswick property back. Unbelievable!"

"Oh. Right." Sarah nodded. "Like you had nothing to do with it."

"I wish I had."

Discomfited by Kelsey's candor, Sarah hesitated a moment before plowing on. "I guess I should just be thankful that you're finally on our side," she said with ill grace. "But how long is it going to last? Hmm? When should Jarred worry about that knife in his back?"

Kelsey drew a breath. Enough was enough. In a steely voice that matched Sarah's own, she said tersely, "I keep reminding him of that every time your name is mentioned. For all I know, you're the one who's been sending information Trevor's way. The way you talk about him is so familiar, as if he were more than just the name of a Bryant Industries competitor."

With that, Kelsey grabbed her purse and tucked it under one arm. It was several moments before she realized that Sarah had gone utterly still, utterly silent. Gazing at her directly, Kelsey carefully examined Sarah's stony countenance. Her lips were knife-blade thin, her jaw tense. In a tone of discovery, Kelsey said, "It *was* you, wasn't it? Gwen thought it was Will, but it was you!"

"You're delusional. Trying to pass the buck as ever."

"No." Kelsey shook her head, her thoughts tripping wildly. "You're the one who's been passing Trevor information. For money or for kicks — I don't know. Was your interest in Jarred just a means to an end?" When Sarah didn't respond, Kelsey added, "Is that what's going on with Will, too?"

"You don't know anything about it!" Sarah strode out of Kelsey's office in the same whirlwind manner she'd burst in. Kelsey walked at a more sedate pace to Jarred's office, her thoughts churning.

"He's at a meeting," Gwen informed Kelsey when she asked for Jarred. "He took a cab. He told me to tell you that afterward he's going home for a physical therapy session and that he would meet you there."

"Oh. Thanks."

She returned to her office and thought about calling Trevor and facing off with him herself, but as soon as she made the call, she experienced serious regrets. Still, when she heard his voice on the recorder asking her to leave a message, she was a bit disappointed not to reach him herself. She needed to confront him. Staring into space, she lost herself in thoughts of the goals and aspirations of the people who surrounded her. Who, she wondered, might be capable of something as drastic and deadly as murder? Sarah? She might be a spy and a home wrecker, but a murderess?

Deciding she needed to clear her head, Kelsey left the offices, entertaining thoughts of visiting her old offices and the condo and tying up a few loose ends. Was she crazy or had she just rooted out the Bryant Industries spy? And if so, what did that mean about overall company security? Sarah Ackerman resided in the upper echelons of the company hierarchy.

And was Sarah's suspected spying even related to the accidents plaguing Jarred?

Joanna stood at the bedroom doorway, arms folded across her chest, her smile beaming with the results of a job well done. "You've made incredible progress," she told Jarred.

He was struggling for normal breath but he was less fatigued than he had been in the past.

These last days were a glimpse of the future: It wouldn't be long until he was back in prime physical shape.

"Does that mean it's over between us?" Jarred joked, wiping his hot face with a towel.

"I think so. But if I were you, I'd keep working those muscles."

"I will."

"What happened to the garage?"

Jarred inhaled and exhaled slowly. "The case of the exploding Porsche."

Joanna looked confused, but when Jarred didn't offer further comment, she observed, "You weren't hurt obviously."

"Nowhere near it when it went off."

After Joanna left, he headed downstairs, impressed that his muscles protested only slightly. His ankle was certainly a trial, but hey, he was lucky with a capital L and he knew it.

Where was Kelsey?

Mary Hennessy stood at the island range top, fussing over a pan of gently sizzling chicken breasts when Jarred entered the kitchen. Seeing him, she jumped right in without preamble, as if he'd asked a question. "I have pear slices and goat cheese, and those need to be placed atop the sliced chicken, which goes on top of the greens in the refrigerator. The greens are in that yellow bowl. The oven's preheated, and these rolls need to be warmed. Fifteen minutes. Let me write this down for you," she said, grabbing a pencil and scribbling on a notepad.

"You didn't have to cook. We're not even staying here. We're on the boat."

"I know. But I wanted to."

"I think I can remember your instructions."

"Better to have it written down." She didn't look up. "I just want to make sure it's right."

Ever since that moment on the stairs, she'd had serious trouble making eye contact with Jarred. *Probably just as well,* he concluded, grabbing an apple from the wire basket on the granite-topped kitchen island. What was there to add anyway?

Sinking his teeth into the apple, he savored its flavor and watched Mary's ministrations. He realized his watching her made her nervous, but he didn't much care. Life was too short to worry about such things.

Mary left a few moments later and Mr. Dog followed her exit, then came back to Jarred and yelped up at him. Jarred petted the golden retriever's head and watched as Felix sauntered through the solarium toward the utility room. He could hear the sound of scratching as Felix found the litter box. Mr. Dog gave the noise a desultory cock of one ear, but kept his eyes on Jarred.

"So the cat doesn't interest you anymore, huh?" Jarred asked, amused. "You bonded the night of the explosion?"

Mr. Dog answered with a short bark.

Jarred checked his watch. He'd left work early for this last physical therapy session with Joanna, but if Kelsey had finished up on time, she should have been here a good twenty minutes ago. He wanted to talk to her. Was desperate to, actually, because he'd gotten a total chuckle out of Trevor Taggart's reaction to Jarred's own secret dealings with the Brunswick people. It had been so easy, too. When Taggart underhandedly made the deal with them, whatever he'd said had left them feeling uncomfortable and soiled. They'd only accepted because Jarred had stalled so long in signing the papers, and that had been because Jarred had wanted to ferret out whoever was spilling information to Taggart Inc. Jarred's accident had prevented him from putting things right with the Brunswicks, but when his memory returned and his health improved, he phoned Neil Brunswick, scion of the Brunswick family.

Eager to put the development deal back on track, Neil asked Jarred to his offices to put things right. The elder Brunswick had never liked Trevor's corner cutting and finagling, and he himself, had refused to sign. Others' signatures were basically meaningless without Neil's — something Taggart blithely ignored.

When Jarred limped into Neil's rosewood office, Neil greeted him like a long-lost son. "Thanks for waiting," Jarred said as Neil signed the documents with a flourish, sealing the deal once and for all.

"Figured there was a reason you were stalling. Just didn't know what it was." Neil's bushy gray brows lifted in an unspoken question.

"It was a personal standoff with Mr. Taggart," was all Jarred offered.

"I just don't like the man," Neil said with a snort. "I'm good at knowing the worth of a man's character, and that man's got debits where there oughta be credits."

They shook hands and Jarred returned to his office and spent the rest of the morning trying to scare up Trevor on the telephone. When they finally connected, Jarred said simply, "I met with Neil Brunswick this morning. He said he'd never signed the final documents with your company."

"Just a matter of time," Trevor responded, but a note of fear entered his voice.

"That time came and went."

Silent shock greeted Jarred on the other end of the line. Without so much as a good-bye, Taggart severed the connection.

Ten minutes later Will had knocked on his door.

"What did you do to Trevor Taggart?" he asked, amused. "Our legal department's been getting an awful lot of calls."

"I can imagine." Briefly he explained about his morning meeting, finishing by saying, "Taggart's fit to be tied, but that's nothing new." He shrugged. "Still, I failed in my purpose."

"What's that?"

"To find out who's been passing information to him."

"You should have told me what you were doing," Will said. "I could have helped."

Jarred smiled and brushed his words aside. How could he say that he hadn't felt he could trust anyone? How could he do that to Will? "I started that game with Taggart. I wanted to finish it on my own."

"Just don't leave Sarah and me out on everything, okay?" he said lightly.

"You and Sarah make all the decisions when I'm not around. I know that."

"Right," Will said, sounding unsure of how to take Jarred's assessment.

Sarah hadn't confronted him about the reacquisition, and Jarred had been running late and unable to talk things over with Kelsey. But that was okay. Let her hear the news from others and get some impressions. Though he didn't truly agree with Detective Newcastle that someone within Bryant Industries was out to get him, he wasn't fool enough to discount a possible snake in the grass. Someone wanted him out of the way. Permanently. And that someone could well be a Bryant Industries employee.

He was just about to call Kelsey's cell phone when he heard her pull up outside the construction area that was once his garage. For a moment he let his mind wander to the events of the night before, when he'd pulled her warm, willing body close to his and made love to his wife slowly and with exquisite, almost painful, slowness while *December's Wish* rocked ever so gently. God, he was like a schoolboy. But best of all, Kelsey seemed as eager for him as he was for her.

"Hey, there," he said by way of greeting as she walked inside.

"Hey, yourself." She glanced around the kitchen. "Something smells good."

"Mary insisted on coming back today and fixing dinner. I told her we weren't staying here, but she didn't care. I think she just wanted to do something."

Kelsey picked up a fork and tasted the chicken breasts. Glancing up, she looked around the room. "It still feels . . . invaded somehow."

"I know."

Wind had disheveled her hair, turning it into a riot of chestnut waves, which curled up enticingly at the ends. Bright spots of color filled her cheeks and her amber eyes sparkled. He wanted to drag her into his arms and make love to her before doing anything else, but she seemed somewhat distracted.

"I was just going to call to find out what happened to you."

She nodded. "I stopped by the condo just to check it. I was thinking I should maybe rent it or something." She brushed back a curtain of shining waves, a frown marring her brow. "There were a ton of phone calls made to my number, but no messages on the answering machine. I checked Caller ID. The calls were from pay phones around Seattle."

"Like your prank caller?" Jarred didn't like the sound of that.

"Maybe."

"Come here."

She willingly slid into his arms. For a moment, neither of them spoke. Then Kelsey forcibly shook off her mood. "I like this," she admitted.

"Mmm. Me, too." He drank in her scent, recalling the soft white curves of her flesh as she had lain across him in bed.

"What do you think we should do next?" she asked softly.

"Hot sex on the granite island?"

Her shoulders shook with soundless laughter. "Sounds like cold sex to me. Cold, uncomfortable sex."

"Then how about hot sex in a warm bed on Lake Washington?"

"Before dinner? What would Mary say?"

"She's not here, and besides, she already thinks I'm completely unsalvageable in that department," he said, and Kelsey laughed, her spirits lifting.

"Let me put this food together. We can eat right here. And then . . . ?" She left the thought unfinished.

"How about a joint shower?" he suggested. "Or a dip in that god-awful heart-shaped tub together?"

"First things first. Bring down the plates and let's get this together."

In a scene of domestic bliss that nearly boggled Kelsey's mind, Jarred did as he was told, and she put the salads together and pulled the rolls from the oven. Jarred discovered a bottle of chardonnay in the refrigerator and uncorked it. Then they sat down together at the kitchen counter. A first, in all their years of marriage.

As the dishes were put away, Kelsey realized she felt slightly drunk, more from this lovely moment than from the effects of the wine. She wiped off the counter as Jarred loaded the dishwasher; then she threw down the sponge and raced for the stairs. "I'll be waiting for you upstairs!" she sang out.

Jarred chuckled but made no move to race after her since there was no chance in catching her, given his current state. "I'll be right there!" he yelled back. A shower . . . or a bath — he didn't care. Either one sounded fabulous.

Remembering the rather elaborate collection of feminine soaps and shampoos and scented scrubbers and such he'd gathered into a box and shoved high on a shelf in the utility room following Kelsey's departure three years earlier, he decided now was the perfect time to bring out the flowery arsenal. He smiled, just thinking about the evening ahead.

Two steps into the utility room and the grin vanished from his face. His head swam. An overpowering smell assailed him. He felt ill. Pressing the heel of his palm to his forehead, he leaned heavily against the washer.

Drugs.

Something . . . Something. What? His head hurt. Throbbed. What was this?

The hospital. He'd woken up in the hospital and thought about drugs. Chance's drugs. That terrible, pungent odor.

Cat urine.

No, crystal meth.

And memory flooded back so quickly and completely it left him dizzy and weak.

Where in the world was Jarred?

Soaped and drenched with water, Kelsey stood in the shower, wishing now that she'd waited for him before she'd stripped off all her clothes and jumped in. Maybe he couldn't climb the stairs. No, he'd been helping her around the kitchen as if he were nearly as good as new; so that wasn't it.

What had happened to him?

After turning off the taps, she unsnapped the glass door and listened. No sound. The fogged mirrors and steam-filled room attested to the length of her shower. She'd been waiting a good ten minutes.

Wrapping a towel around her torso, she stepped outside the bathroom and into the bedroom suite, then padded across to the hallway door. It was ajar, so she stuck her damp head out and listened again. Nothing.

"Jarred?" she called, fear clutching at her

heart. Then, at the top of the stairs, she call his name again.

She scurried downstairs, her bare feet leaving damp marks on the floor as she returned to the kitchen. Jarred was nowhere to be seen.

A nightmare vision of someone grabbing him, dragging him away, and beating or stabbing him to death filled her mind. Choking with fear, she ran through the solarium toward the boarded-up garage.

And ran right into him.

"Jarred!" she declared in a voice shaking with relief. "Oh, my God. What happened to you? I thought all kinds of terrible things when you didn't answer me. Are you okay?" she asked, realizing his face had lost color.

"It was crystal meth," he said in a slightly dazed tone. "Chance and his friend were making it. It smelled just like that." He pointed through the door of the utility room to the litter box.

"Crystal meth?" She didn't understand.

He pressed a hand to his forehead. "I saw Chance outside MacNaughton's one day," he said carefully, as if the thoughts were being pulled from his brain and he didn't trust them. "He was on the street, and I just walked out to talk to him, but he left. I followed in the Porsche. Not exactly a stealth vehicle, but Chance didn't pay attention. He drove to this house outside Silverlake. His place. And I walked in after him and there it was."

"What?"

"They were making it. God-awful smell. Like . . . cat urine. I smelled it and it just hit me."

Jarred closed his eyes and shuddered.

. . . could be temporary? Couldn't it? Well, couldn't it?

. . . opened his eyes twice and spoke. Didn't know a damn thing. Doctor says it happens sometimes after severe trauma . . .

. . . has to remember . . . has to recover . . . Oh, God, what if he doesn't?

Forget it. We could never be that lucky . . .

"Jarred?" Kelsey asked, panic creeping into her voice.

Whose voices were they?

"Chance was in my office," he said, his voice sounding dim and far away.

"When?"

"That day . . . before the accident . . ."

His dream burst onto the screen of his mind. Chance Rowden standing in his office. His hands shaking. His lips cracked, red, almost bleeding. White faced, hollow eyed, scared. *"You've got big problems of your own, but they're not Kelsey. Never Kelsey. But you can smell the problems, can't you? You can smell them. And they're right here. Right here!"*

"Jarred . . ."

He felt Kelsey's arms encircle him. He hugged her close but he didn't want to open his eyes. He didn't want to wake up and lose this moment, this memory.

"It's eating away at everything you have. Erod-

ing like acid . . . Look around you . . . She's *doing it. . . ."*

A door opening. Chance breaking down. A feeling of intense disgust and anger at this pathetic man whom his wife loved. Chance pushing through the door.

"Wait!"

The airport. The engines' roar. Tension in his chest. Worry. Empty thoughts of the future. "Gotta clear my head. Gotta get things right with Kelsey. . . ."

Chance running across the tarmac. Waving at him. Cutting the engines. Lowering the door. Letting him inside.

"You're scaring me," Kelsey whispered.

"Shh. Wait."

Engines loud. Flying low. Distracted by something. Something with the plane. Chance babbling. "She wants what's hers. She thinks you owe her."

"Kelsey?"

"She thinks you all owe her."

Something wrong. Wrong, wrong, wrong.

Jarred inhaled sharply, his heart in overdrive, sweat breaking out on his skin. Slowly he opened his eyes. Kelsey's were huge, scared.

"He tried to warn me about someone," Jarred said in a voice he didn't recognize as his own. "He tried to warn me about a woman."

Chapter Twelve

"A woman," Detective Newcastle repeated, gazing at Jarred across the length of the mahogany office desk.

A woman, Jarred repeated silently. Since his memory had seen fit to return in a blast yesterday he'd run the jumble of words and images in his head over and over again. He still didn't have the entire mosaic; but there were a helluva lot more tiles now. "That's what Chance said. I can remember that day in my office now as clearly as if it happened ten minutes ago." Jarred shifted in his chair, uncomfortable and somehow anxious. Instead of liberating him, this memory dragged him down in a way he didn't fully understand.

He'd explained very little to Kelsey last night. As soon as the memory took hold, he didn't want to talk about it. Why, he couldn't say, but though she'd pressed him, he'd said he wanted to think about it some more before they discussed it. His reticence had made for an oddly strained night together on the boat — not that he could blame her — and not a lot had been said this morning either. But he *had* needed time to think. He still needed time to think. Calling Newcastle had gone against his gut feeling, but with a plane crash and car explosion behind him, he couldn't play the lone soldier and expect to live for long.

"Chance Rowden came to your office to warn you about a woman," Newcastle repeated. There was a whiff of disbelief to his tone.

"The day after I followed him to his house and walked in on him and his friend cooking up something. I'd been at MacNaughton's and I saw him outside, through the window. I just . . . followed him." Jarred grimaced. How could he explain that that particular night? He'd seen Kelsey's lover and he'd acted on instinct, pure and simple. It hadn't been smart. It hadn't even made sense. But he remembered the feeling of wanting to chase Chance down and throttle him or learn the truth or something maybe even worse. "I wanted to confront him," he said now, "but when I got to the house they were making something. Smelled god-awful."

Newcastle smoothed his palms down his pant legs. "Like cat urine?" Jarred didn't move a muscle, but his surprise must have showed on his face because Newcastle shrugged. "That's how crystal meth's described more often than not."

Jarred nodded.

"I told you we checked out Rowden's place after the plane accident," Newcastle said. "There were signs of all kinds of stuff. Those boys were into it pretty seriously. You don't have any idea who the friend was?" he asked without much hope.

"Connor," Jarred said.

Newcastle blinked, pulled out his pen and paper, and asked, "Who?"

"Chance's parents said his cousin Connor lived with him off and on."

Newcastle scribbled away. "Would you recognize him again?"

Jarred considered. Scruffy. Dirty. Nervous and fidgety. "Yes."

"But no woman was there?"

Jarred shook his head. It had been a squalid, smelly room with an aura of desperation and Jarred had been less than kind. "This is where the money goes?" he'd demanded of Chance, for he'd known then where Kelsey's generous withdrawals had been delivered. And he'd hated Chance for it. And himself for caring.

But Chance had desperately grabbed him by the arm, steering him outside. "No, no, no! You've got it all wrong. You don't know."

Jarred's head had been swimming, the pungent odor filling his senses, making him ill, stoking his fury. All he could think about was that Kelsey loved this wreck of a human being. Loved him enough to give him money — loads of money! *His* money. This drug abuser. While he, Jarred Bryant, had been used. Used for years by a woman who couldn't return his love. And he'd wanted to kill Chance Rowden right there and then, but the man was such a sorry excuse for a human being that Jarred had only felt disgust with a bit of reluctant pity mixed in.

Detective Newcastle dragged Jarred back to the present. "So you followed Rowden and then confronted him."

Jarred nodded grimly. "He said I didn't know anything. He told me to leave. To get out and forget it all. His teeth chattered."

"What happened then?"

"I left." *Went home and drank about half a bottle of single-malt scotch.*

He'd been depressed, sick with misery, facing the end of his marriage.

"And then?"

"I went to work the next day and Chance showed up here. Stood by the door and warned me about my business. He said I had big problems. I didn't even know it, but I had big, big problems and that *she* wanted what was owed her."

Newcastle shifted his weight. "No idea who he meant?"

"None."

There was a pause while the detective flipped through his little notebook. Jarred watched him, aware that Newcastle wasn't really looking at anything he had written down. Eventually Newcastle glanced up and met Jarred's eye. "Mr. Bryant, if something happens to you, who benefits?"

Jarred's skin prickled. "Directly?" When Newcastle nodded, he said succinctly, "My wife."

"At the risk of pointing out the obvious, could the woman Chance Rowden was talking about have been your wife?"

"No."

"They did know each other."

"No," Jarred said again in a warning voice. "Chance said specifically that it wasn't Kelsey. Never Kelsey."

"You trust your wife that much?"

Jarred's jaw tightened. "Yes."

"You trust your *memory* that much?"

Jarred's eyes narrowed at the needling detective. This was really getting under his skin. Kelsey was his Achilles' heel. He knew it, and Newcastle knew it. "Yes. Chance showed up here and he was a wreck. If I had to guess on it, I'd say he wanted to cover his ass. I'd walked in on his drug dealings and he and his friend were spooked. So he came here to reason with me. He wanted to shift focus away from his dirty little secret. Everyone always acted like he was this 'dabbler,' this social drug user, but he was addicted, plain and simple."

"Meth users are paranoiacs. They think everyone's after them. He probably thought you would blow his cover. Tell his friends. Your wife, for example. And then his family."

"Everyone knew already. They just didn't talk about it."

"He might have thought he had them all fooled," Newcastle argued. "People have killed over less. Especially under the influence of drugs."

"But it was Chance who died," Jarred argued, completely aware that the detective had a point, but not liking it at all.

"You were the one supposed to be on that plane, not Rowden."

Silence fell again.

Newcastle breathed heavily. "I want to find this Connor and talk to him. There are others involved."

Jarred nodded. His Porsche was the result of those "others."

"Do you recall anything else?"

He'd called Kelsey into his office and tried to tell her about Chance, but she wouldn't listen. "It's not like I was asked here," she'd spat at him. "I was ordered! So don't go telling me that I need to change my attitude, because I'm not the one who treats people as if they're pawns!"

"Mr. Bryant?"

He wasn't about to explain about that fight with his wife, but the memory lingered inside his mind. With an effort, he said, "I remember Chance getting on the plane. I was leaving and he caught up with me. He wanted to talk. I allowed him on board and then things went wrong. That part's still fuzzy."

"Why did you let him on the plane?"

Because I wanted to know the truth about the money.

Once more Jarred hesitated in telling New-castle all. The man already thought Kelsey was culpable. There was no way Jarred was going to throw suspicion on her. And there was no way he was going to admit that he'd feared she'd subsidized Chance's habit and that he'd be-lieved her love for Rowden was deep enough, compelling enough, to allow her to turn a blind eye to his escalating drug dependency.

And that it damned near killed him inside.

"I thought Rowden could tell me something more," Jarred said after a long moment, and the detective let his evasion go by.

"We're fairly certain the bomb left in your Porsche was put there by a local group of drug traffickers. A warning. It may have been that they didn't like what you saw at Rowden's, and when the plane accident failed to kill you, they wanted to let you know they hadn't forgotten."

"I thought you said the accident and explo-sion were the work of two separate factions."

Newcastle nodded slowly. "I believe they are, but I also believe they're interrelated. Some-thing to do with your business or your blind dis-covery of Rowden's meth lab or something involved with your family — I think there's a tie in."

Jarred frowned. "Chance is dead. I can't tie anyone else to that crime except possibly this Connor."

"He's a person of interest," Newcastle said with a slight nod, as if something had been decided. "Although my guess is he's just a link. These are serious crimes — the kind made when someone has serious friends. And those friends are after you."

"I don't know anything."

"Maybe you do."

After the detective left, Jarred prowled around his office. It was some comfort to realize that this mess appeared to be related more to Chance Rowden's drug abuse than Jarred's business. On the other hand, the idea of a shadowy group of drug traffickers wanting him dead didn't leave him with a strong sense of security.

What do I know? What did I see?

Once again he came up against the frustrating wall of his memory. Nothing more to learn. A blank. The worst of it was he had a feeling he might never know. He'd had his breakthrough already. There was nothing left to learn.

A knock on his door. Will looked around the jamb, saw Jarred, and stepped inside. "I'm leaving. I've got some things that need to be taken care of."

Jarred nodded. Will didn't normally check with him about his minute-by-minute itinerary. "I'll see you later then."

"At the Christmas party."

Jarred sucked in a sharp breath.

"You forgot," Will accused with a smile. "Damn good thing I reminded you, or Nola would have your head!"

Due to Jarred's accident, Nola had planned an intimate Christmas party for himself, his father, Will, Kelsey, Sarah, and Gwen, rather than the usual full-blown company holiday event. Jarred had wanted to forget the whole thing, but Nola wouldn't hear of it. They were to meet at the Olympic for dinner and drinks in a private room this evening.

"I forgot to remind Kelsey. I'm not even sure I told her it was tonight."

"Where is she?"

"Running errands," he said for want of a better explanation. He hadn't talked to her this morning. The atmosphere had been oddly strained between them — a recognition that his memory was returning and with it fears of a strain in their relationship. Or something. He wasn't quite certain, but the tension between them had been palpable. His fault, he realized with an inward grimace.

"Sarah's upset with Kelsey," Will confided. "I guess they had run-in over who's slipping information to Taggart."

"I think Sarah can take the heat," Jarred answered dryly.

Will nodded and pursed his lips. He seemed about to say something, but just lifted a hand in farewell. For a moment Jarred stared after him, lost in thought. Then he tried calling Kelsey on her cell phone but only got her voice mail.

"It's Jarred," he said after the beep. "Call me."

Shrugging his shoulders, he tried without

much success to shake off a feeling of impending doom. Newcastle had left him feeling raw and vulnerable, and he didn't like it one bit.

"Tara?"

Tara glanced up from a file of papers on her desk and broke into a smile. "Kelsey! Hey, there, stranger."

"Hello, yourself." With a feeling of being a bit of a turncoat, Kelsey entered the model unit. A stack of carpet samples lay scattered in the corner, and coffee stains littered the papers across Tara's desk.

Catching her gaze, Tara said, "Nothing much changes, does it?"

"Not really. Apart from my employer, I guess. Is Trevor around?"

"Are you sure you want to see him?" Tara's brows inched skyward.

"No, but we have some unfinished business."

Tara gazed at Kelsey as if she'd lost her mind. Then she shook her head and lifted her arms in surrender. "He's on his way here. If you stick around, you're bound to run right into him, but since Phase Two fell through, he's been an absolute bear. And it doesn't help that your husband's the man who pulled the switch."

"I'm sure I'm tarnished with the same brush."

"Honey, you're guiding the tarnisher's hands."

With that ringing endorsement, Kelsey wandered through the model and outside the grounds while Tara returned to business. She felt unsettled and newly anxious. Since Jarred's "breakthrough" of the night before, she'd been firmly set outside his line of thinking. After these past weeks of being his one and only confidante, she found it disconcerting and downright scary. Her memories of the old Jarred were not that distant.

At work this morning she'd been less than useless. Newcastle's disappearance into Jarred's office bothered her as well, and though she knew from the little Jarred had said that his concerns were over Chance and his ties to the drug underworld, she nevertheless felt as if she were on trial, too.

She had to do something. No more sitting on the sidelines wringing her hands. No more worrying and wondering. Time to be proactive. There were answers to learn, and the plodding pace of the police was just not fast enough for either her or Jarred. And though Jarred had clearly changed tactics and decided to fight this battle without her help, Kelsey would have none of it. There were people she could contact, people she could confront. With that firmly in mind, she'd driven over to Trevor's Phase One to confront him about his "spy." Sarah had accused her of being the culprit, and Kelsey firmly believed Sarah was simply covering her own ass.

And Kelsey intended to learn the truth.

Fifteen minutes later, she saw Trevor puffing along the sidewalk from the parking lot to the model unit. He stopped dead upon seeing her. His breath was visible in the cold, dry air.

"Kelsey," he said with a certain amount of distaste.

"Hello, Trevor."

"What are you doing here?"

"I came to see you."

"To gloat? Your loving husband sold Neil Brunswick a bill of goods and cut me straight out of the deal! But I'm sure you know that already."

"You only got close to that deal because Sarah dropped you inside information."

"What are you talking about?" he demanded, but the hand he ran through his thinning hair trembled.

"She accused me of being the spy. Nice tactic. She wanted Jarred to lose faith in me. And it's a tactic she's used before. Except since I knew I wasn't the culprit, it kind of turned suspicion on her."

"I don't have a clue what you're talking about!"

"She first tried to turn suspicion on Will," Kelsey went on thoughtfully, as if the idea were unfurling as she spoke. "She even got Jarred's secretary to believe it, but now she thinks she's got Will twisted around her little finger and she no longer wants him to be blamed. She wants me blamed, but that isn't working. It's almost a matter of elimination: not Will, not Kelsey, then who? There's only one other person with access to valuable information and an ax to grind."

Trevor glared at her, his face red. "Are you finished?"

"I don't believe Jarred's accident had anything to do with this corporate spying. But Detective Newcastle is interested in anyone who has anything against Jarred. Your name's come up."

"Kelsey!" Trevor was aghast. "I — I can't believe you're saying this!" he sputtered. "Are you . . . accusing me?"

"Of buying information from Sarah. I overheard you on the phone the day I quit."

Trevor staggered backward, stunned by her words. For once in his life he looked beaten, dazed, shrunken by his own small-minded desires and machinations.

"I just came by to let you know I'm on to you and Sarah," Kelsey told him, feeling cold inside at the true realization that her suspicions had all been correct. It was a killer to fully realize that people you liked and once trusted could be so self-centered and incapable of returning real friendship. "Good-bye, Trevor."

It was impossible to return to the office. She didn't want to face anyone involved in Trevor's dirty politics, so after wandering around for several hours, she ended up at McNaughton's late in the afternoon. Mac himself came to her table, regarding her white face with concern and sympathy.

"What's wrong then?" he asked. "You look chilled to the soul."

"Very close to the truth, I'm afraid. I could use some of your Irish stew."

He grinned and patted her shoulder. "Coming right up."

Huddling in her coat, Kelsey stirred the savory meat and vegetables around and felt guilty about having no appetite. Her initial energy to learn the truth had deserted her. Trevor's attitude had zapped her and left her feeling weary and forlorn.

With a mental shake, Kelsey pulled up her determination. What was wrong with her? One small rejection from her husband and she was a basket case? Was her belief in his love for her, his change of attitude, so weak that she couldn't abide even the smallest of rejections?

She paid for the stew, apologized for her feeble attempt to do it justice, and left the restaurant under Mac's worried gaze. She had no clear idea of how to proceed, so she drove to her condo, picked up the newspapers stacked outside her door, and walked inside. It was cold as the Alaskan tundra but she didn't touch the heat. Instead she went to the phone, intending to stop her newspaper subscription.

A list of numbers on Caller ID. Nothing on the answering machine. She checked the numbers and felt a shiver dance down her spine. Just like before. Pay phones. From all over the city.

For a moment she stared into space, thinking. A glimmer of an idea formed. Thinking hard, she called the *Seattle Times*, cut off her subscription, then locked the condo and headed for her rental car. Ten minutes later she was driving northward with one hand, digging inside her purse with the other. Grabbing the cell phone she rarely used except for emergencies, she checked the battery and was relieved it had some life left. She saw a message had been received on her voice mail and punched in her security code to hear Jarred's authoritative voice order, "Call me." For a moment she debated doing just that, but she wasn't ready to talk to him just yet. She sensed they were turning a new corner — one she'd somehow been avoiding, the one where the old Jarred and the new Jarred collided. His distance had bothered her this morning, shades of the old Jarred. No, she wouldn't call him just yet.

But she could leave a message on *his* cell phone, which he only turned on when he was outside the office.

"Jarred, it's Kelsey. I talked to Trevor. Looks like Sarah's the one who's been selling him information. I don't know what you want to do with this information, but there it is. I've got some errands to do and I'll meet you at home later. 'Bye."

She almost added, *I love you*, but she just couldn't force herself to do it somehow. *You're such a fragile goose!* she berated herself, but she didn't call back. Instead she called the Rowdens. Glancing up at the darkening sky, she realized distantly how threatening it appeared. Night was falling fast and it looked, and felt, like snow was on its way.

"Hello?" a faint voice sounded through a wall of static.

"Marlena? It's Kelsey," she yelled above the loud fuzz. Her particular cell phone was several years old and had never been all that clear. Marlena's voice was damn near unintelligible right now. One of these days Kelsey was going to have to upgrade. "Are you there?"

"Oh, Kelsey! Yes! Are you on —" The rest of what she said was lost.

"Marlena? Marlena? I'm heading your way," she called. "Can you hear me?"

"Yes!" Some more static. " — to Silverlake?"

"Yes. To Silverlake. I'll see you soon. Okay? 'Bye."

She tried to plug in her phone, realized she didn't have the charger with her, muttered obscenities at herself, then headed into traffic. Before she left Seattle, she stopped at her bank and withdrew several thousand dollars in cash. Back in her car she sat still for several long moments, her gloved hands on the wheel. *What the hell am I doing?* she asked herself. She'd made a habit of giving cash to the Rowdens rather than depositing it into their account. She'd done it to hide her philanthropy from her husband, whom she'd considered ruthless, cruel, and autocratic. She hadn't wanted him to know that she subsidized Chance's parents, and that if they, in turn, subsidized Chance, then so be it. This was her life. The Rowdens were her family. And Jarred was no part of it.

But what a subversive thing to do! How could she demand trust when she couldn't completely give it herself? How was she ever going to make this marriage work if she couldn't be truthful and open? With bitter self-discovery, she realized she couldn't blame Jarred — the old Jarred — for the destruction of their love without swallowing a little of the blame herself.

But she couldn't fix everything at this very moment. In the back of her head she had a plan to help Jarred, and before he withdrew further and the situation turned into a serious problem, she wanted to take care of a few things. With that in mind, she turned the car toward Silverlake and hoped that pending snowfall would wait a while.

Grabbing his coat from the back of the chair, Jarred put another call in to Kelsey's cell. She never had the damn thing on, but she'd been missing all afternoon. He'd left messages at the house, but she still hadn't called him back. Now he regretted his reticence to talk this morning, and he wished he'd told her he needed a ride home when she'd asked. He'd said he'd take a taxi, mainly to keep his independence. He'd just wanted to . . . think. Alone. The Christmas party had completely slipped his mind, and now he was frustrated, needing to head home and change and find his missing wife.

"If this was the old days, I'd think she was

with Chance," he growled under his breath.

The outer halls were empty. Everyone had either left early or closeted themselves in their offices. Gwen, however, was at her desk, swallowing a pill with a glass of water.

"You okay?" Jarred asked.

"Headache." She smiled wanly. "Just a little one. I'll make it to dinner."

"Good. Could you call me a taxi? I'm about to leave."

"Oh, Kelsey's not here?"

"No."

Gwen nodded, picked up the phone, and called Jarred a cab. He mouthed a thank-you and headed for the elevator. Crossing the lobby to the revolving door, he glanced at a low gray sky. He was overcome by an urge to find his wife, take her back to the boat, and make love to her all night, blowing off the dinner party to the horror of his mother. He grinned at the image.

The yellow taxi pulled up the curb. Throughout the journey home he entertained himself with visions of his beautiful wife in the shadow of the boat's gas fire or her face contorted in the throes of ecstasy.

With these thoughts for company, he wasn't going to be able to get out of the car without embarrassing himself!

To Kelsey's surprise, Marlena was waiting on the front steps, rubbing her hands together and huffing out clouds of white vapor in the frigid air. She shifted her weight from one foot to the other.

"How long have you been standing outside?" Kelsey asked, greeting her with a hug and a kiss. "My goodness. Since I called?"

"Yes," Marlena answered, and her tone sent a dagger of fear into Kelsey's heart.

"What's wrong?"

"Oh, Kelsey! Connor was here!"

"Here?"

"He's in terrible shape. Terrible, terrible shape. I know you didn't know him well, but he used to be the sweetest boy. Just like Chance . . ." She broke off on a sob. "He wanted money. He *demanded* money. And he wanted me to talk to you."

"I brought money," said Kelsey.

Marlena waved her away and shook with tears. "It's not right. It's not . . . fair. You can't always be there. You have a husband who loves you, Kelsey. You're part of his family now."

"I'm still part of yours!" Kelsey said fiercely. "Now stop worrying. Please. Come on. Let's go in and get warm."

But Marlena wouldn't let Kelsey guide her to the door. "I don't want to upset Robert. It was hard when Connor showed up. He wanted me to give him your phone number and address. He was raving! I've never been so scared."

Shivers slid down Kelsey's spine. "Has he been trying to reach me?"

"I . . . I think so."

"Do you think he could be at Chance's old place? I know the police checked it and it was deserted, but would he go back?"

Again she shook her head helplessly. "I don't know. I don't know where else he would go. He's not the same. He's really not the same as he was. He waved his arms around like a madman, ranting about conspiracies! He threatened my husband . . ." Now she totally broke down, collapsing within the shelter of Kelsey's arms.

Kelsey soothed Marlena, but her mind was speeding ahead, ticking off thoughts, forming conclusions. Connor. And Chance. And chemical dependency. And drug lords.

And an explosion that had torn out their garage.

"Marlena, let me give you this money." Kelsey drew back for a moment and handed the woman she considered her mother a thick packet. "It's for you and Robert."

"No, I know how this has been a secret from Jarred, and I won't let you."

"Marlena, from now on, I'm not going to keep it secret. The money will be directly deposited."

"I can't take it!"

"You must. We've been through this before. I don't need it. Use it. I've got to get going."

"But you just got here!"

"I want to confront Connor. I need to hear what he has to say. I just wanted to stop by and give you this."

"Oh, Kelsey, it's too dangerous! Call the police!"

"And tell them what?"

"I don't know. I don't know."

"I'm going to say hi to Robert and then head out. Oh, God." Kelsey inhaled suddenly.

"What?" Marlena gazed at her through anxious eyes.

"Nothing. Nothing. I just remembered where I'm supposed to be tonight. Never mind. I might just be a little late."

"You're supposed to be with Jarred?"

"Yes. It's a Christmas thing. Listen. Don't worry, okay? I've got everything under control. Oh, and I need some directions to Chance's."

"Chance's? Kelsey, no! Connor . . . Connor — he's not . . ." she sputtered.

"Shh," Kelsey said, turning her gently around. "Come on. Let's go inside and get warm. Everything's going to be fine."

Jarred stood apart from the group, wondering if he could down the champagne like water and order two more glasses fast. He wore black. Not a tux, for he'd demanded this event be less formal. Actually, he'd demanded that it be scratched entirely but Nola was a wall. They'd argued on the telephone about it twice, and only when Nola nearly broke down and said she wanted Jarred to speak to Jonathan and find out what was eating the man alive did he agree to attend.

And then only when Kelsey had agreed to be

312

with him. Which she wasn't. In fact, he had no idea on God's green earth where she was.

"Another, sir?" The white-coated waiter was their personal host in this upstairs room. Normally it was reserved for a crowd of thirty or more. Tonight, its wreathed windows and twinkling bright lights played for less than ten.

A glittering gold bow adorned the champagne glass Jarred selected at the same moment he handed over his empty. "Don't get too far away," he warned the man, who nodded and turned to Nola and his father.

Jonathan sat in a gold-and-white-striped satin chair. Refusing champagne, he asked for scotch. Father and son exchanged a look — Jarred over the top of his champagne, Jonathan as he reached for the glass of amber liquid.

"Hey, bro," Will exhaled heavily and signaled the waiter. "Pretty dead party, huh?"

"Better than last year."

"How do you figure?" Will asked.

Because I wasn't with Kelsey. Jarred glanced at his brother as he finished off his champagne. Will held a glass in his hand, but his face was red, his color high. He appeared drunk already, given the strange look in his eyes and the slight tremble of his fingers. He saluted Jarred with his drink and knocked it back, half laughing.

"My God, life is strange, isn't it?" he said, not waiting for an answer. "You think you've got it figured out. Then something happens *bam!* right between the eyes." He signaled the waiter again,

313

more impatiently. "What does it take to get a real drink around here?" he muttered irritably.

"You have to ask for it."

"Yeah? Well, it'll be another millennium before he comes back."

Lost in his own thoughts, Jarred hadn't paid much attention to Will or anyone else for that matter. Now he examined his younger half brother carefully. "What's eating you?"

"Have you noticed how frail Dad is? Like he's dying right in front of our eyes."

"I've noticed."

"What do you think that means?"

"I don't know. Nola's worried."

"Nola did right by me," Will said, picking his words carefully. "But she wasn't any kind of mother to me — or to you either. She's not made that way. Don't you think a mother should be more nurturing?"

"Are you drunk?" Jarred demanded.

"If only that were the case," he said, and then he sighed as if the weight of the world were upon him. The waiter appeared at that moment and Will requested a scotch for both him and Jarred. Then he pulled four glasses off the tray, handing two to Jarred and keeping two for himself. "I think it's time I was."

Sarah, in a red velvet dress that hugged her curves and made her appear a trifle less mannish, seemed to pick up on Will's strange vibes. She hurried toward them. Her long, determined stride ruined the effect of the dress, reminding

Jarred how tough and single-minded she could be. For a fraction of a second he felt a bit of Kelsey's aversion to the woman.

Where was Kelsey?

"Oops," Will said. "Here she comes. Before she gets here, one more word of warning: Beware the female of the species. They get what they want."

Jarred stared at his brother's flushed face. "Are you trying to tell me something?"

"Kelsey hasn't been completely truthful about that money. Find out about it before you lay everything at her feet. I don't want you to lose, Jarred. You know, I just want you to be there. Always."

"You are drunk," he concluded.

"Will?" Sarah's sharp eyes examined him from head to toe.

"I was just telling big bro here about the good news," Will said with a sweep of his arm that sent scotch sloshing over the edges of his glass. He took a moment to down the rest of his drink, handed Sarah the empty glass, then downed the second.

Sarah looked startled. She turned to Jarred, momentarily speechless. Something weird was going on, and the hairs on the back of Jarred's neck lifted instinctively.

"Go ahead," Will urged her, his arm jerking in Jarred's direction. "You know I'm behind you a hundred percent. Danielle and I are finished. She's . . . gone. The future's so bright I gotta wear shades." With that, he doubled over in soundless laughter.

Jarred looked to Sarah. She opened her mouth, closed it, thought for a moment, then said simply, "I'm pregnant."

The cell phone fuzzed and beeped, and Kelsey damn near threw it out the window. Useless piece of garbage. She was late, late, late, and she was bound to be later. She'd miscalculated, believed she could continue on her quest and still make it to dinner in time. But she hadn't counted on the weather, which had changed from rain to sleet and ice, and she'd crept the last few miles in a sweat of tension, wondering which way to turn. She was almost to Chance's — and Connor's, she hoped — and there was no way to make it to the dinner now. Should she continue? Or, should she turn back now and at least try to find an area to call Jarred and explain.

A moment of intense decision passed while the car nosed forward, its tires feeling loose and slippery against the surface of the asphalt. She was so close, and she wanted answers.

And that would be a better Christmas present for Jarred than anything else she could come up with.

Her decision made, she tried phoning his cell phone once again, and once again she got static.

". . . was going to invite more people from work, but with your accident and the company in such a state of flux, and then Jonathan . . ." Nola's voice trailed off. She glanced toward the door. She'd just come in from one cigarette and was debating if she could sneak another.

Jarred sat in silence. Sarah's words reverberated inside his head. His scotch sat on the table between himself and Nola. The others were being seated for dinner. His father was out of earshot, at the far end of the table, flanked by Will and Sarah.

"He's seen a doctor?" Jarred asked.

"Well, of course!"

"That wasn't meant as a criticism," Jarred said a trifle brusquely.

Nola swallowed and looked away, across the room toward the gold filigree wallpaper and arched windows. "It's snowing," she said flatly.

Jarred's gaze followed hers. Slick roads. Icy conditions. Inexperienced drivers. He hoped Kelsey had her cell phone with her. He'd left a couple of more messages, but she hadn't called back. His own cell phone was inside the pocket of his overcoat. He'd shoved it there as he'd left the house, intending to use it to call her again if need be. Now he excused himself, went in search of his coat, then pulled the phone from the pocket.

With a start he realized he had a message. He'd never dreamed she'd call his cell phone because he hadn't really used it since the accident. He hadn't even looked at it earlier to see if she'd called him. Gnashing his teeth, he quickly retrieved the message.

". . . looks like Sarah's the one who's been selling him information. I don't know what you want to do with this information, but there it is. I've got some errands to do, and I'll meet you at home later. 'Bye."

Jarred blinked, replayed the message, then replayed it again. He called the house, but Kelsey didn't pick up. Trying her cell phone only granted him another turn with the answering machine. Turning off his phone, he thought hard. Her information about Sarah didn't really surprise him. After tonight, he could believe anything. But she'd said she would meet him at home and she wasn't there.

"What's the matter?" Nola asked when he returned to the table.

"I can't reach Kelsey."

"I'm sure she's fine. She's probably on her way but got slowed down by road conditions. It's your father you need to concentrate on. He's wasting away."

Jarred flicked a glance down the table toward Jonathan.

"Don't tell me you haven't noticed. "Nola reached for the rope of pearls at her throat, unconsciously twisting them with anxious fingers. "It's as if he's the one who collapsed after your plane crash. Only he hasn't recovered. I thought when he saw how well you were doing it would help. But he's been sitting in the corner all night, every night, nursing a drink. But he doesn't get drunk. That would be bad enough. No, this is something else, and he's become embarrassingly devout at the same time."

Jarred wanted to argue with her. Her terminology assaulted his sense of fair play. But her words resonated with a truth that couldn't be ignored, and so he simply nodded.

"You've heard him talk about the Lord. When did that happen? He's never been one to so much as mention God or spirituality or anything even mildly religious. It's like he's someone else!" she hissed in a worried voice, darting sharp looks around the table to check if anyone were listening. "What is happening? I swear, it's as if he's had some epiphany and it's impossible to talk to him about anything else these days. Do you think he could have had a slight stroke?"

Her words pricked Jarred's own fears. "Maybe you should just ask him what's going on."

"*You* ask him," Nola said, plucking at his arm, and Jarred inwardly groaned, realized he was being manipulated by his mother once again. "Try, darling. Please," she entreated.

Jarred swallowed his watered-down drink and silently prayed that Kelsey was all right and would magically appear ASAP.

Jonathan sat shriveled and distant at the end of the table, his eyes focused outside the windows to the white flakes dipping and weaving beyond. Wind whistled and rattled the windowpanes. A ghostly sound.

"If Kelsey doesn't show up soon I'm leaving," Jarred told Nola. "But I'll talk to Dad first."

"After dinner. Please." She fervently clutched Jarred's arm. "Just let's get through this meal."

Shallow-bottomed bowls of white china were placed atop shimmering silver charger plates. Jarred picked up his spoon, swallowed two delicious mouthfuls, put the spoon down, and listened to the clock tick inside his head. The meal was excruciating. Though everyone had asked him where Kelsey was, he had no idea, and he'd been forced to admit that fact, bringing a faint smile to Sarah's lips.

I'm going to fire her, he thought inconsequentially.

Then his cell phone jingled and he snatched it. "Hello? Hello?" The clicking and fuzz on the other end nearly drove him mad. But if it was Kelsey, at least she was able to call. That was something.

"Kelsey? I can't hear you. If you can hear me, we're at the Olympic having dinner. Kelsey?"

Crackle. Fuzz. Then, faintly, she said, "Jarred?"

Her voice! He was overjoyed. "Kelsey!"

Nothing. The connection was lost. He tried to call her back, but there was no answer. Still, she was all right. At least she sounded that way. "I'll talk to Dad," he told Nola and scraped back his chair.

The weather was blasted. Snow now. And lots of it. The kind of tiny flakes that accumulated so quickly that wipers whipping to and fro at warp speed could scarcely fling it away.

"Damn," Kelsey muttered softly, seeing a faint sign ahead. A narrow white road sign on a rickety post. It pointed east toward Marsden Road. The way to Chance's.

Trying automatic dial once again, she slowly herded her car eastward, wishing mightily and futilely for her Explorer. But there was no connection to Jarred. Her cell was dead.

Urgency felt like a bomb inside Jarred, slowly counting down. He'd moved to sit near his father. Then he had been forced to wait to engage him in conversation since Jonathan Bryant seemed focused on his drink and dessert, using them both as a means to stall Jarred's obvious desire to talk. It was all Jarred could do to make himself wait. Restless, he moved apart from the group while his father dawdled, surveying them, yet lost in his own thoughts. Will had failed in his quest for alcoholic oblivion, and he now sat beside Sarah, neither of them saying a lot. Gwen drank coffee, holding the cup in both hands as if desiring its warmth. Nola had searched for a place to smoke outside of the area, and Jonathan now sat by himself at the head of the table, looking tired and worn. As he laid down his dessert fork, Jarred scooted a chair up beside him. Jonathan picked up his drink and refused to meet Jarred's eye.

"I haven't had a chance to talk to you," Jarred said, undaunted.

Jonathan smiled wanly. "Hello, son," he said.

"What's wrong?"

Jonathan sighed and took a swallow of his own watery scotch. "Where's your mother gone off to? Indulging that nasty habit of hers?"

"She asked me to come talk to you."

Jonathan rubbed shaking fingers over his chin. He glanced down the table but only Gwen remained, and her gaze was fixed firmly on Sarah and Will, who were lost in their own world.

"Are you ill?" Jarred asked. "Let me rephrase that: Have you been diagnosed as having some particular disease or syndrome since you're obviously ill. Nola just wants to know what's wrong."

"My life's in God's hands. Where it should be."

"Well, that might be so," Jarred said slowly, picking his way through this minefield of evasions, "but it doesn't explain why you suddenly feel that way. This new faith of yours may be commendable, but it's not like you. In my experience, that means something's happened to change your outlook."

"I've trusted in the Lord," Jonathan said, but his words were a faint whisper.

Jarred leaned forward. "What is it, Dad?" For a moment Jonathan didn't move; then he slowly placed his hands over his face and sat in abject silence. Fear's icy fingers tightened Jarred's chest. "What?" Jarred demanded.

Lowering his hands, Jonathan gazed at his son. "Are you all right, Jarred?" he asked. "Are you?"

"Me? Yes. What do you mean? I've got most of my memory back."

"Physically, are you all right?"

"Yes." His father's intensity baffled Jarred since he was so obviously better. Even the scars were fading, and his left ankle could move without serious pain or impairment. If people weren't told, they would not believe he'd survived a plane crash.

"Then I'm all right, too," was his father's troubling answer.

"Excuse me. Am I interrupting?"

Sarah's voice jarred Jarred and he shot her an angry glance.

"Not at all," Jonathan said a trifle stiffly.

Jarred's brows lifted at this obvious coolness. Maybe Nola wasn't the only one objecting to Sarah's interest in Will. The shit was really going to hit the fan when Sarah's pregnancy came to light.

"Could I talk to you a moment, Jarred?" Sarah asked.

"Not now," Jarred said tersely.

"Go, son," Jonathan urged. "I prayed you would recover. You had to. You had to remember."

Jarred's memory jarred. "I had to recover," he repeated.

"And you did. By God's will."

"Jarred," Sarah said insistently.

Jarred eyed his father thoughtfully. Scraping back his chair, he followed Sarah to the other side of the room, where Will was standing, looking tense. "More good news?" Jarred asked dryly.

"We're worried about Kelsey. Where is she?" Sarah demanded. "What's she doing?"

"If I knew, I'd tell you."

"Would you?" Will questioned. He gave his brother a searching look. "I wasn't kidding when I said you should check out those large withdrawals of money."

Jarred was irked that Will would bring that up in front of Sarah.

"Have the withdrawals stopped since Chance's death?" Sarah asked as if it were any of her business at all.

"I'm not certain."

"You haven't looked, have you?" Will nodded. "Jarred . . ." Unlike Sarah, Will sounded genuinely regretful. "You've had me check Kelsey's account in the past, so I just checked it again. I'm worried about you, and the company. I want you to be sure she's on the level."

"Thanks." Jarred was ironic.

"There's an envelope on your desk at work. The last year and a half of statements on her account. Check it over and see what you think."

"Or you could just ask her," Sarah pointed out.

Jarred's fury at both Sarah and Will knew no bounds. He nodded curtly and walked away. His mood, not particularly pleasant to begin with, had definitely deteriorated. He knew he shouldn't be so deathly angry at them; their suspicions were unfounded and couldn't hurt Kelsey. And he had reason to be more suspicious of them than his wife these days!

At that moment, Nola reentered the room. "I talked to him," Jarred said as he passed by his mother into the hallway.

"Wait! Jarred! Where are you going?" She grabbed his arm. "The streets are an absolute mess. Are you driving?"

"I'll call a cab," he said, aware with an uneasy pricking that Kelsey had been slated to drive him home.

"What did your father say? Anything?"

"He said I had to recover. He wanted me to remember."

"What does that mean?" Nola asked, baffled and a little angry at Jarred's cryptic comments.

"I don't know. He doesn't offer information." He paused. "I think he thinks he's dying."

Nola clutched Jarred's arm a bit more desperately. "What's happening to him?"

Jarred shook his head.

To call the house ramshackle was to elevate its appearance. Through the slapping wipers, she could see a dark, squalid shape with a drooping porch and a disreputable car parked beside a pile of jumbled firewood.

But there was a light in the back. A sliver of illumination stabbing through a tiny slit between dark curtains.

Kelsey had already cut her own lights and coasted up the end of the drive blindly until she'd suddenly approached a clearing. Then there was the house. Marlena's description had been too accurate, and Kelsey had been to enough of Chance's previous residences to understand how this was very likely his last home.

She didn't know what she was doing. She didn't know what she hoped to find. But Connor had wanted to talk to her, and she was fairly certain he was her mysterious caller. Whatever that meant, she couldn't guess. But it was all tied into Chance and Jarred and the airplane crash, and she sensed that drugs were heavily involved as well.

Not a tidy package.

Huddling within her coat, Kelsey cut the engine and pocketed her keys. Stepping into the dark night, she listened to the howl of the wind and felt the sting of snow on her face. Fir trees waved ominously. For a moment she almost got back in her car and turned around. Instead, she walked forward, head bent, calling herself every name for this insipid charge for the truth.

At the door to the house, she hesitated again. A smell reached her nostrils, a strong, god-awful odor.

Cat urine.

Jarred's description. She strained to look through the tiny slit between the curtains.

And suddenly there was a body beside her in the night. A man. Standing at the corner of the house. A scream rose in her throat.

"Who the hell are you?" he demanded, scared.

Shivering, she swallowed. "Connor?"

He jerked, shocked, ready for flight.

"It's Kelsey."

A pause. A moment while her name penetrated his brain. Then he moved swiftly toward her, and Kelsey stepped back on the drooping porch, her hip slamming into a railing that damn near gave way. She flailed and Connor grabbed her arms.

"Kelsey? *Kelsey?*"

"Ye-yes," she chattered.

He gazed at her through narrowed eyes, then shoved open the front door. "Come inside," he said, holding open the door to an untidy room that looked godforsaken and smelled even worse. "You need to help me. Chance said you would."

Chapter Thirteen

If there was ever a sorrier place to live, Kelsey couldn't imagine it. The walls of this once respectable home curved inward, as if swelling from some mysterious edema, and the plaster was chipped, broken, and missing in so many places it looked as if it were some kind of cockeyed design. Still, it wasn't the house itself that hit Kelsey so hard. It was the sense of hopelessness and desperation and the complete lack of dignity or even morality that permeated her surroundings and lent an air of something she couldn't quite name that threatened way down in her soul. Bottles and utensils and pans with blackened bottoms and vials and crystals and scattered pills were strewn around the kitchen. In the living room, a couch and a ripped ottoman sat atop a worn gray carpet smeared with mud and dotted with cigarette burns. A bare lightbulb threw out a yellow halo from a floor lamp A moth frantically circled the bulb. The stench was overpowering. Cat urine wasn't bad enough to describe it. Kelsey's stomach revolted and she fought back a rising taste of bile. Sweat coalesced on her forehead and upper lip. She was simply sick to her deepest heart.

"C'mere," Connor said, waving her into the kitchen. He wore overalls stained with glops of stuff that Kelsey wouldn't even try to categorize. His hair was longish, untamed, uncut, and uncared for. His beard scraggled into the semblance of a goatee. He reeked of desperation.

Kelsey swallowed and managed a quick glance around. There was artillery everywhere. Not one or two guns: artillery. Shotguns and rifles stood against the wall like sentinels. A nest of grenades lay ominously next to a back door whose lock rattled in the rising wind.

"Those loaded?" she asked, indicating the guns with a nod of her head. Stupid question. This wasn't the kind of place where precautions were valued.

"Huh? Oh, yeah."

The odor was like a blanket, thick and enveloping. She fought back another wave of nausea. She could see that Connor had been busy playing do-it-yourself pharmacist. She didn't know much about crystal methamphetamine but she had no doubt that was what she was looking at. And she suspected it was just part of the overall illegal and recreational drug inventory Connor possessed.

Sadness overtook her. This is what Chance had become? This is how far it had spiraled downward? The realization boggled her mind and made her understand his tears and regrets that night before his death. He'd told her how sorry he was. She saw it now. Saw what it meant.

"Don't stand over there," Connor ordered. "Come here!"

"Connor, I just came to find out about Chance," she said, refusing to budge from the center of the room.

He was in the kitchen area, hovering by a plate of crystals. "You know how hard it is to get all this stuff?" he complained, sweeping a hand over the counter. "The ingredients? Hard! And they make it harder all the time. Those fucking bastards, you know."

Kelsey inhaled a shaking breath and told herself to keep a cool head. She wanted to panic. It was so frightening in this room. "You were living here with Chance, before the plane accident?"

"Chance." His face twisted up and she was certain he was going to cry. "It's not my fault! It's those fucking bastards, you know. You know the ones. That suit that showed up here. The fucking bastard you married!" With that, he broke into wailing sobs and clutched his stomach.

Kelsey stayed absolutely still. "If you mean Jarred, he was in the plane, too."

"I know. *I know!* But Chance wasn't supposed to be there! Chance wasn't supposed to be there! Goddamn it. *Get over here!*"

His frantic words persuaded Kelsey to stay put. Calm. Careful. Cool. Collected. "Connor, I don't think —"

He moved toward her snake quick, grabbing her arm, hauling her close. Kelsey instinctively pulled back, stumbled, stood still. Too much weaponry on every wall. Too many drugs. This man wasn't rational. He was something else. Someone dangerous and unpredictable.

She should never have come alone. She should have let Jarred meet him. She'd been a fool to think that she could accomplish something more because she'd been Chance's friend. She needed Jarred's protection far more than she needed Connor's trust — and that trust was a joke anyway. The man didn't know how to trust. All he knew was the power of intoxicants and woe to anyone who stood in his way.

"It wasn't my fault," Connor hissed through stained teeth. "Chance wasn't supposed to be there! You hear me? *He wasn't supposed to be there!*"

"You're right. You're right," Kelsey agreed, her ears ringing from Connor's shouting. "He just showed up at the plane. Jarred didn't expect him."

"What was he doing there?" Connor wailed. "I wouldn't have hurt him. I didn't mean for it to happen like that."

Kelsey's heart nearly stopped. "Of course you didn't," she said, her mind racing. "It was an accident."

"He shouldn't have come here! He was going to the police. Did he tell you that? He was going to the police! And we couldn't have that. And *they* would kill us to keep our mouths shut. They've said so. So when *he* walked in here in a suit like the fucking president of the U.S. of A., goddamn it, Chance went crazy. Just crazy. He was scared. *We* were scared, so we had to do something. Chance had to see him."

Kelsey struggled to follow. "Chance went to see Jarred at his office," she said diffidently.

Connor shook her so hard her teeth rattled. "Aren't you listening? He had to! He had to talk to him. Stop him. And Chance knew things — things he wouldn't even tell me because he knew people. He knew those people at that company — your company. You know," he muttered, frustrated.

Kelsey swallowed. "Bryant Industries?"

"Your suit husband wouldn't listen to Chance. Chance came back and he broke down. Something had to be done, y'know. Y'know?"

Kelsey nodded. Chance had come to see her that night. He'd broken down with her, too. She was afraid to say anything to Connor though, afraid to cut off this tide of confession. She was . . . afraid of him.

"He said you would help me. He told me you would. If I ever needed it. But damn it . . ." He swore violently for several seconds, his grip tightening with each sharp curse. Kelsey held her breath. "He didn't tell me he was going to the plane." He gulped back a sob. "I knew which plane it was. I knew. But Chance wasn't supposed to be there!"

. . . about five foot ten, thin, dark, unkempt hair, blue jeans . . . Detective Newcastle's description floated into her consciousness, too apt to ignore. "You were at the hangar that day," she breathed softly.

"It's that bastard's fault," he said with a catch in his voice. "If he hadn't come here, none of this would've happened and Chance would still be alive."

Connor wouldn't have done a professional job. But he could easily sabotage a plane. Thoughts jumped into her brain, bright and blinding with truth. He hadn't meant to kill Chance.

But he'd meant to kill Jarred.

Licking her dry lips, Kelsey said, "Jarred wouldn't have turned you in."

"Bullshit! He would've. He was going to. He told Chance he was!"

"He told him?"

"At his office! Aren't you fucking listening?" He shook her so hard that her neck ached from the movement of her head. "At his office! I had to do something. I had to. Had to . . ." Now he was seriously sobbing, clutching Kelsey as if she were his sole source of support.

Frantically she sought for some way out. She had to get away. He was too volatile, too emotionally fragile and unstable. Anything could happen. He was a self-professed murderer, for

God's sake! Anything could happen!

The only answer was to run, but Connor's grip was too intense. Her eyes darted around the room. Guns . . . grenades . . . squalor . . . Helpless, she prayed for some kind of divine inspiration.

"Can you help me?" he whispered tremulously in her ear. "Can you?"

"Yes." Kelsey projected as much confidence as she could into the single word. "Yes. I can help you."

Getting a taxi was damn near impossible. The streets were full of cars and slush and cold snow that wisped and blinded and stung. The vehicles moved like molasses in January, clogging the lanes, their headlights blaring sightlessly, windshield wipers flapping. Jarred stood in the front of the hotel and listened in frustration as various bellmen and the main taxi hailer argued and fought with the few taxis that had made their way around the hazards of stopped cars.

A nightmare.

"Jarred."

He turned around and found Nola beside him, shivering. She pulled out a pack of cigarettes, tried three times to extract one with terribly shaking fingers, then inhaled a quivering sob and simply closed her eyes. Jarred took the pack from her, shook out a cigarette, and handed it to her.

"Thank you," she whispered. She withdrew a

gold lighter from her pocket and held it out to him. He lit her cigarette without a word. "What else did your father say?" she asked. "Anything?"

"No."

"It's since your accident. This has happened since your accident."

Jarred didn't respond.

"He's coming out with Will and Sarah's help. I wanted to catch up with you first."

Jarred waited. Snow filtered onto Nola's perfect hairdo and melted in dark spots. She looked so fragile he wanted to bundle her up and take her back inside, but she smoked as if her life depended on it.

"It's no secret he's had other women," Nola said. "I mean, Will's a perfect example."

Jarred turned away. He didn't want to hear this now. No, it was no secret his father had been a philanderer, but it was one generally kept in the closet. And right now he would have preferred it to remain that way. All he could think about was Kelsey and this god-awful weather.

"And now he's going to be a father," she added bitterly, her face screwing up into a look of complete despair.

"So he told you," Jarred said.

"*She* told me," Nola hissed. "Smug as a Persian cat! Darling, you've got to do something! Where *is* Kelsey? Please don't tell me you're having problems again. Not now!"

"Everything's fine," Jarred clipped out.

"Then get on with it for God's sake! What are you waiting for? Your brother to inherit every-thing? I couldn't bear it. You're *my* son. And I married *your* father. You, and you alone, deserve to inherit. It's everything you've worked for and everything I've worked for as well! If you're working through problems in your marriage, just hurry it up for heaven's sake. Make a baby. Stop them all from taking it away from us!"

She gazed up at Jarred. Tears starred her lashes. Cold little bits of ice.

"Nola," he murmured, unsettled to hear her desires expressed so blatantly.

"*Nola!* I'm your mother," she gasped, truly shocked.

"If Will has a baby, and I don't, he inherits the cash equivalent of what was in my grandfather's will on the day Hugh died. But the bulk of Bryant Industries is what's been made since that time and that's outside Hugh's stipulation. Most of the assets have been purchased with money netted since Dad and I took over."

"Since you took over," Nola corrected. "Your father was no shepherd."

"The point is, at the very least, Will deserves what Hugh brought to the table. It was the seed, not the harvest. If this baby ensures he gets that, great. But let me tell you, even without an heir, I'd make sure Will gets an equivalent share. Dad knows this. I'm surprised you don't."

"I know who deserves what," she snapped as the door opened and Will and Sarah helped Jonathan navigate the slippery steps. "And Will doesn't deserve anything!" she added harshly.

"Taxi!" Jarred called, flagging a yellow cab that had miraculously made its way through the snarled traffic. He tried to put Nola into the cab, but she refused. "Will's taking us back in his four-wheel drive. It's right up the street. But I wanted to talk to you. I wanted an understanding between us."

"I understand perfectly what you're saying," he bit out. "I just don't agree with it."

"Jarred, Sarah's not the first woman who's tried to steal a piece of our company. She won't be the last. Pay attention. It's what women do."

Jarred slid into the cab. Nola ground out her cigarette into the amassing snow and stepped carefully toward Jonathan, Sarah, and Will. Grimly, Jarred watched as Will hurried away from the group, heading in search of the car. Jonathan leaned on his cane, gazing at Jarred's cab.

"Wait a sec," Jarred said to the cabbie.

"Man, I've got people stranded. This is a bitch of a night."

"I'll give you a hundred dollar tip to wait for me," Jarred said in a voice like steel.

One swift look to see if Jarred could make good on his word and the cabbie broke into a wide-mouthed grin. "Let 'em freeze to death!"

So much for being a good samaritan, Jarred thought ironically as he hurried to his father's side. "The cab's taking me home. We'll drop you off on the way," he said.

"Will and I are taking them home," Sarah said imperatively.

"Not anymore."

With that, Jarred helped his mother and father into the cab, sketched a salute good-bye to Sarah, then hopped in beside his parents. Once more he tried to raise Kelsey on her cell phone; once more he failed.

"What is it?" Jonathan asked in a frail voice.

"I'm trying to reach Kelsey."

"Where is she?" Nola asked, frowning.

Jarred shook his head. They crept through the streets of Seattle. Tire ruts cut to the pavement through the snow, but that didn't mean cars weren't slipping and sliding. Seattleites were lousy in this stuff. It was a fact of living in the Northwest. About once a year snow fell. Not the fluffy dry stuff they got in Colorado, but the wet, icy, miserable precipitation that looked so beautiful coming down and then turned the highways into a devilish nightmare.

Jarred checked the list of numbers he'd programmed into his cell phone and placed another call. "Who're you phoning now?" Nola wanted to know.

"The Rowdens," he answered tersely.

Connor had a gun in his hand. Held loosely. Waving it about. Sometimes he actually pointed it at Kelsey, but generally that was only to make a point.

On the chipped range top of the stove, one of the burners was in use. Kelsey could see its angry, hot, red spiral, as a small pan rattled furiously atop it. Nearby and moving throughout the house, the air was thick and strong, as if a heavy fog had crept into the room unannounced. The odor seemed to have a physical presence. Kelsey automatically narrowed her lashes to protect her eyes. She was sweating from heat and fear.

Connor frowned at the pan. He'd edged away from her momentarily to check on its contents. She'd taken the opportunity to inch backward as soon as he released his grip. Thoughts of escape filled her brain as the smell pervaded her senses. But he read her mind. Quick as lightning, he grabbed her arm, his eyes dark and staring. She stood frozen to the spot.

"You said you'd help! But you're movin' away. Aren't ya?"

Kelsey didn't respond.

"Aren't ya?" he screamed at her. "What are you thinking? You thinking I did it *on purpose?*"

The handgun was dark. A deep gray hue that shone ominously in the uncertain light. She could neither see nor think beyond the gun. An ironic inner voice reminded her that she'd charged into this quest to save the day. But even in this detached state she could feel the thundering of her heart. She was scared. She'd blundered into this because she hadn't really listened to Detective Newcastle's warnings about drug addicts.

"I'm not moving," she whispered.

He nodded, quieter. A respite from the yelling. But she wouldn't fool herself into thinking it was because he trusted her. That he might actually listen to her. No good thinking that way. A sure plan to get herself killed. Better to just wait and see.

"Y'know what this is?" he asked, jerking his head to the concoction on the dirty countertop.

"I — no, I don't know."

"Come on. You're a smart girl. Chance said you were smart."

She licked her lips. Her lids were lowered. She couldn't quite meet his eyes. Better to be passive anyway. "Crystal methamphetamine."

"Aaahhh . . ." He was pleased, as if she'd finally said something he wanted to hear. "Chance and me — we dabbled, y'know."

Dabbled. Yes, she knew. Maybe that was every addict's answer. Dabbled. A confession that was more denial than acceptance of responsibility. Her mouth was so dry she could scarcely swallow.

"Why'd he have to come here? Huh? Y'know? Why'd he come here?"

"You mean . . . Jarred?"

"He's a fuckin' suit, man. A suit! And he was pissed off at Chance. I could tell he wanted to kill him. Why? *Why?*"

Kelsey cleared her throat. "I think he ran into Chance by accident and followed him here," she whispered softly.

"But *why?*" Kelsey wasn't sure how to respond, so she remained silent. A mistake. Connor drew closer to her. She flicked him an anxious look. He stared at her through bloodshot eyes. Lifeless eyes. Drug numbed. " 'Cause of you? 'Cause he wanted Chance to leave his little wifey alone?"

Don't argue. Don't move. Don't breathe! "I think so."

He nodded. "I can understand that, y'know. I really can. A man hates sharing a good woman. Or any woman for that matter. But women . . ." He lifted his free hand, pointing at her with his index finger until the tip of it brushed her nose. Kelsey flinched. He snorted and did it again. And again. The inadvertent shudder that passed through her slim frame was like a flame to his senses. He yanked her close, squeezing his body against hers, pushing her backward until she stumbled. "Hold on, hold on," he said, almost crooning.

Revulsion filled her, nearly replacing her fear. Her heel slammed up against the wall and he pressed his body against her. The cold metal of the gun lay against her hip, resting.

Wild thoughts gripped her. Knee to the groin. Up, slam, jerk. But the barrel of the gun was sliding toward her stomach. Would he really kill her? she wondered vaguely. A wave of nausea swamped her. Of course he would. He'd tried to kill Jarred.

When he kissed her, she simply shut her mind

down. But mutiny simmered deep in the pit of her stomach. She would rather die than be raped, she decided rather calmly, surprising herself. She was Jarred Bryant's wife, and by God, no other man had a right to touch her and she sure as hell didn't want to be touched by them!

Suddenly he grabbed her hair. "It's not my fault!" he yelled again. "It's her fault!"

"Her fault?" Kelsey repeated.

"*His* fault! His fault!" he corrected himself, then seemed confused. "You don't want to know about her," he whispered. "Chance was really worried about her. She really caused a lot of problems, and she's not gonna stop."

"Who?" Kelsey asked, confused.

"Women."

A woman. Jarred's words. A woman. From his deepest memory. Yet the danger was Connor. He'd confessed to killing Chance while meaning to kill Jarred. But . . . but . . . "The Porsche," she said. "There was a bomb."

"No, no, no. You can't think that. I didn't do it! That was them!"

"No one thinks you did it," Kelsey said truthfully.

"Yes, yes! That was the men in the black car. They're tricky friends."

Kelsey's lungs felt poisoned. Too much fog. "Whose friends? Yours?"

"Everybody's friends if you want 'em to be."

"Her friends?" Kelsey guessed.

"She's not what she seems," he whispered. "She's a chameleon. That's what Chance said."

"Sarah?" Kelsey guessed, gulping. She was the link. The only person besides herself who knew Chance well.

Connor shook his head. "You just don't like her," he accused.

"Well, then, what do you mean?"

Then he was kissing her all over, running his hands down her body. Kelsey froze. The pan rattled and jumped. Swearing, Connor pulled back. "Gotta take care of that," he said dully, swiping at a limp strand of hair that flopped in his eyes. "Dangerous." He took a step away. Then another. He reached a hand toward the stove. Toward the knobs.

. . . volatile chemicals . . .

Kelsey blinked, lifting a hand to shield her eyes. How many newspaper items had she seen about meth labs exploding? Lots. But in her mind's eye it had been a lab — a concrete basement with stainless steel sink and Erlenmeyer flasks and calculating drug dealers who doubled as white-coated scientists. In reality it was scummy, dirty, desperate rooms filled with desperate people. That was what exploded.

Oh, God . . .

She turned. One step. Another. Running. Smacking against the floor lamp. Stumbling. Cursing. Crying. The gun. He could shoot her.

"Hey!" he yelled.

Hand on the doorknob. Twisting. Yanking.

343

Praying with the fervency of the truly devout.

A blast of frigid air. Swirl of snow.

Click.

Sound of a trigger.

She leaped onto the porch, her shoes skidding. Knee banged the rail. Fear. No pain. Stumbled down the stairs. Fell into the snow. Cold. Biting. Teeth chattering madly.

Get up. Run. Get up. Get up!

He was screaming. Cursing. Spitting foul, furious words.

Kelsey pulled a foot beneath her. Jumped. Slipped. Zigzagged toward the car, which seemed miles away. Impossible. Impossible.

Three steps. Fall. Cheek in snow. No air. Breathe. *Breathe!* Up again, stumbling. Stumbling. Closer . . . closer . . .

And then the world exploded around her. A tremendous hot blast. Sizzling. Deafening. Knocking her down into three inches of snow. Raining her with fiery bits of wood. Shrapnel.

Something struck her leg. Burned. She crawled. Crawled. Crawled.

Reached the car. Touched the tire. Dared to look back.

An inferno raged into the snowy black sky where the house had been moments before.

"Please come in," Nola begged. "Your father is so ill and I need your help."

The taxi waited. Its engine humming, wipers rhythmically flicking snow into little heaps on either side of the windshield.

"I'll make sure you're settled, but I've got to go," Jarred clipped out.

"Jarred, aren't you making too much of this? She went to see Chance's cousin. It's not a life-or-death situation!"

Jarred neither had the energy nor inclination to explain. Marlena Rowden had bubbled over with worry and relief to hear Jarred's voice. She passed the information willingly. She was scared for Kelsey. Worried that Connor was unstable and possibly even criminal. She said Kelsey wanted to help him.

Wanted to help him? God! The best thing she could possibly do was stay out of it! Jarred didn't know what the hell was going on, but he damn well wanted his wife to be out of the line of fire. What in God's name was she thinking?

"She thinks they're all a bunch of recreational users," Jarred said through his teeth, fear coming out in fury. "But they're addicts."

"Jarred?" Jonathan called from his study.

"See?" Nola hissed in his ear. She tugged on his sleeve, pulling him away from the open front door.

"Wait!" Jarred called, pointing at the taxi driver, who shrugged.

Jonathan sat in his favorite chair, his pallor gray, his face lined into small crevasses, his body limp and exhausted. He looked a thousand years old. His deterioration even since dinner was un-nerving.

Jarred paused, shocked. "Dad."

"I never wanted anything to happen to you. Or to Kelsey. Nothing, nothing to my family. I just couldn't be faithful. I'm weak, son. And I've asked God to forgive me."

"I've got to go find Kelsey. I'm going to ask Nola to call your personal physician."

"No. You've got to listen to me. It's my fault. I made bad choices. And it's a crime. A crime!" He coughed harshly, his whole body shaking.

"Jarred," Nola said in true fear, coming up behind him.

"Call an ambulance," Jarred told her. "Now."

"But the weather. You don't think . . ." She stared up at him, pinch faced, slack jawed. So unlike herself that Jarred put his arm around her and hugged her close.

"Just do it," he whispered.

Instantly she marshaled her strength. Drawing herself up she strode from the room.

"Dad, Kelsey's in trouble. She's trying to solve this thing, and so she went to see Chance's cousin, who is a meth addict and worse, according to Marlena Rowden. I've got to find her. Now." He paused, hoping this had sunk in but his father showed no reaction to the news. "I'm going to leave you, but the ambulance will be here soon."

"I was never ambitious, Jarred. I should have been . . . more. . . ."

"Dad." He glanced toward the short hallway that led to the open front door. Nola's voice, clipped and artificially courageous, sounded from the kitchen.

"There's nothing to solve," he said wearily. "It's just a love affair with drugs for all of them. It ruins every life it touches."

This was so peculiar for his father to say that Jarred stared down at Jonathan's bent head. But his father's eyes were closed, paper-thin lids over eyes that moved beneath their shade. He stretched and closed his hands in agitation.

Touching his father's shoulder in silent fare-well, Jarred turned swiftly, already thinking of the taxi driver and the conditions of the road and the length of highway they had to travel.

"Good-bye, son. Don't think too harshly of me. I've always loved you and Will."

Another time, another moment, he would have stopped and demanded some kind of explanation for these serious and maudlin remarks. But not tonight.

To the cabbie, he said tersely, "Silverlake. When we get there, I'll guide you."

"Silverlake! Man, I don't feel like it."

"I will give you a thousand dollars," he said through clenched teeth. "Can you make it through this snow?"

"I got chains in the back," the cabbie said, throwing the vehicle into gear.

Kelsey's mind floated. A liquid journey that had neither a beginning nor an end. Time rocked gently back and forth, like a gentle wave.

She was cold. Frozen, perhaps. Snow iced her cheek, burning it a bit. Garish yellow flames and whooshing heat poured from what had been a small ranch-style house.

She lay beside the sedan, one hand stretched toward a tire as if reaching it would somehow help her. How long had it been? Hours . . . lifetimes . . . eons . . . ? Except the sky was still black and snow fell in wispy flurries that were reluctantly lessening. She was covered with the stuff. A half inch on her outstretched arm.

Moving hurt. Something stuck in her leg. With an effort she lifted her head and saw the jagged chunk of glass sticking up like a small sail from her thigh. She sank down again, frightened beyond thought. She was going to die like this. From the elements.

Bullshit. Kelsey raised her head once more, pulled herself onto one elbow, gazed more fully at the thick shard of glass currently skewering her. Clasping it gingerly, for it was sharp and deadly on all edges, she tugged. Pain sizzled up her leg. She gasped. Tears sprang to her eyes, surprisingly hot.

A long moment passed. She focused more thoroughly on the rage of burning timbers and dancing flames. Connor was dead. No question. But his death brought no grief as Chance's had. She felt . . . relief.

It's over, she thought, sinking back onto the cold soil. The snow had melted beneath the warmth of her body.

Sirens. Distant. Nearing? She opened her ears but couldn't tell.

More time. Numbing, numbing time. Was she delirious? Probably. She should be.

Her eyes flew open in sudden wakefulness. The fire raged on in a sinister beauty of orange and yellow and black. Smoke swept by in curtains tossed asunder by the wind, which had picked up and threw pulsing orange cinders and white snow and gray ashes all around. Glancing at the glass shard, she calmly grabbed it with some force and yanked with all her strength. A gasp. More tears. A long wail of agony but the thing was out. It cut the pad of her thumb. A small wound that welled with black blood. She glanced at her thigh. Another black stain against her jeans.

Mental inventory of physical self. Everything seemed in working order. With an effort, she dragged herself to the car, scrabbling for a hold with hands working at fifty percent power. The cold had done that. Pulling up her left knee, she got her uninjured leg beneath her. Moments later, she dragged her injured one to the same position.

One, two, three . . .

With a mighty heave she was on her feet, swaying, clutching the side of the car, pressing herself against it like a lover. *It's over. It's over now.*

More sirens. Warbling way far away. Someone had seen the flames. Had to have. This place was remote, but not that remote.

She waited, quivering, unable to stop. Her teeth chattered in tiny little convulsive movements.

"Come on, come on," she whispered, encouraging those faraway sounds of rescue.

And suddenly sweeping headlights. A car. Turning onto the long driveway, bumping along the lane cautiously. Chained up, she realized. It came into view and she would have cheered if she could have. Instead she waited.

They come in black cars.

For a heart-stopping moment she feared the worst. Then she was both surprised and delighted to realize it was a yellow taxi approaching. It stopped at the edge of the clearing. A man climbed out. The sirens increased. Coming, coming . . .

The man wore a black overcoat and black slacks. Dressed for dinner or a party — a Christmas party. Her heart lurched painfully. "Jarred . . . ?"

Had she spoken aloud? He didn't appear to hear her. His face was stark, ghostlike, staring at the raging inferno behind her. He looked . . . devastated. Shattered beyond bearing.

"Jarred!"

"God, no," he whispered, his gaze dropping to her rental. He stumbled toward it, collapsed on the other side.

"Jarred!" she managed to cry, louder.

He raised his head. "Kelsey?" Sharp. Terse. Disbelieving.

For the life of her she couldn't raise another syllable. She clutched the vehicle and prayed for the strength to keep from falling.

But then it didn't matter. He was there. Beside her. Covering her cold body with the warmth of his own. "My God, Kelsey," he murmured brokenly.

"It's over," she said. "It's over."

He held her close and buried her face against his chest as the wailing sirens rounded the corner of the lane and the fire trucks blasted past the taxi and into the clearing in a carnival of lights and noise and jumping men.

Chapter Fourteen

High tea at the British Tearoom in downtown Seattle was an event that required planning, the right apparel, and a hearty appetite, for it started with a fruit cup and crumpets swimming in maple syrup, moved through tiny watercress and salmon sandwiches, whose crusts had been cut off, slipped into petit fours too rich to even count, while scones and Devonshire cream made certain the calorie count reached an all-time high.

Kelsey sat across from her husband and thought quite clearly, *I am going to throw up.*

Since this would definitely not do in the tearoom, she excused herself, hurried to the nearest bathroom and promptly lost most of what she'd just tucked down with relish. Rinsing her mouth out with water, she considered her still jumping stomach and thought just as clearly, *I'm pregnant!*

She gazed at her face. Ghastly green. Except

352

for the smile brimming on her pale lips. But the next moment reality crashed on her and she wondered just how well her husband was going to take the news this time.

She braced herself against the sink basin for several moments, encountering the curious and concerned stare of another patron. "Are you all right?" the woman asked.

"Perfect."

This answer was met with a lifted brow and a rather frosty look, as if Kelsey were some kind of criminal in not admitting that she looked like hell and was undoubtedly suffering from some strange and incurable malady. But Kelsey's realization was too new, too fragile to share.

And the first person she should share it with was Jarred.

But she couldn't go back there yet. Too much had happened, and this was just one more event to heave upon an already teetering pile.

From the moment Jarred found her outside the blazing house, held her, and allowed her to collapse against him, life had taken a sharp left from the path it had been on. Several complications had happened in succession: *bam, bam, bam!* Jarred believed Kelsey's theory that Sarah had sold Trevor secrets and planned to fire her. But there were complications. Complication one: Sarah was pregnant with Will's baby and Will planned to marry Sarah. Complication two: Gwen had been sick for several weeks and Meghan, Sarah and Will's gofer, had been forced to fill in. Complication three: Sarah, sensing her head was on the block, had worked like the proverbial Trojan these past few weeks, and though Jarred still sought to rid himself of her, since there was really no proof of her criminality, everything was on hold.

Complication four: Jonathan Bryant was at Bryant Park Hospital, languishing and slowly declining from a slow shutdown of his entire system.

And now, complication five: Kelsey herself was pregnant, and though she knew her husband loved her, she hadn't forgotten how cold he'd been on this particular issue in the past.

Slowly, she walked back toward their table. They'd taken half the day off to indulge Kelsey's desire for high tea. It was a frivolous thing, but Jarred seemed to want to fulfill her every wish these days. The night Connor died Jarred had rushed Kelsey to a hospital emergency room, where her wound had been examined, cleaned, and stitched. She'd worried more about inhaling all those fumes, but as time progressed and no serious side effects emerged, she counted herself lucky that nothing worse had happened to her. But Jarred was a maniac about her safety now. Though he didn't say it, her sudden decision to play detective (which had nearly cost her her life) was reason to keep his wife out of harm's way forever. He'd become her constant companion, and even with the replacement of a current model Porsche and the repair and return of her Explorer, Kelsey found Jarred her driver and "bodyguard" at all times.

Not that she minded. Well, as long as he didn't take it too far, and as the weeks had progressed and they'd moved back into the house and survived the beauty and craziness of the Christmas season, he'd relaxed a bit. When she had examined her ghastly pallor in the mirror, she studied the sapphire earrings he'd had specially made to match his grandmother's sapphire pendant. The tiny circle of diamonds surrounding each stone winked at her as if sharing her secret happiness.

Secret happiness . . .

She and Jarred had made love with the joy and interest and abandonment of new lovers, and Kelsey couldn't help pinching herself now and again because nothing — nothing — this good in life ever lasted long. She had to remind herself to just enjoy it, and every time there was a little hitch, she half expected the whole thing to come tumbling down. But it hadn't. At least not yet.

Detective Newcastle had given his usual postmortem after Connor's meth lab exploded. "Bound to happen eventually. Lucky you weren't seriously hurt, Mrs. Bryant." A bit of censure there. A reminder that amateur detectives were always a nuisance to themselves and others. "From what you've said, he confessed to the accidental murder of Chance Rowden. That explains a lot of things, although it's unlikely he set off the bomb in your husband's car."

"He mentioned the people in black cars."

Newcastle nodded. "Dealers. Someone a few rungs up the ladder. The kind of muscle Connor would turn to if he needed a job done."

"He seemed scared of them," Kelsey said, remembering.

"He'd be a fool not to be," was the succinct response.

They discussed Connor backward and forward, needing to clear their minds of all the events that had led to this moment. Exhaustion was all that kept them from talking through the night as they lay cuddled within each other's arms to the gentle rocking of *December's Wish.*

But now, as Kelsey approached their table, her husband rose from his chair. "Are you all right?" Jarred asked, taking in his wife's alarming pallor.

"I'm just not feeling one hundred percent," she sidestepped. Was now the time to tell him? No. Better to wait for the corresponding blood test. Maybe she could get away this afternoon and make certain.

A baby!

If she was correct, and she was sure she was, then Sarah's pregnancy would be a moot point. Jarred's thirty-ninth birthday was on Friday. Maybe she should wait and tell him then. How would he feel to know that his inheritance was safe? Would he be pleased, or would he think she'd somehow diabolically planned this? On this one issue Jarred was completely unpredictable.

"What are you thinking about?" he asked, noticing her smile.

"Sarah's pregnancy," Kelsey admitted.

"Really?" His brows lifted. "You looked a lot happier than I would have expected to be thinking about her."

"You know I asked Connor about her that night."

"About Sarah?" Jarred's brows drew together.

"Connor mentioned a woman. And that's what you said," she reminded him. "The night you remembered about the meth lab. So I asked him if he meant Sarah. He said no."

"I can't really let her go without a reason," Jarred said, "and I don't have enough proof yet that she's "

"Oh, I know. I'm not saying that. If she and Will are really getting married, then I think you should wait. Though I'm sure she did it, I don't know why she would sell out to Trevor anyway. For the money?" Kelsey shook her head. "You're right. There's not enough proof."

Jarred poured them both another cup of tea. Kelsey gingerly sipped from her cup and Jarred asked, "You think Chance and Connor suspected she might be selling secrets to Taggart?"

"She knew Chance from college. She probably knew of Connor, kind of like I did." She shrugged. "It's just that she's the only woman who seems to have a connection to Chance, although I must admit, Chance seemed kind of over-the-top passionate about whoever was eroding your company and this kind of sneaky bit of thievery doesn't seem to qualify. I mean, not in Chance's world. But isn't that the word he used? Eroding?"

Jarred nodded. His cell phone rang and he pulled it from his pocket, frowning at it. Since Kelsey's accident he'd kept it close. "Hello?"

Kelsey shrugged off the Sarah dilemma and let her mind wander down happy avenues as she envisioned baby clothes and baby paraphernalia and baby smiles.

Jarred listened in silence for several moments. Then he said, "I'll be right there," and hung up. Kelsey gazed at him in question. "That was Nola. My father wants to talk to me." He paused. "They don't think he'll make it through the night."

"Oh, Jarred!" She felt sick once more, guilty over her own happy thoughts.

"He wants to talk to me alone. Do you mind if I drop you at the office on the way? I'll pick you up later."

"That's fine."

Twenty minutes later Kelsey climbed into the elevator and pushed the button for the Bryant Industries floor. She hoped they were wrong about Jonathan. It seemed a cruel irony after his son's miraculous recovery.

Meghan was at Gwen's desk, talking on the phone. She waved Kelsey over and whispered,

"It's Gwen. She'll be back tomorrow."

"Good." At least complication two seemed to be getting satisfactorily resolved. "I'm going into Jarred's office for a few moments," she told Meghan, who nodded and returned to her conversation.

Why she wanted to be in his office she really couldn't say. But knowing he was with his failing father made her feel sad and unable to get her head into work. She ran her fingers along his desk, faintly amused at the accumulated dust. Jarred hadn't spent a ton of time in his office lately either. Too many outside influences and decisions to be made.

Kelsey sat down in Jarred's chair and thought about Jonathan. The man had deteriorated in front of everyone's eyes. It was as baffling as much as it was impossible to correct.

"A death of the soul" had been the unsolicited diagnosis from an elderly woman at the hospital one afternoon when Kelsey had stopped by to see him. It had shaken Kelsey and haunted Jarred when she mentioned it to him. Maybe she should go to the hospital herself, get a blood test, learn the truth, and tell him if her belief proved positive. Maybe it would help Jonathan.

She frowned. But learning about Sarah's pregnancy and Will's impending fatherhood hadn't. Jonathan had shrunken almost visibly at the news. Kelsey could empathize. When she'd learned about Sarah, her teeth had actually started to chatter. No one, with the possible exception of Sarah herself, seemed particularly excited by the possibility. Even Will was quiet and acted as if he were facing a very unwelcome destiny. He'd told Danielle the news and she'd answered that it was just one more reason to hurry with their divorce.

There was a small stack of papers shoved between Jarred's phone and a desktop organizer. She fiddled with one end of the papers and considered calling Jarred on his cell phone. But what would she say?

Hi, honey! I'm pregnant. I was just wondering: Should I tell your dad and hope that it makes him feel better?

Kelsey snorted. No, there was nothing to do but wait for Jarred to call her. This was a terrible time for him. Still, if Jonathan were truly that ill, wouldn't he want to know?

The paper slipped from its spot and unfolded in front of her. She realized it was a bank statement and was about to slide it back when she spotted her name. Frowning, she examined the paper thoroughly. It wasn't merely a bank statement. It was a reckoning of every cent she'd spent over the last several years. Even the years when she and Jarred had lived apart.

He'd been monitoring her cash withdrawals all along.

Nola sat outside her husband's hospital room, tense and distracted. She scarcely noticed when Jarred arrived but she squeezed his hand when he clasped her cold one. "Mother," he said gently. "It seems to be what he wishes."

"Will's going to have a baby. That's all your father knows."

Patting her shoulder, Jarred inhaled a deep breath and entered the shadowy room, where his father lay on the hospital bed. They'd gone full circle since Jarred's plane crash. Now it was his father who lay white faced and ill against the bedding.

"Jarred," Jonathan said in a whispery voice.

"I'm here." He pulled up a stool and sat next to the bed.

"I want to talk to you."

"I know," Jarred assured him. When his father's hand reached for him, Jarred clasped it within both of his. He could feel time ticking away and he was almost angry at his father for giving up.

"I've never talked to you about Will's mother Janice. She died a couple of years ago, you know. She wanted me to divorce your mother and marry her."

Jarred's memory of her dropping Will off on the porch was still quite vivid. "Did she give you Will because you refused her?"

"Yes." Jonathan coughed several times, hard. "First she held him for ransom. Then she dumped him. It's never been fair and I've had to make peace with God."

"I know," Jarred inserted quickly, hoping his father would keep on track for a while longer before he got sidetracked by his religious fervency.

"Will's suffered for it. I know that. My fault. You've suffered, too."

"I'm fine."

"The plane crash nearly killed you." His voice was nearly inaudible.

"But that wasn't your fault," Jarred reminded him. "And the man behind it is dead now too. It's over."

"No. It is my fault."

"Dad . . ."

"You've got to be careful. Watchful. God can only do so many miracles."

"Stop that." Jarred was firm. "You are letting guilt eat you alive and it's not even deserved! Don't do this. Get well. Stop letting it take you."

"No, no." He hesitated for a moment, breathing with difficulty. "She wanted you dead," he suddenly said. "She wanted to get back at me. She's always wanted too much. Thought it was her right because she and I had a long-term affair."

"It doesn't matter," Jarred said quickly, not liking the turn of this conversation at all. "She's gone now, too. Don't dwell on it so much."

"She's not gone."

"I thought you just said she died."

"*Janice* died," Jonathan stressed.

Jarred shook his head in bafflement. "Then who are you talking about?"

Jonathan stared at his son. Tears gathered at

the corners of his eyes. "I thought you heard us talking." He inhaled a shaky breath and closed his eyes. "I thought you heard us talking. . . ."

"Dad?" Jarred leaned forward, alarmed, but his father was still breathing sketchily. Jonathan's head lolled sideways. Jarred touched his wrist. The pulse was there. Thready and weak. "Don't go," he whispered.

He waited, but Jonathan was lost in a deep sleep. Swallowing, Jarred regarded him somberly. Had to recover . . . had to remember . . .

. . . *lost all memory. Doesn't speak . . .*

. . . could be temporary? Couldn't it? Well, couldn't it?

. . . opened his eyes twice and spoke. Didn't know a damn thing. Doctor says it happens sometimes after severe trauma . . .

And Jonathan's voice again. ". . . has to remember . . . has to recover . . . Oh, God, what if he doesn't?"

And a woman's voice. Familiar. But hard and full of rage. "Forget it. We could never be that lucky."

Jarred snapped back to attention. "Dad," he whispered urgently, fighting the desire to shake his father awake. "Dad!"

But Jonathan Bryant's slackened jaw told of deep sleep or worse. Jarred froze for the space of two heartbeats, then stabbed the call button several times. He jumped to his feet. A woman. A woman who wanted him dead.

He stumbled outside, where Nola still sat. She

gazed at him blankly. "What is it? What is it?" The look on his face must have spoken volumes, for she suddenly cried, "Oh, my God!" and clambered to her feet, hurrying to her husband's side as a nurse raced to answer his page.

"My father," he said to her, and that was all that was necessary to bring in the doctors and nurses.

The cab dropped Kelsey in front of the hospital in the midst of another drenching rain. Cold as sin and slanted by the wind, it peppered her face and soaked her coat and nyloned legs. She stepped through the front doors and stopped short, shocked to see Jarred standing directly in front of her in the middle of the lobby.

"Jarred?" Kelsey asked, concerned.

They were alone. The deep blue chairs and couches were empty. Kelsey walked slowly toward him, trying to gauge his mood.

"My father's in a coma," he said tonelessly.

"Oh, Jarred. I'm so sorry."

She wrapped her arms around him and pressed her face into the crispness of his shirt. He didn't move, apart from brushing his lips along her hair. "I am so sorry."

"It can't be helped, I guess."

They stood that way for long seconds. Finally, Kelsey said softly, "Jarred, I've got a couple things to say." She hugged him closer. "I found the bank statements in your office. The ones that show all my cash withdrawals. I realized you've been checking on me."

"Kelsey," he murmured in a tortured voice.

"No, shh. I'm not upset. I should have told you before that I was helping out the Rowdens. Robert's illness has created a financial nightmare for them, so I gave them money, but I didn't want you to know, so I gave them cash." Her confession tumbled out faster and faster. "And then I realized how stupid it was to keep it from you and that I'd blamed you for so many things that were wrong in our marriage, but they were my fault, too!"

"I didn't run copies of those documents. Will did. He didn't entirely trust you, and he knew I'd wondered about those cash withdrawals in the past. But I already knew that, whatever the reason, it didn't matter to me. It was your business."

She pulled back to gaze at him. He looked so terribly drawn and tired. Kissing him softly, she said, "And there's something else. Just in case your dad comes out of the coma. I'd like him to know that — well, that I think I'm pregnant."

This time Jarred froze. He gazed at her, hollow eyed. Frightened by his taut expression, she whispered brokenly, "Jarred?"

"You *think* you're pregnant?"

"I was sick at tea today. I bought a home pregnancy test and used it at work just before I came here. It was positive, but I'd like to get a blood test just to make sure."

He stared at her so long without giving a clue to his feelings that her heart lurched with terror. This was just like the Jarred of before. The one who had rejected her love and her baby. Unconsciously, Kelsey took one step backward. But then he suddenly swept her close, his uneven breath fanning her ear. She was touched to realize that he was shaking all over.

"Don't tell anyone," he whispered harshly in her ear.

"Don't tell anyone?"

"I don't feel safe," he said with repressed urgency. "I don't want anyone to know besides us. Promise me."

"Why?"

"Just promise me. Please. I love you Kelsey, and I don't want to lose you. *Promise me!*"

"I promise," she said solemnly, then glanced around the hospital lobby half expecting some strange presence to descend upon them.

"I'm going to take you home," he said. "I want you to stay there."

"At the house?"

"I've got to figure out what my father meant."

"Jarred, you're scaring me. What did your father say?"

"He said there's a woman who wants me dead. For the inheritance. I thought he meant Will's mother."

Kelsey thought of Connor's words. *She's not what she seems. . . . She's a chameleon . . . tricky friends . . .*

"Sarah?" she asked.

"No. He was talking about someone he had an affair with."

"If Sarah has a baby and you don't by the time you're forty —"

Jarred jerked back and gazed at her hard. "Who told you about that?"

"The terms of your grandfather's will?" Kelsey sighed and admitted, "Nola."

"Nola." Jarred made a sound of impatience and weariness. "Did she tell you she wanted you to have a baby to make certain I inherit?" When Kelsey didn't immediately answer, his jaw dropped. "Oh, God."

"It's not like that!" Kelsey said, suddenly seeing the direction of his thoughts. "I told her I wanted a baby. I wanted our baby. The first one. The one you rejected. And she told me to have another one, but I always worried about what you really thought about starting a family because you were so cold. But when you told me you didn't want it because you thought it was Chance's, I stopped worrying. But I want my baby. *Your* baby. And I don't give a damn what Nola thinks!"

She was practically in tears. Turning away, she buried her face in her hands. They were both too emotional. This wasn't the right time. She should have known better.

Gently, Jarred turned her back around to face him. "Don't cry. I'm sorry. There's nothing I want more than to have a child with you," he

367

said through his teeth.

She could scarcely believe her ears. "You — you mean it?"

"I mean it. Nola's got it all wrong and she knows better. Will deserves part of the inheritance. Whether I have an heir or not makes no difference. Most of the company has been built up since the terms of Hugh's will, and that's all mine. I'm going to make sure Will inherits what he deserves no matter what."

"I love you," she blurted out, shocking herself.

"I love you," he responded soberly. "And I want to make sure we have a life together with our child, so I'm taking you home."

The sickness stopped sometime in the afternoon, but that didn't mean she was over it. No, no. Not by a long shot. It was always this way when she was coming down. Sleep like the dead for three days and then wake up sick. But she'd managed to place the call, and the request had been made. By this time tomorrow, no more Jarred Bryant. And probably no more Jonathan, if the reports she got from the hospital were accurate. Well, he'd been a weak link anyway. A man who indulged in sex for the joy of cheating and serving his own pleasures. But she knew a little something about sex that he didn't. It was for profit and for profit only. She'd just made the mistake of giving it away all those years ago. Believed in love. Hah! What a miserable joke that was. There was no love. Only sex and profit.

And she'd be damned if that profit ended up in Jarred Bryant's hands.

Chapter Fifteen

Kelsey sat at the bar in the kitchen, feeling uneasy. Jarred had driven her home and left again for the hospital. There were so many unsettled issues that she felt slightly depressed. Though Jarred had been her shadow for the last few weeks, his father's illness had taken precedence. And though that was as it should be, Kelsey couldn't help wishing she were with him tonight. She needed him. She should be with him during this time more than ever, but for some reason he wanted her "safe," and that apparently meant away from him.

And Friday was his birthday.

"Jonathan, please don't die," she said to the silent room. Her answer was an unsolicited visit from both Felix and Mr. Dog. They sat a foot apart from each other and stared up at Kelsey, and for some reason this brought the tears that had been threatening her for so long.

"Come here," she invited, sliding down to the floor. Mr. Dog lay his head on her lap and gazed up at her with rapidly switching eyebrows, as if trying on new expressions to lighten up the moment. Felix seemed to think about it a moment, then started washing his face. But he couldn't take Kelsey's cooing to Mr. Dog for too long, and he sauntered over and butted his head against her elbow until she scratched his ears.

"Hey, there. We're going to have a new addition to the family. I hope you'll both be as happy about it as I am." She swallowed. "Jarred's happy about it. He said so. But he's got to worry about his dad right now, so we just have to wait. Okay?"

No answer, but both animals regarded her solemnly.

"I'll take that as a yes," she said on a sigh.

Jarred sat beside his father's bed. No change. A coma, yes. But sometimes these things were shorter than one imagined, the doctors had told him. Jonathan seemed fine. Yes, yes. His system has been shutting down, but he'd stabilized. Nothing different from earlier in the evening. Possibly even a slight improvement.

"He asked for a minister," Dr. Wernst added when he'd finally answered all of Jarred's probing questions. "Reverend Thompson is here. He talked to your father yesterday and he's been in and out today. Unfortunately, he hasn't caught your father when he's been awake. Would you like to talk to him?"

Jarred gazed blankly at the doctor. "Yes," he

said after a moment, and then he was shown into a small conference room, where he waited for the minister.

Reverend Thompson turned out to be a man not much older than Jarred himself. He shook Jarred's hand and mouthed good wishes and condolences, and though Jarred had never spoken to a man of the cloth on his own behalf before, he realized how much better he felt just hearing positive thoughts coming from another human being.

"I talked to my father tonight," Jarred said. "He wanted to see me and tell me things."

Reverend Thompson nodded. "He told me he wanted to see you."

"He left me feeling more anxious than relieved," Jarred revealed. "He told me there was someone out there who wished me dead."

The reverend blinked several times, but he maintained his composure. In fact, he stayed very still, and Jarred realized suddenly that this news was no surprise to him. "He told you the same thing, didn't he?"

"We discussed what was most bothering him," was the careful response.

"He didn't tell me whom he meant. He was trying to, but he failed. He said he'd thought I'd overheard."

"I don't know." The reverend looked perplexed.

"I think he meant someone from work, but it sounded as if he'd had an affair with this woman. There's no one there who was even employed while he was there. Except for Gwen, of course, but she's like an institution. She's not the kind who would ever think of a man, as far as I can tell. And everyone else is too young and, like I said, simply wasn't around." Jarred waited, then said, "What do you think he was trying to tell me?"

"People have many motivations. Your father's was to set things right with you."

"I'm asking *you* if there's someone at Bryant Industries who had an affair with my father."

"Your father and I talked privately."

"I realize that," Jarred said with forced patience, "but does that mean you can't help me?"

"I just don't know what you want to hear. Your father was anxious about a lot of things. He's worried about you particularly. That's why he wanted to see you."

"Who would want me dead?" Jarred asked rhetorically.

"Maybe you're taking that statement too literally. Your father still may have a chance to tell you. Don't give up."

With that, he clasped Jarred's hand once more and left. Feeling a tad less uneasy, Jarred walked slowly back to his father's room, where he stared down at the man who seemed to be so full of secrets.

Nola stood by the window. She gazed through the panes. "He came to briefly," she said without turning around. "Mumbled a bit."

"What did he say?"

"Nothing." She sighed and half turned. She looked ten years older than she had at the Christmas party. "Something about Gwen actually."

"Gwen?"

Nola sighed again. "Does it really matter?"

"Yes, as a matter of fact."

She seemed to want to argue, but thought better of it. Instead she lifted her hands in surrender, then dropped them. "He wanted you to talk to Gwen, I think. Something about Jarred and Gwen and Will and Sarah. But not in that order. I don't know." She twisted her necklace in frustration. "Maybe he's worried about her. She was the rock for him at the company when he was in charge."

Silence passed between them. Jarred sat by his father's bedside, lost in thought. A baby. Kelsey and his baby. It left him feeling excited and vulnerable at the same time. He had the image of his life unfurling beautifully only to be snatched away from him.

Kelsey had said it was over with Connor's death, but all that had changed was that Chance and Connor were both gone. Whatever mysteries had plagued his company were still there. He knew as little now as when he'd first woken up in the hospital.

Except your father was talking with someone about you.

It prickled his spine to remember that conversation now, but as he sat in silence he picked each remembered phrase apart, struggling to recall every syllable and his own interpretation. His father's voice had been tremulous, scared, anxious. But the woman's . . . ?

. . . *Forget it. We could never be that lucky* . . .

Anger. And paranoia. A hint of persecution and a tidal wave of fear.

Uncomfortable, he rotated his neck, thinking he'd heard that tone before. Maybe not her voice exactly, but . . .

A moment later, it clicked: the description of a drug abuser. Paranoid. Persecuted. Whomever Jonathan had been talking with was a user.

"Your birthday's Friday," Nola suddenly said from across the room. Her voice caught as she added, "I want you and Kelsey to come to the house for dinner."

Since there was no planning for whatever would happen to his father, Jarred couldn't be certain of anything. But then, neither could his mother. Seeing as there was no reason to argue, he said, "All right." She probably knew it, too.

"How about seven o'clock? I don't have a present. I hate that tradition anyway."

Jarred actually smiled. It was all so ludicrous and painfully tragic. Nola glanced around. She saw his face and her own crumpled. Swiftly Jarred crossed the room and held her close. "You should go home," he told her. "I think I will, too. Kelsey's waiting for me."

"I can't," she said simply.

Nodding, Jarred kissed his mother on her forehead. It was a rare enough gesture for her to leak those silent tears. "Call me if there's any change."

She nodded.

Kelsey heard the hum of the garage door, the slam of his car door, the opening of the back door. She strained to hear his footsteps after that. She was huddled under the covers, anxious for him to come to her. After what felt like an eternity he mounted the stairs, entered the bed-room suite, and strode into the bedroom. He stripped off his clothes and climbed in bed, then wrapped his arms around her.

"How are you?" she asked.

"Don't talk," he murmured, his lips against the hair at her nape. "Touch me."

This she could do. Willingly. She was glad, too, that he felt the need to make love because she felt it like a stirring of her soul. Moving silkily beneath the blankets, she curled her naked limbs against his. She wore a wisp of satin that Jarred's warm hands pulled off her. His mouth touched the flesh at the base of her neck, his tongue circling the skin over and over again, as if he couldn't bear to move on.

His hands moved to her abdomen, paused. She knew what he was thinking. "I'm glad you're happy about it," she whispered.

"I just want you to be safe."

"I'm safe with you."

His mouth moved downward to her breasts. There was a tenderness and urgency in his touch that she sensed at some deeper level. Something was going on within him that she didn't completely understand, but since it didn't seem to have anything to do with her, she simply let go. And when he moved lower yet, she moaned in anticipation, her body quivering and arching, waiting for the soft, slick penetration of his tongue.

For Jarred it was simply a moment out of time. A place to give and receive pleasure and love his wife in every way. When she wound her arms around his neck and cried out, he found the last vestiges of his own control giving way. A delicious mindlessness beckoned, and when Kelsey's hands urgently pulled him close, sensuously sliding over his skin, he moaned his own response, letting her guide his length inside her.

Kelsey gripped his hips with tense fingers, seeking to set the rhythm, but Jarred wanted it slower than she did, which nearly drove her crazy with desire. She writhed and pulled, but he moved with studied caution, each thrust pushing a bit deeper, promoting a quivering response within her from the sheer sweet agony of not receiving it as quickly as she wanted.

"Jarred," she begged.

His answer was a deep groan as his own self-control melted away. The slippery movements of her body were a sweet dance along his flesh. His breathing was labored and so was hers. She matched his thrusts, her body rising and falling in tempo. The delicious excitement seemed to go on and on, but suddenly she was on the brink. With a cry she dragged him to her, as if she could pull him closer, deeper. Jarred's own gasping release followed in swift, frantic drives that evoked sweet waves within her, leaving her adrift and sated and completely pleasured.

In the aftermath she could feel his racing heartbeat against her own sweat-dampened chest. Kissing his temple, she let her hands move down his muscled body. "I love you," she whispered.

"I love you, too," he answered automatically.

"Will we ever get tired of this?"

"I don't know about you," he answered lazily, "but I'd say, for me, that's a no."

She grinned and he kissed her curving lips. "Well, I'm not tired now," she pointed out.

Jarred pulled back to look at his lovely wife in the dark. Light shone on her eyes and he could see the laugh lines bracketing them. "Tell you what. If I tell you where to touch me and how, and you follow along, I don't think I'll be tired long either."

"Show me the way, Captain."

It was the noise that woke her. Something wrong. Something outside, in the dark. Jarred was sound asleep, mentally and physically exhausted, but her mind was still in overdrive. After climbing from their bed, she grabbed a robe and walked toward the window. The hulk of *December's Wish* rocked gently against the dock, a darker form against the screen of an indigo sky. Thin moonlight filtered through a soft rain, running a white strip of illumination across the water, a restless silver ribbon.

But there was no movement between the house and the boat. No dark scuttling human form trespassing on their property. Still, it bothered her, and while she wanted to just jump back in bed and throw the covers over her head, she couldn't forget the night the garage had exploded. Danger was danger. Ignoring it didn't mean it wasn't there.

But should she wake Jarred? If anyone needed sleep tonight, it was he. Wrestling with her own fears, Kelsey slipped out of the robe and tossed on a pair of jeans, a turtleneck sweater, and sneakers. Mr. Dog lay sleeping outside the door, and after a quick thump of his tail of acknowledgment, he glanced sharply toward the front of the house and growled low in his throat — the kind of warning noise that lifted the hairs on the back of Kelsey's neck.

She padded downstairs and the dog hugged her legs as they descended. *Men in black cars,* she thought vaguely, remembering all the arsenal Connor had had around the perimeter of his living area. Yet, in the end, he'd been the victim of his own addiction. No faceless killers to do the job. Just a carelessness born of need.

She reached the front door. Did she dare

open it? Glancing around herself for some kind of weapon, she realized how foolish she was acting. She needed Jarred awake. She needed —

Br-r-r-ring!

She shrieked at the sound of the doorbell. Mr. Dog growled and barked madly, dancing on his toes. For a moment Kelsey didn't recognize what the sound was.

"Kelsey?" Will's voice sounded outside.

She clamped her lips closed, furious with herself and with him for scaring her. But suddenly Jarred was on the stairs, buck naked, running at her as if he were about to tackle her.

"It's Will!" she cried, steeling herself for a flying tackle.

Jarred managed to check himself. He slid toward her and wrapped his arms around her. He was breathing as if he'd run a marathon. "Well, what the hell?" he muttered furiously.

Kelsey started giggling. She covered her mouth to prevent complete, hysterical laughter as she unlocked the door and admitted Will. He gazed at her, then Jarred, then back at her. Under the influence of some personal urgency, he failed to see the humor of the situation, and that made Kelsey laugh harder. She simply sank down on the floor, covered her head with her arms, and laughed until she cried.

"I'll get some clothes on," Jarred said dryly. "Thanks for scaring us to death. What time is it?"

"Ten o'clock."

"Is that all?" Kelsey asked, surprised.

Will nodded. "Sorry. I just had to see you. With Dad and everything. And I've got some things to say."

"I'll be right back down," Jarred said. "Wait in the den."

"I'll make coffee," Kelsey offered, swiping tears of hilarity from her cheeks.

Fifteen minutes later the three of them sat in the den. Kelsey took the window seat, glancing outside at *December's Wish*. Though the house now felt secure, on some level, she would have liked to still be living on the boat. Maybe she should suggest that to Jarred, she mused. Just a few nights a week, for fun.

"Decaf," Kelsey said to Will as he poured the dark coffee down his throat. He treated the hot drink as if it were some life-giving elixir.

"Big bro, I need to talk to you," Will said, his expression bleak. "I've made some heavy-duty mistakes, and I feel like I've really let you all down. No, don't leave," he said to Kelsey, who'd slipped off the window seat, intending to give them some privacy. "I've been unfair to you, too, but that's over now."

"What happened?" Jarred asked.

He grimaced, looked at the dregs in his coffee cup, then glanced at his brother. "Got anything stronger?"

Silently, Jarred opened a lower cupboard of his credenza and pulled out a bottle of scotch. He poured a healthy dose into Will's outstretched cup.

"I've been under the influence," he said, gulping a huge swallow, "of Sarah."

"Ahh." Jarred shot Kelsey a look.

"And I guess I've been working against you because of it," Will admitted. "I knew Sarah was dealing with Taggart. I overheard them on the phone. She tried to cover up, and I wanted to believe her, so I closed my mind to the obvious. She and I were already involved, and any dealings with Taggart were over by that time anyway. You were in the hospital, and we all thought the Brunswick property was gone, so I let it go. Thought I'd talk to you about it later, when you were better, but there appeared to be no hurry."

"You tried to blame Kelsey," Jarred pointed out in a cool voice.

"I thought it was Kelsey at first," Will said, shooting her a look. "Sorry. Really. I let Sarah influence me. I wanted to believe her. Danielle was lying to me and cheating, and Sarah was there."

Kelsey didn't know how to feel. She'd always felt Will's reluctance to accept her, but to hear it so clearly and fully, to *know* that she'd been right, was difficult.

"And then Danielle just became unreachable to me. I felt . . . unhinged," Will admitted. "I wanted to do something. Break something. Man, I took to running around the track at that grade school down the way from my house until I wanted to collapse. Then Sarah told me about the baby."

He gulped more scotch. "That changed things. I just really looked at her, you know. And she's cold. I mean cold. Like there's something wrong there. Even sex feels calculated." With that, he jumped to his feet and paced the room. "I'm not kidding. I think there's something seriously wrong with her. Like she's missing key parts."

Kelsey gazed at Will in surprise, hearing an echo of her own thoughts when she was at her lowest over Sarah. "I agree," she said.

"She's so single-minded it's scary," Will added, fueled by Kelsey's words. "Obsessive. I'd almost go so far as to say sociopathic."

Jarred frowned. "You're the first one to admit that she does excellent work. She's made a couple of deals with some tough negotiators that left us both in awe."

"But don't you see? That's part of it. She doesn't have normal feelings, so she's terrific at working with those hard-edged types. They can't hurt her. No one can hurt her," he added.

"So what are you going to do?" Kelsey asked, realizing Will had come to some kind of decision.

"I'll do right by the baby. But I'm not going to marry her. That's not going to happen."

"Does she know this yet?" Jarred asked.

"I never said I would marry her. She's the one who spread that news. I've just kept quiet. Thinking. But I talked to Dad about it and he agrees with me."

"When did you talk to Dad?"

"This afternoon. Before you saw him. He told

me to get away from Sarah, and it was almost a relief to hear someone else agree with me."

"You could have asked me about her," Kelsey reminded him lightly. "I've never been a fan."

"Do you think she's been involved with drugs?" Jarred said, his eyes narrowed in serious thought. "She was a friend or acquaintance of Chance Rowden."

"I've never seen Sarah use any kind of intoxicant," Will said. "A glass of wine or champagne, maybe, but even then they're left half full. She's too . . . in control."

"What does she want?" Kelsey asked. When both men turned to look at her, she said, "I mean, everybody wants something."

"The baby?" Will guessed, shaking his head.

"That really doesn't sound like Sarah." Jarred was thoughtful. "I realize that she's pregnant and that she probably planned it, but don't you think she'd rather have the whole company? That's the kind of goal she's after."

"Does she know about the will?" Kelsey asked.

"The will," Will repeated slowly. "You mean Hugh's stipulation? No. I don't see how. We've never talked about it."

"I was just wondering if that's why she got pregnant." Kelsey shrugged.

Will turned to regard Kelsey in a way she found totally uncomfortable. She could almost see the tumblers falling into place inside his head. "No."

"Having an heir doesn't matter," Jarred argued. "I've told you both that. Will is part of this family and that's that. All the speculation over Hugh's will is a waste of time!"

"But Sarah wouldn't know that," Kelsey said. "Even your mother doesn't seem to really get it."

"Oh, she gets it," Will said. "She just doesn't like it."

But Jarred sat quietly, filled with growing dread over Kelsey's words. "Sarah wouldn't know that," he agreed. "She might think having Will's baby would ensure both his future and her own."

"God." Will rubbed his face with his hands. "I've been such a jackass."

"And if she thinks that, she might worry that I'll have an heir before I'm forty and then it all goes to dust," Jarred added.

Fear crawled across Kelsey's skin. It was all she could to do to keep from wrapping her arms protectively around her abdomen. "This is all conjecture," she whispered.

"But there's a ring of truth there," Will said.

"I need to tell her the truth," Jarred said suddenly, jumping to his feet. "Then maybe she'll back off."

"Back off?" Will asked.

"From trying to kill me," he said calmly, reaching for his coat, "or harm my wife and unborn child."

The phone rang almost the instant Jarred's Porsche had backed out of the driveway. Kelsey jumped, snatched the receiver, and exchanged a worried look with Will, who had insisted on going with Jarred and been summarily turned down. Jarred wanted to face Sarah. He wanted the truth and he wanted it now.

And he wanted Will to stay with Kelsey.

"Hello?" Kelsey answered.

"Where's Jarred? Is Jarred there?" Nola's sharp voice inquired.

"Umm, no. He just left. He's on his way to see Sarah."

"What? Why?"

"Business issues," Kelsey said lamely, glancing at Will for support. He lifted his hands in surrender.

"His father's awake and desperately wants to talk to him. Get him over here!"

Kelsey held the phone to her chest, muffling her voice. "Did he take the cell phone?" she asked Will.

He glanced at the desk, where the cell phone lay. "You can call him at Sarah's."

"I'll get him to the hospital," Kelsey told Nola before gently hanging up in the middle of her next diatribe about Jarred being always unavailable at the most desperate times.

Will placed the call to Sarah's place, unhappy that he had to spoil the surprise of Jarred's visit, but there was no answer. He left a message, asking Sarah to call him at Jarred's. "She's not there," he said. "Or not picking up anyway."

"Then he'll come back. I'll tell him as soon as he returns."

"I'd better go see Dad," Will said, gathering up his own coat. He hesitated. "Want to come? Jarred won't like to have you left here alone."

"Yes," she agreed after a moment's hesitation. Scratching out a note to Jarred, she grabbed her own cell phone, then followed Will through the cold night to his car.

"Are you really pregnant?" Will asked, as she slid in beside him.

She hesitated before answering. She hadn't forgotten Jarred's urgent admonitions earlier. But Jarred himself had more or less spilled the beans first. Deciding it couldn't matter now anyway, she said simply, "Yes."

He smiled. "Congratulations."

Sarah wasn't in. Jarred stood outside her rather swank apartment on the north side of the city and considered ringing the bell one more time. It would be a waste of time, he decided, though he was surprised she wasn't home. It was near midnight and tomorrow was a workday. Say what you would about Sarah, she was almost never absent nor tardy.

A baby. Even with all the changes flying around him, he couldn't quite get over the humbling realization that he was about to become a father. He could clearly remember how angry and miserable he'd felt when Kelsey had told him about her first pregnancy. It was ironic that he'd believed the child was Chance's merely on Sarah's word.

Sociopathic.

Jarred shook his head. Will wasn't generally prone to drama, so the word was exceedingly harsh. Jarred had known Sarah for years, and no, she wasn't warm. She wasn't even particularly likable, he decided, recognizing with painful irony that he'd never cared for her. He had not been all that likable himself. He'd known it and hadn't cared. He'd nearly lost Kelsey over it. Falling in love with her had thawed him a bit, but the ice had always been there. Protection against a weak, philandering father and an overbearing, self-absorbed mother.

But there was no use making excuses for himself. What was, was. And Sarah was a problem that would have to be faced sooner or later.

Without consciously planning his direction, Jarred found himself driving toward the Bryant Industries offices. Parking in his designated spot in the lot behind the building, he strode through damp air full of drifting fog to the back entrance. Unlocking the door, he stepped into the smallish room that led to the elevators and central foyer. The security guard greeted him with a nod of his head, then returned his eyes to the small TV screen by the desk, which flickered with images.

Inside the elevator, he thought of his father. They'd moved to these offices not long after Jarred had taken over. The business had been in a slow decline under his father's ineffective control, and Jarred had been forced to leave graduate school early to put things right. Which was fine, as far as he was concerned. He'd jumped in feet first and started suggesting ideas to his father. Jonathan had nodded at him and agreed without enthusiasm, and when Nola demanded that he turn the business over to Jarred lock, stock, and barrel, he'd dismissed the whole thing with a smile and wave of his hand. He'd been, in a word, relieved. Relieved to relinquish responsibility. Only Gwen had mourned the changing of the guard. And Jarred had spent more than a few hours getting past her frosty regard, cajoling and comforting and generally making certain she felt needed and safe.

Safe.

Not a word in his vocabulary these days, Jarred thought with a pang of remembrance.

Lights were on in the hallways. Lights were always on. Not a soul remained in the offices however. The place was tomblike and oddly forsaken. A building without people was lifeless and vaguely disquieting.

He stood in his office, staring down at the street. The streetlights fuzzed, blurred by the ever lengthening trails of fog that moved ghostlike through half-empty streets. It was after midnight and Seattle was closing down. Not completely, for the city was never really abandoned, but this section of town, where businesses stood cheek to jowl, wasn't exactly the hot night scene.

Sarah . . . Gwen . . . His father had mentioned them both tonight, along with Will and himself. Glancing around his office, Jarred recalled where Chance had been standing that day he'd come to see him. A door had cracked open and Chance had scurried away.

A woman.

Crossing the room, Jarred opened the door and gazed into the anteroom that housed Gwen's desk. He sat down in her chair and viewed his surroundings from that vantage point. With the doors to the outer hallway open, she could see everyone who entered the offices. She was a sentinel.

Gwen had said she'd overheard Will on the phone with Trevor Taggart, but Will had said *he'd* overheard Sarah. Jarred believed Will. Truth rang from his words. A confession of his sins for falling under Sarah's spell. Gwen had been wrong. She was, after all, frequently out of the office for various ailments, migraines chief among them, and when she was in the office, her effectiveness was hit and miss. Jarred had wanted to let her go, but his father had fervently disagreed, making Jarred feel like an ogre for even thinking about ousting such a loyal employee.

But what were loyal employees made of anyway? he mused to himself, opening the top drawer to Gwen's desk. Could Sarah be considered a loyal employee? Yes, given certain criteria. But what about overall? In the heart. Where it counted. Could an employer even presume to expect that kind of loyalty from people who turned to him for their livelihood? It was a symbiotic relationship at best, a parasitic one at worst.

Paper clips and pencils and tape and scissors and several self-inking stamp pads with the Bryant Industries logos and a myriad of other stuff that made up the daily work of a secretary were scattered throughout the drawer. Jarred closed it and opened another, not certain what he expected to find. Nothing really. But he had a sudden, inexplicable urge to know more about Gwen. Inside the second drawer were current files of work yet to be done. Envelopes and a shrink-wrapped pile of unopened notepads with *From the Desk of Gwen Harrington* printed in red across the top filled it nearly to the top.

The bottom drawer was locked. Jarred gazed at it. Jiggled it. One of those rinky-dink locks that he'd found so easy to unhook with a pen-knife. Grabbing the letter opener from the top drawer, he slid it gently to and fro, and then with more force when the lock failed to budge on the first try. Eventually he pushed through with a metallic thunk and the drawer slid outward as if invited.

Nothing. A pile of papers. A couple of novels with yellowed pages, testimony to how long they'd sat discarded in the drawer. A half-burned candle, faintly smelling of vanilla. A picture frame. A pair of sunglasses.

What was he hoping to find anyway? Some

clue to his father's past?

The frame was buried under the novels. He pulled it out and turned it faceup. It was a picture of Gwen and Sarah, smiling into the camera. Summer. A company event, no doubt. The kind inspired by that overly cheerful woman in marketing. A let's-get-together-and-be-great-friends event meant to bring the members of the company together.

Gwen had her arm around Sarah. Jarred frowned. Something about the photo.

The elevator bell dinged.

Jarred looked up as the doors slid open and Sarah herself strode into view. She stopped short upon seeing Jarred. "What are you doing here?"

"I could ask you the same thing," he returned.

"I mean, with your father so ill. I just talked to Will," she added by way of explanation. "He told me about Jonathan." As an afterthought, she said, "I'm on my way to my office to pick up some papers I forgot."

"Just talked to Will?" Jarred repeated, his thoughts on the photograph. Sarah and Gwen. Gwen Harrington. Sarah Ackerman.

Gwen *Ackerman*.

"She doesn't like the name," he remembered his father telling him when he'd queried about why his secretary had changed it. He'd been seven, maybe, or eight. He hadn't wanted to be at the office at all, but his father had needed to stop by and do some work. "So she changed it."

"You can't just change your name," Jarred had responded self-importantly.

"Well, Harrington's her name, too, so that's the one she's using," was his father's dismissive response.

"Yes, I just left Will," Sarah answered blithely. "We've got plans to make now, you know. I hope your father hangs on. Really. It's so sad. I don't think Will can get a divorce quick enough to make this marriage go through before summer!" she added with a short laugh, her attempt at humor falling flat. "He is going to be okay, isn't he?"

"I'm not sure. He's not doing well tonight."

"What have you got there?" she suddenly asked. "Why are you sitting at Gwen's desk?"

"I don't know," he answered honestly. "Looking for answers, I guess."

"Answers?" She was instantly on alert. It was as if antennae had grown from her head.

Jarred nodded, watching her. "Dad was rambling. Talking and muttering. He's worried someone's out to get me. I got the feeling it was a woman whom he was involved with."

Now she stood stock-still, her eyes wide, more white showing than normal. Her lips quivered faintly, a product of the rapid fall and rise of her chest. "But you're at Gwen's desk."

He glanced at the picture, turned it to face her. "Your mother?"

The color ran from her face so quickly that Jarred got to his feet, intending to steady her.

But she stepped away as if his touch would burn her. "She didn't want anyone to know."

So it was true. Jarred found the idea faintly repellent. Gwen did not seem the motherly type, and Sarah certainly wasn't daughterly. "Why?"

"She hated my father. He left when I was a baby. She felt like a failure."

"Your father?"

"Samuel Ackerman," she spat with distaste. "A drunk. A wife beater. Your father helped her get through the whole thing. I could show you the cigarette burn on my inner thigh, courtesy of my loving dad. It was after that she left him."

This was more information than Jarred had expected. He felt sorry for her suddenly and faintly guilty for not knowing. "Why didn't you ever say anything?"

She actually sneered at him. "Oh, really. Like you're the soul of understanding. You wanted to fire my mother just because she's older."

Her animosity toward him flickered out like hot flames, representative of a burning, furious core. She hated him, he realized. All these years of pretending absorption in him and it had all been an act! He wondered, suddenly, if she felt the same way about Will. "Sarah, you didn't just talk to Will. He's at my house. He's been there a few hours."

"I meant earlier."

Jarred hesitated, but he decided to push for the truth. "And he said you're not getting married."

Abruptly her nostrils flared as her famous control flooded away. "You Bryants! Always so ready to help as long as you get something in return. Isn't that the way it is? So high and mighty, but soulless, every last one of you."

"You said my father helped your mother."

"Some help! A lousy job and sex on command. Prostitution. Spread your legs for a raise, my dear. Why do you think she stayed all these years, huh? For the *benefits?* He promised it to me. He promised it all to me. He said I was as much his child as either you or Will ever were. I might not be blood, but he said it didn't matter. He loved me. Called me his little girl."

Sociopathic.

Jarred saw what Will had seen. Something wrong there. Obsessive. A poisonous snake. Outwardly commanding, but inwardly seething.

And wrong. Jonathan Bryant might be many things, but Jarred knew whom he loved and how he felt. This scenario was all in her head. "If you think your child will inherit because it's Will's, you're wrong. That's not how it works."

"I know how it works. You can lie and lie and lie. I know how it works."

"I built this business up. It's outside my grandfather's will. Eighty percent of Bryant Industries is mine alone. Even if Will were to inherit, it would be a small amount compared to the company's overall worth. That doesn't mean I don't want him to inherit, I'm just saying —"

"Liar!" she screamed. "Lying, lying bastard!

Don't think you can fool me. I'm on to you. And that snide little bitch you married can't bear children at all!"

"You're deluded," he said.

"Where are you going?" she demanded as Jarred got to his feet and headed toward the elevator.

"Home. And you can pack up your things tonight. Your employment at this company is over as of now."

He punched the button for the elevator. Sarah looked ready to scream but she clamped her mouth shut and stalked away. Exhaustion filled Jarred inside and out. She was the soulless one. And she was going to bear Will's child.

"Dad?" Will said gently as he entered the hospital room. Kelsey followed behind.

Nola stood by the bed, holding Jonathan's hand. Seeing Will caused her mouth to tighten into a thin line. "Where's Jarred?"

"On his way," Will said and Kelsey saw fit to let the lie stand.

Jonathan's lips moved, but he couldn't seem to project words. Will bent to listen.

"What is it?" Nola demanded.

"He says he's sorry," Will repeated, shaking his head.

Nola looked at her husband, gazing down at him in that penetrating way that had wilted men of more stature. "For what?" she asked in frustration.

And clearly, though it cost him dearly for the effort, he answered, "For all the Gwens and Janices."

The phone rang imperatively in her small apartment. She could hear it, and therefore she knew she was past the three-day drug-induced stupor that meant she was coming down. But she didn't want to answer the phone.

Still, it rang and rang and rang until her head swam with noise. She reached for it, then she demanded crankily, "Who's calling?"

"It's me," the feminine voice on the other end said around a mouthful of tears. "I just had a fight with Jarred. He fired me."

"What?" *Wake up. Wake up. Wake up!*

"He says there's no inheritance. Will gets nothing. The baby gets nothing! Do you hear me? It's all for *nothing!*"

"No." Gwen's voice was steel. Nothing was what she'd had for too long. Only Sarah's friends from college had given her anything more. A taste of drugs. A way to float away from her small, miserable life.

"He saw the picture of us. He *knows.*"

"Where is he now? What time is it?"

"About one o'clock. He's on his way home, but I don't know. Jonathan's in the hospital. They might all be there."

She collapsed back on the bed. Think. *I called them. I told them. They know he has to be removed.* "If Jarred's out of the way, it all goes to Will."

"Out of the way?" Sarah asked, sounding fearful.

"It's all taken care of anyway. Stop worrying so much! Sweetie, you've got a baby to think about now."

"But Will doesn't want to get married!"

"You're carrying the only Bryant heir, so it doesn't really matter, does it?"

"Unless Jarred has one," Sarah said, rubbing salt in the wound that never quite seemed to close.

For a moment Gwen really resented her daughter. If only she'd been Jonathan Bryant's child! Then everything would have been right. But, no. She had been sired by that sick, torturing psychopath. Luckily he'd run his car off the road in a drunken haze. At least Gwen knew better than to get behind the wheel when she was high. Asshole.

"Mom?"

"He won't have one. He won't be able to." With that, she slammed down the receiver. The phone rang again instantly, so she yanked the cord from the wall.

She had friends who took care of these things.

Chapter Sixteen

If there had ever been a longer day, Jarred wasn't aware of it. He drove through the drifting fog toward his home, stayed just long enough to read Kelsey's note, then turned the Porsche toward Bryant Park Hospital. Just as well. He needed to be near his father and he wanted to be with Kelsey.

He expected Nola, Will, and Kelsey to all be in attendance, but when he entered his father's hospital room, Kelsey was the only visitor inside. She was seated in a chair, thumbing through a magazine, her gaze straight ahead instead of on the slick pages. When she glanced up, her face lightened and Jarred's chest constricted with the bright beauty of her expression. The curve of her lips and soft sweep of her hair were an enticement he couldn't resist. He crossed the room and swept her into his arms, the magazine fluttering to the floor, forgotten before it touched the carpet.

"How is he?" Jarred asked.

"Better," was the surprising reply.

He pulled back to gaze into her thick-lashed eyes. "Really?"

"He had some things to say, and as soon as they were out, he wanted the reverend. We all left the room. Your mother and Will are down the hall in a small conference room."

"Just the two of them?" Jarred's brows rose.

"I'm sure they're waiting for you. I wanted to stay here."

Jarred regarded his father with mixed feelings. He loved him, wanted him to live, was desperate to forge a new relationship, but the revelations of the evening had left him considering the true nature of the man who'd fathered him. It wasn't a tidy picture. Jonathan's weaknesses had divided him from his family in so many ways.

Still, he could see that Jonathan was resting more easily. Breathing deeper. Lines bracketing his mouth and sketched across his forehead somehow diffused.

"What did he say?" Jarred asked.

Kelsey drew him into the outer hallway. The strong lighting caught the shadows of her face, turning it into beautiful planes and angles. Jarred mentally shook himself. He was so worried, so scared for her. She epitomized everything good in his life, and he had this terrible sense of losing her.

"He said he was sorry for having affairs," she said. "He was sorry for the Gwens and Janices."

Jarred gave her a long look. "He mentioned Gwen."

"Jarred, Nola looked crushed. I don't think it ever occurred to her that Gwen was one of his lovers. None of us knew. Gwen and Jonathan hardly even speak to each other. I mean, there's no need, I guess, but it was kind of a shock. Your father was really agitated. Nola walked out and Will calmed him down." Kelsey hesitated. "You don't seem surprised."

"I had a run-in with Sarah at the office."

"At the office? But didn't you go see her at her place?"

"She wasn't there." Quickly Jarred brought Kelsey up-to-date on what he'd learned, finishing with, "That's how I found out about Gwen."

Kelsey grappled with this new information. "Sarah is Gwen's daughter? And she thinks she deserves to inherit?"

"Will was right when he called her sociopathic. I saw that tonight. She just doesn't respond normally. There's nothing there." Glancing back toward the room, he added, "I'm going to check with Will and Nola. Coming?"

Kelsey nodded. "Jarred, Will told Jonathan about the baby. I think it comforted him."

"Did Nola hear about the baby, too?" Jarred asked, wishing he'd kept his own mouth shut. He still didn't feel right about the world knowing. Some basic need to protect, he supposed, but with Sarah's strange designs on the Bryant fortune, he could believe there were goblins out there ready to pounce on his wife, steal her child, and ruin all their lives.

He must have made some sound because she asked, "What is it?"

"Nothing."

Will and Nola sat on opposite ends of a long table. Nola stared at the blank, dark window; Will stared at Nola. He glanced up at Kelsey and Jarred. "There you are!" he said with relief, jumping to his feet.

"Dad's better?" Jarred said.

"Might even be up and around by your birthday," Nola murmured in a flat voice. Then, as if hearing herself, she drew a deep breath. "Good news, darling. About the baby, I mean. I can't tell you how happy I am." She meant it, even though she was too tired to truly inject her voice with her feelings. A dream fulfilled.

"I don't want to publicize that yet," he told her. "I just don't trust people."

"What people?" Nola frowned.

Ignoring her, Jarred said, "So dad's doing better. We don't know what that means yet."

"Confession's good for the soul," Will said, making a face. "He's just been resting better since he talked to us and the reverend. He's worried about you though."

"I'll stay here in case he wakes up again," Jarred revealed.

"And I'll stay with you," Kelsey said.

Will glanced over at Nola, who looked ready

to collapse herself. "I'll take you home if you'll let me."

"Well, of course I will! Whatever do you mean?"

Will gave Kelsey and Jarred a dry look, but they could tell he was pleased nonetheless. "See you tomorrow."

With that, Kelsey and Jarred walked back to Jonathan's room together, settled into chairs, and leaned on each other throughout the rest of the night.

Dreams. They crept in and wound themselves inside your mind and created all kinds of emotional havoc for no better reason than to wake you up. Kelsey's head rested on Jarred's shoulder, but inside her brain, images flashed bright and terrifying. Chance, pleading with her: "I'm sorry. I'm sorry." Sarah, standing back and silently surveying her with a remote look, as if to say, "You are not a part of this family. You don't belong. I will see that you never get ahead of me." Connor, breathing in her ear, touching her, not saying anything, but behind him, stacks and stacks of guns lined along dirty walls and a pan rattling ominously on the stove. And Gwen blaming Will: "I overheard him on the phone. Will's the one. Will's the one."

Kelsey jerked awake. It was just before dawn. The sky was still black outside the windows but fog had descended, making it seem slightly lighter, grayer. She glanced at the bed. Jonathan breathed deeply and normally. She'd always heard about the effects of lightening one's load with the truth, but she'd never truly believed it could make such a difference.

And as if feeling the weight of her gaze, his eyes opened and he blinked several times, a coma victim awakening after a long sleep, a dead man given a reprieve. He met her eyes, took in Jarred's still sleeping form, and smiled at her.

Kelsey gently stirred. Carefully, she extricated herself from her husband and tiptoed toward Jonathan's bed.

"It's going to be all right now," Jonathan said, his face glowing. "I've talked to God, and He's given you a child."

Kelsey smiled in return. She supposed this was not the right time to debate who'd actually given whom a child, and anyway, she understood the sentiment and was just grateful that Jonathan was better. He'd miraculously halted his own steep decline, and if that was God's doing, all the better.

Jarred drew in a breath and woke suddenly. He was on his feet in an instant, looking for danger.

Kelsey winked at him and he came to stand by his father. Jonathan reached for his son's hand. "I should have got her treatment long ago, but she wouldn't let go of it." His eyes pleaded for understanding. "I didn't know how far she would go, but it's the drugs, you know. They got hold of your friend Chance," he said. "And they got hold of Gwen."

"It wasn't ever migraines," Jarred stated.

"Oh, I'm sure she had them, too." Jonathan lifted a feeble hand. "But they were brought on by other things. Sarah introduced Gwen to Chance long ago, and it wasn't a good thing. I knew about it. I should have done something."

Kelsey swallowed, feeling as if she ought to say something positive but not knowing what.

"She was a good woman," Jonathan said as if trying to convince them all. "A good employee. But she always wanted more. Nola knew she wanted more, but she really didn't want to believe it was because of me. Where is she now?"

"Mother?"

"No, Gwen."

Jarred drew a hand through his hair. "Probably getting ready for work. Unless she's talked to Sarah, which is a strong possibility." He told his father about his face-off with Sarah the night before. Jonathan visibly paled.

Alarmed, Jarred asked, "Dad?" in a worried voice.

"I'm okay." He blinked several times. "What a mess I've made." His voice broke as if he couldn't continue.

Kelsey stepped in. Gently, she said, "But Sarah's not your daughter. Any expectations she has are just desperate fantasies inside her own head. And you know what the shame of it is? She's an excellent worker. She could be whatever she wanted to be."

"She wanted to be a Bryant," Jonathan said. "Gwen did that to her. Filled her head with it from the time she was a baby. Be careful of her," Jonathan said suddenly, his gaze turning from Kelsey to Jarred and back again.

"We will," Jarred responded solemnly.

Friday arrived with a thicker blanket of fog and a sense of shifting seasons. Nola's bitter prediction had turned out to be beautifully, unexpectedly true: Jonathan would be home by Jarred's thirty-ninth birthday. For that event, she wanted her family at their house on Mercer Island, and Kelsey and Jarred and Will were the only ones invited.

Neither Sarah nor Gwen had appeared at Bryant Industries since the night Sarah and Jarred had faced off. An attempt to reach Gwen had not been successful; she was either not at home or not answering her door or phone. Sarah was also missing in action. The two of them were like ghosts, gone in the fog.

Meghan sat at Gwen's desk, doing double- and triple-time work. She shrugged off the extra load without a complaint. Will and Jarred divided Sarah's work, tackling those deals that needed an immediate steering hand with barely a blip of interruption.

It almost seemed as if neither woman had ever been there. Especially since Danielle suddenly arrived on the scene, met with Will, and asked if they could sit down over dinner together one evening and reassess their relationship. Even when he explained about his and Sarah's child's impending birth, Danielle took the news surprising well. She was through with her angry fling, she said, sick of fighting and depressed by the thought of a future without anyone who truly loved her and whom she could love in return. She admitted that she'd embarked on her affair only as a means to retaliate against Sarah and Will's growing interest in each other. This was completely to Will's astonishment since he'd always believed Danielle had embarked on her affair before his and Sarah's. He learned, subsequently, and to no one's real surprise, that Sarah had fed Danielle's insecurities when it came to their marriage. She'd led Danielle to believe the affair was in force long before the actual events became true.

As far as Kelsey was concerned, it just showed how quickly a relationship could unravel if it wasn't based on trust. Sarah had nearly managed the same thing for her and Jarred. As it turned out, fate had intervened in the form of a plane crash and a new awakening to the possibilities of their future.

The night of the dinner, Kelsey examined her reflection in the mirror of her bathroom. Then she clipped on the lovely sapphire pendant. She'd pinned her auburn locks loosely atop her head. Instead of a dress, she wore a black silk camisole top and black slacks. It wasn't a huge party, just a gathering of family partly to toast the end of a long, bad season and the beginning of a bright new one.

Gathering up the tiny box she'd hidden beneath their bed, Kelsey headed downstairs, catching her husband on the phone with Detective Newcastle.

". . . don't even know if it's relevant," he was saying. "It's been four days and they're both missing. It's embarrassment or fear of criminal involvement. . . . I don't know." A pause. "No, I'm not worried. Sarah's pregnant. The baby's Will's, and she might be concerned about all the trouble that's been caused, but she's smart. She'll make it work for her somehow. Gwen's involvement . . . once again . . . she had some friends. Those loosely organized gang types you described?" Another pause. "Who's to say? I just want my life back." He slipped an arm around Kelsey's shoulders and dragged her near, inhaling her scent. "Kelsey," he mouthed. She kissed him on the lips, a loud smack that stopped Newcastle in the middle of a long diatribe. "Nothing," Jarred assured him, his blue eyes simmering with humor. "So case closed? You can talk to Gwen about who her sources were, or are, when she turns up."

A few moments later he hung up the phone. Then he dragged Kelsey close and groaned at the thought of having to go over to his mother's again. "Let's just blow them off."

"Oh, sure. After your father narrowly survived

the week! That would go over well."

"You look great, and you smell delicious."

"You don't look too bad yourself."

He wore tan chinos and a black shirt and a lighter expression than he'd worn in the last few weeks. "No gifts," he admonished her when she handed him the package.

"To hell with Nola."

He grinned. Turning the white box with its sky blue bow around in his hands for several moments, Jarred said, "Cuff links?"

"Oh, come on. You hate getting dressed up, and I doubt anything could coax you into a shirt without buttons at the cuffs."

"Tie clasp."

Kelsey sighed. "This is a birthday gift. I was thinking what I would like most for a birthday gift and so . . ."

With no more ado he opened the box. Inside lay a piece of white paper folded up and tied with another, tinier sky blue bow. Mystified, he unwound the bit of silk and read the missive. While Kelsey's eyes danced, he glanced out to the silhouette of *December's Wish* and then back to the paper.

Your December's Wish *is my command.*

"Nothing fancy. Just a little personal party set up for later."

"Set up?"

"Uh-huh. I had some outside help. Although

Mary insisted on adding her own special dishes as well. Whatever did you do to that woman? I swear, you're her favorite man of all men."

He grinned. "Showed her my best side."

They both laughed.

Half an hour later Kelsey escorted her husband up the drive to his parents' house. Caterers swarmed the brick pathways and cars lined the drive. In the glow of a fog-shrouded evening, the outdoor lights looked like halos. Groups of people strolled toward the front door, and by the looks of the womens dresses, this was supposed to be a formal affair.

"Oh, God," Jarred groaned.

"She said it was just us!"

"She lied."

Kelsey glanced down at her black top and slacks. "I'm underdressed."

"That makes two of us," he muttered in a long-suffering tone. "I hope my father can handle this. Is she trying to kill him?"

Kelsey swallowed. "She wants them to know about the baby," she realized.

"No!" Jarred was adamant. "I'll talk to her."

"Be careful."

Jarred muttered something beneath his breath that sounded suspiciously like a string of pungent swear words. Kelsey silently seconded the feeling.

At the door they looked at each other. She knew her lack of makeup, her loose hair, and her choice of outfit were going to make her look unsophisticated and underdressed. In contrast Jarred, in his black, open-throated shirt and tan slacks, looked wonderfully sexy and casually elegant. He could get away with it.

But appearances were the least of their worries.

Jarred tucked Kelsey's hand firmly within the curve of his arm. "We are going to leave as soon as possible."

"Amen," she said, and he leaned over and kissed her temple.

Jarred grabbed Nola as soon as he could. She was smiling and entertaining and looking a far cry from the distraught woman standing vigilant beside her husband's bed she'd been just a few days earlier. "You're not telling anyone about the baby," he hissed in her ear.

"Jarred!" She looked affronted.

"I told you I wanted that kept secret."

She sighed and gazed around the room, her eyes alighting on Kelsey, who had been snatched from Jarred's grasp as soon as they entered the house. Kelsey was currently talking with a group of people whom Jarred knew from other social events around the city. Kelsey flicked Jarred a look and he grimaced in shared misery. She laughed, and he could hear the lilt of her voice across the room.

"Your father's the one who couldn't keep the secret," Nola revealed, waving at an older man who was making his way to the bar. He winked at her and Nola tugged Jarred toward him. Her machinations were transparent enough: She wanted to squire Jarred around herself, as if he were on some sort of parade.

From around the corner Will shot him a commiserating grimace; he knew it was impossible to fight Nola. Jarred saw Danielle's dark head close to Will's and felt a moment of pure jealousy. He wanted to be with his wife, too. But when he tried to pry Nola's fingers off his arm and go in search of his wife, she clung even more tightly. "Please, Jarred. I need this, and your father needs this."

"Like a hole in the head." He snagged the bartender's attention as Nola pulled him past the row of bottles. "Scotch."

Nodding regally to one of Seattle's wealthiest magnates, Nola expertly steered Jarred to a sheltered nook, away from listening ears. Her silver dress shimmered beneath the lights, sending off sparks that seemed almost angry.

"What?" he demanded, losing patience.

"Gwen called."

"*What?*"

"She was ranting like a wild woman. Wanted to talk to your father but I just hung up on her. Gave me a turn, I must say. I nearly canceled the party, but Jonathan said no. You know, it may not seem like it, but he understands about keeping up appearances, too. He's doing well." She glanced to the slightly open door to the den, where various partygoers were hovering around

Jonathan's favorite chair, apparently sharing bon mots with him.

"He damn near died this week, Nola," Jarred reminded her. "And it's because he thought he was responsible for my accident."

"What are you talking about?" But when he opened his mouth to continue, she shushed him. "Never mind. It's all nonsense. Everything's fine now. Just fine."

"With Gwen ranting and raving?"

"I swear the woman sounded out of her mind." *Drugs* . . .

"Forget about her," Nola said. "I have."

Nola was nothing if not consistent. She never varied from the role of society matron, perfectly turned-out hostess, and all-around woman of importance.

"I just would have liked to keep Kelsey's pregnancy a secret for a few more months," he informed her, this time pulling away from her before she could launch into a new line of attack.

With ground-devouring strides he marched through the room in search of his wife. Kelsey, her eyes sparkling with good humor, her hair floating along her shoulders, her lips curved in an enticing smile, was listening with apparent great interest to the story being told by a gray-haired gentleman. That this particular gentleman was one known for barely contained lechery could be evidenced by the way he kept touching Kelsey's arm and waist, as if he wanted to gather her close and was still working out the best way to do it.

It set Jarred's teeth on edge.

"Excuse me," he interrupted, taking Kelsey's hand and peeling her away from the rather loathsome gent, who watched their leaving with regretful eyes. "You're damn lucky he didn't cop a feel."

"He did actually. Or at least tried to. Unfortunately I spilled my sparkling cider down his sleeve."

"Unfortunately," Jarred said, smiling.

"These things happen."

"How many more minutes?" Jarred asked, just as a bejeweled older woman crashed down on him, declaring in ringing tones that he was a "gorgeous birthday boy" and "such a wonderful representation of Nola and Jonathan," and then added, "How happy you must be, my dear, that your father's doing so well. Isn't life grand?"

Jarred murmured that it was, grabbed Kelsey by the hand again, and threaded his way outside. They both gulped damp, thick air. "Who was that?" Kelsey asked.

"Beats the hell out of me. Come on."

Like children playing hooky from school, they ran across the back lawn and to the cars. Luckily, they'd arrived late enough that the Porsche was not blocked in. Firing the engine, Jarred took a last look at the house; then he said simply and much too happily, "There'll be hell to pay later," and backed out of the drive.

414

December's Wish rocked a little wildly on water ruffled by an ever increasing wind. The fog that had lain so thick and stagnant throughout the day dissipated rapidly, as if angrily routed by an unwanted guest. Kelsey held Jarred's arm as they made their way down to the boat, both a little drunk on their own happiness.

"Who needs alcohol?" Kelsey said, giggling a little as she slipped a bit on the brick steps.

"Careful," Jarred warned.

She sobered almost instantly. "A fall would not be a good thing."

"Not a good thing at all," he agreed. "But we're here now."

Indeed they were on the last step. The crescent moon, which had been a dim silver glow behind the curtain of fog, now appeared as cold and bright as a diamond. A strip of water glistened and shivered beneath its frozen light, startlingly bright against the shifting blackness.

And on deck appeared a dark figure.

Jarred saw it first. His grip on Kelsey's arm tightened like a tourniquet. She gazed up at his face, puzzled, saw its grim planes and angles, then followed the direction of his gaze.

The caterers, she thought. The people she'd called to help set up the tiny table with its silver service and draping white cloth. The ones who would uncork the champagne and sparkling cider, lay out the meal, then drift away like the fog.

But even as the thoughts paraded across her

mind she knew she was wrong. This figure waited tensely. Not tall. A woman.

"Gwen," Jarred said, relaxing his grip a bit in order to step forward. The boat heaved upward suddenly on a stronger wave and she staggered a bit.

"Happy birthday, Jarred," she said in a voice that was clearly hers, and yet just as clearly not. Harsh, flinty, yet somehow distant and displaced.

She's drunk, Kelsey thought, then realized it was a darker addiction. The same one as Chance's. Crystal meth users were paranoid, the detective had said. "Don't go any closer," Kelsey pleaded, clutching Jarred.

"What are you doing on board?" he called to Gwen. "Where's Sarah?"

"Sarah is unhappy . . . so unhappy. . . ."

Jarred took another step forward and Kelsey moved with him. "Is she with you," Jarred asked, "on *December's Wish*?"

"You're having a little party. And there're party favors here. Pink and blue ones."

"Oh, God," Kelsey whispered.

"Stay here," Jarred ordered tersely beneath his breath. "No. Go back to the house. Call Newcastle. The number's in my den."

Kelsey turned but Gwen's voice floated after her. "It wasn't her fault. She fell in love with you, then Will, but neither of you wants her. You're as bad as your father, aren't you? She should have *been* a Bryant!"

"Gwen, come off the boat. I can tell you're not thinking straight," Jarred said gently, seeking to placate her.

"Where's she going?" Gwen demanded. "Where's she going? *I know about the baby!*"

Kelsey stopped in her tracks at Gwen's sudden shrieking. Gooseflesh rose on her arms.

"Gwen, I don't want to stand here and explain the terms of my grandfather's will," Jarred answered. "I told Sarah last night. Will inherits. It doesn't matter about the baby."

"You all lie all the time!"

They always shout, Kelsey realized dimly, *as if that makes their thoughts more credible.* Because she knew it was what Jarred wanted, she began walking up the slippery steps again. Carefully. No accidents now. Not while she was so preciously, newly pregnant.

"Come off the boat," Jarred urged.

"You'll try to prosecute. It's not my fault about the plane crash."

"We know that was Connor."

"And the garage and Porsche. I couldn't stop them! Connor told 'em you knew. They had to get you!"

"Gwen, come on."

"They can't be stopped, Jarred. They can't be stopped. They know about you. You and your baby. Do you hear me? They know!"

You and your baby.

Gwen couldn't have offered a clearer confession if she'd seen a priest. The mysterious "they" didn't know about the baby, nor would "they" care. *She* cared. She and Sarah, and a twisted belief that they deserved the Bryant fortune above Jarred's own flesh and blood. She was the one who would harm them.

The wind whipped Kelsey's hair, stinging her eyes. She stopped, pulled the dancing strands away, and recognized Sarah at the top of the steps. She'd been waiting there. Lurking. Listening and watching.

"Sarah," Kelsey said.

"I'm not going to hurt you," Sarah said, walking toward Kelsey in her strong, mannish way. "But I want to get some things straight about my mother. So go back down there."

Kelsey hesitated. She shouldn't listen to Sarah. She should get to the phone and do as Jarred said.

"My mother's got a gun," Sarah whispered in Kelsey's ear. "She'll shoot Jarred if he doesn't give in. She will."

"Give in?" Kelsey asked faintly.

"Turn around . . . now. . . ."

It was a helluva thing to lose to them, she thought, hating them all. Well, not Sarah. Not her own flesh and blood. But sometimes she looked at her daughter's face and saw Samuel, and she wanted to vomit.

And look at all this silver. Glistening. Brilliant. Like the many little mirrors on one of those disco balls.

She'd never given Kelsey enough credit, she realized dimly, looking around at the intimate, beautiful setting for two. She'd actually gotten herself pregnant, the conniving little bitch. And so Sarah was out again.

And now he was on board talking, cajoling, but it was all *blah, blah, blah,* to her. She hated him the most. More than his father. Jonathan she could control, when she had been younger anyway. He just followed his dick, and the rest was easy. Except for that blasted will.

Her head spun. Sarah was mad at her. She hated it when she was high, but too damn bad. At least Sarah was young still. And the baby was Will's, so who knew?

What was he saying?

". . . nothing's going to happen. Newcastle's following the trail of the explosives. He wants to convict the men that set the bomb. They're the ones who were ultimately afraid of my turning in Chance and Connor and leading the authorities straight to them. Gwen, you're not involved with that."

"That's right," Sarah chimed in, her voice high and tinny. "My mother had nothing to do with it. She doesn't want to use. She's just been so abused by your father. It's not her fault."

"Gwen." That was Kelsey's voice. Her pale face swam in front of Gwen's vision. "No one wants to hurt you."

Glancing down, Gwen saw the gun lying loosely in her own hand. Oh, that was right.

That was why they were listening to her. No other reason. It was all lies anyway. They knew she was guilty. They knew she'd talked to the men they wanted. And she'd be damned if she pointed any fingers in that direction. She knew what her friends were like. Kill you while they lit a cigarette, they would.

But she'd talked to them. Just recently. They were going to take care of Jarred. They were. . . .

She frowned, thinking hard. A sudden thought stabbed through the dullness of her mind. "Get off the boat."

"What?" Sarah turned to stare at her.

"Get off the boat."

"Jesus," Jarred breathed. He reached for Kelsey, grabbed her arm, and yanked her toward him.

Gwen stumbled to her feet. "Off the boat . . . off the boat . . . *off the boat!*"

Pandemonium. Sarah's mouth open in an O of astonishment. Gwen slapped her across the face and pushed her.

Then they were above, on deck. Jarred was first, stepping over the rail onto the dock, reaching a hand for Kelsey. Her hand slipped into his. Then Sarah put a foot over. She balanced on the edge, teetering.

Damn it! Hurry, hurry.

Gwen bulldozed toward her, shoved her over. To safety. To the dock. To Jarred.

Distantly Gwen saw Sarah fall into Kelsey. Kelsey into Jarred. Flailing arms, grasping for a nonexistent rail. Pinwheeling outward. To the water. Falling, falling, falling. A short, truncated scream.

And then a tremendous roar from the bowels of the boat that left Gwen frozen and staring into oblivion. Another scream. Blackness. Then nothing.

Chapter Seventeen

Dark water . . .

Her worst fear. Her worst nightmare. But she couldn't succumb. There was a baby inside her. A baby.

Ear-shattering noise. Reverberations that crushed the chest. A sweep of wave like a lifting hand, tossing her about. Away from the wreckage. Into the deeper, fuller waters of the lake. The smell of oil and burning wood. Pieces of shattered boards tossed around.

But fear of dark water was the worst. It was ingrained. Deadly. She floated. She choked. She would have given up, but there was a life inside her and she couldn't die.

Pieces of wood within her hands. Both hands.

How long she floated she couldn't be certain. She would learn later that it was less than twenty minutes. It felt like an eternity. She turned her nose up to the sky and saw the unforgiving moon lighting the water. Wind sang around her ears.

Strangely, the boat was still there. Blasted apart like the Porsche. Sinking, too. Not like the *Titanic* with one end slowly going down while the other rose. No, this was just a pathetic list to one side and a sense of loss.

"Kelsey," she heard faintly above the wind.

"Jarred," she whispered back, but there was no sound.

And then splashing. He was in the water, his dark head not twenty yards away. "Over here."

He grabbed her by the hair, she realized later, in true swimmer's rescue fashion. She didn't care though. Her face was turned up to the unforgiving moon. Her mind buzzing with a litany: *my baby, my baby, my baby.*

On the dock. Artificial respiration. His voice telling her to hang on, hang on, hang on. He loved her. Loved her. Pressing on her heart.

But I'm okay, she thought. *Stop pushing.*

And then suddenly she heaved forward and threw up what felt like a bathload of black lake water out of her lungs.

The flowers around the room were bright splashes of red and white and green, fighting off the dreariness of another overcast Seattle morning. Kelsey heard them talking but she kept her eyes closed, eavesdropping on her own doctor.

"She's in good health," he said for about the umpteenth time. "She's fine. The baby's fine. You're all incredibly lucky."

Lucky. Now there was a word she wasn't sure fitted.

But they were alive. No doubt about that. Except for Gwen. In the dim haze of her rescue Kelsey had seen Sarah sink to the dock, soaking wet, raise her hands to her face, and sob in pure grief.

Moments passed. The ticking of the clock. *I still have my baby,* she thought happily, lazily.

She woke again a heartbeat later. Or was it even the same day? This time she saw Jarred in the chair next to her bed, his cheek lying on the covers beside her hand. Reaching out a hand, she swept gentle fingers along his temple.

Instantly he lifted his head, staring at her with worried, intense blue eyes. "Hi," he said, packing a ton of worry into that one syllable.

She tried her voice. "Hi," she answered a bit scratchily.

His face cleared. Emotion moved swiftly across his eyes. He bent down and kissed her hand with trembling lips.

"I've still got the baby?" she said, making it a question, knowing what she heard but needing affirmation all the same.

"Yes." His voice was choked. "Oh, yes."

"Is everyone okay?"

"Yes, well, not . . ."

"Gwen, I know. I remember enough."

He looked up again and she could see the effort it cost him to maintain that famous Jarred Bryant control. She loved him for it. "Another hospital bed," she said.

"The last one for a while."

"For eight or nine months anyway."

He gripped her hand hard. "I love you. I'm sorry I didn't realize about the boat. I should have known as soon as I saw her standing there. And then the dark water. I knew how scared you had to be and I —"

"You found me. That's all. You found me."

"It's over. This time it's really over. I won't let anyone hurt you again," he vowed. "I love you, Kelsey."

"I love you."

Epilogue

September

"He looks like Hugh," Jarred observed, examining his son's squinched up face.

"What?" Kelsey, at home on the couch in Jarred's bedroom, fluffed up her pillow in annoyance. "Not a chance. All babies look like Winston Churchill."

"Maybe we should name him Winston."

Since he's going to be christened Bennett Rowden Bryant, Kelsey sent her husband a dark look. "Now there's an idea. As if Ben's moniker isn't dire enough already."

"Your choice," he reminded her with a smile, amused that Ben had clamped a tiny red hand around his little finger.

"I'm sure he'll be scarred for life and end up on some psychiatrist's couch, blaming his mother for ruining him at birth."

"I'm sure he won't. Probably name his own son Bennett Rowden Churchill Bryant Jr."

She laughed. "We could have added McNaughton in there, too."

They'd squabbled about the name from the moment Ben had been born two days earlier. Jarred wanted him to be Mac, but Kelsey prevailed with her maiden name as Ben's first. Nola wanted to disapprove, but Jonathan announced that he thought it very appropriate.

Will had simply held the tiny child gingerly and carefully, as if he were afraid Ben might break. Since Sarah's miscarriage two months into her pregnancy, he'd been both relieved and silently grieving. In a moment of surprising confidence, Danielle had told Kelsey they were working on a family, too.

"Look over there," Kelsey directed, pointing to a bright yellow bouquet of tulips on the dresser. "They came this afternoon while you were checking in at work."

"Who from?"

"Trevor." The look on Jarred's face was priceless. She laughed again. "He congratulates us both."

"Surprised he didn't send it in a milk carton," was Jarred's dry response.

"Well, I'd like to give him credit, but I think Tara ordered it. Still, it's a gesture."

Jarred came toward her to hand off Ben, who'd begun to stir and make little, frantic hunger noises. Kelsey lifted her arms and hugged their child close as Jarred sat down beside her, completing the circle of their family.

For a moment they just looked at each other with love. They wouldn't have made it without each other and they both knew it.

The employees of G.K. Hall hope you have enjoyed this Large Print book. All our Large Print titles are designed for easy reading, and all our books are made to last. Other G.K. Hall books are available at your library, through selected bookstores, or directly from us.

For information about titles, please call:

(800) 223-1244
(800) 223-6121

To share your comments, please write:

Publisher
G.K. Hall & Co.
295 Kennedy Memorial Drive
Waterville, ME 04901